LOEDICIA WAS

A WOMAN who discovered it was possible to passionately love two men at the same time—her handsome, hot-tempered, adventurer husband and the gallant Army officer who once again irresistibly entered her life.

A WOMAN forced to tell her son of the shameful blot on his birth and watch him vanish—perhaps forever—on a quest for his lost father and his own manhood.

A WOMAN who saw her enchanting teen-age daughter growing toward enticing womanhood and falling into the snare of intoxicating sexuality.

A WOMAN following a trail of danger and desire from the unmapped forests of America to the great manors of England to the raging seas of the Caribbean. . . .

REAP THE BITTER WINDS

June Lund Shiplett's riveting new historical romance

REAP THE BITTER WINDS

JUNE LUND SHIPLETT

A Sequel to
THE RAGING WINDS
OF HEAVEN

To my four daughters
Maureen, Geraldine, Yvonne, and Laura
I love you all.

SIGNET TRADEMARK REG. U.S. PAT. OFF. AND FOREIGN COUNTRIES
REGISTERED TRADEMARK—MARCA REGISTRADA
HECHO EN CHICAGO, U.S.A.

SIGNET, SIGNET CLASSICS, MENTOR, PLUME, MERIDIAN AND NAL BOOKS are published by The New American Library, Inc., 1633 Broadway, New York, New York 10019

First Printing, October, 1979

5 6 7 8 9 10 11 12

PRINTED IN THE UNITED STATES OF AMERICA

1

Fort Locke, on the shores of Lake Erie—May 1791

Late-afternoon sunset reflected off the lake water, turning it to crimson fire as Loedicia stood on a small knoll watching the surf roll onto the sandy beach. She shaded her eyes and smelled the clean, fresh air that clung to her nostrils and filled her lungs. A frown creased her forehead as she watched the young dark-haired boy leave the warm water and drop down onto the sand some distance away, stretching out on his back to capture the last warmth of the sun before it sank beneath the horizon. As she slowly lowered her hand from her forehead, the frown still remained. How could she keep on pretending? Yet, how could she tell him? How did a woman tell her son that his father is not his father?

When she and Quinn had returned to the wilderness back in 1775 it had never occurred to them that she might have become pregnant during the little while she was married to Roth when she thought Quinn was dead. After all, Rebel was only three months old at the time. And even after Heath's birth, they'd thought nothing of the fact that he had dark hair whereas his older sister Rebel's hair was blond, because Loedicia had dark hair too, but now, as she stared down toward the beach, she could deny it no longer. Heath, as he grew further and further into manhood—he was now a strapping fifteen-year-old—looked exactly like Roth.

A tear rolled down her cheek and her stomach tied into knots as she watched him roll over onto his stomach, cradling his head in his hands. Every time she looked at him it brought back so many memories. He was so much like his father. Roth was easygoing, a man of high principles who rarely lost his temper, yet there was a strength about him that often awed those around him.

She remembered the look on his face the day she and Quinn left to return to Fort Locke and he'd come to say good-bye. He'd held his head high and conceded defeat gracefully, but she wished she could have made it easier for him. She knew his heart had been breaking, because hers was breaking too even though the final decision had been hers. It was hard to put a boundary on one's love, and yet she had, and in so doing had wrenched him from her life.

He'd been wonderful to her in so many ways during the month and a half they'd been man and wife, but then, with Quinn back . . . They were so different, these two men. Quinn with his stubborn temper and lack of conventionality and Roth with his quiet understanding. Why was it Quinn who stirred her heart and brought release to the storm that raged within her? Why couldn't it have been Roth right from the start? She'd loved him, she knew, but it hadn't been the wild tempestuous love that she'd found in Quinn's arms. At least not at first.

She stood silently, remembering the last few nights she'd spent in Roth's arms—those nights so long ago that had haunted her so many times since Quinn's return. She'd finally put Quinn out of her life, acknowledging that he was dead, and given herself to Roth completely. Abandoning herself, as she had with Quinn, holding back nothing, and for the first time in her marriage his passionate possession of her had stilled the raging storm within her and brought the violent release she needed, and she knew, as she reached a wild pinnacle of ecstasy, that she loved him. She had tried not to, but it was no use, he'd forged his way into her heart and she'd loved him with the same violent love she'd once given to Quinn; then Quinn had returned and she'd blindly shoved Roth aside in her glory at having Quinn back, but what if he hadn't returned?

She shook her head. That part of her life was over. That was sixteen years ago. Their daughter, Rebel, was on the verge of womanhood already, and their youngest, Teak, was a stubborn, willful image of Quinn. Following in his father's footsteps, his blond head tall for a twelve-year-old, reaching Quinn's shoulders. But at the moment all she could think of was Heath.

Heath with his dark, wavy hair and dark eyes. The affectionate smile that held none of the impish malice of his younger brother. Often she'd caught Quinn staring at Heath, frowning, and she wondered if he'd noticed it too, but as yet nothing had been said between them.

She sighed, combing back a loose curl that tugged at her mouth as she watched the dark head on the beach raise up, and her heart was in her throat.

He grabbed his shirt from the sand beside him and stretched as he stood up, turning toward the setting sun; then, seeing his mother on the grassy knoll watching, he threw her a kiss and began sauntering away toward the house set beneath the willows at the edge of the sand some two hundred feet from the fort and the Indian village spread out beyond it.

Loedicia was so engrossed, her mind so far away, she didn't hear Quinn's moccasined approach behind her until he suddenly spoke, startling her.

"When shall we tell him?" he asked quietly, his voice strained, and she closed her eyes quickly in disbelief, then opened them again, staring at the boy walking across the sands toward the house. "It isn't fair to him, Dicia," he continued defensively, "and it isn't fair to me either, is it?"

She whirled around and faced her husband, her face drained of color. "I . . ."

"We can't ignore it anymore, can we?" he said as he stared into her violet eyes, misty now with tears. She was still a beautiful woman at thirty-six. Not a gray hair, her figure still able to arouse desires in him no other woman had ever been able to arouse. He loved her so much sometimes it hurt, like now.

"I've tried to tell myself it's not true," she whispered softly as she looked into his intense blue eyes and the crow's-feet at their corners, etched in by the sun and weather, furrowed even deeper with his concern, making the frost at his temples more prominent.

"At first I thought maybe he was taking after you," he said, and reached up, touching the dark curl she'd brushed away from her mouth only moments before. "But now . . . can either of us deny it?" he asked, and she reached up, grabbing his hand hard between her fingers, her body trembling, and she shook her head.

"I didn't want it to be like this, Quinn." She wept softly, pressing his hand against her mouth, her tears glistening on his tanned skin. "My God! I love you . . . would that I could undo all of it!"

"So don't you think, then, perhaps, that it's time he knew?

It isn't right to let him go on believing I'm his father." He pulled his hand from her mouth and this time it was his hand that covered hers as he held it between them. "Besides, it isn't fair to Teak."

Her eyes widened. "Teak? What has he to do with this?" She saw the stubborn look on Quinn's face and pulled her hand from his. "Oh, no, Quinn. You're not going to."

"Teak's my son, Dicia, not Heath," he answered simply.

"But Heath doesn't know that. You're the only father he's ever known. And legally he is your son."

"But not by blood!"

"Does that really matter so much?"

"You know better than that."

"Do I?"

"I told you that one day, when the time was right, I intended to go to England and claim what's rightfully mine. What my grandfather refused to give me—so that my son could have an inheritance. Well, I still intend to do so, but it will be handed down to my son, Dicia, not Roth's. My son, Teak!"

She bit her lip as she glanced toward the house and saw Heath settling himself on the veranda to watch the sun as it fell beyond the horizon.

"Oh, Quinn, he is your son," she pleaded.

"No." His jaw set firmly. "He's not my son and we both know it, and it's time he learned the truth. He talks about going to England and becoming the next Earl of Locksley . . . he knows what I was cheated out of and why. He expects it to be his someday. It can't ever be, not now. He has to be told!"

"Why? So he can do as you've done? So he can hate his mother as you did? So he can spend the rest of his life wondering what kind of a man his father was? Don't force that on him, Quinn."

"I have no choice," he answered angrily. "He's your son, not mine. He always has been. He's always been closer to you. I can't give him the inheritance that belongs to Teak. I just can't," he stated. "I love Heath, but there is no blood tie. He's not mine, Dicia, and it's time we both faced it. And it's time he knew it too."

She sighed and turned from him, her heart tearing to pieces within her. She had known this was coming. She had seen father and son drifting apart as the years went by. Heath was not born to the wilderness as was Teak, and his temperament often clashed with Quinn's because he didn't share his father's love for the frontier. Although he knew the wilderness and could survive in it as well as his younger brother, he rarely found pleasure in its depths and spent his happiest hours on the lake either canoeing on its turbulent waters or swimming along its shores, and reading. He loved to read.

Quinn reached out and took Loedicia by the shoulders, turning her to face him, pulling her into his arms. "I love Heath," he finally said, his voice deep with emotion. "But I want to be fair, Dicia. He has a right to know, no matter how hard it hurts, and we have no right to keep it from him."

She clung to him desperately, knowing he was right. It wasn't right to keep the truth from him and it wasn't right to let him have the inheritance that should belong to Teak. Heath was not Quinn's son. No matter how much she tried to convince herself that he was, she knew it was a lie. Every time she looked at Heath she knew it was a lie.

She pushed herself back, looking up into Quinn's face. "How do I tell him, Quinn?" she asked hoarsely. "How do I tell him about Roth? What do I say? They know nothing about what happened sixteen years ago, only the little we told them, which wasn't much."

He reached up and took her face in his hands. "Then maybe it's time we told them the whole story," he said quietly. "They're old enough."

Her eyes were hesitant. "Heath has to be told alone," she answered softly, and he nodded.

"All right. But he has to be told. We have no right to be silent any longer."

"I'll tell him," she said, and as his hands fell from her face she turned toward the house again, where Heath still lounged on the veranda, wearing only an old pair of trousers, the legs torn off so he could swim all the easier.

"Don't hate me for this," said Quinn as his arms went about her, and he held her close, bending to kiss the nape of her neck, his lips brushing her ear. "I can't help what I am, you know that. I never could. I love you and Rebel and Heath and Teak, but I can't change what I feel inside."

She turned in his arms, feeling his lips against her skin, the old familiar tingle deep down inside. The fire and passion that always overwhelmed her seeping into her now as he held her close. She could never hate him, and he knew it, but her heart cried out in agony now for her son. Her son, not Quinn's!

"I'll tell him now, today," she said softly, and knew it would be the hardest thing she'd ever done in her life as she looked up at Quinn and met his lips, kissing him passionately, trying to fight back the tears that threatened to flood her eyes.

Heath watched his mother and father walking toward him across the stretch of beach between the house and the grassy knoll where he knew she liked to stand and watch the sunset. They were quite a pair. She was so small and dark, he so tall, his blond hair glowing red in the last rays of the sunset.

He wished he could be more like his father. How many times he wished he could love the land like his father did. That he could enjoy their excursions into the backwoods and feel at home with the Indians, but whenever he stood and watched the long expanse of Lake Erie as it stretched for miles on the horizon, and watched the waves on a stormy day as they raged onto the beach, he felt a stirring inside. A yearning to fling himself into the water and turn into a fish and explore the horizons, no matter where they might lead, but he'd never told anyone, not even his mother, of his restless thoughts.

She was so pretty, and he loved her so much. He watched her now as they approached, only for some reason she didn't look the same. Usually her eyes were soft and warm when she looked at him, but at this moment they were sad and forlorn, as if tears were gathering at the corners, and he frowned.

"Something wrong, Mother?" he asked as she took her arm from about Quinn's waist and moved forward to sit on the edge of the steps near his feet. A wistful smile moved her trembling lips, and she reached up, touching his arm.

"I have to talk to you, Heath," she said softly, then glanced over her left shoulder to look at Quinn.

Heath straightened on the chair, his solid frame suddenly alert, his eyes wary. "What is it?" He too glanced at Quinn, his eyes steady, questioning. "What's the matter?"

She squeezed his arm, then reached up and touched his face, feeling the soft fuzzy down that would soon need shaving, and a lump forced its way into her throat. "Something's happened, Heath," she answered softly, then dropped her hand and stood up. "Will you take a walk with me?"

He scowled, bewildered, wondering what the hell was going

on; then he froze inside. They couldn't have heard about the other night. Beau and his sister, Little Fawn, were the only ones who knew, and they'd promised not to breathe a word. How did he know he'd get drunk as a hoot owl on so little ale? . . . And Little Fawn had looked so desirable. Hell, it was the first time a female had ever made him feel so alive, so . . . He'd almost busted his breeches, but he hadn't really done anything, only tried. He'd been a little too drunk. Oh, he'd wanted to. God how he'd wanted to, and the thought frightened him.

"Is it something I've done?" he asked his mother as he stood up, towering over her, but she shook her head.

"No, Heath. It's something I've done," she said, and started to walk away, then stopped, waiting for him to follow.

Quinn reached out and put his hand on Heath's shoulder as Heath descended the steps, and he squeezed it hard as the boy looked at him, puzzled. "Heath, don't let your mother down," he cautioned, and for the first time Heath realized how much his father had aged in the past few years. He suddenly looked tired and worn; the impish twinkle usually present was replaced with a look of apprehension and doubt. "What she has to do . . . you have to understand. Remember that. Whatever she tells you, whatever else you think, you have to understand." And he turned abruptly and walked up the steps Heath had just descended and disappeared into the rambling log house, leaving Heath with a sick feeling in the pit of his stomach. My God! What had happened?

Loedicia began to walk, her son following closely behind, his bare feet leaving deep prints in the cooling sand as shadows began to creep into the trees on shore. She didn't walk to her favorite hill, where she loved to watch the lake; instead she walked to the edge of the water, to where it lapped at her moccasined feet; then she stopped and turned to Heath, her face pale.

"Let's go over here and sit," she suggested calmly, although her heart was pounding, her hands damp and hot, and she motioned to a large half tree of driftwood left by a recent storm.

He followed, and she sat down, both hands clasped in her lap, trying helplessly to put her feelings into words. "Sit down," she said as he stood staring at her, and he complied silently, trying to sift his mind and sort out what was happening.

She covered her face with both hands, then lowered her

hands, threw her head back, and began. "Heath, do you remember a long time ago when Rebel asked where she was born and was surprised to find out she was born in Philadelphia?"

"Yes," he answered softly, still frowning.

She looked over at him. "Do you remember what we told her?"

"Yes. You told her you thought Father'd been killed by Indians and you went east so she wouldn't be born in the wilderness; then, when Father was found alive, you were reunited and came back here together, and Teak and I were born here."

She sighed. "In a way that is what happened," she confirmed hesitantly, "but there's more to it, Heath, something we've never told you. Something we should have told you a long time ago."

Night was falling swiftly, as it often did along the lake shore, and it was hard for her to see Heath's face, but she saw his shoulders straighten a bit apprehensively, and she reached over, taking his hand, squeezing it affectionately.

"Listen to me, please, Heath," she whispered softly, "then hate me if you must, but I hope to God you won't."

"Mother . . .?"

"Hush," she demanded, and freed his hand. "Many things happened years ago. Things you wouldn't understand, and it's no use telling it all, so I'll tell it as simply as I know how. Quinn and I were traveling east, accompanied by Major Roth Chapman and about twenty British soldiers, when the Indians attacked and I thought Quinn was killed. The only ones left alive, as far as we knew, were myself and the major." She stopped and glanced at Heath, flinching at his resemblance to Roth and the strange emotions it stirred within her. "I had known Roth before, when I'd been in Boston . . . we'd been good friends. . . . After Quinn's death, he made sure I reached Philadelphia safely. He was with me when Rebel was born. . . ." She hesitated and turned to face him squarely now, only his face was shadowed. "I thought Quinn was dead, Heath. I thought the Wyandot had killed him. That's why . . . when Roth . . . He was wonderful to me, Heath. He was in love with me. . . ." She stopped, searching for the right words, only they didn't come.

"What are you trying to say?" he asked hesitantly, his voice low and husky, and tears filled her eyes.

"I married Major Roth Chapman, Heath," she whispered,

her voice strained. "Quinn came back to civilization almost two months after the marriage." She turned to him again and grabbed his arm, squeezing it, her fingers tight on his tanned skin. "We never realized, either of us, until the past few years, Heath, but there's no mistake—every time I look at you it's like looking at him. . . ." Her voice faded away as he stared at her face, trying to see it in the growing darkness.

"You mean . . . you're trying to tell me . . ."

"I'm trying to tell you, Heath," she answered reluctantly, "I'm trying to tell you that Quinn Locke is not your father. Your father was Major Roth Chapman," and she heard his quick intake of breath; then all was silent except for the gentle lapping of the waves against the shore.

"You're sure," he finally asked, and his voice broke.

"I'm sure," she answered. "You look exactly like him, Heath, I know there can be no mistake. I must have been pregnant only a few days when Quinn showed up alive, and you were born nine months later. But at that time we never questioned it." Her voice was warm with love for him. "It wasn't until you started to grow that the doubts began. Now there can be no more doubt. You're the image of your father, Heath."

He stood up, and her hand fell from his arm as he walked toward the water and gazed silently into the darkness; then, after a few minutes he turned and walked back to stand before her.

"Where is he?" he asked calmly, and she swallowed hard, trying to hold back the tears.

"I don't know."

"You don't . . . When did you see him last?"

"Sixteen years ago. The day Quinn and I left Philadelphia."

"And you haven't seen him since?"

"No."

"Why?"

She shook her head. "Would it have made any difference?" she asked, and his jaw set stubbornly as she reached out and touched his arm. "Did you want him to suffer all the more, Heath? Wasn't it enough for him to have to put me out of his life? Would it have been fair to flaunt myself in front of him?" Her voice warmed. "I was his wife once, Heath. It isn't easy for a man to give up his wife to another."

"You didn't love him?"

"I didn't say that."

"But you left him."

"I was already Quinn's wife."

"And you didn't want my father."

"It wasn't a matter of what I wanted," she tried to explain, "it was—"

"As I said," he interrupted, "you didn't love him and you didn't want him."

"But I did," she blurted, then gulped back the tears. "I did love him, Heath. He was a wonderful person. Although I thought I wasn't in love with him when we married, I discovered I did love him in a very special way, because he was special. But you must understand—once in a lifetime comes a love that defies everything we dream of, that makes no sense, yet traps us unawares, even when we fight against it. The love I have for Quinn is like that. I can't help loving him any more than I can help breathing, and Roth knew it. Sometimes I hate Quinn because I can't help loving him in spite of all his faults. Someday perhaps you'll know what I'm trying to say. But don't think it was easy for me to say good-bye to your father, Heath, because it wasn't. It was one of the hardest things I've ever had to do."

He reached over and took her hand, holding it in both of his. "What was he like?" he asked quietly, and she sighed as she looked up at her son, trying to see his face and remembering his father.

"He was quite handsome, like you, my son, and just as warm and affectionate. A man of honor and integrity. He was a good husband, and if Quinn hadn't come back, I'd be married to him still, because he was a man a woman could be proud to love."

Heath squeezed his mother's hands as she stood up; then he dropped them and turned again, walking to the edge of the water. He stood quietly for a few minutes watching the waves break on the beach, holding his head high to listen to the sound of the night heron in the distance wakening, and she saw him shiver.

She wanted to wrap her arms about him and hold him close and try to help him, but knew it would do no good. What he had to do would have to be his own decision. She could talk all day and never make him understand what she'd felt for Roth, because she didn't really know herself. Even now, after all these years, there were times when she missed him. She loved Quinn, but he was a hard man to love. He was stubborn, willful, and hardheaded, and they still fought often because of it, but she wouldn't have changed him for the world. To change him would be like pulling the teeth of a tiger. Yet she wondered sometimes what life would have been like with Roth.

She shook her head now, trying to push the thought to the back of her mind, where she knew it belonged, but as Heath turned toward her and she saw his face in the semidarkness, the memory of Roth was even more vivid.

He walked toward her and stopped, staring at her, and she reached out both hands. He took them slowly and pulled her into his arms and hugged her to him, then released her quickly and set her back so he could look at her.

"I'm going to find him, Mother," he stated softly, his voice deep with emotion. "I'm going to find my father."

Her hand flew to her mouth, and she gasped. "No, Heath!"

"I have to."

"But you don't know where to look."

"I can start where you left him."

"But that was so long ago."

He sighed. "I have no choice, Mother, don't you see," he said. "I never belonged here. I think you knew that. I was never a part of all this," and he waved his hand, gesturing about him at the huge log house and the fort and the Indian village where Telak and his Tuscarora lived. "How can you expect me to stay now? Besides"—his shoulders straightened stubbornly—"your husband doesn't want me to stay, does he?"

"Heath!"

"Well, he isn't my father, is he?"

"Heath, how can you say that?"

He reached out and took her hands again. "I don't mean to hurt you, Mother, but you know what I mean. He's always been partial to Teak. Maybe he knew somehow, maybe it was meant to be. He's tried not to show partiality, but it was there. I knew it, and so did everyone else. You always took my side, and that made a difference too. Now I know why you did."

"But you can't leave, Heath. You're too young. You can't go off on your own."

"Father"—and he used the word loosely—"Father was fifteen when he left home. I'll make out."

"I won't let you go!"

His jaw set firmly. "I have to!"

"Why? Why can't you just leave things as they are? Why can't you stay here with us . . . with me?"

He looked down at her, trying to see her face in the darkness. "I have to find him, Mother, don't you see? I have to know what he was like, what kind of a man he was. . . ."

"I told you. . . ."

"But I have to find out for myself." He reached out and put his hand under her chin, tilting her face to look closer at her, because he was so much taller than she was. "Besides, it isn't fair that I should stay here and be a constant reminder to you. Maybe then you and he"—and he glanced toward the house—"maybe you wouldn't fight so much."

She shook her head. "We've always fought, Heath. Even when we were falling in love. It has nothing to do with you."

"Still, it would be better with me not around."

Tears bunched into her eyes, and she drew in a sob. "Heath, please, you can't go, please."

But his mind was made up. Loedicia felt more defeated than she'd ever felt before as she walked back to the house beside her son. Yet she knew there was no way she could stop him.

Quinn had promised to tell Rebel and Teak about Heath, and as mother and son stepped into the sitting room, she knew by the awkward tension and furtive stares that they both knew.

Heath stood just inside the door, blinking his eyes at the light in the room after coming from the darkness outside; then he took a deep breath and exhaled loudly. "Well," he blurted gruffly, "what do you want me to say?"

Quinn stepped from in front of the fireplace where he'd been standing and stood spread-legged in front of him, staring into his tear-stained face, and for the first time, as she looked at Heath, Loedicia realized he'd been silently crying.

"I wish you were my son, Heath," Quinn said hoarsely, his eyes also misty, "and I can understand how you must feel, but I can't claim credit for something that's not mine, much as I wish it were."

Heath hung his head. "Thank you," he murmured softly.

Rebel had been sitting quietly in the chair beside the door; now she knelt on the cushion, raising herself up, her flaxen hair looking even paler with her violet eyes wide and tear-filled.

"What will you do, Heath?" she asked hesitantly, and he swallowed hard.

"He wants to leave," cried Loedicia, and looked quickly at Quinn. "Don't let him leave, Quinn," she wept. "Please, do something. Make him stay." And she grabbed Heath's arm, holding it tightly, and Quinn flinched under her gaze because he knew nothing he said would change the boy's mind.

Instead, he turned and walked back toward the fireplace, the ashes in it cold because the evening was exceptionally warm; then he turned back to face Heath.

"Is that what you want, Heath, to leave?"

"I'm going to find my real father."

"Haven't I been a father to you?"

"Yes."

"Then why do you have to hurt your mother like this? Why can't you just stay?"

For the first time in a long time Loedicia saw hostility in Heath's eyes as he faced Quinn. "You mean stay and watch Teak inherit everything I thought would be mine? Watch him go to England and become the Earl of Locksley? No, thank you. I'll find my father wherever he may be and claim my rightful place with him if there is any."

"And if you don't find him?" asked Loedicia tearfully.

"Then I'll make a place for myself somewhere else," he answered angrily. "But I won't stay here. I can't." And once more tears rolled down his cheeks, and, ashamed of them, he whirled, running outside into the night alone. Loedicia started after him.

"No!" called Quinn, and moved to her side, holding her back. "Let him be. Let him make his own peace."

"But he's only a boy," she murmured, and he shook his head.

"No, Dicia," he answered, "he's no longer a boy," and she knew he was right. She'd robbed him of his boyhood tonight and forced him to become a man, and she wept against Quinn as he picked her up in his arms and carried her across the room and into their bedroom.

Rebel glanced over at Teak as their father shut the bedroom door. Teak hadn't made one move from the chair where he'd been sitting, and he'd hardly said a word during the whole conversation with their father except to exclaim at the fact that he'd be going to England when he was fifteen to become the heir to the Earl of Locksley instead of Heath, and he didn't seem bothered one bit to find out that Heath was only his half brother.

"It doesn't bother you at all, does it, Teak?" snarled Rebel as she slipped from the chair and stood looking at him, his long, lanky frame, awkward and thin, overflowing the chair.

He smiled cynically. "Well, what do you expect me to do about it, cry like you?"

"It might prove you're human."

"Oh, for Lord's sake. So Heath has a different father. So what's so all-fired horrible about that? You'd think the world fell in or something."

"Well, it has for Heath."

"Why? Father doesn't even know who his mother was. At least Heath knows who his father is. He's better off than we are. Our father's a bastard."

"Oh, jolly! You have a beautiful way of looking at things." Her eyes moved to the bedroom door, then back to her younger brother, who stood up now and was a good head taller than she was. "And you'd better not let Father catch you calling him a bastard or you'll get your hide tanned for sure."

Teak grinned impishly. "He's too busy right now to hear anything," he said, and his grin broadened.

"For a twelve-year-old, Teak, you're just a bit too smart for your own damn good," his sister warned angrily, "and one of these days you're going to get your ass bent out of shape and I hope I'm around to see it."

He laughed, then put his broad hand over her face as if to push her away, but she ducked and slapped at him.

"Keep your hands to yourself, you brat."

"Then don't bother me, female," he drawled lazily. "After all, the future Earl of Locksley doesn't have time to bother with insignificant women."

"That's it," she cried, trying to keep her angry voice down so her parents wouldn't hear. "That's all you care about. You don't care about anyone but yourself. You want to go to England . . . you don't care a thing about how Heath feels!"

Suddenly Teak's face grew serious and the grin vanished as if it had never been there. "You think you know me, don't you, Reb?" he stated boldly, eyes narrowing as he stared at his sister, "but you don't. Sure I care about Heath, but what the hell can I do about it? Nothing. That's what. So what good will tears and yelling do? So I've got a half brother instead of a full-fledged brother. So what? It doesn't matter to me. He's still Heath. The only difference is that now I'll get the inheritance. It's the only difference. It doesn't change Mother and Father's feelings toward Heath, only his toward us. The inheritance is the only thing that's changed."

She stared at him, her violet eyes smarting. "Is that what you think, Teak? You think nothing's changed?" She shook her head. "I feel sorry for you, honestly I do." And she turned toward the door and ran out onto the veranda, and Teak made a face.

What did she know, anyway? She was only a girl. Besides, she didn't have to sit by and watch Mother catering to Heath's every whim and fawning over him like he was something special. Well, now maybe he knew why and maybe he felt sorry for his father in all this. What right had they to feel sorry for Heath, anyway, and he stalked off to the kitchen to console himself with a piece of cake left over from supper.

Rebel stood on the veranda at the top of the steps and squinted into the darkness, wondering which way Heath might have gone; then she saw a dark movement on the beach close to the water's edge and she bounded down the steps, then slowed her pace as she came within a few feet of her brother.

"Heath?"

He was sitting in the sand with his toes in the water, letting the waves creep up and lap at them, and on hearing his sister's voice he straightened, then lay back in the sand.

She moved forward and sank to her knees beside him, looking down into his face. "Heath, I'm sorry," she whispered, and he looked up at her.

The moon wasn't up yet, and he couldn't see her face, but the paleness of her hair was clearly visible in the darkness. "What do I do, Reb?" he asked softly. "Sometimes I used to feel like I didn't belong. As if I was out of place with you and Teak, but I never dreamed how close I was to the truth. I just thought maybe I took after Mother more than the two of you."

"Father said you look just like him."

"That's what she said too."

"If you do, he must have been very handsome."

"Do you think so?"

She nodded and reached out, running her finger down the middle of his chest playfully. "You know very well I do. If Roth Chapman looked like you, I can see why Mother was smitten."

"You don't think it's terrible?"

"I think it's wickedly exciting."

"You would."

"Oh, Heath it's not that bad. . . . I know you think it's

terrible, but just think of what Mother's gone through all these years. Every time she looks at you . . . and Father. How horrible to know your wife had another man's child. . . . Heath, we all love you regardless, even Father, and it's been hard for him. Who knows how long he's realized it? And it isn't really anyone's fault, it's just something that happened."

"But it happened to me."

"So find him, then come home."

He grabbed her hand. "You still want me here?"

"You're my brother, remember?"

She was small, like her mother; only her coloring was different, but her face was the same expressive face, and he imagined his mother must have looked like this once, young, warm, and vibrant.

"I guess I can't blame Mother," he said, "but it hurts knowing she didn't love him enough to stay with him."

"What do you or I know about love, Heath?" his sister whispered as she stared down at him. "We're barely dry behind the ears." And he squeezed her hand, remembering what he'd felt the other night when he'd seen Little Fawn bathing and almost made a fool of himself. It wasn't love he'd felt, but God, it was something.

He let go Rebel's hand and sat up. "I'm not all that much a baby," he said belligerently, trying to assert his manliness. "I guess maybe I know why Mother . . . well, how she could have married my father when she was still in love with your father."

Rebel sighed, exasperated. "Your father, my father. Oh, hell, Heath, what does it matter? It happened and we can't change it. So maybe she loved both of them." Her voice lowered. "Maybe she still does."

Heath turned and looked at his sister. "I'm still going away," he stated vehemently, "and nothing you or anyone else says can stop me," and Rebel sighed.

He was so damned stubborn about some things.

Loedicia turned in Quinn's arms, cuddling her head to his shoulder, feeling his shirt, wet from her tears, beneath her cheek. "Why can't you talk him out of it?" she murmured softly. "Can't you think of something?"

"It wouldn't do any good. You know that. Heath's determined to go."

"But what if something happened to him alone out there? He's not old enough to be out on his own."

"I was only fifteen when I left home."

"But you had a good friend with you. You had Burly."

He sighed. "So I'll find someone to go with him."

"Who?"

"Well . . ." He thought a minute. "Beau could go. He's been east enough. He knows his way around."

She sniffed in and raised up a bit, looking down into his face as he lay on his back on the bed. "Do you think he would?" she asked. "Maybe Telak would say no."

"I think I can talk him into it."

She kissed him softly, her lips warm on his. "Thank you, Quinn," she whispered against his mouth. "I don't know what I'd do if anything ever happened to Heath. . . ."

Suddenly she felt Quinn's muscles tense. "What do you mean?"

"What . . .?"

"What do you mean, you don't know what you'd do? Why?"

She laughed weakly. "He's . . . you know what I mean. . . . He's our son."

"No." His voice was slow, deliberate. "He's not our son, Dicia, he's your son. If anything happened to Heath . . . he's yours and Roth's. It's all you have left of Roth!" His voice was harsh, angry. "That's it, isn't it, Dicia?"

She shook her head in disbelief. "No, Quinn. You know better than that. That's over. It's been over for sixteen years."

"Has it?"

"Quinn!"

He reached up and grabbed her hair, pushing his fingers into it, holding tightly as she looked down at him. "Dammit, Dicia. Do you know what it's been like watching Heath growing up? Every day seeing him look more and more like Roth and seeing the bond that's built up between the two of you? Roth's still in your heart, isn't he? Oh . . . you love me, I know that. With you and me it's like a fire that never dies, but he's still there between us. He always has been, and having Heath around's kept him even more alive for you. Dammit! I'll hire an army to go with Heath if I have to, just to get him out of your sight, then maybe you'll forget his father. Maybe you'll forget what it was like with him and be all mine again like you used to be." And as a tear fell on his face, he pulled her down, kissing her passionately, and she wondered as she had wondered for the past sixteen years: Was it possible? Was she in love with Roth and Quinn both? Was it possible to love two men at the same time?

Then she was lost in his embrace and stopped wondering anymore as his lips became more insistent and his body more demanding and she drowned herself in the luxury of his love, letting him possess her fully, giving herself to him wantonly, as she always did. Trying to forget the ache in her heart and the man who'd caused it.

2

Her horse jerked its head sideways, fighting the hold on him as Rebel reined up at the edge of the river and stared ahead at the man standing in her path. She was a good mile from the fort and knew she shouldn't be, but didn't much care. She dug her heels easily into the horse's flanks and sidled him forward as he snorted irritably; then she pulled him to a halt not five feet from Beau.

Wearing only a breechclout and moccasins, Beauregard Dante was far from what he seemed as he stepped aside and stood gazing at the beautiful girl astride the horse. His father was Telak, chief of Quinn's Tuscarora, and his mother was the youngest of Telak's four wives. He was three-quarters Indian and one-quarter French, and unlike his brothers and sisters, Beau looked no more Indian than the blond, violet-eyed girl on the horse, except for the bronzed, olive hue of his skin. His hair was black, but soft and wavy, unlike the coarse hair of his father, and his eyes were green like those of his mother's father, a Frenchman, who had also given him the strong firm chin and classic French features that decreed he was descended from the aristocracy.

Rebel's mother had become instantly fond of Beau when she'd first come to Fort Locke long ago, and over the years she'd treated him almost like an adopted son, even having Quinn send him east to school in Philadelphia, where he learned the ways of the white man. He'd come back to the country where he'd been born to see if he could help others less fortunate, but it wasn't working out too well. Instead he'd become cynical and bitter, because now he felt he wasn't really a part of either world. His Indian name meant "Wild Thunder," and he often laughed at its ridiculous connotation. He felt nothing like thunder, therefore preferred the name his mother had given him after her father, Beauregard Dante.

Rebel stared at him, her eyes shining. He was all of twenty and most braves were married by twenty, but Beau had yet to take a wife. He was a strange one.

"What are you staring at?" she challenged as she threw her head back defiantly and his eyebrows raised.

"Did I do something wrong, my lady?" he asked, and she eyed him impishly.

"You heard about Heath leaving?" He nodded, his eyes hard. "Your mother told me this morning."

"Are you going with him?"

"Is that any of your business?"

She exhaled disgustedly as she looked down at him. "You're insufferable, Beau Dante," she cried. "Why can't you be decent?"

He laughed a low, deep chuckle and she pursed her lips; then her eyes softened. "You are going, aren't you?"

"I said I would, yes."

She grinned flirtatiously as she threw her leg over the front of the horse's neck and slid to the ground, then straightened her buckskin breeches and frontier shirt with its fringed collar. "Did Mother tell you why he was going?"

His eyes bored into hers, and she flushed beneath their steady gaze. For some reason he always made her feel strange inside, and restless. She stretched her arms up and pushed the hair from about her face, where it was stuck to her sweaty forehead, and in doing so emphasized the full firmness of her breasts, developed far beyond her sixteen years.

"She told me," he answered. "And I wasn't shocked, if that's what you're getting at."

"You weren't?"

"Why should I be?" he said nonchalantly. "My father has four wives, why shouldn't your mother have two husbands?"

She cocked her head sideways and saw the smile playing at the corners of his mouth. "You're making fun of me."

He reached out and put his hand beneath her chin, tilting her head so he could look directly into her eyes. "I'd never make fun of you, my lady."

She flushed again self-consciously.

"It stands to reason men would fall in love with your mother, Rebel," he continued. "She's a beautiful woman, as you will be someday." Her eyes sharpened as she glared at him.

She pulled her chin from his hand. "Someday? What do you mean, someday? I already am a woman!"

"At sixteen?"

She straightened her shoulders and put her hands on her hips, eyeing him angrily, watching the muscles ripple across his broad, bare chest; then: "Do I look sixteen?" she asked coquettishly, daring him to look, staring at him defiantly. "Or do I look like a woman?" And his eyes hardened as they moved from her head, the length of her figure, taking in the seductive curves of her maturing body.

He had to admit she was well formed. He'd noticed it more often than he should, and this morning he'd made up his mind that if he didn't get out of here soon he'd probably end up telling her so. She was an enticing little witch and she knew it, and she was feeling the push of womanhood more each day. This wasn't the first time she'd tried to get him to respond, and he wondered what she'd do if he did.

"Well?" she asked provocatively, thrusting her breasts forward in invitation, and he sighed.

"Oh, hell," he exclaimed under his breath, and he reached out, grabbing her wrist, pulling her close against him, and she drew in a quick breath in surprise. "What are you looking for, Reb?" he asked, his mouth only inches from hers, his body taut against her, and she felt him responding, hard and demanding, and her eyes widened.

"I . . . I want you to notice me," she whispered breathlessly, hesitantly, and his eyes devoured her, his voice low and husky.

"So now I've noticed."

Her breath was coming quickly, and she felt warm and trembly inside as she felt him push even harder against her. "I guessed . . . I guessed as much," she murmured.

"That's not all you wanted, is it?" he asked softly, and she felt the warmth of his body against her and realized he was trembling too. "Didn't you want this?" he whispered, and he leaned his head forward, kissing her below the ear, and she felt liquid fire spreading through her veins, settling deep in her loins, and she moved against him involuntarily. "Or was it this?" He sighed, his lips against her ear, and he moved his mouth to meet hers, and she moaned against him, trying to fight the heady feeling that was making her head spin.

He kissed her deeply, his tongue parting her lips, and she felt it to her toes. He drew his head back and looked into her flushed face, instinctively knowing he was the first man to kiss her like this, and he was pleased by her reaction, yet surprised and a bit angry. She wasn't frightened. Instead she was responding, and he liked it, more than he wanted to admit.

"Is that what you wanted?" he asked against her mouth, and she murmured incoherently, pressing even closer to him, meeting his hardness, her heart pounding and he kissed her again, releasing her wrist, slipping his arm about her waist.

His hands began to caress her as she moved against him wantonly, and suddenly it wasn't a game anymore. He'd meant to teach her a lesson, but it wasn't working out that way.

He drew his lips from hers reluctantly. "You'd better go back to the fort," he whispered hoarsely against her mouth. "You're playing with fire."

"I'm not playing," she murmured breathlessly, her arms encircling his neck. "Don't stop kissing me, Beau." Her mouth was on his. "Don't stop now," she begged, and he trembled violently, his heart fluttering wildly.

"You don't know what you're asking."

She was pressed against him as he held her off the ground, and her hips moved instinctively in a circular motion against the bulge at the front of his breechclout, and she sighed at the wondrous feeling pulsating through her, and Beau almost lost control as he looked into her shining eyes, half-closed in ecstasy, and his mouth went dry.

Suddenly, without another word, he pulled her arms from his neck, shoved her away roughly, and grabbed her about the waist, lifting her high into the air, depositing her back on her horse; then, before she could yell in protest, he stuffed the reins in her hand and gave the horse a smack on the rump, sending it careening down the trail.

He breathed a sigh, sweat beading up on his forehead, his breathing heavy as he watched the horse for a few seconds; then he turned and moved hurriedly into the thicket, trying to forget the feel of her body, the touch of her lips on his. Goddammit anyway! He'd vowed not to let it happen. She'd been baiting him ever since she discovered she had something to use for bait. Well, it was good he was leaving.

The shock of being torn from Beau's arms descended on Rebel while she was in full gallop, and she suddenly pulled the reins viciously, stopping her mount abruptly in his headlong flight. She whirled him about and stared wide eyed back on the trail in time to see Beau disappear into the thicket, and her whole body trembled as she moved yearningly on the

she said as she stood looking down at Loedicia, then sat in the chair next to her.

"I worry about Rebel, Lizette," she answered softly. "She's going to be a woman soon, and it worries me. What men are there here for her to choose for a husband? Indians and a handful of white men."

Lizette nodded. "I know. I have seen it myself. She is straining at the bit already."

Loedicia agreed. "Maybe it's good Beau's going with Heath," she offered. "By the time they return, perhaps Rebel will have settled some."

"Or become more restless." Lizette eyed her quizzically. "You think she wants Beau?"

"I think she doesn't know what she wants, just as I was at sixteen, and I'd hate to see her make a mistake."

"Then it is good Beau leaves. I have seen him watch her sometimes. He does not look at her as he does the other girls. Yes . . . it is good he goes."

"Were you terribly shocked when I told you about Heath this morning, Lizette?" asked Loedicia, and Lizette smiled, reaching over to squeeze her arm.

"*Oui*, a little. But it is something that happens many times. At least you were married. Some women just sleep with them, then the husband comes home after being gone two, three years and finds a new baby in the house. But what is a woman to do when her man insists on wandering? Sleep alone night after night, month after month, not knowing whether he is alive or dead? *Ma petite*, this land breeds many such children, even as yours was born."

"Then you don't think what I did was wrong?"

"Wrong? *Sacrebleu!* It would be wrong only if you make it so." She sighed. "But now you let the boy find his father, *ma petite*, and everything will turn out fine. You'll see."

Loedicia smiled, and there were tears in her eyes. "What would I do without you, Lizette?" she whispered, and Lizette laughed lightly and began telling her of a love affair she had once when François had been gone over a year.

As they talked, neither woman saw Heath leave the river's edge and walk down to the beach, then wander away up the shoreline as if looking for someone. He had walked almost half an hour when he heard a sound in the brush behind him and whirled around to face Beau.

"What the hell are you doing here?" he exclaimed, surprised. "Rebel said you were down by the river, and I searched for ages."

"Why?"

"Are you still going with me?"

He nodded as he stepped out to the edge of the sand and brushed some nettles from his breechclout, then rubbed some smaller seeds from his arms. "Why shouldn't I go with you?"

"I thought maybe you'd changed your mind."

"Why should I do that?"

He shrugged. "I don't know, except Reb said you may not want to go now. What did she mean?"

He smiled cynically. "When did you see Reb?"

"She rode out of the woods by the river like there were Mohawks on her tail. What the hell did she mean, anyway?"

Beau looked away, out across the lake, as he sighed. "Your sister's in heat."

"What?"

"She wants the same thing you wanted the other night when I caught you with my sister."

Heath's face reddened. "Oh, Lord," he exclaimed. "She wanted you . . .?"

He nodded. "She wanted me."

"She asked you to?"

"In so many words."

"Christ!"

Beau laughed. "Don't worry, Heath, I didn't."

Heath eyed him suspiciously. "Did you want to?" he asked hesitantly, and Beau's eyes hardened.

"What do you think?"

Sex was something new to Heath. He'd had a few tender inklings of it as he grew up, but nothing like what had happened the other night. Beau, however, was older by five years. He'd probably done it already, and Heath felt inexperienced and foolish talking to him about it.

"I think maybe you wanted to . . .?"

"Maybe I did," Beau acknowledged calmly, "but I didn't."

"Would you, if you had another chance?"

Beau's eyes shot up and he stared hard at Heath. "Maybe I would," he finally answered. "And then, maybe I wouldn't." He shrugged. "So when are we leaving?"

Heath swallowed hard. "Tomorrow morning, if your father agrees."

"He will."

"How do you know?"

"I know my father."

"I wish I knew mine," mused Heath.

Beau put his hand on the boy's shoulder. "Don't worry. If he's around, we'll find him."

"Does everybody at the fort know?"

Beau shook his head. "I don't know. . . . I don't think so. Maybe. Even if they do, it doesn't matter. We won't be here."

"But Mother will."

Beau understood. "Don't worry about your mother, Heath, she's not as fragile as she looks. She'll do fine."

"I hope so," he answered stubbornly, "because if anyone hurts her . . ."

Beau dropped his arm. "I'm heading back to the fort. You coming?"

Heath shrugged as he reached down, picked up a stone, and hurled it out into the lake. "Yeah," he answered angrily, "I'm coming."

Quinn was heading toward the house as Heath and Beau sauntered down along the edge of the shore, and he called, bringing them to the veranda, where Loedicia sat tying off the last knot on Heath's shirt.

"It's all set," Quinn said as he straightened, looking steadily at Heath's face. "You still determined to go?"

"Yes, sir," he answered, and Quinn shrugged.

"Telak's giving the two of you an escort as far as Fort Pitt if you want it."

Beau shook his head. "We don't," he answered, and Heath looked at him sharply. "Two men make less noise and move faster."

Quinn agreed. "I'll give you a list, names, places. It may help. If nothing else, go see the general, he might know," and Heath's eyes bulged.

"You mean President Washington?"

"I mean George Washington. He knows a lot more about the men who served under him than people give him credit for. If that doesn't do it, you're on your own."

Beau nodded. "It'll do." He glanced up at a noise and saw Rebel standing in the doorway licking something from her fingers, and her eyes sifted over him longingly. God, she was enticing, and he felt himself start to respond and looked away quickly.

"Don't worry," he continued, "we'll make out. Now, I'd

better get back to the village. I've a lot to do before morning."

They watched him go, and Quinn stepped over, putting his hand on Heath's shoulder. "Beau may be young, son," he said firmly, "but he's smart. You couldn't be in better hands," and Heath looked up at Quinn, rather puzzled, but didn't answer.

"What's the matter?" asked Quinn as tears filtered into Heath's eyes, and Heath bit his lip.

"You called me 'son,'" he answered huskily, as if he couldn't believe it. "You called me 'son.'" Quinn frowned as his hand tightened on Heath's shoulder; then he smiled warmly.

"There's more to being a father than a one-night stand," he answered affectionately. "Much more," and he saw the look of astonishment in Heath's eyes and turned toward Rebel, still standing in the doorway, and tried to cover his embarrassment. "Now, let's go see what Sepia's fixed for lunch that's tempted your sister so much, shall we?" They turned to Loedicia, who stood up, showing the shirt to Heath, who exclaimed over the ruffles she'd added down the front.

"And you'll take your good coat and breeches and boots with you too, young man," she demanded as they walked into the house. "I'll not have you running about the city in buckskins." Quinn rolled his eyes at her tirade and smiled at Heath in understanding, and for the first time the animosity that had built up in Heath since last night began to crumble. But he was still going. He had to.

It was dark. Rebel moved slowly along the beach watching the moon on the water. She hadn't been able to sleep. It was well past midnight, and Mother would raise a fuss if she knew she'd slipped from the house, but there was no use staying in bed tossing and turning like hot corn on a fire. Heath was leaving in the morning and Beau was going with him. Bad enough Heath wouldn't be here anymore. They were closer than she and Teak, probably because they were only a year apart in age. But now Beau wouldn't be here either.

She threw her head back and looked at the moon. Beau! She'd always teased him. Maybe because he looked so stern and aloof all the time, and maybe because he never seemed interested in any of the Indian maidens or girls from the fort. The other young bucks chased them and made eyes at them. Not Beau. It was as if he was laughing at their stupidity. As if he didn't like women, but she'd discovered this morning that he was vulnerable too. Hard, cynical Beau . . . And she shivered, remembering the way he'd kissed her.

She was barefoot, her nightgown barely touching the arch of her foot, and she lifted it gently as a wave slapped at her feet. She moved back away from the water, on up to the hill, where her mother always liked to stand. She sat down in the grass, then lay back watching the moon and stars overhead.

Suddenly she drew in a quick breath and her heart started pounding as a shadow darkened her face, blotting out the moon, and for a minute she couldn't breathe.

"You shouldn't be out here," said Beau slowly from above her, and she sighed, relieved, and stood up quickly, brushing the grass from her nightgown.

"I couldn't sleep."

"So I see."

"And you?"

"I couldn't sleep either."

"Any special reason?"

He looked at her out of the corner of his eye. "No." He gestured with his hand. "Care to walk?"

She nodded and threw her long blond tresses back over her shoulders, revealing the bareness of her shoulders in the scant nightgown. She glanced at him quickly as they walked, realizing that he was barefoot, bare from the waist up, and was still wearing a breechclout. Probably planning to swim.

"Don't let me detain you," she said as they headed toward the water. "You were going swimming?"

"I had that in mind when I left the village."

She looked back toward the house, then to her right at the fort and beyond it at the bark huts and tepees silhouetted in the moonlight. "You always swim so late?"

"Often."

"I didn't know."

"Too bad."

"What is?"

He stopped and stared at her in the moonlight. She looked like the women he'd seen in books back east, and in the ballrooms, alive, exciting, and he kept trying to tell himself she was barely a girl. Not even out of her teens. But it wasn't working.

"You'd better go back to the house," he said huskily, his feet touching the cool water, but she stood her ground, staring directly into his eyes. They stared at each other silently for the longest time, and something seemed to pass between them; then, without saying another word, he walked into the water and dived headfirst at the waves breaking onto the shore, disappearing beneath their frothy surface.

She backed away from the water and stood watching him for a minute hesitantly, then suddenly lifted her nightgown, pulling it from her head, throwing it behind her, where it caught on a piece of driftwood, and she plunged in headfirst after him.

Beau's head broke the surface and he cleared the water from his eyes, looking behind him, then gasped as he saw her swimming toward him, her head barely visible in the choppy waves. His feet found the bottom and he stood up, just over waist-deep, feeling the slap of the waves on his back, the pull of the undertow at his feet. He stood motionless as she swam toward him; then she pulled herself erect, standing naked in front of him, her hair drenched, falling in tendrils onto her full bare breasts, the nipples standing taut and firm as water dripped from them.

"You're crazy," he whispered as she stood staring at him, the moonlight turning her into something almost unreal.

"So are you," she answered, and reached out, touching his bare chest, running her hand straight up the middle of it, raising gooseflesh on his arms.

He caught her hand as it reached his chin, and opened it, pressing his lips to her palm, and she took a quick breath, pulling her hand away, then plunged backward into the surf, her bare body stretching tantalizingly for a moment before it disappeared under the waves.

He plunged in after her, and they swam in and out of the water like seals at play, diving and cavorting, until suddenly he reached out and grabbed her by the arm, standing up, pulling her to her feet, and she gasped.

"What are you doing?"

"I'm taking you back to the house," he explained breathlessly, but she balked.

"No!"

"Rebel, please! Behave yourself!"

She sank both heels in the sandy lake bottom and pulled against him, but he fought her.

"You're going to the house!"

Suddenly she changed her tactics and made a flying leap against his chest, almost knocking him over, her breasts pressing hard against him, her arms entwined about his neck, and he released her arm, grabbing her about the waist, feeling her wet flesh beneath his hand.

"What are you . . . ?"

Her eyes were shining as she stared up at him. "Kiss me like you did this morning, Beau," she begged, her breasts rubbing against him, and he groaned deep inside.

"My God, Reb!"

"Make love to me," she pleaded, and his hands moved down her graceful body, caressing her hips, and he pulled her closer toward him. "Please, Beau," she whispered, and relaxed against him weakly, and he swung her into his arms, carrying her onto the beach, away from the water, to the edge of the dunes, where the grass was soft, and he laid her down on her back in the grass, stretching out beside her, looking down into her face.

"Is this what you want, Reb?" he asked softly, and she sighed.

"Yes, Beau, yes. Let me feel as I did this morning."

"Why me?"

She shook her head. "I don't know. I only know I want you."

"Reb . . ."

She pulled his head closer, her lips parted, waiting, and his hands began to caress her passionately.

He stared into her eyes, his hand moving to one of her breasts, cupping it gently, his other hand stroking the silky wet hair from her forehead. She was enough to drive a man crazy. Her eyes were soft and warm, her lips trembling invitingly, and her body moved sensuously.

He bent his head closer, his lips barely touching hers, brushing against them, the tip of his tongue tracing the line where hers began to part; then they moved to her neck, and he buried his face, nibbling at her ear, and felt her body move closer beneath him.

"No," he whispered into her ear. "I can't do it to you, Reb. I can't take the chance . . . you might get pregnant."

"I don't care. . . . I won't. . . . Please, Beau, give me what I need . . . please," she begged recklessly. "You want to, I know," and she reached down, her hand touching his hardness, and he groaned hopelessly against her ear.

"I can't . . . but I'll give you something," he whispered, and his hand moved slowly down her body, spreading her legs, and he began caressing her as his mouth sought hers, and he kissed her passionately for what seemed an eternity as his fingers stroked her over and over again, and she moaned beneath him, pushing her hips up to meet the rhythmic movements of his hand. He kissed her alternately on the mouth and neck, whispering to her softly, lovingly, until she wanted to crawl inside him, begging him to take her.

Suddenly she jerked forward, pushing hard against his hand, her body on fire, and she groaned ecstatically, letting out a low cry; then she lay still, her body throbbing wondrously.

He pressed his hand hard against her, his tongue searching her mouth; then he too shuddered spasmodically, shivering as if he were cold, moaning helplessly, and he relaxed, almost lying on top of her, pulling his lips from her mouth, burying his face in her neck, breathing heavily.

After a few moments he drew back and looked down into her face.

"What . . . what did you do?" she gasped breathlessly, her eyes soft and dreamy. "You didn't . . ."

"You know I didn't," he answered huskily, his mouth only inches from hers.

"But you did something. What did you do?"

"I gave you a taste of what might have been," he said, and bent down, kissing her softly. "Did you like it?"

She murmured something incoherent against his mouth, and he kissed her again more deeply, thoroughly.

"But you . . . ?"

"I'm all right."

She reached down, and her eyes stared into his. "You're not as hard anymore."

"No, and I'm a mess." He ran his hand up her body lovingly, then started to get up, grabbing her hand, pulling her with him. "Now you're going to get your nightgown on and go back to the house, and I'm going to take another dip and get clean, and tomorrow you're going to forget this ever happened. Do you understand?"

"Are you going to forget?" she asked boldly, and he stared into her eyes, warm and soft in the moonlight.

"Yes," he said emphatically, but she grinned wickedly.

"I bet you won't."

He reached out and pulled her to him, kissing her roughly until she was breathless, then picked her up, carried her back onto the beach, grabbed her nightgown from the piece of driftwood, and raised her arms, pulling it down over her head, his hands caressing her body as he did so, pulling it all the way down.

"You won't forget. I know you won't," she whispered seductively as his hands moved onto her hips and she smiled beguilingly.

"To hell with you!" he answered harshly, and ran his hand up to her crotch, savoring its softness for just a moment; then he turned, running, and plunged into the surf.

She watched his head bob up again a short distance away, then turned and headed back toward the house in a state of rapture. She still wasn't going to be able to sleep.

The next morning they stood at the gates of the fort saying good-bye. Loedicia hugged and kissed Heath at least six times before the final parting, and Quinn hugged him and shook his hand vigorously, then shook Beau's hand and hugged Heath again. Teak was a bit quieter, merely shaking Heath's hand when he said good-bye, and Rebel frowned at him disgustedly.

She hugged Heath, her eyes filled with tears. "May I walk to the edge of the river with you?" she asked, and he smiled.

"You want to ride a ways?"

"Can I?"

He looked at his father.

"Go ahead," agreed Quinn, and Rebel thanked him, then glanced at Beau, who was watching her out of the corner of his eye as he nuzzled his horse's nose. "I'll get her a horse," offered Quinn.

"No need," said Heath. "She can ride with one of us."

"She's welcome here," offered Beau, but she gave him a haughty glance.

"I'll ride with Heath."

Heath checked his horse, then turned, shrugging. "No room, Reb," he said. "I've got too many bundles already. Sorry. You'll have to ride with Beau."

Beau was wearing buckskins today, and he sprang to his horse's back and looked down at her, his eyes like steel; then he reached out for her hand.

She had on a blue dress instead of her usual buckskin pants and frontier shirt, and she reached up, gave a small jump, and he pulled her onto the horse in front of him, seating her sideways.

They rode bareback except for a blanket, and she settled against him, very aware of his closeness. His left arm went about her, and he felt her tremble, but neither said a word.

Good-byes were said again; then Heath mounted and the three rode off with a caution from Loedicia for Rebel not to go too far.

Horses and riders skirted the bark huts and tepees, saying good-bye to old friends; then they turned and waved vigorously as they headed for the river.

"Will he come back, Quinn?" Loedicia asked as Quinn put his arm about her shoulder, and he sighed.

"I hope so, Dicia," he answered. "But it may not be for a while."

"Just so he comes back," she whispered, tears running down her cheeks, and her heart wept too as they turned, heading toward the house, the horses disappearing along the river path.

Beau was letting Heath lead the way as they moved along beside the river, and he tagged close behind with Rebel. Once she felt his lips brush her hair, and his hand moved up, gently caressing her breast, and she leaned back against him, not daring to look at his face, but there was an intimacy about it that pleased her.

They were out of sight of the fort now, and it'd be a good ten-minute walk back from where Beau reined up near a big overgrown, gnarly maple. "This is as far as she goes, Heath," he said, and Heath nodded and reined in, slipping from his horse; then he walked over and reached up, helping her down.

She hugged him hard, kissed him on the cheek, then ruffled his hair. "You be careful, you hear, fella," she said, her voice breaking. "And hurry back."

"Not till I find him, Reb," he answered quietly. "And you take care, don't let anyone hurt Mother."

She fought back the tears. "I won't." Then he kissed her again and turned, jumping onto his mount, ready to ride as he glanced over at Beau, who was sitting his horse lazily, making no effort to move.

"You ride on ahead," ordered Beau from the back of his horse; then he looked at Rebel, who had turned her back to him. "I'll catch up with you in a bit."

Heath stared at Rebel's back for a second, looked quickly at Beau, then slowly nodded and nudged his horse in the flanks and moved on down the trail. He slowed once or twice and glanced back, frowning, then shrugged and moved out of sight, and Beau slid from his horse.

Rebel was standing next to the maple, her back still to him, staring silently into the river water.

"Aren't you going to say good-bye?" he asked, and she turned slowly toward him, leaning against the trunk of the tree, but she didn't answer.

He reached out with both hands and touched her breasts gently, caressing them, the calico material of her dress hampering him, and their eyes met; then his hands moved up to her shoulders, slipping down her back, and he drew her to him, his mouth covering hers. He kissed her slowly, savoring her sweet mouth as it moved against his lips.

When he finally drew back, her face was flushed, her eyes warm with desire. "Don't go," she whispered softly. "Don't go, Beau."

"I have to."

"No. Stay here with me."

"If I stayed with you, I wouldn't be satisfied with the way it was last night, and you know it."

"Neither would I."

"I'd want more."

"I know."

"That's why I have to leave."

Her eyes grew misty. "I'm almost seventeen, Beau. When you come back—"

"I'm not coming back," he interrupted, and she stared at him, frowning, her eyes bewildered. "I'll send Heath back, but I won't be with him."

She shook her head in disbelief. The warmth was gone from his eyes; they were hard and callous. "I don't understand. . . ."

"Don't you?" His face was like granite. "Would you be content to be one of four wives?"

"But you don't have to . . ."

"No, I don't have to, but I'm an Indian, Reb, don't ever forget that. I'm not part of your world. I was never meant to be."

"My world's this wilderness, Beau. What other world do I have?"

He reached up, burying his hand in her long blond hair. "You're young, beautiful, and someday you'll go to England with your parents and rub elbows with royalty. You don't want to be stuck with an Indian in your bed." His voice was harsh and bitter. "I'm not for you, my lady. Much as it might be fun."

Her arms went around his neck, and she clung to him longingly. "It doesn't make any difference, Beau, please. I don't care . . . just come back," she whispered, her voice pleading, but he steeled himself against it.

"No," he answered, shaking his head. "It's no good, Reb. Last night I told you to forget it, and I meant every word." He pulled her arms from about his neck. "I was going to let you down easy, but . . . it didn't mean a thing, Reb, do you understand?" he told her irritably, shattering all her illusions. "I've made love to girls before. I enjoy it. Last night meant nothing. It was an interlude, it was fun, but that's all it was. You threw yourself at me, and I obliged as far as I could without making a peck of trouble. That's all there was to it. You've got stars in your eyes, little lady. I'm not coming back to you or anyone else."

She stared at him, dumbfounded. "You . . . you don't love me?"

He smiled cynically. "Love? Did I mention the word even once?" He saw the pained look in her eyes. "Well, did I?"

She shook her head, unable to answer.

His fingers twined about her long flaxen hair, and he leaned forward. "You were right, Reb, you're quite a woman," he whispered as he drew her head closer, and he kissed her long and hard, feeling the salty tears beneath his mouth; then just as suddenly he released her and turned to his horse.

"I hate you, Beau Dante!" she whispered savagely from behind him, the tears streaming down her face. "I hate you!" And she saw his shoulders stiffen. "You're just saying this . . . you're making it up," she cried. "You're doing this just because you're an Indian, because you . . . you . . ." She sniffed in hard. "You won't forget, any more than I will . . . you won't, and I know it!" she flung at him, but he whirled around, contempt on his face.

"Won't I?" he answered huskily as he stared at her for a moment; and then he mounted and turned back to face her. "Don't bet on it, honey," he said viciously. "You don't mean a damn thing to me." And he dug his horse in the ribs and headed down the trail. Rebel stared after him, her young heart breaking.

"I hate you, Beau Dante," she whispered softly to herself, licking the tears from her lips as he disappeared from sight, "I hate you," and she sank to the ground and cried.

3

Beau caught up with Heath some hundred yards ahead and they set an easy pace. By nightfall they'd left some thirty miles of dense wilderness behind them.

"At the rate we're moving, we should be in Philadelphia in a couple of weeks," said Beau as they cooked a rabbit for supper over a slow fire.

"How do you figure?"

"We're moving slow now, but we can make up over two hundred miles by going straight instead of heading for Fort Pitt."

"You know the way?"

"I can find it."

Heath stared over at Beau. He hadn't said a word to him this morning when he'd joined him again on the trail after saying good-bye to Reb, eyes flashing angrily, but it bothered him.

"I take it your good-bye to Reb didn't go too well this morning," he ventured, and Beau glanced at him sharply.

"So what?"

"After last night, then this morning, the way the two of you looked at each other . . . I thought . . ."

"What about last night?"

Heath's face reddened. "I heard Reb sneaking out, it was way past midnight . . . she was gone a long time." He looked at Beau sheepishly. "I know you swim a lot at night, and her hair was wet this morning."

Beau's eyes narrowed.

"Don't worry," offered Heath, "she made some lame excuse to Mother about it being too warm last night and sweating."

Beau stretched out, watching the flames lick at the rabbit on its spit, remembering last night.

"Did you get another chance?" asked Heath as his face turned crimson, but Beau didn't answer. "I'm not supposed to ask, am I?" he finally acknowledged, and Beau stared at him sullenly.

"Well, good God, Beau, how can I ever learn about women and know what to do if nobody tells me anything?" he said disgustedly, and stood up, poking at the fire, stirring up the flames.

"I want it to cook, not burn," said Beau, and Heath sat down again.

"I don't even know what it's like to kiss a girl," Heath said, embarrassed. "I was so drunk that night with Little Fawn, all I can remember was how warm and soft she felt in my hands." He leaned over confidingly. He was young, but his body was almost that of a man, broad-shouldered, slim-hipped; he could easily have passed for nineteen or twenty, and he didn't know what to do about it and had always been a bit shy when it came to girls. "You've done it already, haven't you, Beau?" he asked softly. "What's it like? How does it feel?"

Beau suddenly grinned and lay back with his arms beneath his head.

"Did Rebel fight or kick?" continued Heath, and Beau sat up.

"I didn't take Reb last night, Heath," he finally said emphatically. "First of all, you get that notion out of your thick head, understand? But if you want to learn about women"—he remembered Reb's body beneath his hands last night—"we've got a long way to go and I'll oblige. Now, suppose we take a breather for tonight and start in the morning. I'm tired and hungry and . . . well, I just don't feel like talking, understood?"

Heath frowned, then nodded and shrugged. Sometimes he just didn't understand Beau, but he began to understand him more as the days went on.

Beau was proud of his Indian heritage, yet stifled by it. Broader of build than Heath and a bit taller, he'd inherited a hairless face from his father and only occasionally had to pluck a stray hair or two here or there from his chin, and he teased Heath a few days later on the trail when Heath began to shave with his hunting knife, explaining that it made him feel more grown-up, but he also kept his promise and tried to explain to the younger man all he knew about women.

He was wise beyond his years in many ways, especially

when it came to women, and how to treat them seemed to come natural to him, a trait perhaps inherited from his French grandfather. Yet, there were savage streaks in him that often surfaced, the combination serving to attract women even more. Still, he was in many ways as much a white man as Heath and seemed to live in both worlds comfortably.

Both were expert woodsmen, reared to life on the frontier, and neither feared the loneliness and isolation of the journey they'd set out on, although Heath, being younger, often rattled on incessantly, talking about everything and anything. Beau was moodier and listened stoically, commenting only when necessary and sometimes shaking his head and smiling. They'd been fairly close over the years, even with the wide age difference, and were almost like brothers, so Beau understood.

They followed the same trail as the Allegheny Trace, instead of going toward Fort Pitt, but stayed off the main trail, working their way toward the mountains, because the Mohawk and Seneca had been moving farther south lately, dissatisfied with the influx of settlers into the wilderness, and the Shawnee, Cherokee, Chippewa, Miami, Sauk, and Fox were moving northward, banding with them, so they had to keep a sharp watch, and it made the trip more hazardous.

Once they almost ran head-on into a party of Mohawk returning from a raid, and they watched from a vantage point, not daring to even breathe, hands on their horses' noses, praying they wouldn't be heard, because they were outnumbered twenty to one, and there was no guarantee what kind of reception they'd receive, since Beau was Tuscarora and Heath white. But the Indians passed on, oblivious of the two men watching from an outgrowth of underbrush a short distance away.

Several times they had to leave the trail to skirt war parties, their only advantage the fact that they had horses and knew if it came to a showdown they could always run. However, this didn't always help, because more and more the Indians were acquiring horses in their raids, and Beau was certain that within a few years there'd be no warriors left on foot. Because of this, they'd moved farther into the Alleghenies than they'd planned and had to find a suitable place to ford the river, then moved up into the mountains, traveling down again through Sandy Lick Creek, the narrow, low valley, lowest pass in the Alleghenies, their eyes constantly watchful for hostile tribes.

Late in the afternoon, about three days beyond Sandy Lick Creek, they were moving slowly amidst the giant trees, eyes alert, having seen signs of a small, fresh camp that morning, when Beau reined in, hand in the air, and Heath brought his mount to a stand beside him.

Both men slid quietly from their horses, tethered them to a nearby bush, then moved ahead on moccasined feet, keeping low, their bows ready. About a hundred feet ahead a split-rail fence abruptly emerged in front of them, and the trees, suddenly less abundant, opened to a large field where corn, barely a half foot high, was stretching toward the scarce sun and a half-grown garden tried to peek its head above a growth of weeds.

They dropped down and crept up to the fence, peering between the rails. At the edge of the garden, with half a row of weeded plants behind him, was the body of an old man sprawled in the dirt, half covering the plants he'd tried so hard to save from the parasitic weeds, an arrow protruding from his back.

As they looked toward the house, Heath's teeth clenched tighter and Beau's eyes hardened. It was a log house, maybe three or four rooms, a bit bigger than most, with a summer kitchen on one end. Behind the house was a barn, flames already licking at the lower boards and smoke beginning to pour from the open door of the loft. Between barn and garden lay two dead oxen and a dead cow, the body of a young boy sprawled nearby, scalp missing.

As their eyes moved toward the house, Heath swore under his breath. The body of a woman hung half in, half out of one of the windows, and a man's body was hunched over in the doorway. Another body, that of a man, hung, swaying jerkily from a rope at the well, only the head and shoulders visible, the pail dangling against it, swaying slowly back and forth.

Between well and house stood two braves, their painted bodies glistening in the sun, and one of them was holding a young girl in front of him, her arms clasped together behind her while she cried, tears streaming down her face, and both warriors watched the house intently as Heath and Beau realized they were waiting for another Mohawk who was setting fire to the house as he had the barn. They watched flames appearing, first at one window, then another.

"She doesn't have a chance," whispered Beau as they watched through the weeds that almost hid the fence, and he motioned toward the young girl, who looked to be about Rebel's age. "They'll take her with them and use her on the way, then turn her over to the women."

"Can we take them?" asked Heath.

Beau studied the situation quickly. Two outside, one in the house, and from the way the two outside talked and gestured, and from the evidence at the remains of the camp they'd found earlier, probably about six or seven more not too far away. He surveyed the situation quickly. The others were out of sight.

"Use your bow," he said, pulling an arrow from his quiver, holding it against the bowstring, ignoring the rifle strapped to his back. "Then, when the one from the house breaks loose, try to catch him in the doorway. I'll get the one with the girl, you take the other one. Left shoulderblade, low, two inches to the right," he said, and Heath nodded, knowing that was exactly where Beau's arrow would land and hoping he could follow suit on his target.

"The one in the house?" he asked.

"He's yours. Take it as it comes, but don't use your rifle unless you have to. I'll grab the girl."

They were close enough, and both men aimed over the top of the fence, the unsuspecting Mohawk faces registering shock as the arrows hit their targets simultaneously.

The Indian's hands clenched tighter on the girl as he felt the arrow thud into his back; then he fell forward, pinning her beneath him, his arms spread-eagled.

Heath's arrow wasn't as accurate, and the other Indian crawled frantically in the dust beside the well, trying to reach the tomahawk that had slipped from his hand; then his face contorted with pain and blood gushed from his mouth as he thrashed about for a few more seconds, then lay still.

Both men were halfway across the yard as the young girl managed to slide free from beneath the Indian who'd held her captive. Her brown hair was caked with dirt and blood, her nose swollen and battered and her face tear-streaked as she managed to crawl to her knees.

"You all right?" asked Beau as he reached her and pulled her to her feet.

She nodded.

"Can you walk?"

"Yes!"

She was barefoot. "Your shoes?"

"In the house!"

At that moment a low rumbling moan pierced their eardrums, ending on a high note that made her hair stand on end, and the Indian from the house stood poised in the doorway, his face writhing in fury. His arm was pulled back with a tomahawk poised in midair, only Heath was swifter and his rifle echoed over the clearing, penetrating deep into the woods as a ball of shot embedded itself between the man's eyes and he slumped forward over the body of the man hunched on the doorstep.

"Let's go," cried Beau viciously, and half-dragged the girl hurriedly across the small expanse of lawn, through the garden, and over the fence as faint shouts could be heard filtering through the woods beyond the house.

They pushed aside bushes and branches, heading for the horses, the girl wincing with every step as she walked on sticks and stones, and Heath kept one eye behind as Beau pulled her frantically along.

Beau bounded to his horse, then reached down, dragging her up behind him. "Hold tight!" he yelled through clenched teeth as Heath reached the back of his mount, and both horses whirled, heading into the woods.

They made a half circle, then headed southeast again as the shouts died off in the distance.

"They'll follow," called Heath ahead to Beau.

"On foot," he yelled back, and the girl's arms tightened about him and he urged his horse faster.

They moved swiftly, plunging deeper into the thicket, then slowed a bit as Beau took his bearings. They continued on to where they reached a small stream, and they waded in on horseback, following it downstream, riding in the water about a mile, then moved to the bank again, and Heath jumped down easily, grabbing some stones from nearby, placing them gently over each horse track, then dusted away his moccasin tracks with a tree branch. He hopped back on and they kept moving.

"They won't still be following, will they?" the girl asked from behind Beau, and he nodded.

"They don't like interference," he answered. "They'll follow until they can't read sign anymore."

"You think we can lose them?"

"We'll sure as hell try."

The going was slower now, thick with underbrush and thorn trees, and Beau swore. "We've gotta get the hell out of here or end up with a lame horse," he said, and reined north for almost a mile, then turned southeast again, skirting the wild-thorn-apple orchard, but they'd lost good time.

Reaching another creek, they headed up about a hundred feet, then backtracked again and headed downstream until the stream began to widen into a deeper pond. Leaving the water the same way they had before, they moved up the bank and across a small clearing, then climbed to the top of a hill close by that overlooked the valley they'd just moved through.

The hill was high enough so they could look out across the valley some distance, and Beau pointed off to the right to where the thorn-apple orchard was. Beyond it, moving fast, were seven men, reading the ground as they moved.

"They look like ants," said the girl at his shoulder, but his jaw set hard.

"Have you ever watched one ant attack another?" he asked, and she shook her head. "They're vicious," he said, "and those men are just as vicious."

He turned and looked ahead. The hill they were on was a large knoll, and looking down the other side, he spotted something that brought relief to his eyes.

"Come on," he said, digging his horse in the ribs, "make for that water hole just north of here," and Heath followed close behind.

An hour later they moved through the trees, scaring away two deer as they headed for the salt lick at the side of the water hole; then they moved out the other side and skirted the area in a wide circle.

A short while later Beau stopped and pointed ahead. In a small clearing near an outcrop of rocks a short distance ahead was a herd of deer heading for the salt lick, and Beau grinned.

"Give them a bit of a shove, Heath," he said over his shoulder, and Heath nodded.

He moved forward and rode to the edge of the herd, nudging them forward noiselessly, and they moved faster, shying away from him, heading directly toward the salt lick.

"By the time the Mohawks reach the lick, there should be at least thirty deer covering our tracks," mused Beau. "Now, let's get lost," and he whistled softly for Heath to rejoin them.

By sundown they were miles away, and now Beau led them across rocky shelves into an area of caverns spreading out in the semidarkness as far as the eye could see.

"We'll bed down here," he said as he reached around and grabbed the girl's arm, helping her to the ground; then he slid down after her. "No fire," he continued, "and we take turns at watch."

They'd ridden all afternoon, eating on the run, stopping only long enough to run into the bushes and quickly relieve themselves, and now for the first time Beau got a good look at the girl.

She was about seventeen, slight of build, her brown hair matted with blood and damp from sweat. Dark brown eyes regarded him coolly as he unfastened his bedroll and threw it to her, and her full mouth almost pouted as she hugged it to her, rubbing the end of her tip-tilted nose where it was swollen and blood had congealed beneath it.

"Maybe tomorrow you can get a bath," he said apologetically. "But there's no water here."

She shrugged. "At least I'm alive."

Heath fastened his horse near a small patch of grass nearby, then came after Beau's horse and fastened it beside his as the girl just stood staring.

Beau sighed, then stepped up, took the bedroll from her, and spread it out on the shale rock behind her, bunching the end into a pillow.

"But where will you sleep?" she asked, and he pointed to a rock above their heads that overlooked the whole area.

"I'm a mountain goat," he answered, and Heath laughed.

"He'll keep first watch," he offered, then reached over, spreading his bedroll beside hers. "What's your name?"

She sank down onto the rough blanket, pulling her clothes together in front, fastening the buttons on her dress, glad she had buttons left and that they hadn't popped off. "Name's Cora," she answered quickly. "You think they're far enough behind?" she asked, looking at Beau, and he shrugged.

"Maybe, maybe not. I'd feel better, though, if a few more elk, moose, and big bucks would wander into that salt lick, but sometimes Indians can smell a white man miles away."

She laughed skeptically. "That's silly," she said. "How could they smell a white man?"

Beau's eyes darkened as they stared at her.

"He knows," answered Heath. "He's an Indian." Cora frowned, then stared at Beau as if she'd just laid eyes on him, and without saying another word, he walked to the horses and took down one of the bags tied across the front of his horse and took out some jerky, walking back, handing her a piece.

"Cora what?" he asked, and she scowled as she tried unsuccessfully to tear off a piece of the jerky.

"Cora Richmond," she answered, and tried again, managing a small piece, but hurting her teeth in the process.

"Your folks back there?"

She nodded as she chewed. "And my future husband. He'd come to help Pa dig a new well. 'Stead, he's hangin' in the old one."

Beau eyed her skeptically. "You don't seem too sad."

"I ain't."

Heath frowned. "How come?"

She laughed a low chuckle. "Is he for real?" she asked Beau, and Heath blushed.

"You weren't in love with him, right?" guessed Beau, and she nodded.

"I was marryin' him because he was the only man within fifty miles, that's why," she answered bitterly, then spit out a piece of the jerky and wiped her mouth. "We've been here almost two years. You wouldn't know what it's like. Grandpa yelled at me, Pa beat me, and Ma treated me like I had no reason to be alive. Besides, I wanted a man to love me, to make me feel like somethin'. Well, I waited and I waited and I waited, then last winter Gabe showed up. He got lost in a blizzard," she explained. "I took my chance. He was big and ugly and smelled like horses, but he was a man and he treated me decent . . . least he tried to . . . but . . . well, no . . . I ain't sorry he's dead, 'cause I don't know as I could of took it much longer. Every time he touched me it almost made me sick to my stomach, but now"—her face reddened—"now I don't have to. Now maybe I can find a man who takes my fancy 'stead of grabbin' anything that comes along. I feel sorry for my brother, Danny, though. Poor kid didn't have a chance."

Beau's eyes steadied on her. "At least you're honest."

"Where're you headin'?"

"Philadelphia."

"The capital?"

"I'm going there to find my father," offered Heath.

"You'll take me with you?" she asked, and Beau glanced quickly at Heath, then back to her.

"You know anyone there?" he asked.

"No . . . but I imagine I can take care of myself better

there than out here," and she made a sweep of the place with her hand. "I don't know nothing about no Indians."

Beau's eyes darkened. He didn't like having a female along, especially one who'd announced she was looking for a man. Heath was too itchy. But there wasn't much else he could do.

"All right," he answered. "I was planning to go through Millersburg, but we're too far south, so I figure we'll make Clark's Ferry, then down to Harrisburg." He glanced at Heath, then back to Cora. "You'll ride my horse, behind me," he said irritably, and she shrugged.

"No matter. Just so's I get there." She smiled, stretching her arms above her head, the tight dress pulling across her firm breasts, and Beau saw the look in Heath's eyes. Damn women anyway! Always upsetting things. Well, they were stuck with her, that's for sure.

He and Heath took turns on guard during the night; then they moved out at dawn, keeping the sun in front of them.

About four hours on the trail Beau reined up and pointed to a creek a few hundred feet away and reached around, grabbing Cora's arm, lifting her to the ground.

"We clean up," he commanded, and slid down after her as she stared at him reluctantly.

"Well, come on," said Heath as he too dismounted, then walked his horse to the edge of the water, letting the animal take a long, cool drink.

She stood watching as they stripped off their shirts; then both of them got on their bellies, leaning over, washing face, head, and arms in the cold stream. Reluctantly she followed suit, but left her dress on. There was no soap, but her face came clean, and even the mud and blood washed from her hair. When she finally looked up, water dripping in her face, Heath grinned.

"You look like a boy." He laughed, and she scowled at him.

"You don't look so good yourself," she answered haughtily, and flung her long brown hair in the air, trying to rid it of the excess water; then, while it was wet, she separated it into three strands and made a braid that hung down her back, knowing all the while he was watching her.

"How far is Philadelphia?" she asked Beau. Instead of answering, he stood up, looking off toward a thicket behind them, then raised his finger to his lips for her to be still.

All three of them stopped, motionless, as a rustling noise

perked the horses' ears, and they watched breathlessly. Within seconds a young deer nudged its nose through the bushes and stared at them wide-eyed.

"Anyone for venison?" whispered Beau, and Heath's amen was barely audible. No one moved, and the suspense was agonizing as they waited. The animal eyed them cautiously for a long time, then with a flick of its head stepped into the clearing and began nibbling the leaves of a small bush.

Beau's arm moved in one quick motion, whipping the knife from its sheath, spinning it through the air, and the deer fell over without even a cry, the blade embedded deep in its shoulder.

"We take time to cook it?" she asked as both Heath and Beau slipped their shirts back on and began to skin it, and Beau nodded.

"If we tried taking raw meat with us, we'd have every wildcat and wolf on the trail following us," he answered. "There's been no trace of Indians all morning, and a fire isn't as easy to spot in the daytime as it is at night, so we should be all right. We lose a few hours, but we eat, and there'll be plenty to take with us."

Beau showed her what kind of wood to gather that made little smoke, and kept her busy while they skinned the deer, made a fire, and built a spit; by late afternoon they left the stream with enough cooked venison slung across the horses' backs to last for a number of days.

It was slower going now with Cora and the venison, but Heath didn't seem to mind. The two talked back and forth most of the day about an endless array of things, until Beau wanted to scream. He liked the quiet silence of the woods, the soft trill of the birds, and the nostalgic whisper of the leaves through the trees.

"Look," he finally said one morning a few days later as they got ready to break camp and he thought of the tedious day of constant chatter ahead of him, "why don't you climb on behind Heath this time, Cora, that way the two of you won't have to shout back and forth at each other. You're scaring game and making enough noise to warn any Indians on the trail that we're coming, and besides . . . it's driving me crazy."

Cora laughed as she walked up and offered her hand to Heath. "He's sure a sourpuss, ain't he?" she said as he pulled her up behind him, and she wrapped her arms around him, pressing her breasts against his back, and Heath grinned sheepishly as a slow tingle warmed him to his toes.

"He's just quiet, I guess," he answered softly, his face flushed, and for the rest of the way they rode along steadily with Heath telling her about his search for his father while he thrilled to the feel of her body soft against him, and Cora complained about her life on the farm as she warmed to the masculine feel of him as she held him tightly, and Beau silently rode along, remembering a pair of violet eyes, a mass of flaxen hair, and a midnight swim.

4

One day moved into another as they made their way across country, eating off the land, bathing in its streams, sleeping under the open skies, stopping now and then at a farmhouse carved out of the raw land or a settlement that had practically sprung up overnight.

The buckskins Beau and Heath wore automatically marked them as backwoodsmen, a breed of men most people looked upon with awe. They'd managed to find breeches, an old frontier shirt, a jacket, and a pair of moccasins for Cora, but horses were rare so she continued to ride behind Heath, stubbornly clinging to him, determined to reach Philadelphia.

Beau had to admit she was plucky, but the looks that passed between her and Heath bothered him. The boy was feeling his manhood, he knew, but he didn't like the idea. Cora wasn't good enough for him. She was restless and struck him as the type of woman that needed more than one man to satisfy her, and besides, she was uneducated and crude. Heath was made for better than Cora Richmond. But then . . . He shrugged. Maybe it was better he sow his wild oats on someone like her rather than take a chance on some doxy in Philadelphia who'd give him the pox. Yet, he didn't like the idea and was glad Heath had managed to control himself so far.

Homesteads were becoming more frequent, and Heath finally came to the conclusion that they'd left the backwoods behind as they moved along a road toward Clark's Ferry. Now and then they passed a wagonload of settlers heading west, and every so often they passed men on horseback, trappers, peddlers, tinkers, chandlers, tailors. Some even had wagons and carts. People were walking and riding. Anything that could move or be pulled or pushed was making its way on the rutted road.

Heath stared every time they met someone, and people stared back. "What's the matter with them, Beau?" he asked as they passed by a couple of wagons, the people gawking at them wide-eyed.

Beau grinned one of his rare grins. "A man in dirty buckskins with a rifle on his back and a bow slung over his shoulder is a rare treat for these people, Heath," he answered as they jogged along. "We're known to fight grizzlies, ride mountain lions, and eat Indians for breakfast. Is there any wonder they'd stare?"

Heath grinned back. "Hell, that's funny."

"Don't laugh. You may have to try to live up to that reputation someday, and believe me, it's not funny when you've got a drunken sailor ready to split your throat from ear to ear just to prove he's a better man."

Heath frowned.

"Don't worry," cautioned Beau, "we'll change clothes in Harrisburg and show up in Philadelphia as proper gents." Then he eyed Cora. "But I don't know what the devil we're going to do about you."

She smiled as she hugged Heath a bit tighter about the middle. "Don't worry about me, Beau," she offered as she leaned her head on Heath's back. "I'll manage." He scowled. That was the trouble, he was afraid she'd manage too well.

When they finally reached the ferry, it wasn't crowded at all as they moved forward, and fortunately the rush of traffic was heading west, not east, but all the crowd was on the other side of the river waiting to come across.

Clark's Ferry crossed the Susquehanna about twenty miles north of Harrisburg, and as they pulled up to the riverbank, Beau studied it lazily. It was late afternoon and the ferry was across the river taking on a wagonload of furniture while the driver argued over the price and three families of settlers argued that it was their turn.

Only one man waited on their side of the river, a peddler with a small two-wheeled cart pulled by an undersized mule.

"What's the fare?" asked Beau as he sat his horse, looking down at the bewhiskered man, who spat a chaw of tobacco before he answered.

"If you got paper money, forget it . . . if it's gold or silver, you can buy the whole danged ferry . . . but the goin' rate's two coppers to a shilling," the man answered matter-of-factly, and Beau nodded his thanks. Quinn had given him money, and he reached in the pouch about his neck, extracting a few shillings. "Don't get in no hurry, though, son," offered the peddler as he watched Beau. "The way they's arguin' over there, we got a long wait," and he was right.

It was over an hour later when the flat-bottomed ferry boat, held in place by ropes and pulleys, finally brought the wagonload of furniture across and poled up to the bank where they waited, then took them back to the opposite side, and the trio walked ashore, followed by the weary, talkative peddler.

A small settlement had sprung up on this side of the river, and Beau nodded. "Maybe we can eat in style tonight, how about it?" he suggested as he watched the look on Cora's face as the aroma of fresh bread drifted down from one of the buildings where a sign hung with a picture of a loaf of bread and a mug on it and letters spelled out "Welcome, Ordinary," and below these the words "Food and Drink," and he saw her hold her head back, sniffing the air.

"Do we have enough money?" asked Heath.

"For a decent meal, but not lodging," said Beau. "It won't hurt to sleep under the stars again, but it might do good to have something solid in our bellies," and they headed for the building some two or three hundred feet from the edge of the river.

After turning their horses to graze in a patch of grass out front in the care of a freckle-faced youngster with two missing front teeth, the trio opened the door and stepped into a noise-filled room of fast-talking men and women that slowly grew silent as they stopped what they were doing and stared at the newcomers.

The long table was half-filled with steaming food, and the group were already gathering chairs around, and Beau stopped, head high, staring back at them.

The silence was deadly; then suddenly: "Here, here," said a tall woman, her thick graying hair braided in a coronet about her head, her apron smeared in front, and she hurried toward them, breaking the silence. "Ve haf more guests, Hans," she said, glancing across the room at a thick-bodied, red-faced man with a bulbous nose who was obviously her husband. "Pull up t'ree more chairs und don't eferybody stare," she yelled, waving at the crowd, who began lowering themselves to their chairs at the table, still unusually quiet, and the man named Hans pointed to three more chairs at the side of the table and lifted one, motioning for Beau to take it.

All eyes were on them now, and Beau knew why. They

were trying to figure out whether he and Heath were Indians or white men. They were both dark-skinned, mostly from suntan, although the coppery hue of Beau's skin was all too obvious and the steely look in his green eyes was enough to make anyone uneasy.

"Ve haf more dan enuff," the buxom woman continued nervously as she motioned toward the food, trying to bridge the awkward reception they'd received, and Beau shrugged as he stepped up and took the chair from the fat man, and Heath and Cora followed suit, the three of them moving up to sit at the edge of the table.

Cora's eyes twinkled as she realized what was going on, and she leaned forward knowingly as she started to sit down, and she addressed the group.

"Please," she said, her voice husky, "don't be afraid. They aren't Indians." Then she glanced at Heath. "At least, he isn't, and they saved my life. If it wasn't for these two, I'd be hanging over some Mohawk's fire letting the squaws roast my innards. Least, that's what Beau says," and she glanced over at him. "He's Indian, but not all Indian. . . . Well, anyway . . . if it weren't for them, I wouldn't be alive," and at this revelation everyone gasped, starting to ask questions, and by the time the meal was over, Heath and Cora had everyone convinced that Beau was not only the smartest backwoodsman on the frontier, but the greatest hero that ever lived, although Cora was sure Heath fitted in there someplace too.

Later, as they rode away from the ordinary, Heath laughed. "They were really afraid of us, weren't they?" he said, and Beau agreed.

He'd sat stoically watching through the whole meal. "Petrified," he answered as they jogged along. "You'd be surprised how many men come roaring down from the mountains, sweeping everything in their paths, with no regard to morals or decency. Most men who live beyond the hills are a strange breed. You've met them, you know. Men like your father, George Clark, and Daniel Boone are rarities. The average mountain man is a cross between a hermit, a cougar, and Henry VIII, and when one walks into a room, the people there aren't just quite sure which kind he'll be."

Heath shook his head. "How much farther to Philadelphia?" he asked.

"About a hundred and twenty miles, give or take a few. We'll camp along the river tonight and reach Harrisburg in the morning sometime."

At dark, Beau reined off the main road, down an embankment, with Heath and Cora following close behind, then slid from his horse at the edge of the water where it was screened by some elderberry bushes and dense shrubbery.

"This should do," he said, and turned to his horse, grabbing the bedroll.

The weather was hot, the night still, with not a breath of air stirring, and since they'd already eaten, there was no need for a fire, so he spread his bedroll at the foot of a small poplar tree and stretched out, settling back comfortably as he watched Heath spreading a blanket out for Cora, then unfolding his own bedroll.

Beau lay on his back, hands beneath his head, watching the stars as they came up one by one out over the river, listening to the water as it gently flowed along, and he wondered what purpose there was to all this. Heath had a reason to be here; he was looking for something. A place in the world, his spot under the sun. But what was he looking for? Was he looking for the same thing?

Silently he cursed the Frenchman who'd given him his name and put the white man's blood in his veins, because it made him restless. Who was he? What was he? An Indian? Not really. Where was his place in the world? He guessed he wasn't so different from Heath, only older. He was looking for the same thing. A place to call his own, if there was one.

After a while Cora stirred restlessly and sat up, sighing, fanning the top of her shirt in the heat. "God, ain't it hot?" she exclaimed, and blew a strand of hair from her face as Heath grunted in agreement. "I ain't remembered it bein' this hot for years," she said, standing up and stretching; then she stepped quietly to the edge of the water and stared into it, watching it trickle past her feet; then she turned to Beau.

"You asleep, Beau?" she asked, and he grunted, and she went on. "How deep you reckon the water is?"

"Two, three feet near the edge. Over your head in the middle. Why?"

" 'Cause I'm gonna cool off," she answered matter-of-factly, and started strolling around the corner of the elderberry bushes that lined the bank.

"Hey," yelled Heath, "be careful."

She grinned as she looked back in the darkness. "Don't worry. I ain't gonna drown," and she was lost around the corner.

Beau held his breath as he tensed up, sensing Heath's restlessness, and in a few minutes sounds of light splashing filtered from beyond the bushes.

Heath exhaled loudly and turned again on his bedroll. He was remembering the feel of Cora's breasts in his back and the feel of her hands as they circled him, sometimes moving lower than necessary, making him tingle all over; and Beau listened to Heath, knowing what was going through his head and hoping he'd forget it; but he didn't.

Suddenly Heath sat up and sighed; then he stood up and stretched. "Damn, she's right," he said, his voice husky, and his whole body quivered as he took a step toward the bushes that concealed Cora.

"Heath!" Beau's voice was harsh, and Heath stopped, staring down at him in the darkness.

"I have to, Beau," he whispered urgently, "I have to. I can't take it anymore. I have to find out," and he kept going behind the bushes and Beau relaxed again without trying to stop him. What was the use of fighting him? Each man had to find himself in his own way, and yet, he hoped he was doing the right thing.

Heath stopped on the other side of the bushes. The moon was rising above the trees as Cora stepped from the water and raised her arms, letting her wet hair fly; then he stepped from the shadows, and she stopped. She stood still, staring, her eyes wide, lips parted, and then she smiled.

"Come on in, the water's fine," she said, so low he could barely hear her, and Heath swallowed hard. He'd watched her before a few times when she'd bathed, and he knew every curve of her body, the lift of her breasts, the way the skin flattened across her stomach and was lost in the dark patch below, and the thought made his blood flow hot through his veins.

He stripped slowly, his eyes never leaving her as she stood watching him; then, as he stepped from his breeches, she stepped forward hesitantly, letting him wait for her until she was directly in front of him.

"I was wondering when you'd finally make up your mind," she whispered softly, and reached out, touching him just below the navel, running her fingers across his stomach, and he felt himself begin to harden even more than he already was.

She stared down at him in the moonlight and sighed. He might be only fifteen, but, God, he could have made Gabe jealous, and she moved her eyes to his face, then ran her hand up his chest to his ear. To his surprise, she leaned forward and kissed his chest, running her tongue across it.

He began to sweat, his breathing short and labored, and he reached out, touching one of her nipples, trying to remember what Beau had told him, gentle but firm, soft and loving, yet passionate and demanding, and he cupped her breast in one hand as he reached out and pulled her head up, his mouth covering hers, and he couldn't have turned back now even if he'd wanted, and he didn't.

Beau listened to the faint sounds from behind the bushes, knowing what every groan, every sigh meant, and he died a thousand times remembering Rebel, wishing now he'd taken her anyway. He'd wanted to for so long.

Minutes lengthened into an hour; then the noise stopped abruptly, and he heard a soft splashing; then the splashing became fainter, and he looked up as Heath, wearing only pants, pulling his shirt on, almost staggered from behind the bushes.

Beau raised his head and watched as Heath moved to his bedroll and sat down, shaking his head slowly, spent and breathless.

"You all right?" asked Beau, his voice barely above a whisper, and Heath nodded.

"Oh, my God!" he sighed breathlessly, his voice husky, and Beau could hear his heavy breathing, and he seemed to shiver. "Oh, my God, Beau, I had a woman," he exclaimed incredulously, as if he couldn't believe it. "I had a woman. Holy Christ! I never knew it'd be like that. . . ."

Beau smirked in the darkness. "Sounds more like she had you," he said, and Heath fell back on his bedroll, staring up at the star-filled sky and the moon hanging directly over the river.

"Whichever way," he whispered wondrously, sounding completely exhausted, "I don't really care. I finally did it. I did everything you said, and she liked it." He sighed again and swore under his breath, pleased with himself. "Jesus, thanks, Beau," and he stretched his arms above his head and relaxed. "Thanks." And as Beau listened to the gentle splashing of the water still coming from the river, Heath, contented, fell into a deep sleep.

Beau listened to Heath's deep breathing as he slept peacefully, wondering how much longer Cora was planning to stay in the water; then all at once the splashing stopped, and he waited.

The moon was bathing this side of the river now, and he stirred, sitting up, holding himself on both elbows as he watched her, still naked, step from behind the bushes.

She glanced quickly at Heath, realizing he was asleep, then turned back to Beau and stared at him as she moved forward, her hips undulating seductively. She stopped above him, staring down, breasts firm and high, a half smile on her lips; then suddenly she dropped to her knees beside him in the dirt of the riverbank.

"How does an Indian make love?" she asked softly, and her eyes bored into his.

He should have been surprised, but he wasn't. "Those bucks back at your pa's farm would have showed you," he answered, leaning his head back on his bedroll. "Maybe I should have left you there."

She smiled. "But you didn't," she whispered, taking a deep breath. "I think I got cheated, why don't you show me?"

He tried to keep his voice down. "Wasn't Heath enough for you?"

She reached out and touched his face, then picked up his hand and set it on her breast, cupping his fingers around it, and Beau stared hard at her. "That was the first time for Heath," she whispered. "It was fun, but he ain't experienced enough, and he came too quick. I have a feelin', though, that you're somethin' special," and she pressed his hand harder on her breast, but Beau frowned. He wasn't having any. He was right. Cora would never be satisfied with one man.

Instead of caressing her breast, his fingers pinched, digging into the nipple.

"Hey!" she yelped, trying not to wake Heath, backing away from him, rubbing the end of her breast, her eyes blazing. "What the hell you doin'?"

"You might as well know, Cora," he answered lazily, as if he didn't give a damn, "I don't rouse all that easy. It takes more woman than you'll ever be to take what I can give out, so you might as well stick to junior there," and he motioned toward Heath. "At least you'll keep him happy for a while."

She leaned back and stared at him angrily. "You know, you're somethin'," she said through clenched teeth. "You don't look Indian. You don't even act Indian, most of the time that is, but you've got a mean streak, Beau. Hell, all I wanted—"

"I know what you wanted, but forget it. I'm not your type." He leaned back again, taking his eyes from her, staring overhead at the stars, and he felt her move away from him, slipping back into her clothes; then she walked over again and stood looking down at him.

"You're a funny one," she finally said, half smiling, and he sighed.

"Yeah, I know."

"No hard feelin's?"

"No hard feelings."

"You can't blame a girl for tryin'."

"I guess not."

" 'Night, Beau."

" 'Night," and he watched her walk over and drop down beside Heath and stretch out on her back; then he could have sworn he heard her whisper, "But I bet it sure would have been somethin'," and he rolled over, shutting his eyes.

They reached Harrisburg the next morning, late, and managed to get rid of the buckskins, bows and arrows, everything that breathed of the frontier. Heath already had his clothes. A deep green velvet coat with buff trim and gold buttons and the shirt his mother'd made with ruffles down the front and a pair of buff breeches tucked into shiny black riding boots. The only thing he had to buy was a hat, and it was low-crowned with a buff feather at the brim, and he wore it cocked forward jauntily.

Beau had to buy his clothes and picked out a dark gray broadcloth coat with black trim and silver buttons, black pants and black riding boots, with a low-crowned black hat and a ruffle-fronted shirt with more ruffles at the wrist. Beau's clothes were secondhand, but good, and fit him well, and both men cut quite a figure as they stood in the leather shop picking out saddles and bridle.

"What do we do about Cora?" asked Heath as he glanced out the shop window, where she stood in her old clothes, the long braid hanging down her back, a disgusted look on her face.

Beau sighed. They sure as hell couldn't get her a horse of her own. As it was, they'd traded almost everything they had to get what they'd acquired. The last thing to go was the rifles, and Beau felt uneasy without one, but he still had his knife. And she needed a dress too, and a bonnet. . . . Well, they had some coffee left, and a few other things. Maybe . . .

Beau bit his lip. "Don't worry, Heath, she'll have to keep

riding with you, but I'll see she gets some clothes," and they left the leather shop.

Three days later when they crossed the Schuylkill River into Philadelphia and headed down High Street, Heath's stomach was fluttering worse than it had the night he took Cora for the first time. She pressed close to him. Her plain yellow dress, straw bonnet, long stockings, and button shoes, paid for with the last of their salt, were not the latest fashion, but they were serviceable, and she still wore her long hair in one braid down the back.

Beau had to admit, with her large brown eyes, small nose, and full mouth, she was attractive enough. Oh, well, he left her to Heath, who seemed content, for a new intimacy had developed between the two. One that made Beau nervous, however, because he was afraid Heath was falling in love, and there wasn't much he could do about it.

This was Heath's first visit to a city the size of Philadelphia, and he was in awe. But Cora and her parents had passed through on their way west, and Beau had attended school here, so it was nothing new to them.

It was late afternoon when they rode into the noise and clatter, and Heath frowned. "Is it always like this?" he asked as they made their way through the crowds at the center square at High and Broad streets, and Beau nodded.

"It'll be worse tomorrow."

"Why?"

"Market day. Wednesday and Saturday." He reined to the right, Heath following his lead, as a pig squealed, running beneath the horses' feet, heading for the garbage at the side of the road, where another pig tried to defend a half-rotten head of cabbage. "On market day you're lucky you can get through." Beau maneuvered his horse alongside a small carriage, missed an ice peddler and a man selling ice cream from a trundle barrow, then moved back to the center of the road, avoiding a wagonload of furniture that rumbled by.

"Do you know where we go first?" asked Heath, shouting to be heard above the din that was almost deafening as men and women shouted at each other, children screamed, horses clattered on the cobblestones, dogs barked, and now suddenly church bells began to ring.

"Butter bells from Christ Church," exclaimed Beau, yelling back, pointing toward the sound of the bells. "They always ring the day before market day." Then he motioned forward with his head as he answered Heath's question. "Up ahead there's an inn." As they rode on, Heath saw a sign with a blue anchor painted on it, and the words "Blue Anchor Inn." Beau pulled up to the edge of the brick pavement, sliding down, fastening his horse to a hitching post, and Heath did the same, then helped Cora down after him.

The Blue Anchor Inn wasn't the best of inns, but it wasn't the worst either, and it was in the main section of town, close enough to the market, yet far enough not to be right in the thick of it.

Beau and Heath straightened their clothes, and Beau nodded toward the door. "This used to be the Green Lantern sixteen years ago, Heath," he offered as they walked toward the door. "Your mother stayed here when Reb was born, and she and your father were married here."

For the first time since they'd left Fort Locke, Heath felt that sickening feeling in the pit of his stomach, the same feeling he'd felt the night his mother had told him the truth. This was the beginning of the search, and both men squared their shoulders; then Heath took Cora's arm and tucked it in his, and they stepped inside.

5

About ten people sat at the tables eating and talking, and none paid attention to them as they came in. They walked into the center of the room and stood looking for the proprietor, then glanced toward the back as a short, well-rounded woman with graying blond hair stepped in from what looked [illegible] kitchen.

Suddenly she stopped, staring, a puzzled look on her face as her eyes fell on Heath, and she scowled even harder as she slowly walked toward them.

She screwed her face up as she continued to stare. "Don't I know you, young man?" she asked, frowning, and Heath glanced quickly at Beau.

"Not him," answered Beau. "But you may have known his father," and the woman glanced at him sharply as he asked, "Are you Polly, by any chance?"

She scowled. "Aye. I'm Polly, but who be you?"

"May we talk privately?"

She shrugged, gesturing about at the people in the room, who seemed quite uninterested in them. "This is private enough," she answered.

"As you wish," said Beau, then asked, "Sixteen years ago this inn was known as the Green Lantern, was it not?"

She nodded. "Aye."

"And do you remember a young woman who worked for you? She had a small baby you helped bring into the world. . . . She married a British soldier . . ."

Suddenly the woman sighed, her hands moving to her cheeks, face flushed, eyes alert. "The little missus," she cried happily, nodding. "Aye." Then she pointed at Heath. "You . . . But it can't be. . . ."

"I'm his son," offered Heath, and the woman's hands rested on her breast as she sighed.

"Aye." She nodded. "It brings back memories. Those two. So young they were, and he loved her so. . . . It was so tragic."

"Tragic?" asked Heath.

"There were rumors." She shrugged. "You know how it is. Her first man came back when they thought he was dead. . . . He never talked about what happened. That was so long ago. But tell me, where is he?"

Heath's eyes faltered. "I was hoping you could tell me."

"Me?"

"That's why we're here."

Beau explained the situation, and Polly shook her head. "Oh, mercy. I wish I could help," she said sadly as he finished. "But I haven't seen him since shortly after the war. He used to come here afterward once in a while and talk, and he and my John would have a drink together." She reminisced. "So lonely he was." She shook her head again. "It's been years . . . so many years."

"Do you have any idea?" asked Beau. "Did he have any friends?"

She thought. "The Newells', where they lived for a while, then there was a French lady. I remember he brought her here once. She reminded me a bit of your mother, but I don't remember her name. A few years later he came in, said he was leaving, but didn't say where he was going, then he just disappeared."

Disappointment covered Heath's face, and Polly smiled. "But I'll tell you, young man," she went on, her jaw set firmly, "you and your friend shall have a room here for as long as you wish, free of charge, while you hunt for him. That's the least I can do for you."

Beau nodded graciously. "We're in your debt, madam," he answered, using a charm Heath only now realized he had. "But would it be too presumptuous of me to ask if perhaps you could use a serving girl in the inn?" He explained about Cora, and Polly's big heart was once more tied in knots as she looked her over, noticing the warmth in Heath's eyes when he looked at the young girl; then she nodded, smiling knowingly.

"It's so hard in these times," she said. "But I think maybe something can be arranged. If not here, then I have friends," and Beau smiled.

"We'd be ever so grateful," he answered and Polly's eyes sparkled.

"If only John were here to see, but he died two years ago," she muttered as she walked ahead, taking them to their room; then she had Cora follow her back down to the kitchen, where she'd have a room near the pantry.

"What makes you think Cora wants to be a serving girl?" asked Heath as the door shut behind the women and he began to look about the room.

"What else would you have her do? Lie on her back and collect from the sailors down at the wharf?" answered Beau, and Heath glanced at him sharply, realizing that suddenly it was as if Beau were different. In the woods he was Indian, quiet and aloof; now, instead, he was charming and glib, as if he'd been born to the drawing room with a charm of speech and manner befitting a gentleman of breeding, yet he was hard and callous—"cynical" would be more the word for it.

"What's wrong, Beau?" asked Heath as he opened the window and leaned out, then looked back at his friend.

"You really don't know, do you, Heath?" asked Beau, and Heath raised his hands, questioning.

"Look at me," demanded Beau angrily, gesturing toward himself. "Take a good look. I look white, I pass for white, but I'm not white. Does that answer your question?" he said bitterly, and Heath shook his head. "You don't know what it's like, Heath, to go to balls and parties, accepted by men as an equal, talking with them as you would your friends, dancing with beautiful women who hang on your every word and toy with you, flirting as they would with any other man, giving you open invitations—they smell of sweet perfume, their eyes deep and passionate, their bodies waiting to enjoy what you know you can give them, yet you know that one word, Indian, and the men would snub you, the women shrink from your touch. The light in their eyes would turn to hate. I've seen it and I loathe it. . . . And the women back home, Indians. Women with coarse black hair and dark sloe eyes that hold no attraction for me. Women I have nothing in common with. Dammit, Heath, what am I? My mother's one of four wives, my father a savage, yet I feel like a white man." His jaw set hard. "What am I?"

Heath stared at him, and suddenly he understood his bitterness and felt maybe now he understood him more than ever before. "You're a man, Beau," he answered hesitantly, staring at his friend. "You can be whatever you want to be, because you are a man."

Beau sighed. "I don't agree," he said, and walked toward

the window, leaning out, staring toward the waterfront, where he knew the wharves would be crowded with ships, and his eyes were pained. "If I had my way, Heath," he finally said, "I think I'd like to go down to the wharf, get on a ship, and sail away and never come back." Then he straightened, squaring his shoulders. "So much for that," he said, turning to Heath as if to brush his former words aside. "Now, which shall we do first, hunt for the Newells or try to locate what's left of the Philadelphia Light Horse Troop?"

Heath gestured with his hand. "You're leading the way," he said. "Whatever you say."

Beau smiled acknowledgment. "Then let's start with the soldiers," he answered, and they left the room, closing the door firmly behind them.

It took no time at all to learn where headquarters was for the Philadelphia Light Horse Troop; however, the last entry on their records for a Roth Chapman had him listed as a colonel, a promotion Heath had been unaware of, and it was written on the day of his discharge, September 8, 1783, with no forwarding address, but a list of citations behind him that would cover the chest of any hero with medals, and it brought a lump to Heath's throat. At least his father wasn't a coward. But where was he?

The officer they were talking to tried to be helpful, but he'd been in the troop for only about six years. "I don't have the faintest notion where he might be, lad," he said as he closed the ledger in front of him. "We don't keep track."

"Would anyone else know?" asked Beau.

"I doubt it. Some men are still here who served under him, but I remember one night, not too long ago, we were talking about the old days, and Colonel Chapman's name came up . . . some of the men wondered what had happened to him, but nobody seemed to know." He scratched his chin. "They talked about some French lady he knew, can't remember her name, though. . . ." He turned to another soldier at a desk in the rear of the room, a man in his early forties with dark piercing eyes. "Hey, Lieutenant, you remember the name of that French lady the men said Colonel Chapman used to escort about town when he was here?"

The man's eyes shifted to the two young men standing before the captain's desk, and he bit his lip. "Who wants to know?" he asked, his face expressionless.

"The lads here. They're trying to locate the colonel."

The man stood up, straightening himself, trying to look

tall, but he was still shorter than both Beau and Heath and a bit heavier. "Why?" he asked as he walked over and stared at them, looking exceptionally hard at Heath.

Beau tried to be polite. "Does it really matter why, Lieutenant?" he asked.

"It could." The man didn't look too pleased. "May I ask your names?"

"I'm Beauregard Dante, my friend's Heath . . ." He hesitated.

"Heath Chapman," finished Heath, and Beau's eyes softened. "I'm the colonel's son," Heath explained proudly, but the lieutenant's eyes narrowed.

"The colonel wasn't married."

Heath's face reddened and his jaw tightened. "I'm afraid you've been misinformed, sir," he answered, trying to keep his voice calm. "Now, do you happen to know the name of the lady in question?"

"I know it."

Beau's patience was running thin. "Would it be too much to ask for it, sir?"

"You're French?" the man asked Beau, and Beau glanced at Heath, then nodded.

"Yes, sir, part."

The man shrugged. "I shouldn't tell you, but, hell, what's the difference? It was Madame Dubonné," he finally said. "Madame Marget Dubonné."

"You know where she is today?" asked Beau, but the man shook his head.

"That, sir, I don't know," he answered, then smiled a sneering half smile. "And if you're going to start looking for her, I wish you luck, gentlemen, you'll need it." Beau looked at the captain, who shrugged his shoulders as the lieutenant returned to his desk.

"Why?" asked Beau as the lieutenant sat back down at his paperwork.

"You'll find out soon enough," he answered. "Just do me a favor, though, gentlemen, don't let anyone know I was the one who gave you her name. I wouldn't appreciate it." Both Heath and Beau looked puzzled as the captain at the front desk stared at the lieutenant, then shrugged, shaking his head.

It was too late to look for the Newells that evening, so they returned to the Blue Anchor. Polly shook her head as she served them supper.

"I don't know what to do about your young miss, gentlemen," she said, rather worried. "I've got her working in the kitchen, and I need the help, but she doesn't know much of anything, does she?"

Heath glanced at Beau, who looked at the woman apprehensively. "She lived on a farm, surely she can cook."

Polly shook her head. "She can serve tables, but not much more. Maybe I can teach her, though. I'll try tomorrow." She shook her head. "I sure can use the help."

"By the way," Beau said as they began eating, "we learned the name of the Frenchwoman Heath's father used to see. Ever hear of a Madame Dubonné?"

Polly frowned, unaware that two tables over, a pair of heads suddenly jerked to attention at the mention of the Frenchwoman's name and two pairs of ears strained hard to listen to the rest of the conversation. "There are so many people in the city," Polly said. "I remember the name now, but if she's here, I've never heard it mentioned since."

Beau glanced at Heath, then back to Polly. "Would there be any reason why . . . the lieutenant at the headquarters acted strangely? Do you have any idea who Madame Dubonné was?"

"No. The young major—he was a colonel by then—he brought her here, as I said before, once, maybe twice. They ate, then left. I didn't remember her name until now, but as I say, she spoke with a French accent and looked a bit like the little missus." She looked at Heath. "That's what I used to call your mother." Heath smiled.

As Polly, Heath, and Beau continued talking, the two men at the next table finished their meal and left, having paid for it in advance, and as they stepped from the inn, the elder man, tall, with graying hair, turned to his companion.

"Do you know those two?" he asked, and the man frowned.

"I've never seen them before, M'sieur LeFleur."

The taller man stood staring ahead, his eyes hostile, the nostrils in his hawklike nose flaring slightly; then he sighed. "You will find out, Claude, and report back to me as soon as possible. And you will say nothing to M'sieur Gereaux as yet."

"Oui," the man said, and when M'sieur LeFleur moved on down the street, Claude melted into the shadows and stood watching the Blue Anchor, his large greedy eyes glued to the doorway.

Heath and Beau had stabled their horses in a nearby livery, and first thing the next morning they headed back out High Street, up Broad Street to Vine, and out toward where the Newell estate had been, according to the directions given to Beau by Quinn.

As they rode along on the dusty road, a short distance behind them was a small nondescript man with chin whiskers, dark inconspicuous clothes, riding a roan gelding. He stopped whenever they stopped and started whenever they started, but only Beau seemed aware of it as he glanced quickly behind them at intervals, but he said nothing to Heath.

The large stone mansion was easy to spot even after all the years, and the name Newell was still clearly visible on the sign out front that was almost covered by rambling-rose vines with huge roses hanging from them, and as they rode between the stone pillars at the edge of the drive and headed toward the house, Heath pointed to the small stone cottage at one side, almost dwarfed now by the huge willow tree in the front yard. It was where his mother said she and his father had lived during the short time of their marriage.

They rode up to the front of the house, and a young black boy ran out, greeting them as they reined up at the steps, taking their horses' reins, and holding them, while both men eyed each other with raised eyebrows, surprised at this luxury; they thanked him as they walked up the steps and lifted the heavy iron knocker, letting it fall in a tattoo of rhythm.

The house was very impressive, and Heath stared at it in awe as the door was opened by a young woman in a dark gray dress and white apron, wearing a mobcap, her slightly protruding teeth overly exposed as she smiled graciously.

"Yes, sirs?" she asked as she stared at them curiously, and Beau doffed his hat, bowing graciously.

"Are the Newells at home?" he asked, and her eyes studied his dark handsome face; then she glanced to the younger man at his side, who was equally nice-looking.

"May I say who's calling?"

"Mr. Beauregard Dante and Mr. Heath Chapman," answered Beau, and the girl curtsied.

"Wait here, please," she said, and showed them inside; then she shut the door and disappeared from the foyer down a long hall.

The house was more than Heath had imagined a house ever could be. Raised in the wilderness, he'd seen houses like this only in paintings in the books his mother had sent for from back east.

"To think a place like this really exists," he said to Beau as they stood waiting. "And my father actually knew these people."

"Let's hope they know where he is," answered Beau, and both men turned as the maid came back.

"Mrs. Newell wants to know what you want," she said.

Beau exuded charm. "Inform her that we're old friends of the family, in a manner of speaking." The maid shrugged, disappearing once more down the elegant hall with its elaborate flowered wallpaper and highly polished floors beneath plush red carpeting. A curved staircase with the same red carpeting was at one end of the foyer, and crystal chandeliers hung overhead from the high ceiling.

A few minutes later Heath and Beau were escorted into a huge sitting room toward the back of the house and on outside to a terrace of flagstone, where a woman sat on a low wrought-iron bench, embroidery in her lap and a small table with a cool drink on it beside her.

Beau was the perfect gentleman as he stepped forward and introduced himself and Heath.

The woman was in her late thirties, hair stiffened and piled atop her head in the latest fashion, her pink satin dress trimmed with rows of lace about the neck and sleeves, the hoop beneath holding it so her dainty satin slippers showed, and a black velvet choker graced her slender neck, shortening its length, making her more comely.

"You're friends of the family?" she questioned as she offered them a seat, and Beau's face reddened slightly.

"I'm afraid I stretched the truth a bit, madam," he apologized as they accepted her invitation to sit down in the wrought-iron chairs opposite her, and he continued explaining about their search for Heath's father as Mrs. Newell listened attentively; then she sighed, shaking her head.

"It's a strange story, and I wish there was something I could do," she answered. "But I'm afraid you've come for nothing. I'm not the Mrs. Newell you're looking for. You want my husband's aunt and uncle. They were childless. His aunt died first, and when his uncle died, he left everything to my husband, and we've been carrying on ever since. I'm sure John didn't know the man you're looking for. We moved to Philadelphia only a few years ago."

"Do you still have the shipyards?" asked Heath.

She nodded. "Yes."

"Perhaps someone there knew him." She thought a minute. "Perhaps. There are a few men there that worked for John's uncle for a number of years. You might try there. You'll have to go to the docks. The main office is near the corner of Pine and Penn at the waterfront. Naturally the actual building is down at the edge of the river. You'll find my husband at the main office. I only wish I could help more."

Beau expressed the same wish, then begged her leave, and both men left, disappointed again. They had barely begun, and already things weren't going too well. Then, as they headed back toward town and the waterfront, Beau spotted the same roan gelding with the same inconspicuous man following not far behind, and now he really began to wonder.

Without giving an explanation, he took Heath back a different way, traveling farther down Vine Street, past Broad Street to Second Street, then heading straight to the market, and still the small man on the gelding was never far behind. There was no doubt now that he was following them.

When they reached the market, Heath reined his horse to a standstill beside Beau and just stared at everything. He had never seen a market like this before. No one rode inside the market area itself, and it was about four city blocks long, right in the center of High Street. There were sections for vegetables, fruits, fish, meat.

"You can even buy possum and bear meat," shouted Beau as a group of young boys almost knocked into their horses, chasing some chickens that had gotten loose.

"Lord, where do all the people come from?" asked Heath, and Beau smiled.

"Every farmer within fifty miles makes his way to the market, and the ships bring in the rest." He pointed to one section, where oranges, figs, and spices were on display. "There's something you've never seen, Heath. Fresh oranges. Well, not too fresh, but not dried peel, either," and Heath nodded. It was fantastic.

Beau pointed across the way, and Heath followed his finger in time to see Polly and Cora moving through the market, Polly picking out produce, putting it into a basket Cora carried on her arm.

Both men nudged their horses a bit closer and watched the two for a few minutes as Polly haggled over her change with the man selling eggs; then Beau caught her eye as Polly looked over, and she motioned for him, that she wanted to talk.

The two women moved to the side of the market and sidled toward one of the openings where they could speak to Beau and Heath.

"Did you have any luck?" asked Polly.

"None," answered Beau. "Mr. and Mrs. Newell are both dead, and the nephew owns everything. But we're heading for the Newell shipyard offices now, someone there might know something."

Polly frowned as she leaned closer to Beau, while Cora made soft doe eyes at Heath. "I think you'd better be careful," she cautioned Beau. "Something strange happened today after you'd left the inn."

Beau leaned closer to be heard above the din. "What's that?"

"Two men came in and sat down to eat, and that in itself weren't unusual, but they started asking questions about you and Heath."

"What kind of questions?"

"Where you were from, what you were doing here, and why were you looking for Madame Dubonné."

"Did you find out who they were?"

"They wouldn't say . . . they just avoided my questions, and when I told them it was none of their business, the looks they gave me were enough to make my hair stand on end. They didn't look like respectable gents—mean and unsavory they were."

Beau straightened in the saddle and glanced about him at the crowd, once more spying the roan gelding with the little man on its back. The man was trying to be nonchalant, watching the crowd, but Beau knew his eyes were aware of them at all times.

He didn't like it. Not at all, and he cautioned Polly. "Be careful, Polly," he said as he leaned down toward her. "I don't know who they could have been or why they're so interested in what doesn't concern them, but I have a feeling they're up to no good."

"My sentiments exactly," she said. "But don't you worry, they won't learn nothin' from me." Then she looked about the market. "I guess I'd best be gettin' the rest of my shoppin' done afore the best is all picked over," and she nudged Cora. "Come on, child, let's be on our way. We've got food to cook when we get back to the inn, and time's a-wastin'."

They said good-bye, and Beau and Heath watched them disappear among the crowd; then they turned their horses about and headed for the docks.

"I have a strange feeling, Heath," said Beau as they rode slowly, picking their way through the crowds, "that finding your father isn't going to be as easy as we thought, and I also have a feeling that for some reason finding Madame Dubonné is going to be equally as hard."

"Well, I won't give up," answered Heath as he reined his horse aside for a young woman who gazed at him flirtatiously, then smiled and moved on. "I have to find him if it takes forever." He frowned. "Do you think that little fella following us has any connection with the men who came to Polly's?" he asked suddenly, and Beau glanced at him surprised. "You didn't think I noticed, did you?" he said. "I may be dumb about some things, Beau, but I've followed enough trails to know when somebody's following mine."

Beau turned down Water Street with Heath close beside him, and the crowd began to thin out. "I was hoping you hadn't noticed," he answered. "Somehow, in some way, I think we've stirred up a hornet's nest, and I sure as hell wish I knew why. When we're through at the Newell shipyards, if we haven't gotten a lead, I intend to stop at the President's."

Heath looked at him sharply. "Do you think we'll have any trouble getting in to see him?"

"We shouldn't if he and your father were really as good friends as your father claims."

"Quinn Locke's not my father."

"You know very well what I mean," he answered, and Heath frowned as they turned down Pine Street toward the corner of Penn Street, where the Newell main offices were located, hoping they wouldn't have to search further.

As they stepped into the rather dingy offices and stood looking about, both of them felt a bit out of place. A group of men were in the back working noisily around desks and tables, all of them with their shirt sleeves rolled up, and there were three men at one side perched atop high stools, drawing boards in front of them, their shirt sleeves also rolled up, and they were working on paper drawings that would someday emerge as ships. They were trying new designs. Sloops, schooners, brigantines, two-masted square riggers, single fore- and aft-rigged masts, two-masters with square sails, three-masted barks. Anything that floated on water and could be built was turned out at their drawing boards. They were the heart of the Newell shipyards.

The room had an old wood smell, the kind that seeps up when the sun has baked wood for a long time, and Beau wrinkled his nose slightly as he touched Heath's arm and they moved to a small glassed-in cubicle in the side of the room, where two men were seated, arguing rather heatedly over something.

The men looked up as they approached, and the younger of the two, a man perhaps in his early forties, stood up and walked to the door, addressing them.

"Something for you, gents?"

"Mr. Newell?" asked Beau, and the man confirmed Beau's question. "If you could spare a few minutes of your time . . . your wife said you may be of help."

"My wife sent you?"

Beau motioned toward the gentleman seated in the chair in Mr. Newell's office. "We didn't mean to interrupt," he apologized. "We can wait."

"Not at all. That's perfectly all right." Mr. Newell didn't seem perturbed. He was a pleasant man. A bit paunchy and red-faced, but friendly, with bushy eyebrows and large brown eyes that studied both Heath and Beau intently. "Mr. Brinkman can wait. We were just discussing the price of lumber. A bit exuberantly, I'm afraid. I'll just give him some time to think about my offer." The gentleman at the desk turned, scowling, then harrumphed as he turned his back to them again and waited as John Newell stepped from the small office. "Now, what can I do for you? Buy a ship? A schooner maybe . . . a small sloop?"

Beau smiled, then glanced across the room at the scale model of a full-rigged frigate nestling in the window at the front of the shop, with a sloop on one side of it and a brigantine on the other. "I wish I could afford one," he answered. "But our business is of a more personal nature. We're trying to locate my friend's father," and he glanced quickly at Heath, then back to John Newell. "He was a good friend of your uncle's, and although your wife said she didn't think you'd ever met him, she thought there may be someone here who knew him. His name was Roth Chapman and he was a colonel in the Philadelphia Light Horse Troop, discharged about eight years ago."

John Newell frowned. "Chapman . . . seems I remember the name. I think I met him a few times at my uncle's house, but"—he shook his head—"I wouldn't have the faintest idea where he might be today." He raised his hand as Heath started to say something. "Wait a minute, lad," he said, then turned and called toward the three men working on the high stools. "Henri?" One of the men turned, cocking his head. "May we speak with you a minute?" The man slid from the stool, wiping ink-stained hands on his leather apron, then adding another ink smear to his face as he rubbed a knuckle across his chin.

"Oui?"

John Newell addressed Beau. "I didn't hear your names, sir?" and Beau realized he hadn't given them.

"I'm Beauregard Dante," answered Beau, putting his hand on his chest, and he gestured to Heath "and Heath Chapman."

Mr. Newell acknowledged their names; then: "Henri," he said, motioning toward Heath, "Mr. Chapman here is looking for his father. He was in the Philadelphia Light Horse Troop some years ago. You've been here for some time and used to visit my uncle a great deal. Maybe you know him or know of him. His name was Colonel Roth Chapman," and as John Newell spoke the name, Beau saw a look of recognition cross Henri's eyes, and they narrowed as he studied both of them for a minute.

"Colonel Chapman was not married," answered Henri finally, his French accent very heavy as he looked suspiciously at Heath. "He had no son."

Heath straightened his shoulders. "You're wrong, sir," he said harshly. "My father was married for a very short time, and I assure you, I am his son."

The Frenchman wasn't a big man, but gave the impression of being big because he was stocky and broad-shouldered, with dark, graying hair, a sharp nose, and a receding chin that he tried to stick out stubbornly as he regarded Heath.

"Why did he not speak of you, m'sieur?" he asked slowly. "He never talked of a wife or son."

"He didn't know about me. It's a long story. The marriage ended suddenly . . . Then you did know him?"

Henri nodded. *"Oui.* I knew the colonel. I met him during the war."

"Do you know where he went when he left Philadelphia?"

The Frenchman shook his head. *"Non.* He resigned his commission." The man shrugged. "Some say he went back to England, some say to France. He bought a ship from Mr.

Newell, an old relic that he restored, and he sailed to . . . who knows where," and Heath's heart sank.

"What of this Madame Dubonné?" asked Beau. "Would she know where he went, or could she have gone with him? Everyone we've asked about her seems so vague."

At the mention of the woman's name the man's face turned pale, and a look of fear filled his eyes. "You have been asking around about Madame Dubonné?" he asked hurriedly, and both Heath and Beau were surprised at the look on his face.

"Yes," answered Beau, and the Frenchman's eyes hardened.

"Then I suggest, m'sieurs, that you leave Philadelphia as soon as possible if you value your lives? To ask of Madame Dubonné is a death warrant," and he turned sharply on his heel, walked back to his desk, and climbed upon the stool as Heath, Beau, and Mr. Newell stared after him.

Beau followed Henri across the room, with Heath and John Newell close behind. "What did you mean by what you just said?" he asked the Frenchman, but the man only looked at him stubbornly, refusing to answer.

"Good Lord, Henri," exclaimed John. "At least you could tell them something."

Henri's eyes grew dark, his jaw set firm as his fingers rubbed together nervously. "I do not wish to die, m'sieurs," he finally answered. "As far as I am concerned, there was never a Madame Dubonné, she never existed, and if the young gentlemen will take my advice, they will forget they ever heard the name. I will say no more," and he turned back to the drawing board with finality and pretended to become engrossed in the sketch of a ship on the table before him, but his hand was trembling.

Beau turned to Mr. Newell, who shrugged his shoulders.

"You must understand," said John Newell. "Henri is French by birth, and right now in France things are not too good. King Louis is fearful of his crown, the people are restless. Perhaps this woman is mixed up in it all, who knows? Maybe his advice is good. Perhaps you should leave well enough alone."

"I must find my father," said Heath stubbornly. "Whatever it takes, I'll do it, and if he's with this woman, I'll find him."

Beau sighed. "You see how it is, Mr. Newell. We'll keep searching." They turned to go. "Thank you for your help, and if you hear anything, we'll be at the Blue Anchor."

Mr. Newell said good-bye, then headed for his office as Beau and Heath moved to the door, and as they went out they could hear him in the office once more arguing over the price of lumber with Mr. Brinkman.

6

"Well, what do we do now?" asked Heath as they stepped onto the pavement and he glanced at Beau.

"We do like I said," answered Beau. "We see the President. But we go tonight. He's probably at the State House or with the assembly this afternoon, and I'd rather see him at home. Meanwhile, we'll go back to the inn. It's way past noon, and I could do with a bit of food," and they headed for their horses.

They bypassed the marketplace this time and took Front Street to Spruce, then moved up Dock Street to Third, then Chestnut to Eighth, and on to High Street, and Heath still couldn't get over the size of the city with all its noise and clatter. They passed shops and businesses that catered to ships and to the men who owned and sailed them, with taverns, coffeehouses, warehouses. The air smelled of fish, rope, and tar, combined with the smell of decaying garbage in the drainage ditches, and Heath turned up his nose in disgust. He was used to the fresh green smell of the woods.

Few people in the city could read, so along with the names written on each sign above shops and taverns was a picture to identify it, such as the blue anchor that hung above Polly's place, and this too fascinated Heath. His mother had insisted that her children have an education, and it seemed so natural to Heath that all men should read and write. To find out that they didn't was rather a shock.

The city was such a paradox. Past the rough waterfront area were hat shops, cobblers, tailors, bakeries, print shops, and houses of all kinds. Rich men mingled with poor. The literate with the illiterate, the gentle with the cruel, and he just wasn't sure whether he liked it or not. Especially as he and Beau glanced behind them and were well aware that the small man on the gelding was still there. No, he wasn't quite sure.

They took their horses to the stables, then walked around the corner to the Blue Anchor, and as they reached the door, Beau stopped, his hand on the door handle.

"Look back over my shoulder, Heath," he said softly as he let go the handle and reached down, pretending to take something from the sole of his boot. "We've picked up another friend."

As Heath glanced back, a man ducked into the doorway of a bake shop across the street. Then Heath turned and glanced back the other way, spotting the small man on the gelding again as Beau straightened up and opened the door. "Do you think the two of them are together?" he asked Beau, and Beau frowned.

"Let's find out," he said, and as they stepped inside, closing the door behind them, he moved to the front window and peeked through a small slit in a curtain; then his eyes narrowed as the man on the horse joined the man in the doorway and they stood talking. "They're together," he said, and turned around, almost bumping into Heath, who was looking over his shoulder.

"Because of this . . . this Madame Dubonné?" asked Heath.

"Probably."

"I wonder why."

"Who knows? Maybe Mr. Newell's right. Maybe she's connected with what's happening in France."

"But France is so far away."

"That's right," answered Beau. "But that doesn't always stop people from getting involved."

"Who's getting involved in what?" asked a voice from behind them, and they turned around to face Cora, who held a large tureen steaming with food. "I bet you're both hungry as a bear," she said as she smiled, and her soft brown eyes were warm for both of them, but Heath didn't seem to notice that she looked at Beau the same way she looked at him.

"Lead the way," he said, rubbing his stomach. "I'm starved."

She led them to a table in the corner, and within minutes they were enjoying a chicken stew with brown bread and cider to wash it down, and fruit cobbler for dessert.

When they finished the food, they sat relaxed, sipping at the cider, and neither noticed as two men entered the inn and stood looking about; then, spotting Heath and Beau, they walked directly to them.

Both men were of medium height, wore white powdered wigs, but other than that, were nondescript. The kind of men hard to describe. Plain and ordinary except for their fancy clothes that marked them as men of wealth. They moved slowly across the room, stopping beside the table where Beau and Heath sat, and Beau's eyes studied them warily.

"M'sieur Dante?" asked one of the men, and Beau nodded, taking the mug of cider from his lips.

"You wish to speak to me?"

"To you and your friend," the man went on. "If we may have a few words."

The men were French, which didn't surprise Beau, and he motioned for them to sit down.

"We received word that you are inquiring about town as to the whereabouts of one Madame Dubonné, is that not so?" asked one of the men as they both sat down.

Beau nodded. "That's right."

"May I ask why?"

"Do you know her?"

"That's beside the point."

"On the contrary," answered Beau. "In the first place, it's none of your business why we're looking for her . . . unless you can tell us where she is. In that case I might be persuaded to tell you."

"What makes you think we know where she is?" asked the other man.

Beau smiled cynically. "Oh, come now. You wouldn't be here if you didn't."

"Touché, M'sieur Dante," remarked the same man. "But we ask again. Why do you seek her?"

"Is it a crime?" asked Heath, and both men's eyes darkened.

"At the moment, m'sieur, it is not a crime, but a very dangerous undertaking," answered the same man warningly. "However, if we knew the reasons, perhaps it would make a difference, who knows?"

Beau took a long drink of cider, then spoke. "All right, gentlemen," and he proceeded to tell them of the search for Heath's father. When he was through, the men stared at him apprehensively.

"That's the only reason?" asked one of them, and Beau's jaw set hard.

"The only one," he answered, and the man sighed as he looked at his companion and motioned to him with his head, that they'd better be leaving.

"We will be in touch," he said, his voice barely above a whisper; then both men stood up and left without saying another word.

As Beau and Heath watched them leave, Cora slipped from the kitchen, where she'd been watching. "What did they want?" she asked breathlessly, and Heath frowned.

"They wanted to know why we were looking for Madame Dubonné," he answered, and looked surprised as Beau left the table and once more stood peeking through the slit in the curtain at the front windows.

He watched as the two men walked down the street, and minutes later the man who'd been hiding in the doorway of the bakery slipped from the shadows and started trailing after them, leaving the small man who'd been riding the gelding waiting at the corner to take over his duties, and Beau scowled. It was quite obvious now that the last two callers were not acquainted with the man from the bakery and the man on the gelding. And it was also obvious that Madame Dubonné was going to great lengths not to reveal her whereabouts because someone else was going to equally great lengths to find her. This was getting interesting, most interesting, and Beau rubbed his chin, pondering, as he turned and went back to the table.

They arrived at 190 High Street just at dark, and Heath straightened his shoulders as they walked up the marble steps of the three-story brick house. "Are you sure this is where he lives?" he asked, and Beau smiled.

"At the home of Mr. and Mrs. Robert Morris," answered Beau. "And from what I learned earlier, he should be home tonight."

Heath stood looking about, and suddenly felt a hollow feeling deep down inside as Beau lifted the door knocker.

They waited nervously for what seemed like endless minutes, and finally the door was opened a small crack by a middle-aged woman in a dark dress and mobcap, and her face wrinkled pleasantly as she questioned them.

"Yes, sirs?"

"I sent a note earlier today with a young lad," explained Beau as he bowed to her. "Is the President at home, and will he see us?"

"And who be you, sir?" she asked in sprightly fashion.

"Mr. Dante and Mr. Chapman, at your service, ma'am."

She curtsied. "If you'll wait, please, gents," she said softly, and shut the door, leaving them standing on the door stoop.

"You mean it's this easy to see him?" asked Heath.

"Not exactly," Beau answered. "We may not even get in. The door's kept locked, and that little old lady, I hear, is a formidable watchdog. No one sees the President without her permission, and it's said she has some aides of the President's inside who back her up if need be. So don't get cocky."

They continued to wait silently; then suddenly the door was opened wide this time and the little lady gestured them in.

"The President will see you," she said cheerfully. "If you'll follow me."

The house inside was as magnificent as the Newells', and it amazed Heath that people lived like this. He was used to the log house with its handmade furniture—crude but serviceable. An elegant staircase in the huge foyer led up a flight of carpeted stairs, and it was up these stairs the little lady pointed, then led the way, with Beau and Heath close behind. She ushered them into a spacious drawing room on the second floor, and as she faded into the background, announcing their names, a tall, impressive man left the chair by the fireplace where he'd been sitting and approached them.

His hair was powdered, but he wore no wig, and his clothes were casual. He wore no coat, and the ruffles on his white shirt frilled to the waist, where his shirt was tucked into blue velvet breeches, above white silk stockings that covered his slippered feet.

"You'll excuse me, gentlemen," he said in his deep resonant voice after greeting them and introducing himself, "but it feels good to relax after a long day of speeches and wrangling. I swear . . . just once it would be heaven if every man were to agree on something without having to argue about it first." Then he gestured to them. "But I'm wandering on . . . Come in, please, sit down, and tell me what this is all about. Which one of you is Quinn's son?" and Beau glanced quickly at Heath, who took a deep breath.

"Actually, neither, sir," apologized Beau, and the President scowled.

"But the note . . .?"

Beau cleared his throat. "Heath was raised as Colonel Locke's son, sir," he said, "but it takes some explaining. . . ."

The President nodded. "Well, go ahead young man, explain."

"Do you remember a Colonel Roth Chapman, sir?" asked Beau, and the President smiled.

"Indeed I do," he answered; then suddenly he took a good look at Heath, and his eyes studied him intently; then they widened as he stared incredulously, and all at once he understood. It couldn't be, but it was. This boy, this young man. "By God!" he exclaimed slowly, hesitantly, his face pale as he stared at him. "It has to be," he said, as if to himself; then he shook his head as if in disbelief, and Beau swore he saw a tear in his eye. "They were married such a short time," he said, his voice soft as it broke in mid-sentence. "No one dreamed . . ."

"That's right, sir," agreed Beau. "It was only as Heath grew up that they realized the truth."

"You're Roth's son, lad?" he questioned, and Heath nodded.

"Yes, sir. My mother is Loedicia Locke," and the President sighed as he leaned back in his chair, and for a few minutes there was silence as he stared at the ceiling, remembering that evening so long ago when Loedicia had pleaded with him to make both men understand. And now this. He closed his eyes.

"I've come to find my father," offered Heath, his voice barely above a whisper. "Do you know where he is, sir?"

The President straightened, opening his eyes as he stared at the young man, and his heart went out to him, but he had no answer. "I wish I did, young man," he answered compassionately. "Your father was one of the finest men I've ever known, but I'm afraid I haven't seen him since eighty-three, when he resigned his commission and left Philadelphia."

"Then how about a Madame Dubonné?" asked Beau, and the President's eyes sparkled.

"Ah, yes, Marget. No doubt you heard he escorted her about town. I think he was trying to forget what happened to his wife, but to pick Marget was folly. She may have looked much like your mother, young man, but I'm afraid there the similarity ended."

"But who is she?" asked Heath.

The President sighed. "Marget Dubonné is a cousin to King Louis XVI and was once lady-in-waiting to Marie Antoinette until she married General Dubonné, a close friend of General Lafayette's. She and her husband came to the colonies with General Lafayette, but unfortunately her husband caught the fever and died only a few weeks after their arrival. Madame Dubonné stayed on for some time, and she and Roth became rather close friends. In fact, they both disappeared from Philadelphia about the same time. Some people thought they left together, but I doubt it. I knew Roth too well. I've heard rumors of late that she's married to someone else and back in town. I haven't seen her, however, and so far it's just hearsay."

"I think it's more than that," said Beau. "We've been followed ever since we first spoke her name, and we've been warned to forget we ever heard of her."

The President pondered a minute, both hands clasped in front of his mouth as he stared at the two young men. "You must remember there are men in this city who fight for both sides of France," he answered frowning. "There are those who would welcome a revolution, who would die for their beliefs, and also those who support the king, and they're just as zealous. At the moment, things are bad in France, as they were here once. It hasn't been quite two years since the storming of the Bastille, and I fear that was only the beginning."

"Then you think this Madame Dubonné is mixed up in it somehow?" asked Heath.

"But I also think that if anyone knows where your father is, she does," he answered, and Beau agreed.

"But how do we find her?"

"Perhaps you've already done the right thing," he said. "You've dangled the bait, now let her come to you," and the rest of the visit he talked to Heath of his father's exploits in the war, during the battle of Philadelphia, and the friendship they'd enjoyed together, and by the time they left the house on High Street, Heath's head was swimming with new, even more lasting impressions of his father.

For the next few weeks they hit a dead end. No one approached them regarding Madame Dubonné, yet they were followed constantly, and it was getting on their nerves. About two weeks after their arrival they ran out of money, and Heath watched reluctantly as Beau auctioned off one of their horses at the market on a Saturday afternoon to get enough money to tide them over. Now they had only one horse left and still had turned up nothing.

They bought some work clothes so they wouldn't look conspicuous, and haunted the taverns, coffeehouses, and streets day and night asking questions, getting no answers, and every night came back to the Blue Anchor, where Beau tossed sullenly and Heath found solace in Cora's arms.

If Polly was aware of the liaison between the two, she never mentioned it, nor did Heath mention it to Beau, although Beau was well aware of his midnight wanderings that led him to Cora's small room off the kitchen, and it worried him, because he knew by the way she acted that she was only using him until something better came along, and she was determined that that something better was going to be Beau himself.

He found this out the hard way late one afternoon as he sat on the edge of the bed with a chair to one side in front of him, using it as a desk, writing a letter to Colonel and Mrs. Locke to let them know how things were going. He was almost finished when the door opened and he glanced up.

Cora hadn't even bothered to knock, and now she shut the door, leaning back against it, stretching seductively; then she straightened and walked toward him.

"What are you doing?" she asked curiously, and her mouth pouted provocatively as she stared at him.

"As you can plainly see, I'm writing a letter," he answered, and she smiled.

"To your lady friend?"

"I have no lady friend."

She moved closer and stood directly in front of him, his head even with her breasts, and he realized her dress was unbuttoned all the way down the front to the waist, showing just enough soft curve to make it inviting.

"Heath won't be back for quite a while, will he?" she said, and Beau knew very well she knew Heath had gone on an errand for Polly and wouldn't be back for at least an hour. He didn't answer.

She reached out and put a finger under his chin, tilted his face toward her, and studied it. "Your eyes give you away," she whispered softly as he looked up from her breasts into her large brown eyes. "You like what you see, don't you?" and Beau shivered.

What man wouldn't? She was young, her body firm, but she was Heath's. At least Heath thought so, and he couldn't betray a friend. Besides, when it was over, there'd be nothing. No love, no warmth, just the animal craving satisfied. The girl was a slut, yet his body was responding to her, and he cursed it.

"You misjudge me," he answered huskily. "If I'd wanted you, I'd have taken you a long time ago, but I don't."

She sneered, then suddenly leaned over, her mouth pressing against his, and she kissed him long and hard and he fell back on the bed from the weight of her body against him, and suddenly his arms were around her and he was kissing her back, his hands caressing her as she lay on top of him.

She drew her head back and looked down into his face as she felt him hard against her, and she moved sensuously. "I knew you weren't all that cold and indifferent," she whispered breathlessly, undulating herself forward against the bulge in his pants. "You just needed a bit of coaxing," and she reached down, moving to one side on top of him, beginning to unbutton his breeches.

"What about Heath?" whispered Beau, and she looked at him sheepishly.

"He's a boy, Beau. I've been trying to teach him, but he's still clumsy. I need a man who don't tire out," and he felt her hand begin to caress him, and her eyes grew wild, intense; then suddenly, as he stared into them, he felt sick, as if he wanted to vomit.

This was insane. It was nothing like it had been with Reb. Reb was something special, something . . . Her eyes had been warm and soft. This girl was no better than a whore.

His eyes hardened, and he reached out, grabbing her hand, pulling it from him, and he held both her wrists in a vicelike grip as he pushed her back, setting her on her feet, her dress in disarray, breasts hanging out.

"What the . . . what—?"

"Don't!" he cried softly, his teeth clenched. "Don't say anything. Just get the hell out of here," he ordered angrily. "Leave me alone, and if you ever try that again, I'll tell Heath, do you understand?" and she stared at him, bewildered.

"What did I do?" she cried, holding her hand against her breasts. "I only wanted . . ."

"As I told you once before, I know what you wanted, but you aren't going to get it from me. Not now or ever," and her brown eyes blazed as she stared at him, and her hands trembled as she pushed her breasts back inside her dress and buttoned it up.

"You think you're somebody, don't you, Beau Dante?" she said, her voice shaky, face livid with rage. "Well, I'm somebody too, and someday I'm gonna be somebody important, you'll see. Right now all I got is Heath, but someday I'm gonna have me a real man, one with money and position who'll keep me in style, and when I do, you're gonna be sorry you missed your chance, and I'm gonna look down my nose at you and laugh, because all you are, Beau, is an Indian. You pretend you're somebody, but you ain't nobody!" His face went white as she yelled at him, heading for the door. "You're nothing but a goddamn Indian!" and she went out, slamming the door behind her.

From that day on, relations between Beau and Cora were so strained that even Heath remarked about it one day.

"It seems like the two of you are just plain avoiding each other," said Heath as they sat down to eat one evening, and Beau sighed, unable to tell him the truth.

"Heath, why don't you forget about Cora and find some other girl?" he offered, knowing it was useless to argue, but giving it a try. "She doesn't even know how to read and write," but Heath promptly enlightened him with the fact that he was teaching her; therefore, Beau wasn't surprised a few days later when he walked into the kitchen and found her reading a recipe a friend of Polly's had given her for a special cake, and he didn't know whether to be mad or glad. Whatever, she was Heath's problem now, and he continued to try to keep his distance.

Time seemed to drag on, and after weeks of nothing Beau and Heath sat in a grog shop one evening, disgruntled and discouraged, dressed in their old clothes, listening to the talk around them and hoping to hear something, when a short sandy-haired man sidled up to their table and lurched, dropping a note directly in front of Beau, almost dropping it into his mug of ale.

Beau glanced down, surprised, as he reached down, covering it surreptitiously; then he opened it furtively, and his eyes narrowed as he read it.

"Finish your ale," he told Heath, trying not to sound too anxious. "We've got an appointment," and he handed him the slip of paper.

Half an hour later they stood at the corner of Dock and Third streets waiting for a carriage and a man who would ask them what kind of weather they were having in Boston, and they were to say, "The moon's up in Boston, but rain's due tomorrow." The carriage was on time, the question asked, and within minutes Beau and Heath found themselves in a carriage, their eyes blindfolded, riding to an unknown destination.

It seemed like they rode for well over an hour, and suddenly the carriage stopped. Not a word had been spoken by the man who accompanied them since they'd entered the carriage, but neither seemed to mind. Beau was content to listen to the sounds of the city and try to count the curves and turns the carriage made, and if he was right, he was sure when the carriage finally stopped that they'd merely moved about the city and were still within a short radius of the center square.

The door was opened and they were helped down, then led across what felt like soft grass beneath their feet and through a door that had a slight squeak, and the blindfolds were removed as they finally stood in the center of a large drawing room.

Both men blinked their eyes, squinting as they became accustomed to the light, and as they stared, a dark-haired woman draped in a rich red silk dress seemed to float from a dark corner of the room across the Persian rug toward them.

"You are looking for me?" she asked softly as she stood before them, and both men looked at her face, only to see she was wearing a mask that had narrow slits for her eyes and a ruffle that covered her mouth.

"You're Madame Dubonné?" asked Beau, and she sighed, her voice soft, melodious, and very French.

"Oui. I was Madame Dubonné, but that was years ago." She walked closer and reached out, touching her fingers to Heath's chin, tilting his head toward the light from the candelabrum on the harpsichord in the center of the room. "You are the one," she whispered passionately. *"Oui.* I could not make the mistake. You are Roth's son?" and Heath's eyes searched the dark, mysterious eyes that glared at him from behind the mask.

"Yes," he answered, and she dropped her hand abruptly.

"But Roth was not married."

"He was for a short time. He married my mother, thinking her first husband was dead, but her husband showed up alive about two months later. Her second marriage was declared void, and she returned to her first husband. I was born nine months later and raised as his son. The mistake wasn't realized until I began to grow up."

She smiled wistfully. *"Oui.* You look exactly like him, and it hurts," she said, touching her hand to her heart. "What can I do for you, and how can I help you?"

Beau let Heath carry the conversation. "Do you know where he is?" he asked. "I've come a long way to find him."

She shrugged. "Perhaps. *Mais oui* . . . in a way. I was much in love with your father, but he could not forget her, this woman he loved. We quarreled . . . he did not want me as his wife. . . . Hurt pride is a bad thing. He bought a ship, took on a crew, and sailed for England . . . and I sailed for France. That is all I can tell you."

"You mean he went to England?" asked Beau, and she nodded as she twisted her hands nervously.

"Oui. His family was still in England, and he said something about his father being ill."

"Do you know where he was from in England?"

She shook her head. *"Non, m'sieur* . . . but I think somewhere along the coast. One of the port cities. I am afraid he never said."

Heath looked at Beau, and his heart sank. England was such a big place, and it was so far away.

"Well, at least that's more than we knew before," he said. "But England. How do we get to England?"

Beau straightened his shoulders as an awkward silence filled the room. "I guess we sign on a sailing ship," he finally said, and saw Heath's face brighten.

"That's right," he answered, and his eyes were once more alive and glowing; then suddenly he looked deflated again. "But we can't do that. They make you sign on for a two- to three-year stretch."

"Then we work and pay our passage," said Beau. "However we do it, we go to England," and he turned from Heath to look at the woman standing in front of them, her dark hair shining in the candlelight. "We thank you, ma'am, for your trouble," he said graciously, then paused a moment. "If you don't mind," he said, "I think it only right, since you helped us, that we warn you." He saw her eyes harden. "We aren't the only ones looking for you, madame," he offered hesitantly. "I don't know why or what's going on, but I ask you to be extremely careful."

They could see a faint hint of a smile beneath the gauze skirt of her mask. "Thank you, m'sieur, of this I already know." Her voice sharpened instinctively. "That's why I have taken these precautions," she said, gesturing about her and at the mask. "Now, you will tell no one of our visit, and you will forget you met anyone named Madame Dubonné, *n'est-ce pas*?" and both Heath and Beau bowed graciously and kissed the hand she offered them as they said good-bye.

They were taken back in the same manner they'd been brought, and it was well past midnight by the time they were helped from the carriage, the blindfolds removed, and they found themselves standing in front of the Blue Anchor.

"Polly's probably worried sick," said Beau as they watched the carriage disappear down the street, and he looked toward the inn, where a faint light shone inside.

They started toward the door, talking in low tones, when suddenly Beau stopped and touched Heath's arm as his eyes stared into the darkness of the doorway ahead of them. "Wait," he said, "there's someone standing in the shadows at the door," but it was too late.

As a man emerged from the doorway, pistol drawn, two more, the small man who'd ridden the gelding and the one from in front of the bakery, moved up behind them, also with pistols drawn, and Beau swore.

"It would not be to your best interests to run," advised the tall man in front of them, his hawklike face etched sharply in the faint light from the inn as he saw Beau's hesitation. "Claude and I are excellent shots, m'sieurs, so one bullet is all we need," and with that he signaled, and in seconds another carriage moved into view, but this time Beau was apprehensive. He didn't like the looks of these men.

The one in front of them had eyes of steel, and the one he called Claude seemed exceptionally nervous, his eyes shifty.

"If you will, m'sieurs," said the tall man, motioning toward the carriage, and Beau looked at Heath.

"I guess we haven't much choice, have we?" he said, and Heath agreed, so they climbed into the carriage and once more submitted to blindfolds.

This time the trip took only a short time, and suddenly they found themselves in another drawing room, but not quite as elaborate as the one where they'd met Madame Dubonné.

As their eyes once more became accustomed to the light, a man entered the room and motioned for the men holding pistols on them to lower them, then offered Heath and Beau a seat on a green plush sofa in front of the fireplace.

"Well, m'sieurs," the man said, his voice trying to conceal his anxiety as they walked to the sofa, "tonight you paid a visit to Madame Dubonné, am I right?" and Beau stared at him, neither he nor Heath answering as they turned and sat down.

The man sat in a matching chair opposite them and began tapping on the arm of the chair with his finger, and it made Beau nervous, only he tried not to show it. He was a portly man, his hair a bit longer than usual, with thick graying sideburns, his eyes a faded blue set in a heavily masculine face, and the black velvet frock coat he wore made his eyes shine like agates beneath heavy brows. He could perhaps have been handsome if he'd been about forty pounds lighter, but the paunch in front and the slight double chin ruined his looks and made him appear sinister.

"There's no use denying it, m'sieurs," he continued as he stared at them. "We know Madame Dubonné is in the city somewhere. It is only for us to find her."

"I wish you luck," said Beau, and the man's mouth hardened angrily.

"Where did they take you?" he demanded, and Beau shrugged.

"We have no idea. We were blindfolded."

"The whole while?"

"No."

"Ah . . . then what was the place like?"

"Much like this," answered Beau, gesturing about them to the candelabrum on the desk at the far wall and the marble-manteled fireplace in front of them. "Just a drawing room with little light in it."

The man stared at him, his face like granite, unhappy over Beau's apparent flippancy. "Perhaps you don't realize the seriousness of your situation," he said as he stood up and began to pace the floor. "I intend to learn the whereabouts of Madame Dubonné, no matter what the price!"

"May I ask why?" asked Beau, and the man's face became livid.

He stopped pacing and stared at Beau and Heath as if trying to decide whether to tell them, then exhaled loudly as he made up his mind.

"On the twentieth of June, according to all our reports," he answered vehemently, "King Louis and his queen, Marie Antoinette, were to have left France on a ship, and if all went well, at this very moment they are on the high seas headed for this country. We have sent men to stop them, but they may have failed, and if so, Madame Dubonné will be waiting to greet them and smuggle them ashore in Philadelphia, where they will hide in exile." His eyes blazed. "This must never happen! It cannot be!" and his mouth trembled with rage as he stopped pacing and stared at them, his breathing heavy and labored. "Now, will you tell us what you know of the woman?" and both Heath and Beau felt a tingle down their spines as they realized the men they were with were in deadly earnest. They weren't just fighting for themselves, they were fighting for a cause.

"We told you already," answered Beau stubbornly, sticking to the truth, although it was getting them nowhere. "We had no idea where we were taken. Why didn't you just follow the carriage after it left us?"

"We did. It was taken to a livery stable, and from there the men with it just melted into the darkness and we lost them." He ran blunt fingers through his long hair. "This . . . this Madame Dubonné, she gave no indication as to where you were? Did you see her face? Could you recognize her if you saw her again?" The man was desperate, but Beau shook his head.

"She wore a mask."

"Sacrebleu!" He cursed as he walked to the mantel and stood looking down into the cold ashes in the fireplace, and his eyes blazed. "We have searched the town, pulled it apart at the seams, but still she eludes us. Somewhere, someone knows who she is, where she is. . . . It seems impossible!"

The hawk-faced man leaned forward, his face stern. "So what do we do with them now?" he asked, gesturing toward Heath and Beau, and the man with the agate-blue eyes straightened up, turning to look at them as both of them stared at him warily.

"They've seen my face, so we have no alternative," he answered, and Beau tensed, taking a deep breath.

If they were going to die, it wouldn't be without a fight. He started to move, and the man they called Claude raised his pistol, pointing it at his head.

"Non," cautioned the man in the black velvet coat, and Beau sat rigid. "I think perhaps this time it would be a mistake if they were to turn up dead. After all, they are friends of President Washington; besides, we will leave no blood on our hands. This is not our country, and I don't wish to hang. Tie their hands, blindfold and gag them, and bring them," he said, and Heath and Beau breathed a sigh.

But what did they have planned? As they were gagged, their hands tied, and their eyes blindfolded, they listened intently to the conversation going on about them, learning that the man in the black velvet frock coat with the agate-blue eyes was M'sieur Gereaux and the hawk-faced man with Claude was M'sieur LeFleur.

When the blindfolds and gags were securely in place, their wrists secured behind their backs, they were hustled from the house and forced to lie down in the back of what seemed to be a heavy farm wagon, and a light blanket was thrown over them.

"Remember, Claude," warned M'sieur Gereaux as he moved up to the wagon seat. "The *Sea Queen.* Don't make any mistakes," and they heard Claude mumbling as he flicked the reins, starting the wagon forward, and Beau and Heath both realized as they heard him breathing that the hawk-faced man, LeFleur, was sitting next to them in the wagon with his pistol handy at his side.

They'd been moving for some five or ten minutes when the wagon suddenly stopped, and Beau strained his ears. A carriage was on the road, and he listened as it approached, then slowed and stopped beside the wagon.

There was silence for a minute; then a soft feminine voice floated back to them. "Claude, *mon Dieu!* Where are you off to at this time of night?"

Beau could tell the man was hunting for the right words as he stammered, "Ah . . . ah . . . Madame Gereaux. I thought you were at the house."

She laughed. "Tonight is an important night, Claude, have you forgotten?" Her voice was warm and vibrant, and suddenly, as Beau heard it, he sighed and smiled to himself. "The theater was grand," she went on, "and the party afterward superb. The next time, though, I will insist that my husband accompany me, even though he doesn't like the theater. I am tired of making his excuses." She sighed. "But you didn't say, where are you off to?"

He cleared his throat. "Ah . . . M'sieur Gereaux had a few things he wanted taken care of for the morning," he answered reluctantly, "and seeing as tomorrow's the fourth of July, the town will be a madhouse, so we thought we'd take care of it tonight."

She laughed a low melodious laugh. "Oh, *oui.* Now I remember. You are hauling the pig for the roast on the green," she answered. "I almost forgot he promised to donate it. Well . . ." She paused, and then, her voice gay, "Hurry, then, Claude," she urged. "Don't let me detain you."

Her voice faded from them as Beau heard the carriage start up again, and suddenly he laughed, this time out loud beneath the gag, only to be kicked by M'sieur LeFleur's boot, but he didn't care. He knew the answer at last.

The wagon lurched forward again and moved steadily down the road, lumbering along for about half an hour; then suddenly, cobblestones grated beneath its wheels, and Beau's muscles tensed. They were back in the heart of town, and a few minutes later a crier's voice was heard in the distance, "Three o'clock, and all's well", and Beau moved a bit in the bottom of the wagon. His muscles were stiff from being in the cramped position, and he felt Heath beside him, alert and listening, and he wondered if he too had realized the truth.

The strong smell of fish, tar, and river water seeped beneath the blanket that covered them, and it mixed with the stench of garbage from the gutters when a short time later the wagon rolled to an abrupt stop.

Beau heard Claude climb down, and there was hurried mumbling; then a few minutes later the blanket was yanked off them, they were pulled from the wagon and forced to stand. Huge hands pushed them forward, and they moved reluctantly, trying to fight the ropes that bound them, the gags that almost suffocated them, and the blindfolds that blinded them.

They were pushed along for some distance; then without any warning Beau's head spun and he staggered forward from a blow on the back of the head, and his knees buckled as everything went black; and seconds later, Heath too followed him into oblivion.

Beau's eyes felt like heavy weights as he tried to lift them, and he reached up, rubbing his head, wondering how long he'd been unconscious, realizing his hands were free now and there was no longer a gag in his mouth. He opened his eyes slowly and looked around, as Heath too began to come to, and both of them rubbed the back of their heads, moaning as they tried to adjust their eyes to the darkness that surrounded them.

"Where are we?" asked Heath as he rubbed his mouth where the gag had been and licked his dry lips.

Beau looked around. It was pitch dark. Not a crack of light anywhere, and the smell of tar, rope, and lumber still filled his nostrils, mingling with the smell of the river water and garbage. He lay still for a minute, feeling the gentle motion beneath him, then sighed. "I'd say we're on a ship," he answered slowly as he moved to his knees, then gingerly stood up, leaning against the side of the wall.

"A ship?"

"We've been shanghaied!" he exclaimed. "And if the feel of it's right beneath my feet," he said cautiously, "I'd say we're moving," and Heath stood up beside him, rubbing his head.

"But why?'

"What better way to dispose of unwanted cargo?" answered Beau, straightening, trying to brush some of the filth from his clothes. "We end up sailing around the world for a good two years, and by the time we reach Philadelphia again . . ." His voice trailed off; then he started to chuckle, a low furtive laugh, and Heath frowned.

"What's so funny?"

"They are," he stated, amused. "Didn't you hear it, Heath?" he asked as he walked to the side of the hold they were in and started feeling around for a door. "Didn't you hear the voice of the woman who stopped the wagon earlier?"

Heath was puzzled. "I heard."

"And you don't remember hearing it before?"

Heath stood quietly, trying to remember, trying to figure out what Beau was talking about; then suddenly it dawned on him, and he grinned, his eyes widening. "Madame Dubonné!" he exclaimed incredulously. "That voice . . . like silk . . . warm and soft. . . . My God! M'sieur Gereaux is looking for his own wife and he doesn't even know it!" Heath tried to laugh, but the tensions of the past few hours and frustrations of the past few weeks caught up to him, and instead, he expelled a choking sob as his mouth tightened, and he tried to hold back the tears. "For this we lose our freedom," he groaned bitterly as he slowly sank to the floor. "I wanted to find my father, and now . . ."

"Now we get to England," answered Beau, seemingly unperturbed as he found the door, pulled on it, then cursed and gave up when it wouldn't open.

Heath leaned his head against the wall of the small hold they'd been thrown into, and Beau turned, trying to see him in the darkness.

"You did want to get to England, didn't you?" he asked.

"But like this?"

He made his way to where he heard Heath's voice in the darkness and dropped to the floor beside him. "What's the difference how we get there?" he said. "It would have taken us months to get enough money to get to England," and he tried to shift into a comfortable position.

"But we don't even know where we're headed."

"We'll get there eventually."

"And in the meantime?"

"You've been wanting to feel the deck of a ship beneath your feet for years," answered Beau, remembering the times Heath had told him of his dreams. "Now's your chance."

But it wasn't the feel of the ship Heath was thinking about at the moment, it was the feel of something else. Something he hadn't known before. An emptiness flowed through him, and he closed his eyes as he thought of the feel of her lips on his mouth, the warmth of her body against his as he made love to her, and he cried inside because Cora was in Philadelphia and he was on a ship bound for God knows where. It wasn't fair! He clenched his fists in frustration. He needed Cora, and his heart cried out with longing.

"We have to get off, Beau," he whispered desperately, his voice shaking. "I don't care what we have to do, anything, swim ashore, fight them, I don't give a damn about the ship, but somehow we have to get back to Philadelphia," and Beau sensed what was wrong.

"Don't be a fool, Heath," he answered, knowing what these men were like. "Cora's not worth it."

"I'm in love with her."

"You don't know what love is."

"And you do?"

He had to make him understand. "Love is more than taking a woman to bed, Heath," he answered, feeling for the right words, trying to ease his hurt. "A man can take a hundred women in his lifetime, but that doesn't mean he loves them, yet he could love a woman without ever taking her. Love comes from inside. From the heart. You're not in love with Cora. Any woman can do for you what Cora did, and it wouldn't be love. She's the first woman you've made love to, and right now you'd swear it was the real thing, but believe me, what you feel for Cora isn't love."

"How do you know?"

"Because I've traveled the road already and I know how you feel, and believe me, Heath, Cora's not worth it."

"She was all I had!"

"But not what you deserve. You deserve better than Cora

Richmond, and there are women out there who can give you better."

"But they're not Cora! Besides, she's all alone!"

"Cora can take care of herself." He sneered, his voice cold. "Don't ruin things and get yourself messed up. The men who sail these ships can be vicious. Take it as it comes, and don't buck them."

Heath hesitated as he stared toward Beau in the darkness.

"I mean what I say," Beau went on angrily. "These men don't play games. Many a sailor's stretched his neck from the rigging for contemplating what you've suggested. Now, which is it? Are you going to take the chance that we might reach England and your father someday, or are you going to die fighting to get back to a girl who's probably already found someone else to warm her bed?" and Heath's heart sank as he gulped back the tears.

"Who means more to you, Heath," Beau asked, "Cora or your father?" and Heath sighed softly, defeated.

"You know the answer to that, Beau," and Beau breathed easier as heavy steps shuffled outside the door and it was flung open, letting a dim shaft of light into the hold.

"All right, you two," boomed a gruff voice from the other side of the doorway. "Hold to. The tide's going out and we've taken sail, and the captain wants you up on deck. He paid good money for two healthy hands, and he don't want 'em pissin' their time away when there's work to be done, so get a move on," and Beau reached over, helping Heath to his feet, and they stumbled into the light, coming face to face with a huge man whose face looked like it was carved from stone, a thatch of curly hair topping it, a pair of bloodshot eyes chiseled into it, and a cruel mouth etched below.

The man reached out, grabbed each by the shoulder, and shoved them toward the stairs, yelling as they stumbled up ahead of him.

"Up to the quarterdeck, gents," he bellowed as his mammoth six-foot frame followed close behind. "You're on the *Sea Queen* now, headed for the West Indies, so you might's well get used to it." As they stepped onto the deck into the early-morning air, they heard the first crack of fireworks as bells began to ring out the dawn of another fourth of July and the city that was slowly moving farther and farther away from them began coming to life.

"It looks like the celebrating's started," said Beau as he touched the sore spot that still smarted on the back of his head and felt the breeze lift his hair as the ship moved farther from shore with every breath of wind.

"And here we are on this goddamn ship," snapped Heath, wincing, and Beau glanced toward the water, then back at Heath.

"Care to swim ashore?" he asked, but Heath's jaw tightened as he took a look about them at his new shipmates, and he felt a queasy feeling in the pit of his stomach, as if he was looking straight into the barrel of a loaded rifle, and he swallowed hard, knowing it was no use, he'd never make it to the ship's rail.

"We sail for England . . . by way of the West Indies," he agreed reluctantly as he turned to Beau, and Beau sighed, relieved, as the sailor who'd brought them above deck gave them another push forward and they joined the rest of the crew hustling to the first mate's orders, trying to learn their job in the routine of setting sail.

A few minutes later, as the huge ship drifted farther away from the city, each new sail unfurling, catching in the wind, sailing out into midstream, the sounds of the celebration slowly faded in the distance and the sun began to clear the horizon beyond the river, signaling the new day. Suddenly both young men stared apprehensively out across the water as they worked, sweat beading their now-bare backs, and they caught glimpses of the skyline of the city as it disappeared from view, and they wondered, each for his own special reason, just how long it would be before they touched the shores of home again.

7

Fort Locke, on the shores of Lake Erie—April 1793

The first tender rays of dawn filtered through budding trees, turning the lake into a mirror of white as Quinn finished tightening down the bundles on one of the four packhorses they were taking with them. It was a wet morning, having rained the night before, and Loedicia jostled her horse ahead through the wet sand to the top of the grassy knoll near the shore so she could get one last look from her favorite spot.

She was wearing buckskins, her long dark hair tied in back with a ribbon, a small fur hat on her head, and her feet in warm moccasins as she straddled the horse bareback, looking out over the lake. There was a chill on the morning air, along with the dampness, and she could see her breath as she exhaled, and she pulled the buckskin jacket a bit closer in front.

This was it. The day Quinn had been waiting for all winter long. What he'd been saving for all these years. She reined her horse about and looked back at the house once more where it nestled among the willow trees, a soft drift of smoke trailing from one of the chimneys. Sepia was to stay in the house while they were gone, but for some reason, as the first rays of dawn fell on the house, making it look so warm and inviting, she had a strange foreboding that it was the last time she'd see it. That she should take a good long look, one to last a lifetime.

She'd had this feeling last night as she'd stood in the bedroom before slipping into bed and looked at the children's drawings that covered the log walls, hearing the willows sighing above the house and the night hawk's call from the woods.

Quinn had promised her they'd come back. She'd made him promise, but sometimes . . .

She bit her lip as she watched him by the veranda, steadying the horses, giving instructions to Rebel, Teak, and Lizette, who were already mounted, and greeting some of Telak's men, who were to escort them partway. She didn't want to go. She'd never wanted to leave here. The wilderness had become a part of her from the day he'd first brought her here so long ago. She never missed the ballrooms and parties, the afternoon teas and musicals of Boston. She'd missed India at first because she'd been born and raised there, but her home here at Fort Locke had replaced India in her heart now, and the thought of never seeing it again brought tears to her eyes.

She didn't want to go to England. She hated going to England, but Quinn had become obsessed over the years with the idea of claiming his inheritance, and now they were going, and there was nothing she could do about it. If only Burly hadn't been killed during the war. Good old Burly. He'd been Quinn's best friend for so long, maybe he could have talked some sense into him. But Burly wasn't here, he was dead, and there was nothing she could do alone; she'd tried, to no avail. Sometimes Quinn could be so stubborn and bullheaded.

She hadn't been east since 1775, and the long journey ahead and the thought of civilization frightened her. How should she act after all these years of isolation, seeing only Indians and the few white men and women who were at the fort, and occasionally some stranger passing through? She had changed over the years. At least she felt she had changed. She was no longer the naive young girl who'd defied all conventions to marry Quinn Locke, rebel and outlaw. She was a woman, a mother with half-grown children, and there were no longer stars in her eyes; instead, there were tears as she said good-bye to her home.

Quinn waved to her, and she dug her heels into the horse's side and moved back down the hill to where everyone waited.

"Are you going to say good-bye all morning?" he asked as he mounted and she reined up beside him. "You act as if you're never going to see it again."

She winced as she gazed again at the house. "I have a strange feeling I won't."

"We're only going to England and back."

She avoided his eyes and looked at Sepia standing on the porch, her bronzed face worn and sad. She'd been with them since their return, when Rebel was a baby, and Loedicia wished she were coming with them. But at least she had

Lizette. Quinn had promised her Lizette could come, and she looked back at her in line beside Rebel in front of the packhorses, trying to quiet her horse.

Lizette wasn't used to horses and rarely went riding, but she wasn't about to be left behind, not when Loedicia needed her.

"And you do, *ma petite*," she'd told her only a few weeks before. "You need me as much as I need you and Quinn now that François is gone. I will keep your dresses in order and take care of the children's needs."

"But I want you to go as a friend, not an abigail," protested Loedicia, at which Lizette pooh-poohed her until she gave in.

So now Lizette sat astride, the only one using a saddle, wearing buckskins, which she never wore, and swallowed hard, trying to quiet her skittish mount, her sharp eyes noticing the apprehension on Loedicia's face, and she was glad she was going along.

Loedicia wanted to cry out, "I don't want to go, I won't go," but instead she looked at Quinn, her violet eyes misty but determined.

"If you say we'll be back, we'll be back," she answered stubbornly, and Quinn grinned.

"That's my girl," he said, only he failed to see the tear that ran down her cheek as he dug his horse in the ribs and they moved out past the fort, past Major Holmes and all the men he was leaving behind who wished them farewell, through the Tuscarora village, saying good-bye to Telak and all their Indian friends, then picking up the trail that followed along the riverbank.

The sun came up as they rode, filling the spring air with the smell of fresh earth, and birds sang from every treetop, hoping the newly budding leaves would hide their nests from view when they unfolded, and Loedicia glanced ahead of her to Quinn, tall on his horse, challenging the day as if he dared anyone to stop him.

He'd been planning this day for so long. Teak had been fourteen in January, and it would take them about a month to get to Philadelphia, another three months to England, and he figured about four or five more months to tie all the legal ends together, and by the time Teak turned fifteen, he, Quinn Locke, would legally be Lord Quinn Locksley, Earl of Locksley, and Teak would be his heir, the next Earl of Locksley.

She glanced at Teak riding beside Quinn. He'd grown so

the past two years. He was past Quinn's shoulder already, only he hadn't started to fill out yet and was still lean and lanky, but he had the look of Quinn about him. Especially his blond hair, blue devil-may-care eyes, and the impish grin that turned the corners of his mouth. He was nothing like Heath.

Heath! It was the first time she'd really allowed herself to think of him for so long. Heath! Heath! She said his name slowly, sweetly to herself. He and Beau had been gone for two years, and the only word from them was a letter Beau had written from Philadelphia shortly after their arrival, saying things weren't going too well. Since then, nothing. Where was he? What could have happened? He could be dead by now.

She glanced at Quinn's back, wondering if he cared. She didn't dare even mention Heath's name anymore. Oh, Quinn never came right out and said it, but she knew. He'd promised to sail from Philadelphia and inquire about Heath and Beau, but he'd been belligerent about it, acquiescing only to make her happy, and only after a violent argument. He thought when Heath left she'd no longer think of Roth. Without Roth's son as a constant reminder, he was hoping she'd put Roth out of her life once and for all, but it hadn't helped. It had only made things worse. She missed Heath terribly. When he had been here, he was so much like Roth that it was as if Roth were still with her, at least part of him. Now, with Heath gone, she missed them both, father and son, and she knew Quinn sensed it, even though she tried to hide it, and things just weren't the same.

She still loved Quinn. You didn't stop loving someone you'd loved for so long, but some of the fire had gone out of their love the past few years, and it had started with Heath. Quinn hadn't been the same since Heath had left. He was restless, irritable, and she knew he sensed the void Heath's going had made in her life.

If he'd merely grown up and gone off on his own, she could have accepted it, but whenever she looked at Quinn, much as she tried to fight against it, she was reminded that he'd forced her to tell Heath about his father and that the truth had driven him from her. Heath would be here yet except for Quinn, and without wanting to, she hated him for it. She hated him, yet loved him. Oh, God! Her world was so mixed up. She couldn't even explain this strange feeling she had whenever she thought of Roth, and it annoyed her, because she'd thought it was going to be so easy to forget him. It hadn't been.

She glanced quickly back at Rebel and Lizette riding behind her as they followed single file along the riverbank, and she studied Rebel for some time, realizing how happy she seemed about the trip; then she sighed. Maybe it was good they were going after all. Maybe England would do Rebel good. She'd been restless and spent so much time alone in the woods lately. At least she'd meet some young men for a change, and suddenly she brushed the cobwebs from her mind, tearing the irritable doubts from her thoughts. It was foolish to worry and get so upset.

Maybe this trip to England would be worth it if Rebel found someone she could love, and as Rebel looked at her and smiled, Loedicia's heart warmed and for the first time in days her apprehensions began to ease. Maybe Quinn's decision hadn't been so bad. Maybe they'd find more in England than a title, and her eyes danced as they looked her daughter over. It would do the girl good. She was eighteen now and had grown into quite a young lady, her hair still as fair, her eyes still like the violets in the woodland meadows. She was beautiful, and Loedicia almost felt sorry for the young men in England, because she was sure they were about to meet one of the most beautiful, unpredictable, independent young ladies who ever existed. Yes, England might prove profitable after all, and she hummed softly to herself as the sun moved higher in the sky and the warm spring air sifted through the trees, heralding an even warmer afternoon. She had to forget this anger and foreboding. Forget the past and try to be happy for Rebel's sake, if not her own, and she made up her mind that she wasn't going to spoil things. Not if she could help it, anyway, and she smiled, breathing deeply as she took off her hat.

The caravan moved steadily along—Quinn, Teak, Loedicia, Rebel, and Lizette, with close to twenty of Telak's best braves escorting them, leading the packhorses, and scouting the trail ahead.

Quinn had been back to the coast a good many times since the war, but mostly to Virginia and Boston, and only a few times to Philadelphia. Rebel had never been east, and neither had Teak, and Quinn wondered what they'd think of the city as he jogged along leading the way.

He stared at the trail up ahead, conscious of the warming sun and new buds on the trees ready to break forth. Conscious also of the spring beauties being trampled underfoot by the horses as they rode along. He hated to see beauty spoiled. Even these delicate little flowers. The woods was awakening to spring, but he wouldn't be here to see it.

The frontier, this land, was a part of him, as were his children, but there was another part of him too. A part that had never died as he remembered the sound of his grandfather's voice bitterly telling him he was not a Locksley, that all his father would have possessed had he lived would go to Quinn's cousin, Lord Varrick, his father's sister's son.

He could do nothing about it then, but now Lord Varrick was dead and no longer a threat to him, and he had his father's letter to prove that he was a Locksley. An illegitimate one, but a Locksley, and he'd been waiting for years for just this day, yet he was disturbed.

He glanced back at Loedicia following behind Teak, her hat off now to the morning sun, guiding her horse slowly along the trail. She was still so beautiful, and his heart ached. What was happening to them? Life just didn't seem the same anymore. When had it started?

He tried to put his finger on a sign, a thought, a gesture, a single moment in time and space when things went wrong. When had the fire in her eyes begun to dwindle and die?

Heath! He tried to block the name from his mind, but it was no use, and he knew why. He remembered holding him as a baby, proud of the son she'd given him. A little boy the image of his mother. Then slowly, as he grew . . . an affectionate three-year-old laughing at his new baby brother. At eight putting worms on a fish hook, squirming his face up as they slid between his fingers, then suddenly, a look on his face, the semblance of a smile that was vaguely familiar.

That was when it started. The doubts, the nagging suspicions, until there was no longer any way to deny it, and he felt a bitter gall in his stomach as he thought of what Roth had done to him. Damn him! Roth's face filtered across his mind, dark eyes compelling, and he cursed as he remembered how he'd looked that last day when they'd said good-bye so many years ago. But it hadn't been good-bye. Not really, because she'd never forgotten him. How could she, with his son as a constant reminder? Roth stood between them now even more than he had then.

Quinn glanced back at her again angrily, only she didn't notice, she was looking away, watching a pileated woodpecker staring at them from a dead tree a short way off the trail. What did she expect from him? He'd given her all the love he had to give, yet every time he took her in his arms the ghost of Roth was there between them, subtly filling his head with doubts. How much had she loved him? What did she really feel inside? And there were times when he made love to her that he knew she hadn't been completely satisfied, when his lovemaking seemed only to leave her restless and discontented, as if her body cried out for more. For a release that wasn't there, and he wondered if she'd been thinking of Roth, of the way he'd made love to her.

It had been that way almost from the very start, but he thought the doubts and fears would leave over the years. Instead, they got worse, because of Heath, and it hurt deep down inside.

His son Heath. . . . No, not his son, Roth's son! Was it possible to love and hate at the same time? He loved the boy Heath had been, yet hated the man he looked like.

Quinn stared on ahead as they started to move into a small valley. When he had first started making plans, he was going to go to Virginia and take a ship from there, but Dicia and he had argued and she'd made him promise to go to Philadelphia and inquire about Beau and Heath before they sailed. Why had he promised? Why couldn't he have said no? He knew why. The look in her eyes as she pleaded with him had torn at his heart, and he'd been unable to fight her any longer. He couldn't hurt her any more in spite of his pride. He loved her beyond all reason, yet every day, because of this boy, because of Heath, she was being torn from him and he didn't know how to fight it. How did you fight something you had no control over?

He dug his horse's ribs a bit harder as they moved away from the river and headed eastward onto a new trail that led clear to the Susquehanna. Maybe by the time the trip was over things would be better. All he could do was hope. For now he was going to pretend nothing was wrong and enjoy the journey, and he slackened his pace, joining Teak, calling to Dicia and the others to join him as he spotted a huge flock of cedar waxwings off to the left, and for a short time both of them forgot their anxieties as they watched the birds covering the tops of the trees. This was his forest, his land. He'd fought and almost died for it, and by God he was going to come back to it. He'd promised her he would, and he meant it.

Suddenly he looked at her, his eyes filled with love, and

she smiled as he reached out and took her hand. "We will come back, Dicia," he stated firmly. "I promise we'll come back," and she sighed, her eyes softening.

"I know," she whispered, "I know," and she squeezed his hand hard, letting him know that she understood, and for a while again it was all right. Everything was all right, but for how long? He wondered.

The journey cross country was long, tiresome, and dangerous. Joseph Brant was leading the Indians of the Ohio and Susquehanna valleys in an uprising that was scaring the hell out of every settler in the northwest territories, and Quinn's small band had a tangle with them a little over a week out.

About twelve to fifteen warriors pounced on them in a surprise attack one afternoon, killing two of Telak's men and one of the packhorses before finally being driven off. Afterward, the remaining three packhorses groaned under the added weight that had been on the fallen horse as they set out again.

The rest of the trek was without incident, and Telak's men left them about a hundred miles east of the Susquehanna River, and Dicia sighed as she watched them go.

"Well, we're really on our own now," she said to Quinn as they watched them disappear back down the trail they'd just traveled.

"Are you glad?"

She shook her head. "I've gotten used to having them around."

Quinn relaxed on his horse and stared at all of them. Loedicia and Lizette looked tired, but were taking the rough trip well, and he knew that a few days' rest in Philadelphia would revive them. Rebel and Teak, however, looked strong and healthy as ever, and he prided himself on their strength. They looked like they had energy to ride on forever.

"You take the rear guard, Teak," he said, motioning to the back, and he handed Rebel the guide rope for the three packhorses. "And you lead the packhorses. Let your mother and Lizette stay directly behind me," and they lined up once more, heading east again away from the cooling afternoon sun.

They arrived in Philadelphia the first week in May as a warm spell blew down from the Appalachians and the city crawled out of the late winter into a land newly greened and flowered with dogwood, wild plum, apple and cherry trees all in bloom.

It was late afternoon as they rode away from the Schuylkill River along High Street toward the center square, and Loedicia sat her horse in awe, unaware of the people who stared at them apprehensively. Men in buckskins were still not too common, but women in buckskins, especially three pretty ones, were a rarity, and Loedicia, Rebel, and Lizette had no idea of the furor they were causing.

"It's changed so," said Dicia as she rode beside Quinn, trying to take everything in at once as she dodged the carts and carriages, children and animals, and cautioned Teak to help Rebel with the packhorses.

"It's been almost twenty years," answered Quinn. "Times change."

"And us with them," she said. "I feel old all of a sudden."

He looked across the distance between them directly into her violet eyes and ignored the crowded street. "You look as young and beautiful as you did when I first saw you," he answered, and she grinned that impish grin he knew so well.

"I was dressed like a boy when you first saw me."

"Don't get cute," he cautioned. "You know what I mean," and she flushed beneath the newly acquired tan on her face.

"Yes, I know," she answered, and looked away as a carriage barred their way and they had to maneuver around it.

Quinn reined close to her and motioned for Lizette to follow, yelling to Rebel and Teak so they wouldn't get lost in the crowd as they continued to move forward.

Rebel was amazed. She and Teak were having a hard time trying to see everything, stay out of everyone's way, and still keep track of the packhorses. It was Wednesday, a market day, and the streets were jammed. She'd never seen anything like it. And the shops! She almost pulled a muscle in her neck twisting to look at a milliner's shop, a bakery, a silversmith's, a printer's, such an array. Everything a person used was here at your fingertips. You didn't go out and shoot supper, you bought it at the market. And if you wanted a plate to eat from, you bought it at the china shop or potter's, you didn't dig the clay and shape it, then fire it. And the material for dresses was already woven like the dresses her father had brought her from Boston, and she stared as a cart went by with bolts of material piled high on it, all shades and colors, like the rainbow. It was fascinating.

They moved steadily along, being jostled about, Quinn in

the lead; then suddenly he reined his horse toward the pavement and stopped in front of an inn at Fifth and High streets and dismounted, reaching up, holding the bridle to Loedicia's horse.

"I'll go in and see if they've got rooms," he said. "All of you wait here."

He was gone only a few minutes while they waited, then came out shaking his head. They tried five more inns, finally finding some rooms at the Copper Kettle, a small inn on the north side of town near Cherry and Sixth streets.

They had three rooms. One for Teak, one for Rebel and Lizette, and another for Loedicia and him, but before going up to their rooms, Loedicia addressed the proprietor, who'd looked at them rather apprehensively as they walked in.

"Could you tell me, sir," she asked, her voice warm and soft as they stood, arms full of bundles, "could you find someone to do some clothes up for us?" She reached down, touching her filthy buckskins, then brushed a curl away from her dust-streaked face. "We've had a long journey and I'd appreciate a chance to get a nice warm bath and put on some decent clothes again. We've everything with us, but it'll need a good pressing."

The man scowled. "You can pay?"

"I wouldn't ask if we couldn't."

His eyes eased. "I can find someone. Just bring the things down when you get them unpacked." He reached up and took three keys from a rack, handing them to Quinn. "The last three rooms at the end of the hall, but the bath'll cost you a shilling apiece and you'll all use the same water. It ain't Saturday night, you know."

Loedicia glanced at Quinn, who winked at her. They were used to swimming in the lake every day in the summer and taking frequent baths in the winter, something, she forgot, which was not done in fashionable society. Some people thought bathing every day was unhealthy. A bunch of nonsense.

"I'll set the tub up in the back room off the kitchen like I do for Saturday nights," he offered. "But it'll still take a while." He looked hard at Loedicia, taking in her violet eyes, the small tip-tilted nose and warm mouth. In spite of the suntan, disheveled hair, and dirty clothes, she looked and spoke like a lady of quality, and the tall giant with her—he had an air of distinction and authority about him. The proprietor had a suspicion they weren't just ordinary travelers. "Mebbe you'd care to eat while the water's heating," he suggested. "There's a table yonder. I'll have the girl bring you some victuals after you've put your things upstairs."

Quinn nodded. "Much obliged. And is there a place for the horses?"

"Around back. Got a small stable. You can bed them down there."

Quinn was pleased as he helped carry the things to their rooms, then left Loedicia to unpack while he went to take care of the horses.

She met him a short time later at the foot of the stairs, the dark green velvet dress he'd bought for her six years before in Boston slung over one arm and his good breeches, a black frock coat, and white shirt across the other.

Rebel, Teak, and Lizette had already brought their things down, given them to the proprietor, and were sitting at the table waiting, but Loedicia had been undecided on just what to wear.

She had only five dresses. The two light gray cottons she wore around the house, her gold lawn for summer, black wool for winter, and the green velvet, her favorite, but since Quinn had promised her some new clothes before sailing, she'd decided to wear the velvet.

He smiled his approval, the clothes were handed to the proprietor, and they joined the children and Lizette at the table, where they all feasted on ham, beef, potato soup, thick slabs of cheese, wheat bread, and raisin pie washed down with cider for the children and a smooth port wine for the adults, after which they started their baths in a copper tub set up in the back room.

Rebel was first, then Lizette and Loedicia, with Teak and Quinn last on the list.

Loedicia, her bath over, waited for Quinn now in their room, sorting out the rest of the clothes so she'd have them ready to put into the trunks he said he was going to buy. For now, she took down the wooden hangers and hung the rest of the wrinkled dresses up. She'd have them pressed tomorrow, along with everyone else's things, and she hung Quinn's green velvet uniform jacket beside them with his buff breeches, belt and sword, and his brown broadcloth jacket and brown breeches.

The underthings she tucked into the old dresser on the wall near the clothes press, then surveyed the dingy little room, wondering how long it would be before they'd find a ship heading for England. Not too long, she hoped, and glanced quickly at the straw-tick bed held up by a latticework of ropes. It looked hard and uncomfortable after the feather bed back home, but at least it wasn't as hard as the ground she'd slept on for the past few weeks.

She looked into the mirror above the dresser and surveyed herself, unhappy over what she saw. Why did people have to grow old? She studied her chin line and saw the slight sagging of the muscles, the tiny crow's-feet creeping near her brow when she frowned. Soon her hair would turn gray and her teeth would go bad. Thank God she had fairly good teeth. Many of the women her age were half toothless by now. God had been good to her, but why did she have to grow old? She was old enough to be a grandmother already, yet sometimes she felt like she was still twenty, and then again there were times, like now, she felt eighty.

She reached down onto the top of the dresser and picked up a pair of small gold earrings, slipping them into her pierced ears as someone knocked on the door.

"Come in."

Rebel stepped into the room, her deep russet dress making a soft swish as she swirled it, closing the door behind her, and walked over, looking at her mother. "You don't look happy, Mother," she said as she watched her mother pinch her cheeks for color and moisten her lips, and Loedicia sighed.

"I don't mean to spoil things," she answered. "But I feel so out of place here. It's been so long."

"I bet you were the belle of the ball when you were young."

Loedicia eyed her daughter curiously. "Is that what you want to be? The belle of the ball?"

Rebel's eyes grew soft, excited. "I want men to notice me, Mother," she said enthusiastically, smoothing her dress, showing off her small waistline. "I want them to court me and treat me like a real lady. I saw so many handsome men when we rode in today. If there are this many in Philadelphia, I bet London's full of them." She reached up and lifted her hair, letting it fall sensuously between her fingers, closing her eyes dreamily. "When Father said we were going to England, I was ecstatic," she whispered slowly. "And I've decided I'm going to marry a count, or maybe a marquis." She opened her eyes and looked at her mother provocatively. "Are Englishmen marquises, Mother, or is a marquis

French?" Then her face looked dreamy again. "Or maybe I'll marry a duke. That's it, I'll be a duchess. . . ."

"Why stop there?" interrupted Loedicia sarcastically. "Why not a prince? After all, when you're aiming high, you might as well go to the top."

Rebel hesitated and stared at her mother abruptly. "You're angry with me?"

"No. Not angry. Not really."

"You are."

She frowned, irritated. "Rebel, please don't set your heart on wealth and a title; that's not for you. You'd never be happy. Don't ever marry anyone unless you're in love."

Rebel laughed, and her laugh was anything but gentle, cutting Loedicia like a knife. "Oh, come now, Mother," she answered, and for the first time Loedicia saw the effect the past few years had made on her daughter. "You married for love, and what did it get you? Are you happy?"

Loedicia couldn't answer.

"Well, are you?" She looked disgusted. "All you and Father do anymore is argue. Even on the trip. Oh, yes, you slept in his arms every night. Not because you wanted to, but because it was a habit, so what's the difference, Mother? Marry for love and have it grow cold over the years, or marry for money and a title and at least one can make you happy."

Loedicia was speechless, her face white as she stared at Rebel's flushed face. "You have no right," she whispered hoarsely, finally finding her voice. "What's happened between your father and me . . . you don't know. You can't possibly understand. . . . That's not how it is. I love your father very much."

"I'm not a child, Mother," answered Rebel. "I know you love him, but love isn't everything, is it? It can't always bridge the wrongs, the mistakes, the faults, and rather than take the chance and find myself hurt and bitter, living on nothing but memories and dreams, I'll compensate with money. After all, if I'm not in love with my husband, then the things he does won't bother me, will they?"

"And what happens if you happen to meet someone and really fall in love?"

"I won't let that happen, ever," she said, her face determined. "I don't have to fall in love if I don't want to."

"Oh? Just like that?"

"Just like that!"

"Rebel, love isn't like that. Nobody asks to fall in love, it just happens, even when we don't want it to. If we could turn ourselves on and off like you seem to think, life wouldn't become so complicated. You can't tell your heart not to love someone."

"I can and I will!"

"But love is—"

"Love is fickle! I thought Father loved Heath, but he doesn't. If he did, he wouldn't get mad every time we mention his name. And if he really loved you as much as he says, he'd forget what happened, but he won't. Love is supposed to conquer all. . . . Ha! What a laugh!"

Tears welled up in Loedicia's eyes as she listened to her daughter's tirade. "Don't," she whispered softly, looking into Rebel's angry eyes. "Please, Reb, don't let what's happened to your father and me spoil life for you. Everyone needs love."

"Not me! I can play the game as well as anyone else, and that's all it is, a game. Well, I'm going to make sure I play by my rules."

Dicia shook her head. She should have seen it coming long ago. The quiet moods, the irritability, the sarcastic remarks to Teak, the restlessness. Always flirting, yet never letting her guard down. She never walked around starry-eyed as most young girls did, at least not for the past two years. She'd grown up cold and callous.

Dicia reached out angrily and grabbed her daughter's face between both her hands so she had to look into her mother's eyes. "Reb," she whispered harshly, trying to make her understand, "don't harden your heart to what life can give you. Marriage isn't just a few words said in front of a preacher. It goes much deeper than that. It's the little things that count. The everyday living. The laughter, the anger, the warmth, the tears, the repressions, but most of all it's sharing a bed with a man, and God help you, unless you love the man you give yourself to, life will be a living hell. I know." Her hands dropped to her sides as Rebel stared at her, puzzled.

She knows? "I don't understand. Heath told me you said you loved his father."

"It has nothing to do with Heath's father or your father. Don't try to understand. Just believe me, dear. No money can compensate for the touch of a man's hands if there's no love to go with it. I'd rather have a dozen fights with your father and make up a dozen times than spend one night in the arms of a man I didn't love." She took a deep breath. "It's as simple as that."

She didn't know what to say and stood transfixed, remembering the day Beau left, the way he'd mocked her and made fun of her for thinking herself in love. The bitter tears she'd shed over his rejection and the anger that had finally erased the ache in her heart. Oh, yes, love was grand for someone like her mother. She'd never been rejected. She didn't know what it was like to ache inside for just a touch, a word, to feel his arms about her, his lips on hers. Well, she wasn't that calf-eyed little girl of sixteen anymore, she was a woman, and as a woman she could shape her own destiny. And it wasn't going to be subdued and submissive, eating her heart out over a man. She'd seen Indian girls married to men they hardly knew, and they didn't look like they were suffering any. Her mother didn't know what she was talking about. She was just trying to get her to change her mind. Who was she to say? How did she know?

"It won't work, Mother," she answered. "It's a good try, but I've got my mind made up." She stepped past her mother and surveyed herself in the mirror, pleased with what she saw. "With the right clothes and the right introductions, it shouldn't be too hard to catch an eligible man."

Loedicia shook her head as Quinn opened the door and stepped in, gazing at his daughter proudly. "And what eligible man is this you hope to catch?" he asked as he straightened his black frock coat, pulling down the sleeves so they covered his shirt cuffs.

"I've decided to catch myself a husband," she answered gaily, ignoring the hurt look in her mother's eyes. "London ought to have at least one titled bachelor with money who'd be willing to walk me down the aisle."

"It's a title you want?"

She smiled. "Why not? Like father, like daughter."

He frowned. "You're jesting."

"No, Father, I'm not," she said seriously. "I loved Fort Locke and I loved the wilderness, but it can get awfully lonely all by yourself. I've often wondered what it would be like to live in a big house, have servants, and be able to entertain lavishly and wear all the latest fashions."

"You'd get tired of it," stated Loedicia, and Quinn glanced at her quickly, sensing that something was wrong.

"You don't approve?" he asked.

"Not if she's planning to get married just to get a rich husband, I don't. There are some excellent reasons for marriage, and money isn't one of them."

His eyes narrowed as he stared into Loedicia's eyes, and something passed between them that made him feel strange inside.

"Your mother's right," he said slowly as he turned reluctantly from Loedicia and looked at his daughter. "If you fall in love with a rich man, fine, but don't marry a man you don't love for the sake of his money. It wouldn't be fair to you or to him."

"Him?" Rebel looked at her father, surprised. "Oh, Father, you're as bad as Mother. Three-quarters of the marriages are arranged by parents between people who hardly know each other, and nothing's even mentioned of love. So what's wrong with it?"

Quinn's voice was deep, yet soft. "Because it's wrong for you. You're a different breed, Reb. You're not a submissive young lady who's grown up crocheting doilies and embroidering linens, you've had free rein to live life to its fullest. You couldn't stand the shackles of a loveless marriage."

"Let me be the judge of that, shall we, Father?" she answered flippantly. "After all, it is my life, and you did tell me you'd never stand in the way of my happiness."

"But that doesn't mean you're to sell yourself to the highest bidder."

"Why not? What has love done for you? If the past few years of listening to you and Mother is any indication of what love can do for me, then no thanks. I want no part of it. I'll marry my way." She swung her long hair back over her shoulders. "Now, if you two don't mind, I think I'll go see if Lizette knows anything about whether marquises are French or not," and she left abruptly as Quinn stared after her, speechless.

"Of all the . . ." he finally blurted as he found his voice again. "Who does she think she is, talking to me like that?"

"She's a very confused young woman," stated Dicia soberly.

He whirled about, his face stunned. "What the hell did she mean, the past two years . . . what's she talking about?"

Dicia flushed scarlet, and her heart turned over inside her. She had to tell him. They'd avoided it for too long already. It had to be brought into the open once and for all. "Don't you know, Quinn?" she answered softly. "She thinks because we quarrel so much that we don't love each other anymore," and he stared into her eyes, his own questioning as he saw the strange expression on her face.

He studied her for a long time, his eyes probing hers deeply. There was something . . . Was Rebel right? Had his anger and frustration killed the love between them, or was the memory of Roth driving her from him? Was that what he saw in her eyes?

He stepped toward her and reached out, touching her face, cupping it in his hand, his thumb brushing a tear from the corner of her eye, and he stared at her anxiously.

"Is Rebel right, Dicia?" he whispered huskily, swallowing hard. "Is there nothing left for us anymore?"

She tried to speak, but instead tears rolled down her cheeks into her mouth.

"If I could kill him, I would!" he cried violently, close to tears himself. "He's always there between us!"

"No!"

"Yes!" His voice trembled as he dropped his hand and turned his back, walking to the window to stare out into the alley behind the inn as darkness began to descend on the city. "It was bad enough knowing he'd made love to you, but the bastard had to get you pregnant so I'd have a reminder for the rest of my life."

"That's not how it was, and you know it."

"Wasn't it?" He turned quickly. "You went to him willingly, and he wanted to make sure I knew it."

"He had no way of knowing I'd get pregnant."

"And he didn't much care, did he?"

"That's not fair. He saved my life and sanity. You should be thankful."

His eyes blazed. "Oh, yes! I should be thankful. The man's ruining my life, and I should be thankful."

"Your own petty jealousies are ruining your life."

"I'm not supposed to be jealous?"

"It's been eighteen years," she answered slowly, emphatically. "Eighteen long years, Quinn."

"That's right! And have you forgotten him after those eighteen long years?"

She stared at him angrily, her face flushed crimson as his eyes hardened.

"Well, have you?"

"No . . . but I—"

"You loved him!"

"Was I supposed to hate him? A man who loved me and treated me like a queen. Was I supposed to hate him?"

"You were mine. You didn't have to fall in love with him!"

"Didn't I? You know what Roth was like. How could I live with him without loving him?" Her voice throbbed. "You thought I was dead. What if you'd found someone else?"

"Maybe I did," he shot back furiously, the veins on his neck tightening. "Maybe I did find someone else," and he saw the startled look on her face. "You didn't know that, did you?" he said bitterly. "I never had the guts to tell you before, but there was a woman. A beautiful, sensitive Indian girl. God help me, I tried, but I couldn't do a damn thing. . . . Do you understand what I'm trying to say? Do you understand me, Dicia? I tried to make love to her, but it was no use. I couldn't get your face, your eyes, your lips, your body out of my mind. I couldn't even do it because it wasn't you. . . . But you—you not only gave yourself to him, you enjoyed it."

The back of her hand flew over her mouth as she stared at him wide-eyed. He'd never told her. In all their years together, he'd never said a word, and her heart sank. No wonder he felt betrayed. "Oh, Quinn . . ."

"Sometimes I wish I could hate you," he whispered savagely, "but I can't. You're like a fever with me. I love you so much it hurts inside."

"That night you came back," she whispered, crying softly, "I told you I loved Roth. You knew it. I told you I was all mixed up, that I didn't really know what I felt, but you made me choose, and I chose you. You knew how I felt about him, yet you wanted me anyway. Why?"

"I thought I could make you forget. . . . Maybe I would have if it hadn't been for Heath."

"Don't bring him into it," she answered, trying to hold back the bitter tears. "It's not his fault. It's between you and me."

"And Roth!"

"Yes." Her voice lowered. "And Roth. I love you, Quinn, I always have, but I can't hate Roth simply because you order it. I'm sorry. . . ." She sniffed in. "He was a good husband, a good father, and he loved me very much. I haven't seen him for eighteen years and I probably never will again, but I can't help thinking of him once in a while. I can't erase all the memories. Condemn me for that if you want, I can't help it.

I can't completely forget him, and I'd be a liar if I said I did, but I'm willing to give you all the love within me, yet instead of accepting it you've let things fester inside you, believing that I loved Roth more than I loved you. For God's sake, Quinn, I don't really know what I feel for Roth anymore. That was so long ago, yet you act like it was yesterday. You drove Heath from me because of your hate. Are you trying to drive me away too? Why can't you accept it? Why can't you just love me as I am and let me love you? Why?"

He stared at her, his eyes dark, lips parted. He wanted to hit her, shut off her words, cover his ears, kill the memory of the man who was coming between them, but he couldn't. So, instead, frustrated, he turned, walking angrily toward the door.

"Where are you going?" she asked breathlessly as he reached for the doorknob, and he didn't even turn around.

"Out!" he shouted back over his shoulder, his knuckles white on the knob as he turned it. "Just out!" And he left, slamming the door behind him, leaving her standing in the middle of the room, a stunned look on her pale, tear-streaked face.

It was late, well past eleven, when Quinn finally returned, opened the door, and slipped into the room, then leaned back against it, his face drawn, eyes weary. He felt weak and drained. He'd been walking and walking for hours, and still it did no good. He couldn't forget. He'd never forget, yet he'd never stop loving her.

He straightened and looked toward the bed, but all he could see was a vague lump in the center, because she'd left only a small candle burning on the mantel and the room was barely lighted. He walked over and took off his coat, hanging it in the clothes press, then did the same with his shirt, pulled off his boots, shoved his stockings inside, and set them by the dresser, then hung his breeches over one of the chairs.

He stood for a minute and stared at the candle, then cupped his hand around it and blew, plunging the room into darkness; then he walked to the bed, bent down, and slipped beneath the covers.

He lay on his back for long minutes listening to her steady breathing, feeling the heat from her body next to his, and the warm vibrations it aroused. Dammit! Why did she do this to him?

He swallowed hard. "Dicia?"

The sound of his voice was almost lost as he whispered, but her answering voice was like music to his ears.

"I love you, Quinn."

He turned in bed and gathered her in his arms, holding her close, and he felt as if he'd explode.

Her face was barely discernible in the darkness, but his mouth found hers and he was kissing her passionately, the storm within him unleashed.

She returned his kiss, her mouth answering his hungrily, feeling the familiar longing in her loins, pressing against him, her breasts tingling as they waited for his caress, and he began to stroke them tenderly, his hands gently, but firmly arousing her, making the nipples hard beneath his fingers.

"I'm sorry, Dicia," he whispered against her mouth, his breath warm on her face. "I can't help loving you, forgive me, please. It's just when I think of you with him—"

She pulled his mouth against hers and kissed him again, silencing him.

"Not now," she whispered, her lips warm on his mouth. "Make love to me, darling. Help me to forget everything but now and us. I need you . . . I want you." Her body moved sensuously beneath his hands, crying for release, and for the first time in months she felt alive and whole again as he took her, her release like a dam that burst inside her, flooding every nerve, filling her very soul, and he too felt it as he came, exploding inside her like a tempest, then gathering her in his arms afterward, fondling her lovingly, knowing regardless of what was before or what was to come, she belonged to him, whether he wanted it to be or not. There was no one else in the world for him but Dicia, and he slept soundly for the first time in months, and she was glad.

8

Loedicia stirred slowly, feeling the warmth from the covers, the soft silkiness of Quinn's arms about her, the hair on his chest brushing her chin as she felt his arms slip from about her, and she rolled over onto her back. She sighed, then slowly opened her eyes, looking straight up into his as they looked down at her.

"I love you," he whispered softly, and she wanted to cry as she reached up and touched his face.

"Is it all out of your system?" she asked, and he grabbed her hand, kissing her fingers.

"I've been a fool," he answered softly. "A damn fool, but it's been so hard."

"I know."

"You can't imagine what it's like. . . . I don't want to share you with anyone."

"You don't have to. Whatever happened before is over, Quinn. Neither of us can forget it, but we can live with it as long as we never stop loving each other. Don't ever stop loving me, darling, I couldn't stand it."

He pulled the covers back, baring her breasts, and leaned down, kissing the valley between them, smelling the warm woman smell of her; then he looked back up at her face.

"I walked for miles last night," he said softly. "I wanted to strike out, hit something, anything to ease the hurt, but most of all I wanted to kill him. Yet, your words kept pounding in my head until there was no escape, no matter how far I walked, and slowly I discovered there never will be. I can't run from it, Dicia, because I love you more than life itself, but you'll have to be patient with me. I'm a selfish, jealous man."

"I know."

"I can't help it." He reached out and traced the side of her face intimately with his finger, looking deep into her violet eyes. "I'll try to understand," he whispered, "but I can't make any promises. I don't think I'll ever forget, but I think maybe I can live with it now. You hit me with a few hard truths last night."

"You needed it."

He frowned. "I guess I did, but it still hurt."

"I didn't mean to hurt you."

"I know."

She reached up and pulled his head down, kissing him softly on the lips, sipping at them lovingly. "I love you," she whispered, her mouth against his. "Don't be too harsh on me, Quinn, and forgive me my mistakes."

His lips answered hers as he kissed her deeply, then let his hands begin to caress her again, and he made love to her once more, this time slowly, deliberately, savoring each moment, thrusting into her rhythmically until she came, then he could hold back no longer and she felt him tremble above her, her own body still quivering with rapture.

"I have to go now," he whispered a few minutes later as he still lay on top of her, his lips against her ear, and she held him tightly against her, shutting her eyes, never wanting to end the ecstasy she always found in his arms.

"I wish we could stay like this forever." She sighed, and he took a deep breath.

"If we only could."

She loosened her arms from him, and he slid off her, bending over to kiss her as he left the bed; then he straightened up, the chill in the room raising gooseflesh on his bare skin. He washed himself, then picked up his underwear where he'd thrown it the night before and began dressing as he talked while she lay in bed watching him. "If I intend to get anything done, I'd better get going," he said, pulling on his breeches and shirt. "I've got trunks to buy, horses to sell, and a stomach that's growling for food."

She laughed as she rolled onto her side, bunching the pillow beneath her head, gazing across the room at him, her eyes warm and soft. "It always did give you an appetite, didn't it?" she whispered, laughing, and he grinned at her as he slipped on his coat and walked to the bed.

He sat on the edge, put on his stockings, then pulled on his boots as she curled around him, teasing him playfully. Suddenly he pulled on the last boot, turned, and made a grab for her, and she tried to duck under the covers, but wasn't quick enough. He wrestled her until she lay breathless beneath him, and he gazed down into her eyes, then stared at her full breasts turned up to him, and he leaned his head down, kissing their rosy tips, running the tip of his tongue across each one, making her tremble.

"You're shameless," she cried breathlessly, and he laughed, then kissed her hard on the mouth.

"That should do you until I get back," he said firmly. "Now if you want me to go see if I can learn anything about Beau and Heath, I suggest you quit trying to seduce me again," and he saw the light shining in her eyes.

"Is that where you're going?"

"First to the docks, then to the Blue Anchor, then to see George. But first I'll stop by Teak's room so he can go along. I'd like him to meet the President," and Dicia smiled warmly.

"Thank you, Quinn," she whispered gratefully. "Thank you so much," and his eyes softened as he stared at her.

"For what?"

"For loving me," she answered passionately, and he kissed her again, then left the room, leaving her still sprawled on the bed on her back, her body alive with desire. It was as if she couldn't get enough of him.

She watched the door close behind him and lay motionless for a long time, finding pleasure in the memory of him. It had been so long since he'd made love to her like this. For the past few years their lovemaking had been strained, more of a physical release than anything else. A habit. The tenderness and warm intimacy replaced by a tension that was slowly smothering the fire that burned inside her. But now . . . She hoped, now that he'd come to grips and started facing his doubts and fears, he could banish them forever and things would be all right again, but she knew the battle wasn't going to be easy.

She moved slowly, reluctantly, and crawled from the bed, cleaned herself off, washing thoroughly with the cold water Quinn had left in the basin on the washstand, shivering in the chill of the morning; then she slipped into her clothes and brushed her hair; finishing her toilet just as Lizette knocked on the door and called her name.

"Come in," she answered as she set the brush down and turned to face her friend.

Lizette had on a plain black dress, her salt-and-pepper hair tied atop her head with a white ribbon wound between the layers of curls, her piquant face expressing everything she felt with dark eyes that spoke from the heart.

"It is all right again?" she asked as she eyed Loedicia anxiously. "I heard him leave last night."

"I think everyone did."

"But I heard him return too," she said, her eyes twinkling. "And this morning he was whistling as he stopped by Teak's room."

"Do I dare hope, Lizette?" she asked, holding out her hands to her friend, who knew without having to be told what was happening between them. "He was his old self this morning."

"Ah, *oui,*" she answered. "If he can keep fighting the demons that torment him, maybe it will be as it was. Today, for a while he forgets, but tomorrow . . . What of tomorrow? Perhaps he will remember, and the anger will come again. For your sake, *ma petite,* I hope I am wrong, but a man like Quinn . . ." She shook her head. "He is intense. His anger rides high, unbridled, and his love is the same—fierce and possessive. It takes a strong man to purge away the kind of hatred Quinn carries in his soul, and I only hope he has the strength."

"He has to," answered Loedicia, squeezing Lizette's hands affectionately. "Otherwise I'll die inside, and I think he knows it."

"Then he will fight all the harder," she said, and eyed Dicia fondly. "And this morning was a start?"

Dicia's eyes softened and her face flushed warm. "Yes, this morning was a start," she confessed, then sighed and stood akimbo. "Well, now, shall we be about our work or shall we stay lazy, gossiping about my love life all day?" and Lizette's eyes sparkled mischievously as they turned to the clothes press, gathering the clothes together to take downstairs.

Meanwhile, Quinn and Teak stood at the end of Chestnut Street and gazed at the ships in the harbor. There were well over fifty. Teak had never seen anything like it. The smell of rope, tar, fish, and garbage filled his nostrils, and it was alien to him, yet fascinating.

Men in leather aprons scurried about with boxes and crates in their arms and on their shoulders, joking back and forth as officers from the various ships barked out orders that no one seemed to be rushing to obey, and wagon after wagon rumbled, wheels grating on the cobblestones as they simultaneously emptied and filled with cargo. Everything from furniture to chickens.

Father and son began strolling along the wharves slowly side by side, the younger man a fair facsimile of his father, and those who took time to notice them smiled at the proud look on the older man's face as he took time to point out something special to his son here or there about the ships and the men on the docks.

The walk to the waterfront had also fascinated Teak. The first early rays of the sun had shone on colorful awnings that graced the rows of close-fitting houses, the front doors opening directly onto pavements with not a blade of grass in sight, and Teak thought it was an awful way to live until Quinn explained that they all had huge backyards filled with trees and grass.

But what surprised him most were the women scrubbing the marble door steps of the houses. They looked like an odd congregation in prayer, on their knees, with their mobcaps, brushes, and wooden scrub pails.

"It's an old custom," explained Quinn as one of the women glanced up at them as they started past, and Teak, noticing everything, realized the woman looking at them was far too young to be the lady of the house and was probably a servant girl. She smiled, sitting back on her knees, watching him, her dark eyes warm and tempting, and he smiled back, his father unaware of the slight flirtation as he continued his explanation as to how the custom started. But it was right then and there Teak decided maybe he'd like the city after all.

Then there were the brightly painted signs that hung above every shop telling customers what went on within. "Because over half the people can't read," offered Quinn, and Teak was astounded. To him reading was as natural as eating and sleeping. These city folks sure were weird.

He stood now gazing at the ships in the harbor, and he felt strangely alive. Like he always did just before a hunt.

There were close to half a dozen shipping offices on the waterfront, and at the third one they found a ship leaving in two days for England. It was a full-rigged three-master called the *Tempest* on its way from Jamaica, but the price was a bit higher than usual. Twenty-five dollars a head.

"The going rate's twenty," argued Quinn, but the shipping agent held firm.

"She's a new ship. Just over a year old, and her cabins are worth it at twice the price."

"Hell, you sound like it's got feather beds," said Quinn, and the man grinned.

"The next thing to it. There's even carpets on the cabin floors."

"And a motley crew, I don't doubt."

"The captain's an Irishman. As for the rest"—he shrugged—"as good as any."

Quinn hesitated.

"You'll find none better, but then, if you care to go looking . . ."

Quinn wanted the best. It took long enough to sail to England without ending up on a miserable excuse of a ship with cabins that were merely an afterthought, dingy and dirty, no better than the filthy holds that held the cargo.

"You're sure of the carpets?"

"I'm sure."

"I'll need three cabins."

"She's got six, and only two booked. Most folks'd rather save the money than sail in comfort."

Quinn had a large leather bag with a long strap slung over his shoulder, and he opened it and reached in, pulling out a small doeskin pouch tightened with a drawstring. He loosened the strings and reached inside, then from it he counted out two fifty-dollar gold pieces, a twenty-dollar gold piece, and five Spanish silver dollars, setting them on the counter in front of the man, then put the doeskin pouch back in the bag.

"That pays for five," he stated confidently, and the man nodded, reaching for the ship's passenger list.

"You won't be sorry."

"I'd better not be," offered Quinn, "because if they're not everything you say, you'll live to regret it. This doesn't happen to be a one-way trip."

The man smiled confidently as he set the ship's list on the counter in front of him. "I don't look worried, do I?" he asked, and Quinn's eyes crinkled in the corners. "Now, what's the name?"

"Quinn Locke, with an E on the end," he answered.

"And the rest?"

"Mrs. Locke."

"First name?"

"Loedicia," and he spelled it for him. "My daughter, Rebel . . ." The man glanced up at him curiously for a second, then wrote the name. "My son, Teak . . ."

"Like the wood?"

"Like the wood," agreed Quinn. "And a family friend, Madame Lizette DeBouchard," and he spelled the name for the man.

"We sail at six Saturday morning," the man said as he set aside the passenger list and made out a receipt, handing it to Quinn. "If you want, you can board the night before, or you can wait till morning."

"We'll wait till morning," said Quinn, and put his hand on Teak's shoulder. "Well, son, let's be off," he said casually. "Our next stop's the Blue Anchor, and the man watched curiously as father and son left the office. Strange pair. Looked a bit too rugged and out of place in city clothes, with their tanned faces and lengthy stride, and he wondered what would prompt a man like that to want to take his family to England.

The Blue Anchor was practically deserted as they stepped inside and looked about. Two men sat in the corner eating; a man and woman were at another table arguing softly; and a short, round, dark-haired man with a huge mustache emerged from curtains in the back that evidently concealed the kitchen.

The man scowled, bushy brows twitching above dark piercing eyes. "I can do something for you?" he asked as he wrung his hands on the apron hanging about his neck and down over his rotund stomach.

Quinn had purposely avoided the Blue Anchor when they rode into town yesterday because he didn't want Dicia to have to stay in the same inn where she and Roth had become husband and wife, even if it did have another name and was no longer the Green Lantern.

The gnawing jealousy that he'd pushed aside last night began to rise within him as he thought of it, and he clenched his fists as he stared at the mustached man, fighting his thoughts; then his fingers relaxed again as he pushed it aside and spoke. "We'd like to speak to the owner if we may," he said, his voice still strained from the effort it had taken to submerge his jealousy. "There are a few questions we'd like to ask."

The man dropped the apron and smoothed it over his stomach. "I'm the owner," he acknowledged, and Quinn nodded.

"We're looking for two young men, both dark-haired, nice-looking. One of them, part-Indian, was named Beauregard Dante, and the other went by the name of either Heath Locke or Heath Chapman. They passed through here in May and June of ninety-one and stayed here at the Blue Anchor, but the owner then I believe was named Polly Mason."

The man nodded. "Polly Mason died last August," he answered, then shook his head. "And I'm sorry, I never heard of the young men, sir."

Quinn sighed. No use going any further here. He thanked the man, and he and Teak left, heading back down High Street toward the marketplace. Suddenly he stopped in front of one of the houses and glanced at the door, looked down at the marble steps, then sighed.

"You always said you wanted to meet the general, Teak," he said as he turned to his son. "Still want to?"

Teak's eyes widened, the blue orbs shining as he smiled. "Is this where he lives?"

"One-ninety, High Street. Only he may not be in."

"And if he isn't?"

"We head for the State House and wait till recess, but it's early yet." He stepped up the marble steps, followed by Teak, and lifted the door knocker.

A few minutes later the door was opened by a gray-haired woman, her face full of smile lines, but she frowned slightly as she spoke, looking them over closely.

"May I help you, sirs?"

Quinn smiled as he bowed. "Is President Washington in?" he asked.

"He's just finishing breakfast, sirs. May I say who's calling?"

"Quinn Locke from Fort Locke and his son, Teak," answered Quinn, and the woman nodded, then shut the door.

She was gone for some minutes, and they waited in silence.

"It's been a good many years since I've seen George," stated Quinn after a while, breaking the silence as they waited. "He was at Mount Vernon then, about two years before the election."

"I wonder if he's changed?" mused Teak, but Quinn didn't think so.

"If I know George, he's still the same. He couldn't change if he tried. I remember shortly after the war—"

He was interrupted as the little gray-haired lady opened the door. "The President will see you now, sirs," she said, smiling, her eyes twinkling as she opened the door wider. "He's eating breakfast out back," and she led them through the house and out to the backyard, where President Washington sat finishing the last of his hoecakes, honey, and cold tongue with a cup of hot tea to wash it down.

He stood up, wiping his mouth with a napkin, and held out his hand to Quinn as they stepped up to the small table set beneath a blooming apple tree near the back door, and both men shook hands vigorously.

"My God, Quinn," commented George as he held his hand firmly. "How long has it been?"

Quinn grinned warmly. "Somewhere near six years, George," he answered as the President freed his hand.

"Sit down, sit down." He motioned to the chair opposite him, then glanced at Teak. "He has to be your son, right?" he asked, gesturing toward Teak.

Quinn put an arm about Teak's shoulder. "My son, Teak Locke. Teak, may I present George Washington, President of the United States."

Teak shook hands, his face beaming, then both of them sat opposite the President while a maid brought more tea.

"I enjoy eating here in the yard," offered the President, his deep voice almost throbbing. "The fresh air, birds, smell of the blossoms." He offered them a bite to eat, which they declined, having eaten earlier at the Copper Kettle; then he sipped at his tea. "So what brings you to Philadelphia?" and Quinn frowned as he once more began to remember that night so many years ago when this man now sitting across from him had stepped between himself and Roth, stating that since Quinn was still alive, Loedicia's marriage to Roth was void. The gnawing jealousy began to seep into his thoughts again, and he fought once more to shove them aside, and his eyes hardened as he spoke.

"I raised another son, George," he said softly, his voice strained. "I believe you met him two years ago."

The President stared at his friend across the top of his teacup, at the strange look in his eyes, and he remembered the dark-haired young man who'd stood in the drawing room upstairs and listened as he'd told him about some of his father's exploits during the war. A handsome lad, big for his age, and the image of Roth Chapman.

"I remember the lad well," answered George. Then he winced as he realized what Quinn must have gone through over the years. "I'm sorry it turned out the way it did, Quinn," he apologized, "but none of us had any way of knowing—"

"It's over . . . done," interrupted Quinn quickly, then tried to shake away the bitterness that was once more trying to engulf him. "But the lad's disappeared, George. There was a letter written from Philadelphia by the young man who accompanied him . . ."

"Ah, yes." George's eyes shone. "The Indian. A remarkable young man. When he told me his father was chief of your Tuscarora, I was amazed—he was so learned, so charming, so—"

"So debonair and worldly wise?" asked Quinn.

"That's it," he said enthusiastically. "He reminded me more of a Frenchman than an Indian." He paused. "And speaking of Frenchmen, I wonder if they ever found Marget Dubonné."

"Marget Dubonné?"

He nodded. "She was the last one to see Roth before he left Philadelphia, but they were having a rather hard time locating her." He mused. "I know why now, but I didn't at the time, and I couldn't be much help to them." He shook his head, then continued. "Do you remember hearing back in June of ninety-one about King Louis and Marie Antoinette trying to escape from France?" He saw the look of recognition in Quinn's eyes. "That's right, my friend. Marget Dubonné was his agent here in the United States. Unfortunately, or fortunately, depending which side one's on, the plot was nipped in the bud and the king never reached the ship that was to bring him here, but in the meantime your two young men stirred up quite a furor in their search for her. Whether they found her or not, I don't know. They stopped by to see me several times while they were here, but never came to say good-bye. I thought it strange at the time, but young men are foolish and full of pride, and I thought perhaps he hated to admit to me that he had failed, or maybe they'd found a lead and just taken off without thought to anything else." He studied Quinn hard. "He never came home?"

"His mother's been frantic. There's been no word of any kind since that one letter."

The President frowned. "Maybe he found his father. . . . It's possible."

"But not probable."

"Would you like me to make inquiries?" asked George, and Quinn sighed.

"If you think it would help."

He shrugged. "Perhaps. I don't like to worry you, but we did have an epidemic of yellow fever that year. Perhaps . . . But then, I doubt very much . . . If one of them had gotten sick, I'm sure the other would have come to me. . . . I imagine Loedicia's terribly worried. How is she?"

"As beautiful as ever."

He smiled. "You'll bring her to dinner this Sunday," he said, but Quinn declined.

"We sail Saturday morning for England," he announced, and the President's eyes looked at him knowingly.

"You've finally decided to go back," he stated, and Quinn put his hand on Teak's shoulder.

"To claim what's rightfully mine and my son's."

George caught the note of finality in Quinn's voice, and now he suddenly realized what had driven Heath away from Fort Locke, and he felt sorry for the boy. Yet, could he condemn Quinn? How would he feel under the same circumstances? After all, it was hard enough being a father to step children; what would he have done if he'd raised a son as his own, then discovered another man fathered him? No. He couldn't blame Quinn.

"Then bring Loedicia this evening," he said. "And I imagine little Rebel has grown into quite a young lady by now. I want the whole family. I know my host won't mind." He stretched a bit as he took the watch from his pocket and checked the time. "I'll expect you about six." He saw the reluctant curve of Quinn's mouth. "And you won't refuse, my friend," he said as he stuffed the watch back into his pocket. "Because I don't have time to argue and coax. Congress waits, and I'm going to be late as it is."

He pushed his chair back and stood up, then kept talking as they moved into the house. He made them wait until he retrieved his hat, then walked to the door with them, and all the while Teak stared at him, amazed, saying hardly a word, but taking everything in. No wonder the man had been elected President, he had a magnetic personality that seemed to shine from within, yet he was anything but good-looking. In fact, his nose was a bit long and his eyes a bit small and his mouth a bit too straight, but sincerity dwelt in those eyes. They were the eyes of a leader, and Teak knew why his father was proud to call him a friend.

They walked a way with him, talking about old times, until Quinn suddenly stopped in front of a leather shop, explaining that he had trunks to buy yet, and both men shook hands; then once again the President shook hands with Teak.

"Make sure your father doesn't forget dinner tonight, young man," he said firmly. "I'm expecting the whole family."

"And Lizette?" asked Teak.

"Lizette?"

"My mother's friend. She's sort of a friend anyway. She's been around for years."

"Lizette DeBouchard is the widow of one of my men, and an old friend," explained Quinn. "Loedicia insisted she come with us, although she claims she's traveling as an abigail. Did you ever know of an abigail who acts more like a mother-in-law?"

"A mother-in-law?" George laughed. "Good God, man, she can't be that bad."

"She's not," said Quinn affectionately. "She just has a sharp tongue where I'm concerned, and for some strange reason she always makes me feel like a naughty little boy . . . if you know what I mean."

George sighed. "I have a cousin like that, and I'm glad she doesn't come visiting too often. It can be a damned nuisance." He checked his watch again, then apologized for having to leave, making Quinn promise to be there at six and promising to see if he could find out anything about Heath and Beau.

When Quinn and Teak arrived back at the Copper Kettle late that afternoon, Loedicia was almost in a state of shock. Four huge trunks had arrived early that morning, followed a few hours later by a dressmaker and two assistants with enough clothes for ten women instead of three, carrying needles, thread, and scissors with them, and as they tried one dress after another on the three women, tucking in here, letting out there, adding lace here, a bow there, Loedicia kept insisting they must have made a mistake. Quinn couldn't have had enough money for all this, she argued, but they just kept on, unmindful of her protests.

The clothes were lovely, but she was skeptical. He'd never actually shown her all he'd saved, but this seemed like so much, and she thought of the hundreds of furs he'd trapped over the years and the countless trips east he'd taken, investing the money, saving for this trip like a child saves for a new toy.

She looked up quickly as Quinn entered the room; then she frowned, puzzled at the look on his face as he stood dumbfounded, staring at her, until she happened to remember and glanced down at the dress the dressmaker was fitting on her. It was the same violet color of her eyes. The color of the dress she'd worn that night he'd come back eighteen years ago when she thought he was dead and found her married to Roth, and she saw the pain in his eyes.

Quickly she brushed the dressmaker aside and ran to him, flinging her arms about his neck, her lips reaching shamelessly for his mouth. The kiss was long and hard; then suddenly Quinn flinched.

"Hey," he exclaimed as he disengaged himself from her embrace. "You're full of pins!"

She smiled impishly, trying to recapture the carefree abandon she'd felt when he'd made love to her that morning. "You mean you're going to let a little thing like a few pins keep you from kissing me?" she whispered wickedly, and his eyes, hard just seconds before, half-smiled.

"Take that damn pincushion off, madam, and you'll end up with more than just a kiss," he answered, and the dressmaker and her assistants glanced furtively at each other, trying to keep from giggling as Quinn set Dicia aside and stepped farther into the room.

He glanced at Lizette, being fitted into a black dress, severe and undecorative except for white collar and cuffs. "And what are you supposed to be?" he asked curiously. "I told them to find dresses fit for royalty. You look like you belong to one of those Quaker societies."

Lizette clucked hurriedly. "I told you before, *mon ami*, that I do not want the pretty gowns. I am to be treated as a servant, and servants do not parade about in silks and satins."

"You're as stubborn as a jackass," remarked Quinn. "How I ever let Dicia talk me into bringing you is beyond me."

Lizette smiled mischievously, her eyes crinkling. "You would be lost without me, *mon ami*, and you know it." She chortled, smoothing the white collar beneath her animated face. "Besides, let an old woman have her pleasure—"

"Old?" he interrupted. "You're younger than I am!"

"But older and wiser in years," she continued, waving her finger at him. "And you'll quit back-talking or I'll refuse to accept even the new dresses you are forcing on me, and I will arrive in England wearing the same old clothes I wore about the fort, *comprenez-vous?*"

"You wouldn't dare."

"Don't tempt her," interrupted Dicia. "She's just liable to, and she deserves new things."

He reached out and picked up a gray dress, obviously also meant for Lizette, with its severe lines, and held it out to Dicia. "But these? Everyone'll think she's no better than a servant."

"Which I want to be, *mon ami.* Please"—she frowned, cocking her head sideways at them—"humor me in this, please. I don't wish to be the grand lady and go to the balls or dress like the *beau monde.* I want to be me, Lizette, with no frills, no pomp. If I had wanted to be of the *beau monde,* I would never have left Paris to marry my François. I would have stayed with the bourgeoisie, I would have become a—how you say it—lady of leisure." She shook her head. *"Non,* my life is better spent doing things, and I wish for to go to England with you and keep doing things because you need me. Both of you. Now . . ." She waved the back of her hand at him, gesturing that her words should put an end to his protest, and Quinn sighed.

"I guess I'll never understand women," he said, tossing the dress back on the bed. "But if that's what you want . . ."

"It is what I want, *mon ami,*" she confirmed, and Quinn shrugged as he turned to Loedicia, who was being hovered over again by the seamstress who was pinning her bodice smaller.

He stared hard at his wife, taking in the curvaceous lines of her bosom above the seamstress's hands, remembering the way she'd lain on the bed beneath him this morning, and he tried to push the thought aside as he walked to Rebel, who was standing by the window while the other assistant worked on the pale apricot satin dress she was wearing, with its mounds of draped and tucked skirts.

"George invited us to dine with him and his friends this evening," he stated huskily as he eyed his daughter appreciatively, and Loedicia looked at him sharply as Rebel gasped.

"You mean the President?" asked Rebel, and Quinn nodded.

"The President," he confirmed, and looked at Dicia. "We're to be there at six."

Loedicia's face tried to mask the feelings that were creeping into her body. Strange, alien feelings. It had been eighteen years since they had stood on the streets of Philadelphia beside General Washington and watched Roth ride out of their lives. Could she bear to see the man again, or would it bring back too many memories?

She stared back into Quinn's eyes. They were warm and alive, yet wary, waiting to see her reaction. For the telltale look of pain and doubt that would once more kindle the agonizing jealousy within him and bring it to the surface.

No! She wouldn't let it happen, and instead she forced a gay smile to her lips and her eyes grew soft with love as she stared at him. "Should I wear this dress?" she asked softly as the dressmaker put in the last pin, then stood back and eyed her handiwork, and Loedicia was rewarded by the answering look in Quinn's eyes.

Yes, she'd wear this dress, and Quinn would wear his uniform, and Rebel the apricot satin, and Teak would wear his buff breeches and the blue velvet coat that matched the blue of his eyes, and Lizette would be prim and severe in her black dress with white collar and cuffs, and they would go to dinner and she would drown her thoughts with idle chatter, steel her heart from the past, and everything would stay all right. It had to!

Dinner with the President went well. There was leg of lamb, a roast duck, beef, ham, various vegetables including glazed young carrots, fresh peas, and cabbage leaves with sausage rolled inside cooked in a cream sauce, two huge plates of butter with white and brown bread and numerous jellies, ending with spiced fruit, cream pie, and two different kinds of cake.

Loedicia was amused at the gluttonous look in Teak's eyes as he watched one dish after another appear on the table, and a smile cracked the corner of her mouth. He had a ravenous appetite that never seemed to be appeased, but she was sure that this evening, at long last, Teak, if he had his way, would leave the Morrises' house with a full stomach. Perhaps too full, and she hoped he didn't get a stomachache. The food was far richer than the simple fare Sepia had always served them.

"Do have just one more piece of spice cake, young man," urged the President's wife as Teak licked the last of the frosting from his fork, then took a large swig of his cider, but Teak declined seconds for the first time that evening, and Quinn laughed.

"I do believe you've finally managed to fill him up," he said as Teak blushed. "I swear I don't know where he holds all he eats. At home he drives Sepia to distraction. Ten minutes after dinner he's prattling about the kitchen, under her feet, coaxing, looking for more," and Martha was surprised.

"You have your own cook on the frontier?" she asked.

"An Indian woman, but I'm afraid her skills can't be compared to the cook who prepared this meal, ma'am, it's superb."

"We're blessed with a French cook, Colonel Locke," answered Mrs. Morris as she signaled for the serving girl to add more wine to her glass and refill the glasses about the table. "And he is also a connoisseur of good wine, as you may have noticed."

"Indeed, ma'am," answered Quinn. "The whole meal has been a delight."

"Then I suggest," said George, settling back in his chair, "if we are through with the delectable practice of filling our stomachs, we should take our wineglasses and retire to the drawing room, and perhaps your daughter could entertain us on the pianoforte, Quinn," he suggested, eyeing Rebel, who stood next to her mother as they all pushed back their chairs.

She was a strikingly beautiful girl with the astounding contrast of her mother's violet eyes and her father's almost platinum hair, and she had an air of independent charm that astounded him. There was a confidence in her walk and the tilt of her head that declared: Here I am, I'm somebody. And she was somebody. Somebody quite extraordinary.

"But she can't play the pianoforte," announced Quinn.

"I'm sorry, sir," Rebel apologized, confirming Quinn's announcement. "Unfortunately, to get a pianoforte to the shores of Lake Erie would have been an incredible feat, even for my father," and the President laughed. "But I can play a stringed instrument called a guitar," she offered, "and I know some songs Telak's wives taught me."

"Wives?" gasped Martha, wide-eyed, as they headed for the drawing room. "Did you mean plural?"

"Oh, yes, ma'am," she answered nonchalantly. "Telak has four wives and eighteen children."

Martha's hand moved to her bosom, covering the lace that trimmed the bodice of her green satin dress. "Mercy. How can a man have four wives?"

"It's very simple," answered Reb with no thought to propriety. "He keeps a bark hut for each family and shares his time among them."

"But aren't they ever jealous of one another?"

Reb shrugged. "Mostly they get along fine and work together pretty well. But sometimes, I know, even though they won't admit it, they get jealous if he spends too many nights with any single one."

"Oh?"

"Well, how would you feel knowing you had to share your husband with three other women? I don't think I'd like it one bit. In fact, I'm sure I wouldn't. That is, if I was in love with my husband," she said as an afterthought, and suddenly an awkward silence fell on the group as they entered the drawing room, and Dicia swallowed hard as she glanced quickly at Quinn, both of their faces turning quite crimson.

"Well, suppose you sing us one of your songs, then, young lady," suggested George, rescuing the conversation as he offered her a seat near the fireplace, then walked to the corner and came back with a pear-shaped instrument with a long neck and strings, handing it to her as Rebel smiled warmly, unaware that her outspoken frankness had caused the lull in the conversation.

For the next half hour she serenaded them with the songs she'd heard about the Indian campfires and the rousing, rather bawdy songs sung by the men at the fort, quite unconcerned that the words were causing any consternation, until finally Quinn suggested perhaps it was someone else's turn and Mrs. Morris happily moved to the new pianoforte in the corner and continued the entertainment.

As the evening wore on, more guests arrived. Business friends of the Morrises', friends of the President. By nine o'clock there were at least thirty people milling about the drawing room, talking and laughing, and as Loedicia stood near the open window to get a breath of fresh air, the President moved up behind her and spoke.

"You look a bit hemmed in, my dear," he said as she felt the cool breeze from outside caressing the dampness of her forehead, and she straightened, turning from the window.

"It's been a long time since I've been to a party of this sort, sir," she answered faintly. "I'm afraid the wine's going to my head."

"Perhaps," he mused. "Or is it more the memories you've been fighting all evening? You're a good actress, Loedicia, but I daresay I've learned to judge people by their eyes, and yours, my dear, are a dead giveaway."

She stared at him, pursing her lips, the wineglass slippery

in her perspiring hands. "I dare not think of it, sir," she answered primly, her voice trembling.

"But you do."

"Yes," she whispered. "I do."

"And it hurts."

"But it shouldn't."

"And why not?"

"Because I love Quinn. Roth was so long ago. If it hadn't been for Heath, I would have forgotten."

"Would you, Loedicia?"

She stared into his eyes, his question seeping into her thoughts, rankling.

"Well, would you, my dear?" he asked again, and she frowned. "Or did you love Roth enough that you'll never truly forget him, no matter how hard you try?"

She winced. "Th-that's impossible," she whispered, her voice faltering, but he stood his ground.

"Impossible? You mean that you can't love two men at the same time in the same way?"

Her hands tightened on the wineglass as she stared at him. "That's right."

His eyes warmed, and a softness seemed to enfold them. "Don't be so sure of that Loedicia," he answered softly. "May I tell you something in the strictest confidence?"

Her eyes were puzzled as he went on.

"Tonight you met my wife, Martha. She's a wonderful person, and I love her dearly." His face paled a bit as he spoke; then it turned a rather light shade of pink. "But I've been in love for years, my dear, with someone else who happens to be beyond my reach because she already has a husband. I used to fight it at first, trying to rationalize my feelings, until I suddenly realized that love is not a rational state of mind. Now I accept the fact that I will always love her, even though I cannot have her, but it has made the loving of Martha easier. So you see, it is possible to love more than one person. I don't say it's wise, nor do I say that everyone in the world is capable of the feat, but it is possible, and whether we want it to or not, it can happen, and you, my dear, are not the first to experience it."

Loedicia glanced quickly across the room to Martha Washington, her kindly face animated as she talked with her friends; then she glanced at Quinn standing by the fireplace talking to a group of men, and her hand tightened on the glass of wine as she fortified herself with another sip.

"Your confession is appreciated, sir, for what you're trying to accomplish," she answered weakly, taking the glass from her lips. "But I believe our circumstances are far from parallel."

"How's that?"

She turned from the guests in the room, once more looking deep into his eyes, and he saw the pain she felt inside. "Because I doubt very much if your Martha even suspects that there is another woman, and I can bet you never fathered a child by her. Quinn knows about Roth, and Heath is Roth's son. Therein lies the difference."

He drew in a quick breath. "I see," he said softly.

"So I continue watching my husband fight against a man who may as well be a ghost, and hope he wins, because if he doesn't, if the next few years start resembling the past few years, I'm afraid there'll be nothing left between us."

"It's that bad?" he asked.

She twirled the glass slowly, nervously in her hands. "I can't give my love freely unless love is given in return, sir," she said. "And when hate rules the heart and mind, there's little room left for loving."

The President's eyes saddened. "Perhaps it would have been better had I not interfered and let you choose for yourself that night," he said, but she shook her head.

"I did choose for myself," she answered meekly. "After you left the house with Roth, I became mixed up about my feelings and I didn't know what to do. Quinn made me choose. He made it plain that I couldn't have both, and I chose him."

"And are you happy with the choice?"

"That's not fair!" Tears filled her eyes, and he reached out, touching her arm affectionately.

"I'm sorry, Loedicia. It wasn't fair," he whispered. "I know you love him, but I also know Quinn's a violent man by nature, the exact opposite of Roth, and sometimes, although perhaps your love for Quinn is stronger, I feel you would have been happier with Roth, and life would have held fewer complications."

He saw the tears in her eyes as she turned toward the window. "Last night we quarreled violently," she whispered, "and I said some things that I probably shouldn't have said, I don't know, but for the first time since Quinn realized Heath was Roth's son, the love between us was as it used to be, and I don't want it to change again. Yet I'm so afraid it won't last, that I'll do or say something, that the constant reminders will begin to rankle again."

"He asked me to inquire about Heath."

She nodded. "I know, and I thank him for it, but it bothers me that he isn't concerned himself. It doesn't seem to bother him where Heath is, just so he doesn't have to look at him."

"The lad does look like Roth, doesn't he?" he conceded.

She nodded, unable to speak.

"Be patient, Loedicia," he finally said as she continued to stare out the window. "What Quinn has to fight isn't easy. I'm sure he loves the boy in his own way; give him time."

She turned to him and tried to smile. "I know, only it hurts."

His eyes answered her far more than words ever could, and she knew he understood. He straightened, looking out across the room, then felt uneasy as he noticed that Quinn was staring at them, frowning, a puzzled look on his face, as if he sensed what they were talking about. This would never do.

"Are you looking forward to England?" he asked self-consciously, feeling it best to change the subject under the circumstances, and she glanced at him quickly, then caught a glimpse of Quinn out of the corner of her eye and understood what he was doing.

"I wasn't at first," she answered, looking back out the window. "Then I had afterthoughts and decided maybe it'd be a chance for Rebel to meet some nice young men." She turned back to him, frowning. "Now I'm not so sure again."

"Oh?"

"She has the idiotic notion that she's going to marry a title and wealth, with not a thought to love."

His eyes surveyed the room, resting on Rebel standing on the other side of the room in animated conversation with two young gentlemen who'd accompanied their parents to the gathering. Her face was glowing, and the young men looked enthralled with her, hanging on her every word, and he smiled.

"She'll change her mind when the time comes," he said, but Loedicia didn't agree.

"You don't know Reb. She's got a stubborn streak like her father, and I'm so afraid she's going to let her head rule her heart and be sorry afterward." She turned away from the window and followed the President's eyes as they stayed on Rebel. "And another thing," she said as she blushed. "She's had too much freedom. We've let her run loose on the frontier, and let's face it, life there is more open. We live differently than they do in the drawing rooms of London, and I'm afraid Rebel's forthright speech may be offensive. To her the fact that Telak has four wives and the sharing of their connubial bed is quite an everyday occurrence. To London society it would be shocking. I hope she isn't hurt by her unconventional behavior." She shook her head. "I've tried to caution her and make her understand that the things she says aren't ladylike, but I guess she's a lot like I was at her age, and I think sometimes she purposely says things to see the effects they have on people."

"A regular renegade, just like her mother, eh?"

"God forbid," she answered, sighing, "but I'm afraid you're right, and it worries me."

"Have no fear, Loedicia," he said as he watched the concern on her face, then glanced back at Rebel, his eyes amused. "I have a feeling that Rebel Locke is one young lady who'll have all London at her feet. She'll be the toast of Saint James's."

Loedicia looked skeptical. "I don't know," she answered hesitantly, frowning. "Maybe you're right, but I certainly hope she acquires a little more propriety before we reach England," and George smiled to himself as they both continued watching Rebel.

Quinn, who'd been watching them furtively out of the corner of his eye for the past few minutes, since he'd spotted them by the window talking, excused himself from the conversation he was in the middle of and strolled over, trying to look nonchalant, but he wasn't. Something about the way they were quietly talking, the two of them standing alone away from the others, had begun to annoy him.

"Why the frown?" he asked Loedicia as he joined them, hoping he didn't appear too anxious.

"We were discussing your daughter," explained George as he glanced quickly at Loedicia, then back to Quinn, seeing the anxiety in his eyes. "She's quite a young lady."

Quinn stared at him for a moment as if he was about to say something, then apparently changed his mind as he too turned to look at Rebel; he had to agree with George, and for the rest of the evening, at least for all outward appearances, Roth Chapman seemed completely forgotten as they talked about Rebel, Teak, the weather, the city, politics, and their voyage to England.

But Roth was far from forgotten, and Loedicia knew it by the look in Quinn's eyes, the tone of his voice, and more than once she winced, fighting back tears at the sharpness of his remarks.

When the evening was finally over and they rode back to the Copper Kettle in the carriage, Quinn was quiet, staring hard at her, wondering if he'd been right—that she and George had been talking about Roth when he'd interrupted them. He swore softly to himself, trying to fight back the anger that kept gnawing at him. He'd promised her he'd try, but it was so hard.

It was late, and they were all tired, arriving back at the inn well past eleven, so the children and Lizette made their good-nights brief and they all headed for their rooms happy with the thought of bed. At least the children were happy. Lizette was apprehensive, as she sensed something was wrong again between Loedicia and Quinn; and Loedicia, recognizing Quinn's mood, was almost in tears.

She undressed quickly, hanging her things in the clothes press, helping him hang up his things, but saying little to him; then she slipped into bed, and he climbed in beside her, stretching out, feeling her warm, naked body beside him, and his stomach tied into knots. She'd been nervous tonight, he knew, and quiet, trying to hide her feelings. Trying to pretend it didn't matter, but it did, and he knew it, and seeing George had brought it all back to her. They shouldn't have gone, but how could he refuse? Now, there it was between them again. The anger he felt. The horrible silence. The tension and restraint. He couldn't let it happen. Not again!

He turned in bed and reached out in the darkness, barely able to distinguish the outline of her face, and he ran his finger down her cheek to the corner of her mouth, his heart literally in his throat.

He felt her tremble as he touched her, and she turned her face so his fingers touched her mouth, and she kissed the tips of them, sending warm sensations through him.

"I'm sorry," he whispered huskily as he felt the loving touch of her lips on his fingers. "I've been letting him get to me again."

She reached up, grabbing his hand, holding it tightly against her. "It's my fault," she answered, a sob in her voice, but he shook his head.

"I should have told him we couldn't come!"

She moved closer to him, her breasts brushing his chest,

feeling the strength of him next to her. "No," she said softly. "It had to be. We can't keep running every time something reminds us. We have to face it, remember?"

His arms went about her, and he held her close. "I don't want to remember anything except that I love you," he cried. "Dammit, Dicia, I'm trying!"

"I know," she whispered, snuggling closer, moving sensuously against him, burying her face in his neck as she kissed him, sending shivers to his toes, and he groaned.

"My God!" he gasped. "How can I think clearly when you do that to me?"

"You're not supposed to think. You're supposed to make love to me."

He sighed as she tilted her face up to his, and his mouth covered hers, drinking in the warmth and love that were waiting for him, and he pulled her even closer, his body responding to her. Oh, God! How much he loved her.

His hands began to caress her, feeling the velvet touch of her skin, her wanton response, and this time he took her hungrily, satiating his need for her with a savage passion that almost frightened her, yet left her trembling with ecstasy. So once more the air between them had cleared and everything was as it should be as she nestled in his arms afterward, looking forward to their trip to England, where she knew there'd be no more reminders, nothing to threaten the love they shared.

The next day was spent with the dressmakers again, preparing the rest of the dresses, and two delivery boys arrived in the morning with the accessories—hats, gloves, capes, shoes, stockings, underthings. Then, in the late afternoon some clothes arrived from the tailor's for Teak and Quinn. New breeches, coats, vests, a cape for each of them, with hats, shoes, stockings.

When Dicia protested he was spending too much, he only grinned and teased her for being a shrew.

"There's more than enough," he explained cheerfully as he gave her a hug and a kiss. "Now, on with the packing," and he slapped her playfully on the rear as Rebel grinned furtively and Teak watched them curiously. It had been quite some time since he'd seen intimate byplay like this between his parents, and he seemed amused.

By evening, with all of them working hard, all four trunks were stuffed full and Quinn had to run out to locate two large traveling bags for the overflow. They welcomed bedtime, tired and exhausted, glad to get a few hours' sleep before getting back up in the wee hours of the morning to leave for the ship.

Long before the first rays of dawn scared the night away, they all stood on the wharf, their eyes heavy with sleep, watching the trunks being loaded, then followed them aboard and settled everything in the cabins, which, to Quinn's delight, were everything the ship's agent professed them to be. And as it grew closer to dawn, Loedicia and Quinn stood apart from the others on the deck of the ship, their cloaks pulled about them to ward off the cool night air that would soon be replaced by the warming sun, and Quinn sighed.

"At last," he said, taking a deep breath as they watched the ship being loaded in the dim light just before dawn, and Dicia glanced at his face, studying him intently. "I've waited for this moment for years," he went on, glancing at the men on the rigging as they readied the sails, taking in the activity that was filling the harbor with constant noise as other ships besides theirs began loading cargo.

His face looked almost young, eagerness and determination glistening in his eyes as he watched. He was going home to a world that had turned its back on him, and now he was going to show them who he was, that Quinn Locke was a man to reckon with. She pulled the cloak tighter about her arms, praying that his hopes and dreams wouldn't be in vain.

The *Tempest* was a sound ship, her three masts reaching skyward like sentinels wrapped in white shrouds, ready to unfold and catch the wind as it attacked with the morning light. But she rode exceptionally low in the water, her holds filled to capacity with over a hundred barrels of flour, two hundred blocks of cheese, five hundred wicker baskets, fifty boxes of candles, close to eight hundred fur pelts, and an assortment of smaller items such as salt, sugar, spices, and household goods.

As the last box was loaded, the hatch secured, and the first rays of the sun began to shove aside the darkness, they all stood at the ship's rail. They watched the sails unfurl one by one, and as they caught in the wind, the ship slowly stirred like a giant sleeping animal and heaved up, leaving her moorings, moving slowly, cautiously out, away from the wharf into the river, and Quinn looked at Loedicia, smiling.

"Well, we're on our way," he whispered slowly, and put his arm around her, holding her close, as the others too stared out at the horizon. "We're finally on our way." Loedicia looked back at the city, watching it move farther and farther away with each minute that passed, and for a brief moment she wished again that they hadn't had to leave. She knew, as the ship moved, that she was leaving part of herself behind. Heath was back there somewhere. He had to be, yet where? Even the President's probing had turned up nothing, and now they were leaving and she wondered if she'd ever see him again, if he were lost to her forever. A tear left her eye and rolled slowly down her cheek. She'd return. She had to. Quinn had promised, and she held back the rest of the tears as she snuggled closer against him, feeling a physical ache in her heart, comforting herself with his strength. With the love she knew he had for her.

The ship moved faster, taking on more sail, catching the strong wind that had blown up, and the city of Philadelphia was left behind. Only the river lay ahead of them. The river and the ocean. They were on their way to England. To England and royalty and to the inheritance Quinn had always wanted and never been able to have.

9

England—August 1793

They waited nervously in the large salon in the house on Grosvenor Square—Loedicia, Rebel, and Lizette shuffling their feet beneath them as they sat on the sofa, Teak twiddling his thumbs while he sat across the room in one of the plush velvet chairs, looking quite handsome, Loedicia thought, in a deep indigo coat and buff breeches, his blond hair curled about his ears in an attractive, yet almost careless fashion, and Quinn pacing the floor, his red velvet coat making his flushed face look even redder.

"I can't understand why the servants don't seem to know anything about our coming," he said as he stopped for a minute and addressed Loedicia. "The letter I received from Jules said he'd be extremely happy to have us stay with him and he'd be expecting us. In fact, he said he'd be quite put out if we didn't. I just don't understand."

Loedicia smiled at him reassuringly and tried to soothe his anger, but she'd been surprised too.

Quinn had been planning the trip for over a year and had written to an old friend of his who had lived on the estate next to the Locksley estates, asking him if he could help find accommodations for them while they were here, and had received a welcoming letter insisting that they would stay with him in London. Since the season wouldn't be over yet, they could enjoy some memorable times together and have a chance to catch up on the years between.

The duke and Quinn had grown up together from the time Quinn was two years old and his father had brought him to live at Locksley. They'd ridden together, gotten in trouble together, and gone to school together until Quinn's father's death, when Quinn had learned his grandfather refused to recognize him as a grandson. It wasn't that his father hadn't wanted to marry his mother, but he already had a wife. Locked away and completely out of her mind, but a wife. She had died when Quinn was six years old, but his own mother had already been dead for four years, so there was no way to make right the wrong. Rejected by his grandfather, Quinn had left England at the age of fifteen, taking one of his grandfather's servants with him, a young man named Burly who'd often joined the two young men on some of their more adventurous escapades. Burly was dead now, having been killed during the revolution, but Quinn had kept in touch with Jules off and on over the years, so it was natural that he write to him for help.

Jules hadn't married until he was forty-one, and unfortunately his wife had never given him any children, even though she was younger than he by some twenty years. He had taken over the title of duke at his father's death some ten years before, and although Quinn suspected the young lady had married him more for title and money than love, the letters between the two friends had convinced him that at least Jules seemed content.

Now Quinn stood, pacing the floor, wondering what the devil could have happened and why no one seemed to know what was going on.

Suddenly the knob on the door to the salon turned, and all eyes fastened on it as the door slowly opened and a bewigged servant stepped in, standing at attention just inside the room.

"His Grace, the Duke of Bourland," the man said in his stiff-necked English, head held haughtily, and Quinn's eyes widened as he stopped in his tracks and stared at the gentleman walking through the door.

He was young, perhaps close to thirty, with tawny brown hair worn carelessly, in the fashion of the day, just brushing the collar of his white-and-gold-brocade coat that was worn over a gold satin vest. The delicately ruffled lace cascading down the front of his shirt was set with gold thread and contrasted beautifully with his cream-colored satin breeches that were tucked into delicately embroidered silk stockings, and the shoes on his feet were black velvet and heeled with diamond-encrusted buckles.

He stopped abruptly, staring at Quinn, his gold-flecked brown eyes taking in Quinn's height, which was a good deal greater than his own, and the intense blue eyes set in the deeply tanned, ruggedly handsome face; then his head turned slowly as he looked first at Teak sitting across the room, then to the women on the sofa, resting uncomfortably long on Rebel. His eyes sifted over her, noticing the similarity of looks between her and the dark-haired woman sitting next to her, realizing the dark-haired woman was older and wondering perhaps if they were sisters, although their coloring, except for their eyes, was so extremely different. Their eyes were a deep violet color, and as his eyes caught those of the younger woman, he felt a quickening inside. My God! She was gorgeous.

He was pulled from his fascinating analysis by the tall blond giant addressing him rather coarsely.

"Duke? Where's Jules?"

He turned to the man, looking down his strong aristocratic nose at him, a slightly cynical turn to his mouth. "If you're referring to my uncle, Jules Grantham, sir, he died some months ago," he answered, his voice edgy. "You knew him?"

Quinn straightened, making his height even more conspicuous. "We've been friends for years," he said, then frowned. "You're Annie's son?"

"I'm Lady Ann's son, yes, sir," he answered, making it plain that he resented his mother being called Annie.

Ann Grantham was Jules's sister, younger by a few years, and Quinn remembered Jules writing that she had married and produced first a son, then four daughters. Apparently this was the son.

"When on earth did Jules die?" he asked, his face saddened by the unexpected news. "I received a letter shortly after Christmas telling me to come."

The duke stared at him curiously. "May I inquire first, sir, as to who you might be?" he asked, and Quinn cleared his throat, apologizing.

"I'm sorry, your Grace. The name is Quinn Locke. My father was Martin Locksley, the son of the Earl of Locksley." He turned to Teak. "My son, Teak." Then the women: "My wife, Loedicia, our daughter, Rebel, and a family friend, Madame DeBouchard."

He watched, frowning, as the duke, instead of shaking hands or greeting them more appropriately, merely nodded his head toward all of them as if they were not worth bothering about, then looked back at him.

The young popinjay, thought Quinn to himself, but continued as the duke stared at him. "I've returned to England to try to claim my inheritance. Although at the moment I'd rather no one knew of my real intentions," he went on. "By all rights I should be the Earl of Locksley," and he saw an amused look on the duke's face.

"I wish you luck, sir," he answered. "The present earl is one of King George's favorites. To denounce him will take something near genius."

Quinn's eyes hardened. He didn't care much for this young man. He was too affected, too haughty. How could Jules have been an uncle to something like this?

"That, your Grace, will be my problem," he answered firmly. "But you still haven't told me what happened to your uncle." Quinn reached in his pocket and took out a letter, handing it to the duke. "This is the letter I received from him, and as you can see, if you'll read it, I'm not fabricating."

The duke took the letter from Quinn and opened it, reading it slowly, then nodded. "I think I understand a bit more now," he said as he handed the letter back to Quinn. "My aunt Rachel was away the day he died, visiting a friend in the country. Sometime during the day Uncle Jules had a caller. The doorman said it was a young man with a letter for him. The young man was dismissed readily after Uncle Jules had read the letter; then he retired to the library. An hour or so later he emerged and started to ask one of the servants to find a boy to deliver a letter for him, then changed his mind and said he'd do it himself. He was gone quite some time and arrived home shortly before dinner. No one had any idea where he had been. Unfortunately, not quite half an hour before aunt Rachel arrived home he had a heart seizure and never fully regained his faculties. He kept mumbling something about a letter and having to tell his wife." He stopped for a moment and straightened his shoulders, trying to appear taller in the presence of the giant he was addressing, but it did little good. "It must have been this letter he had sent in answer to yours, and he never had a chance to tell us."

"But what happened to my original letter?" questioned Quinn.

"He had a letter in his hand and was stirring up the fire when he had the seizure," explained the duke. "I presume it must have been the letter you'd written. As he fell, the letter dropped onto the edge of the grate and caught fire. All we managed to retrieve was one corner of the envelope and a small smidgen with a few blackened words on it. Not enough to distinguish the sender, and there was no way to discover where Uncle Jules had delivered his letter. He undoubtedly took it to one of the ships in the harbor." He sighed as he looked over at the women, then glanced at Teak, then back to Quinn. "It seems, sir, I am obliged to honor my uncle's gesture of friendship," he said rather reluctantly, "much as it inconveniences me at this time, but since the house is large, we shouldn't be in each other's way too much."

His attitude rankled Quinn. "Under the circumstances, your Grace, I wouldn't expect you to accommodate us," he answered irritably. "I came here solely because Jules insisted. We'll be glad to find accommodations elsewhere."

The duke raised his hand in protest. "I wouldn't think of it," he said. "There'll be no more said. My home is open to you for as long as you require it."

"But I dislike inconveniencing you, your Grace," insisted Quinn.

"Pay no attention to him, sir," interrupted a low, sultry voice from the open doors of the salon, and all heads turned to stare at the woman standing on its threshold, and she smiled as she stepped into the room. "I'm afraid my late husband's nephew has let his title go to his head," she continued sweetly as she walked toward them. "The only inconvenience there will be to him is that he won't have to bear the deadly silence of this lonely house anymore, and I'm sure he'll agree with me that at times it can become frightening."

The duke looked disgustedly at his aunt. Rachel Grantham was close to his own age, with soft chestnut-brown hair piled high on her head, scattering curls above and behind each ear. Her hazel eyes were large and comely, with gently arching brows above them, and her small tapered nose accentuated a full rosy mouth below. She was an attractive woman, made even more so by a delicate use of makeup, and the black silk dress she was wearing with its low-cut bodice brought out the red highlights in her hair.

She smiled at the duke with her eyes. "Oh, come now, Bran," she admonished affectionately. "Don't be such a goose. You know very well you won't be put out a bit. This house has been like a tomb since Jules died." She turned to Quinn. "Brandon is from the country and knew few people in London society. When my husband made him his heir, it was somewhat of a shock to him, and he still hasn't been able to cope with everything. He spends most of his time at Brooks or the races with his newfound friends, and since I am still in mourning for another month . . ."

She glanced quickly at Teak and the women still seated on the couch, then back to Quinn. "I'm afraid I've been unladylike and listened from the hallway, Mr. Locke," she confessed as she blushed slightly, "and I've heard most of your conversation. It would pleasure me if you'd forget Brandon's rather rude remark of a few moments ago and stay. I'd welcome the company."

Quinn was at a loss for words.

"When my husband died," she explained, "there was one provision of Brandon's inheritance, and that was that I was to live wherever I chose, in any of his houses, until the day I remarry. I choose to live in London at the moment, although I don't know why." She shook her head. "God knows I can go to no balls or join in any festivities, but at least I can look out at the streets and go to the shops. But being shut up in this house is as bad as being shut up in the country with no one to talk to but the servants."

The duke frowned. "Aunt Rachel, I'm sure Mr. Locke is quite uninterested in our family situation," he said, tugging at his vest, trying to look important. "I've told him he's welcome to stay. If he goes elsewhere, that's his doing."

Rachel looked at him angrily, as if he were a small boy she was reprimanding. "If he goes elsewhere, I'll never speak to you again, Brandon Avery," she said heatedly. "I've spent enough time talking to empty rooms, and if it's the present Earl of Locksley's friendship you're afraid of losing, forget it. He's not worth the bother. You may think he's your friend, as does the king, but more than once he's talked behind your back, and Grantham Hall has never known a moment's peace since he's lived next door. You know that yourself. He'd like nothing better than to own all the land down to the sea itself, and Grantham Hall and the Bourland estates are all that's in his way."

Quinn frowned. "I presume Lord Varrick's cousin Elton Chaucer is still the present earl?" he asked, and Rachel remarked that she was surprised he knew. "He came forward and claimed it after Lord Varrick's death," affirmed Quinn. "I guess since there was no one else to dispute it, the title went to him along with the land. At least that's what Jules wrote me. Elton and Kendall Varrick were like two peas in a pod when they were young. His mother and Kendall's father were brother and sister, and he used to come to Locksley all the time on visits in the summer. I couldn't stand him."

"He's probably not much better now," exclaimed Rachel. "His wife takes the back seat to his mistress—"

"You have no proof," countered the duke, but she smiled knowingly.

"Don't be so sure of that, Brandon," she said quickly, then continued. "And his two sons are absolutely obnoxious."

Suddenly she realized that Loedicia was staring at her rather curiously, and her face flushed. "Oh, gracious," she remarked, and her hands flew to her cheeks in embarrassment. "Here I am prattling on like a guinea hen and you're all tired from your journey." She looked quickly at the duke. "Brandon?" Her soft sultry voice was a command.

He threw back his head, unable to argue with his aunt, but unwilling to look defeated. "I'll have the servants take your things to your rooms, and you can clean up," he answered firmly, then looked directly into Quinn's eyes. "My aunt is right, Mr. Locke," he confessed reluctantly. "But I was only thinking of her when I spoke before. I thought perhaps house guests would look rather strange during her time of mourning, but since the time is almost up and she seems discontented with things as they are, it will be a pleasure to have you and your family as our guests."

Quinn was surprised at his capitulation, because he had a feeling that the pretty clothes were all an act. There was something hard and forceful about the young man.

Rachel Grantham, though, seemed genuinely pleased to see them, and greeted Loedicia, Rebel, Teak, and Lizette with enthusiasm, inviting all of them to follow her upstairs.

"Jules read me every one of your letters," she said to Quinn as they went up the beautifully carved staircase, then walked down the long hall, where she showed them their rooms. "Except the last one, unfortunately. But I'm sure we can make up for it."

She talked incessantly as she extolled the virtues of each room, apologizing that they hadn't had a chance to air the rooms and change the sheets, but it would be done before bedtime. When everyone was settled comfortably, she excused herself and went back downstairs.

Brandon Avery had removed to the library and was waiting when his aunt returned alone, and he frowned as she stepped into the room, closing the door behind her.

"What on earth were you trying to do with that display you put on?" he asked abruptly, and she smiled.

"I wanted to see what his reaction would be."

"You're a fool," he said as he poured himself a drink and downed it hurriedly, but she continued smiling.

"On the contrary, Bran. One look at Quinn Locke and I had the strangest feeling he was the answer to our prayers."

"You think he can stop Chaucer?"

Her eyes hardened. "I do."

"A backwoodsman from America? A man who fought against the crown?"

"He's a man with determination," she said as she walked over and looked out the window into the courtyard at the back of the house. "After all, how long has it been?"

His eyes flashed. "When Sir William asked my help, I told him it couldn't be done overnight."

"But a year, Bran? It's been almost a year, and all you've found out is that he has a mistress. Instead, you've managed to almost let him bleed us dry in those card games of yours at Brooks, and he still hasn't pulled you into his circle of intimate friends."

"And you think he will now? With his enemy in my house?"

"Sometimes what can't be gained one way can be gained another. Your act of friendship doesn't seem to be working, so perhaps Mr. Locke's battle will turn the tide."

"Oh, come now, Rachel, all it will do is incite Chaucer to try all the harder to put me in his debt. As it is, I've had to maneuver out of his clutches enough times in this ridiculous charade."

"Then why did you promise to go along with the prime minister's suggestion? Why didn't you tell him no?"

"You think I plan to hang about in England for the rest of my life playing cards and living a life of ease? I didn't study law and politics and learn what I could in the army to end up lulling my time away in drawing rooms. He promised to get me an appointment as governor of Grenada if I thought I could successfully invade Tobago and Trinidad and seize them for the crown. It's a small start upward, but a start."

"And all you care about is power, right?"

"What else is there? To hang about here being a nobody?"

"You're a duke."

He smiled cynically. "A duke. Oh, jolly. I get to order around a few tenants and go to the king's court wearing a jeweled crown and ermine robes and have men bow down and scrape and call me 'your Grace.'" He walked to the desk. "That's not the kind of power I want, and you know it. Unfortunately, I wasn't born a king, so I'll take the next best thing."

"Emperor?"

He smiled at her, and she stared at him intently. He was too ambitious. He always had been. She'd warned Jules that to make him his heir would be a mistake. There was a cruel streak in him. He liked to order people around, and sometimes it frightened her. Lack of money and position had held him back before, but now, as the Duke of Bourland he was determined that someday the power he'd always dreamed of as he grew up would be his.

For the moment, however, he was a long way from seeing his dream come true, unless he could turn the tide for the prime minister. Sir William Pitt disliked the influence that Lord Chaucer, the Earl of Locksley, had with the king. His ideas were harmful and treasonous to the throne and to England as a whole, yet King George listened with enthusiasm. Since the Locksley estates bordered Grantham Hall and the Bourland estates, Sir William had asked Brandon Avery's help in exposing Lord Chaucer as an enemy of the crown, as Sir William suspected him of being. So far he hadn't been successful. There were a lot of suspicions, but nothing could be proved.

Brandon moved forward, and his arm circled Rachel's waist as he looked into her eyes.

"Don't you want to go to the West Indies?"

"As the governor's aunt?"

"Every man should have such an aunt," he whispered softly, and pulled her closer in his arms, kissing her thoroughly.

Brandon had always thought his uncle's choice of a wife was a good one, and often flirted with her behind the duke's back, so it was inevitable that he take advantage of her loneliness after the duke's death. He wasn't in love with her, but she fascinated him. Besides, it wasn't every man who could have his mistress under the same roof and yet avoid scandal. He knew Rachel wasn't in love with him; in fact, he was glad. If she were, it could complicate things. They'd become more of a convenience for each other, and a pleasant one at that.

He released her and sighed. "With them here we'll have to be doubly careful."

"I know that."

"Yet you think it was wise?"

"It'll be fascinating to watch Jules's old friend at work. Besides, he's quite handsome."

"But out of reach."

"No man is out of reach unless I want him to be, dear boy," she answered, but he grabbed her arm, twisting her wrist, his fingers biting into the flesh.

"Don't call me 'boy,' " he whispered angrily. "I've told you before."

She winced, yet her eyes looked steadily into his. "You're too sensitive, Bran."

"I may be three years younger than you, Rachel, my love, but I'm more of a man to you than my uncle was, and you know it."

Her eyes softened. "Are you going to show me tonight, Bran?" she coaxed softly, but he frowned and released her wrist.

"Not tonight, my dear. Tonight we have guests to entertain, thanks to you."

She straightened, her eyes studying him. He was dangerous. He used people for what they could do for him, even her. He gave the impression of being a dandy, but he was far from being weak. He'd given up a commission in the army to inherit his uncle's title, hoping it would further his ambitions, and he had some unique ideas on how a country should be run. In a way, she pitied the inhabitants of Grenada if all went well; yet she couldn't cross him. They were in this together, and she'd learned at a rather tender age to look out for herself above all else. Besides, she enjoyed his lovemaking, and her eyes smiled at him seductively as he poured himself another drink.

Upstairs, Loedicia stepped out onto the balcony of the huge bedroom she and Quinn would share, and she smiled to herself as she remembered the look on Rachel's face when she'd tried to give her and Quinn separate but adjoining rooms.

"My wife and I have slept in the same bed for twenty years now, your Grace," he stated emphatically as he stared at the small bed in the room she was allotting to Loedicia, "And I don't see any reason to change the habit now. So do you happen to have a room with a bigger bed?"

She wondered what the duchess would think if she knew

they almost always slept in the nude, and the thought made her smile all the more.

The bed in this room was certainly bigger, and Loedicia peeked back through the curtains on the French doors that opened onto the balcony and watched Quinn bouncing on it to test it as the servants carried the trunks into the room.

The bed was mammoth, with deep green velvet draperies surrounding it and a spread of white brocade with goose-down pillows bunched at the head. The top of the bed, above the curtains, was splendidly carved mahogany and fastened into the ceiling with posts from ceiling to floor at the foot and head, and sheer white lawn panels hanging at the wall between the headposts that gave it an ethereal look. The furniture was from an earlier century too, large and intricately carved, with a mahogany-manteled fireplace on the inside wall.

She watched as Quinn got up from the bed and strolled over by the fireplace to examine the pale green plush sofa and chairs that were set before it; then he gave a quick glance toward the trunks as the servants opened them and began unpacking. He studied them for a few minutes, then frowned and headed for the balcony.

"Jules lived in style, didn't he?" he said as he stepped onto the balcony, watching the afternoon sun as it caught in Loedicia's dark hair.

"I feel out of place."

"Nonsense." He straightened, taking a deep breath of air. "Unfortunately, the city smells like the city," he said, wrinkling his nose distastefully. "It's the new mills and factories. Sometimes I wonder if progress is really worth it. When I was a lad, the air of London was clean and clear except for soot in the winter. But now, with these new steam inventions . . . Even the better parts of the city can't escape it."

"The house is beautiful, though."

"Indeed." He stared down at the courtyard below him with its overabundance of roses, delphiniums, daisies, and peonies, his eyes following the slate walks that wound between each bed of flowers and the green hedges that bordered the walk that separated the gardens from the house. He looked up across the courtyard to the other wings at the back, where the servants stayed and worked. The house was magnificent, and he felt a strange sensation, because the splendor of Bourland Hall reminded him of Locksley with its numerous wings and high Norman towers built centuries ago.

Could he do it? Would the earl marshal see fit to restore what his grandfather had refused him? Would he once more walk the halls of Locksley and this time be able to call it his?

"I wish to hell Jules hadn't died," he suddenly said as he grabbed the wrought-iron rail and leaned over to watch a cat curl up on a bench below and close its eyes for a nap. "He was with me in this all the way, but I'm not so sure about his nephew." He looked quickly at Loedicia. "What do you think of him?"

She brushed a strand of hair back from the side of her face. "To tell you the truth, I don't know what to think of him," she answered. "But I know one thing. I didn't like the way he looked at Rebel."

Quinn's eyebrows raised. "Oh?"

"I had a chance to watch him while you and the duchess were talking. He looked at her as if . . . as if he were a starving man with a plate of food held just beyond his reach."

Quinn's eyes softened. "Maybe it was love at first sight."

Dicia shook her head. "Not love, Quinn, lust maybe."

"You're sure you're not just being a typical mother?"

She looked at him sheepishly.

"After all," he went on, "you do have a lovely daughter, my dear, and I'm sure the duke is not the only gentleman who will appreciate that fact." He took her by the shoulders, feeling the softness of her gray silk traveling dress beneath his hands, the fragrance of the scent she always wore seeping into his nostrils. "And what did you think of the duchess?"

Her violet eyes looked hesitant. "She's lovely."

"That's all?"

She flushed. "Well . . ."

He leaned forward and kissed her on the nose. "Well, what?"

She grinned at him impishly. "Well . . . I think the duchess loves the duchess and money in that order. Anything else she may be fond of is only a means to an end. And I don't think she'd be all that friendly with us either if you weren't who you are."

"And what is that supposed to mean?"

"It's obvious she and the duke and the Earl of Locksley are at odds. I think she plans to let you fight their battles for them."

"Is that so wrong?"

"It is if you get hurt."

"Who says I'll get hurt?"

She reached up and touched his cheek, looking deep into his blue eyes. "You're not used to this sort of thing, Quinn. The courts, the intrigue, the subtle manipulating of one man against another—this isn't your kind of war."

His arms tightened about her. "Then I'll make it my kind of war." But she frowned.

"Darling," she said quietly, "the king still hangs his enemies," and his eyes stopped smiling as he stared at her.

"You're really worried, aren't you?"

"He's a king, Quinn, and from what President Washington and others we've talked to have said, not a very stable one. What if he holds your past against you?"

He put his fingers to her lips to stop her. "I won't hang, Dicia."

"How can you be sure? After all, they had a price on your head once. He may not forget it, especially if you rile him."

He laughed softly. "That was a long time ago."

"I hope so," she answered. "But I don't like it. We're all alone here."

"Maybe the present duke has more influence than we give him credit for," he offered hopefully. "And surely the duchess knows all her husband's old friends." He took one arm from around her and caressed her ear lobe affectionately, then cupped the back of her head in his hand with his fingers tangled in her long dark hair. "I know I counted on Jules, my love, but I'm afraid we'll have to do with what's available. But don't worry"—his voice deepened—"I didn't come all this way to wind up at the end of a rope," and he pulled her head closer, kissing her, trying to still her fears, fears he knew were very real, because although he hated to admit it, the prospect of going on without Jules didn't appeal to him either. But he wouldn't give up. He'd do anything, and he kissed her all the harder, trying not to think of it and hoping he was right about the young duke.

10

The next morning Quinn started to stir in the big bed, then stopped and gazed down at Dicia. She was nestled against him, half on her stomach, her face turned toward him, using his outstretched arm as a pillow, with her right hand directly in the middle of his bare chest. He watched her for some time as the first rays of the early-morning sun crept into the room. She was still so lovely, and he warmed down to his toes just looking at her.

"Dicia?" he whispered softly. "Dicia?" and she took a deep breath, sighing, then exhaled contentedly. He put his hand up and touched her face, stroking a few stray hairs back affectionately. "I have to get up now," he whispered as she fought sleepily to open her eyes.

"Mmhmmm," she murmured, and snuggled closer.

He smiled and kissed her forehead. "I have to get up," he whispered again, his lips against her forehead, and this time she moved reluctantly, lifting her head to look at him, her questioning eyes warm with sleep. "The duke and I are going to leave for Locksley this morning, remember?" he reminded her. "We made plans after dinner last evening. We're to leave shortly after daybreak."

"Damn the duke!" she answered petulantly, and he grinned as his arms went about her.

"You're a shameless hussy, Mrs. Locke," he admonished, and she wrinkled her nose at him, moving against him seductively.

"Why? Because I like to feel your body next to mine? Because I think it's a pleasure, not a duty, to let you make love to me?"

He stared up into her violet eyes, feeling the desire for her becoming more acute by the minute, even though he'd made love to her only last night. "I'm going to be late."

"Who cares?" she whispered and bent down, kissing his neck, and he groaned helplessly.

Almost an hour later, as he hurriedly washed and dressed, he could feel her eyes on him, watching him intently. She lay curled up in bed, the covers to her chin, her face still flushed, her body still warm from his caresses.

God! What she did to him! And things had been so good between them lately. It almost frightened him. He kissed her good-bye long and hard, then straightened his coat and threw her a kiss as he headed for the door, but she held out her hand coaxingly.

"Oh, no," he said firmly as he opened the door. "You're a vixen, and if I get near you again, I'll be later than I already am." He winked. "Be good till I get back, and remember," he reminded her, "we'll be gone for a day or two," and as he shut the door behind him, she sighed, pulling her hand back beneath the covers, and shut her eyes, savoring the remembrance of him.

As Quinn entered the dining room, the duke was finishing the last of his breakfast, and he looked a bit annoyed.

"You're late," he said as he wiped his mouth on a napkin and surveyed Quinn from head to toe, taking in the black traveling coat, dark green silk vest, white shirt with its cascade of ruffles down the front, and buff-colored breeches tucked into highly polished black boots. Quinn wore boots most of the time, hating shoes and silk stockings, condescending to wear them only when protocol occasioned it.

"First time I've overslept in years," answered Quinn nonchalantly, but the duke looked amused, as if he sensed the real reason for his tardiness.

"I thought perhaps you'd changed your mind."

Quinn sat down in the chair one of the servants pulled out for him. "On the contrary. I'm pleased at the prospect of seeing Locksley again."

"We can't go into the main estate grounds," explained the duke. "As I said last night, I'm not on intimate terms with the earl, only speaking terms. But we can ride about the shire and get an idea of how he's taking care of things. I imagine his farms are quite prosperous, however. I've never paid much attention, but I know he's never without funds when he needs them."

"He spends liberally?"

"Very."

The duke waited while Quinn ate, and the two men talked

cordially, Quinn asking questions and the duke answering when he was able.

The duke insisted Quinn call him by his given name. " 'Your Grace' is fine sometimes," he remarked. "But it can be annoying too," and Quinn was relieved, for it seemed strange to call a man so much younger than he was "your Grace."

Breakfast over, they walked to the hall and collected hats, then left the house. The duke was driving his high-perch phaeton, and the servants had already put two small trunks with their extra clothes below on the front transom and back axle tree, fore and aft. The horses were sleek and tawny, a bit high-spirited, and champed at the bit as Brandon accepted the reins from his stableman.

Quinn would have preferred to ride, but since the duke was intent on driving, he didn't want to put up a fuss. He climbed up and sat back easily beside Brandon, who gave the reins a flick, but as the phaeton jerked forward abruptly, jostling him against the side, he glanced down at the distance between himself and the ground and decided that the high-perch phaeton was a far more uncomfortable conveyance than an ordinary carriage. Damn thing's dangerous, he thought to himself as they swung through the gates and bumped maddeningly onto the cobbled streets.

It was a warm August day and the ride would have been fine if Brandon had been more skilled, but Quinn came to the conclusion early that driving was not one of his talents. He treated the horses with little concern, forcing them to his will, the reins tight so they fought the bit.

Once out of the city the roads were smoother, although somewhat rutted, and Quinn was able to enjoy more of the scenery. It seemed strange to be back after so many years, and although he thought he'd be glad to see the land he'd been raised in, it was alien to him and he began comparing it to the wilderness. He'd forgotten there were no maple trees here, but the countryside was abundant with white oak, beech, willow, aspen, and ash. Not as tall and majestic as the great forests along the shores of Lake Erie or the foothills of the Alleghenies, but comforting to the eye.

They passed hedgerows of white hawthorn, yards and fields dotted with honeysuckle, briar, and holly, and he remembered as a young boy trampling through the woods and meadows in summer in search of primrose, hyacinth, columbine, buttercups, and a dozen other woodland flowers to make into a grubby-looking bouquet he knew nurse would make a fuss over when he got home, and he smiled as he thought of his old nurse. She'd loved him like a son, and he'd been heartsick when his grandfather had insisted she leave shortly after his tenth birthday. His father had tried to argue him out of it, but it had been no use. That was so many years ago.

They stopped at a posting inn for lunch, where they received preferential treatment because of the duke, a fact that pleased Quinn, because the food and service were better than most, and they were on their way again in no time.

By evening the duke pulled into the yard of the Foxes' Den and sighed. "I'm afraid we'll have to spend the night here and should reach Locksley by early afternoon," he said as he handed the reins to one of the stablemen and left instructions for him to take care of the horses; then he had the trunks carried into the inn after he'd secured rooms for them.

As they sat down to eat, the duke suddenly straightened as he stared at the door to the dining room. Quinn's back was to the door, but he heard a slight commotion behind him.

"Don't turn around," said Brandon as the serving girl set down a large bowl of beef and vegetables on the table in front of them, "but Elton Chaucer's two sons, Bertram and Peregrine, just walked in."

Quinn looked at the duke hesitantly. He'd been afraid of this, because almost everyone in this part of the country knew Brandon, so they already had arrangements made that the duke would introduce him simply as Mr. Locke. He didn't want Lord Chaucer to know he was in England just yet. Not until he saw the lay of things.

"They're coming this way," said Brandon. "I guess we don't have a choice."

The two young men sauntered across the room as if they owned it, and stopped abruptly by the table where the duke and Quinn were sitting.

"Your Grace," said a nasal voice, and Quinn glanced up quickly at the two men, momentarily startled to see they were twins. Both had sandy hair with dark freckles splashed on their faces, as if they'd been splattered with mud, and iron-gray, arrogant-looking eyes. They were a bit taller than average, their mouths wide and severe beneath prominent noses that were a trifle too long. They looked to be in their mid-twenties, and Quinn was reminded of their father, Elton, when he was young. "What a surprise," continued the young man. "We had no idea your Grace was in these parts."

Brandon conjured up his best look of indifference. "I don't generally announce my comings and goings to the local populace," he answered nonchalantly. "Does that meet with your approval?"

Quinn fought to keep from laughing as he saw the two young men's faces turn pink beneath the freckles.

"Oh, to be sure," muttered the other twin. "It was just a surprise. We don't generally see you in the Foxes' Den."

Brandon glanced about at the inn. It wasn't the best by far and was in much need of repair, and the food needed improving. He usually stayed elsewhere when traveling through, but darkness had caught them and he had little choice. "If you look about you, you can see why," he said deliberately. "But since there is no other inn close by, I'm afraid I had to prevail upon it for the evening. A mistake I plan to rectify in the future."

"I hope you and your friend will be comfortable, your Grace," remarked the first twin and glanced quickly at Quinn.

"Forgive my negligence," said Brandon. "May I present Mr. Locke. Lords Bertram and Peregrine Chaucer, Mr. Locke, the sons of the Earl of Locksley," he introduced, and the twins stared.

It was unusual for the duke to be traveling with a plain gentleman. "Mr. Locke?" asked Bertram emphasizing the "Mr.," and Quinn straightened in his chair to his full height.

"All of us are not fortunate to be able to use a title, Lord Chaucer," he explained. "After all, we can't all be lords and dukes, or princes for that matter," and Bertram sneered.

"You're not from England?" the other asked, and Quinn's eyes narrowed defensively.

"You're observant, young man," he answered. "I'm not from England." But he made no attempt to tell them where he was from.

"Would you care to join us for dinner?" asked Brandon in a tone indicating he was merely being polite and he'd rather they refuse, but either the young men were extremely stupid or perhaps arrogant enough not to care, for they did join them, making the meal one of the most unpleasant Quinn had endured for some time.

They were pushy and arrogant, flirting with the serving girls and complaining about the quality of the food loud enough so others could hear, and thought nothing of asking questions about matters that were none of their business. Now Quinn knew why the duchess had referred to them as obnoxious.

By the time he and the duke retired for the evening, they were never so glad to get rid of anyone as they were the Chaucer brothers, and thank God they wouldn't be traveling with them in the morning, for Bertram and Peregrine were heading back to London, in the opposite direction. They had been abominably curious during the course of the evening, and Quinn's conversation was strained as he tried to avoid answering their impertinent questions without being downright rude. The duke, however, didn't seem to care, and Quinn saw another side of him as he continued to flip witty, cutting insults at them, but unfortunately, they went completely over the young men's heads.

The next morning they left directly after breakfast, glad not to encounter the twins, since the pair had ridden off barely after sunup, and according to the innkeeper, who was glad to get rid of them, they made the trip regularly back and forth from London to Locksley and always stayed at the Foxes' Den.

It was shortly before lunchtime when the duke slowed the horses and they passed a sign that heralded the village of Locksley, and Quinn began to look about critically. He was hardly impressed.

On each side of the road as they moved slowly along were fields of vegetables almost ready for harvest. The plants were none too strong, scraggly and insubstantial, and would yield only a sparse crop. The fruit trees were heavy-laden, but the fruit was small in size, and although some of the branches almost touched the ground, the fruit on them looked inferior. As they rode farther on by the pastures, cattle moseyed up to the fence to gawk at them, cattle that looked as if they could have been fatter and better cared for, and few yearlings stared back at them through the wooden fences.

Suddenly Quinn frowned and reached out, touching the duke's arm. "Stop," he commanded sharply, and Brandon pulled on the reins, bringing the horses to an abrupt halt. "Look," said Quinn, and nodded beyond the horses' heads.

It was a farmhouse. At least what he supposed to be a farmhouse. The thatched roof was in shameful need of repair, as were all the outbuildings, the shutters falling off, some of the boards split and missing; the children playing in the yard wore no better than rags on their lean, half-starved bodies.

"I thought you said he was prosperous?" questioned Quinn, and the duke frowned, explaining that he'd made few trips to the country and paid little heed to his surroundings when he did.

"Drive on," ordered Quinn, and each farm they rode by was a repeat of the one before, but when they reached the gates of the main house, Quinn's eyes hardened as they stared through the iron bars with the Locksley coat of arms emblazoned in the middle of them.

Tall stately poplars lined the drive that disappeared around a bend; then, as they moved forward and reached the top of a high hill, the duke stopped his phaeton again and they looked back. Now the whole estate was in view.

Beyond the stone walls and hawthorn hedges, on a hill almost like the one they were on, was spread a stone mansion built like a fortress with a large tower in the front center, and smaller towers at the end of each wing that spread out from the main hall. In front of the castle in the lawn between the circular drive that went past the front door was a small lake with swans swimming on it. The whole place reeked of wealth and prosperity, with elaborate gardens spread out beyond the courtyard in the back and extensive stables with a horse run to one side, where the drive curved around back.

"It seems my cousin lives in a style much more opulent than his tenants," offered Quinn, and Brandon had to agree, although he did speculate that perhaps there was a reason.

They continued down the road some distance until Quinn caught the strong smell of the sea; then Brandon wheeled the phaeton into the long winding drive to Grantham Hall. It was a beautiful place with a huge, rambling stone house set at the edge of the cliffs that bordered the sea, and not twenty miles away, across the Strait of Dover, was France.

They were greeted by the servants who kept the house in order even when the duke was absent. and Quinn was sure he caught a general air of tension in their faces as they scurried about, but he put it to the fact that the duke's arrival had been a surprise.

Dinner was served to them in the huge dining room, after which the duke called for his riding boots and ordered two horses to be saddled, and they rode across the fields of Bourland toward Locksley to get a more personal look.

All afternoon they visited the tenants, casually, as if just passing through, but asking questions as subtly as they were able, and each farm they came to had evidence that its tenants were in a sorry state of neglect, yet were forced to produce to capacity and often punished if the crops were not right or the cattle not fat enough.

"I wish I could talk to Chaucer's manager and secretary," said Quinn as they rode back toward Grantham Hall late in the afternoon. "It seems the earl's draining all the profits from Locksley for his own use, even making them pay for the food and milk they consume. Why, a tenant should be allowed to own his own cows and chickens and have his own gardens. This is no better than slavery."

"You don't approve of slavery?" asked Brandon, and Quinn glanced at him quickly.

"You do?"

"Under certain conditions."

"And what are those conditions?"

"Some people are unfit and illiterate, unable to cope with their own lives and the world around them. Sometimes they can live better when they have someone else to do the worrying and thinking for them."

"You think the earl is worrying about these people?" he asked, gesturing with his hand to take in the countryside. "He could care less."

"But if the right man were in control, one who cared that his tenants were properly cared for, would you still be against slavery?"

Quinn's face hardened. "I'm against slavery in any form, Brandon," he answered stubbornly, "whether it be meted out by private individuals, governments, or kings. For one man to own another is an abomination."

The duke raised his eyebrows. "You're a unique man, sir," he said. "Most men enjoy running other people's lives."

"There's a difference between ordering and guiding," Quinn answered. "At Fort Locke I was leader of over a hundred men. I gave orders regularly and ran the fort with a firm hand, yet not one man, woman, or child was my slave. We worked together for the good of all, and anyone who wanted to was welcome to leave anytime. They stayed by choice."

"You're an idealist, sir," stated Brandon.

Quinn held his head high. "Rather an idealist than a tyrant."

"But your own president has slaves, so I'm told."

Quinn scowled. "So that makes it right?" He reined his horse in, and Brandon reined in beside him and they gazed ahead across a meadow where a small herd of deer grazed lazily. "The King of England does many things of which his subjects disapprove, and his doing them doesn't make them right," said Quinn. "One day, when it's expedient, things'll change."

The duke eyed him curiously. "You really think that?"

"Men are tired of shackles. They've become weary of serving masters, and the world is ready for change. I say before long slavery will be abolished, not only in America, but around the world."

The duke smiled cynically. "Keep your dreams, Quinn," he answered. "They'll make nice fairy tales to tell your grandchildren on a cold winter's night."

"You don't think it's possible?"

The duke sat firm in the saddle. "As long as there are men with power and authority, Quinn, there'll always be slavery in some form. It's inevitable."

"I hope you're wrong," stated Quinn. "I'd hate to think that humanity would progress so little in the years to come."

The duke sighed. "Thank God we don't all think like you, sir," he remarked as he held his horse in check beside Quinn, "or you wouldn't be having a title to lay claim to."

"On the contrary," answered Quinn. "If I succeed, Brandon, I'll prove to you that a man can rule as well with kindness as with an iron fist. That a title doesn't give anyone the right to own another, but gives him a responsibility to others as human beings. That I can live comfortably without bleeding my tenants of the necessities of life. Even you'll agree that the earl has overstepped himself. There's one thing to have a slave and another to abuse him, and these men are supposed to be servants, not slaves, yet it seems the earl has chosen to treat those entrusted to him as animals. Even you must admit I'm right."

Brandon studied the herd of deer as a rabbit moved into the clearing and scared them, frightening them off; then he turned to Quinn. "Slavery I condone, sir," he answered firmly. "And each man rules in his own way, but as you say, the earl perhaps has gone too far." He drew his horse's head back defiantly. "And now, shall we head for Grantham Hall, or did you wish to see more?"

"I've seen enough," replied Quinn, and they spurred their

horses forward, heading for the woods beyond the meadow that stretched to the back of the Bourland estates.

They stayed overnight at Grantham Hall, and after an evening meal of stuffed pheasant, roast lamb cooked in onions and mushrooms, cauliflower and peas in white sauce, biscuits and butter, and a delicate claret wine to enhance the taste, topped off with frosted pasties filled with nuts and sugared creams, they retired to one of the salons, where Quinn, during the course of the evening, had a rare insight into the complicated personality of Brandon Avery.

A graduate of Oxford, where he'd studied law and political science, he'd championed the underdog and almost gotten himself thrown out once for helping incite a rebellion that almost disrupted a session of Parliament, but was stopped just in time. He'd accepted his punishment gracefully, but continued to frequent taverns, giving speeches that irritated his superiors.

Shortly after graduation, with the help of his uncle, and promising to behave himself, he secured a minor post in the government, where he kept his eyes and ears open and managed to talk his way into a position of some authority as aide to the ambassador to France. However, as time went on, seeing no chance for advancement in the near future, and with French negotiations somewhat at a variance, he resigned and bought himself a commission in the army, where he soon proved himself a born leader.

When he stepped into the role of the Duke of Bourland, he tried to disguise the inherent ambitions he'd nurtured for years, afraid he'd frighten off the very men he knew could help him to achieve his lifelong dreams, but now as the two men talked in the drawing room at Grantham Hall, he was unable to successfully hide his quest for power from Quinn. It showed in the way he ordered his servants about and the way he talked of the people with whom he associated and the small mannerisms and words he let drop as they talked, and Quinn wasn't sure he liked what he learned. But he needed Brandon as he'd needed Jules. Besides, there was no indication that the young man would ever realize his dream. Many men dreamed of ruling the world, but so far no one had accomplished it, so Quinn would accept his friendship as offered, but keep an eye on him, for some men didn't care how they achieved their ambitions, and often their friends suffered as well as their enemies. Yet, he had to admit that Brandon, in spite of his ambitions, was a likable enough fellow once you got past the foppish clothes.

After a good night's sleep they left at sunup, lunching at the Foxes' Den, then spending the night in a small inn closer to London, arriving in the city in the early afternoon.

Quinn swung Loedicia into his arms and planted a firm kiss on her mouth as she greeted him on their return, and Brandon looked past them at Rachel and smiled.

"I never saw a man so glad to see his wife," he commented as Quinn set Dicia back on her feet, her face flushed and warm. "But then I never met a man quite like Quinn Locke before," and Dicia glanced at him, her eyebrows raised.

"My husband surprises you, your Grace?"

"The name is Brandon, ma'am. Brandon Avery," he said warmly. "And, yes, he surprises me. He's here to claim a title that would make him one of the nobility, yet I have the distinct feeling he'd rather be in his backwoods tracking game or sitting about a campfire swapping stories with his Indian friends."

Loedicia smiled. "It's stubbornness that drove him away and stubbornness that brought him back," she said. "And he'll never be happy in England, no matter how many titles he has." She glanced quickly at Quinn. "But he's a man of principle. The title belongs to him, and that's all that counts."

"Brandon's offered to help," explained Quinn as he gazed at the younger man, then looked at Rachel. "And if we might have a promise of help from the duchess . . ."

Rachel smiled. "As I said before," she answered firmly, her eyes glowing, "I can't stand the present earl." But to herself she was saying silently: Besides, I don't think I've ever met a man quite like you either, Mr. Locke. Just looking at him did something to her, something neither Jules nor Brandon had ever done, and she liked it. "I'll be glad to help all I can," she finished aloud, "although it's two weeks yet before my year of mourning's up."

"And then we can have a ball," ventured Brandon. "In the meantime"—he turned to Quinn—"are you still determined to keep your identity a secret?"

Quinn nodded. "Until I learn more of my enemy, yes," he answered. "As far as anyone's concerned, I'm merely Mr. Locke."

But unfortunately Quinn's anonymity was short-lived. Later that evening Rebel was wandering about Bourland Hall like a lost soul. There was nothing to do. At least back home she could ride or hunt or visit the Indians or swim or half a dozen other things, but here it was sit and stare into space unless she sat embroidering all the time like the duchess, and Reb hated embroidering. While her father was away she'd played whist and other games with her mother and Teak, but now, with her father back, her mother was preoccupied and Teak had disappeared. The last she'd seen him, he was standing in front of one of the mirrors admiring himself. What a conceited ass. But she had to admit he was getting handsome enough, and he was probably flirting somewhere with one of the servants right now. She'd seen him making eyes at that little dark-haired girl who helped the chambermaid, only she hoped to God he wouldn't get himself in trouble. He could be impetuous, and who knows when he'd start feeling his oats? And if she knew Teak, he'd be nothing like Beau had been.

Beau! She turned, gazing out the window, thinking of him as she had a hundred times over the past two years, and as always, a hardness crept into her heart. A hardness filled with sweet pain and bitterness. She'd been foolish to throw herself at him, but what was she to do? The strange yearnings of her body, the torturous agonies of her sudden desires had been more than she could bear. Even now sometimes she didn't even understand her body. All she knew was that whenever he was near she'd felt so strange, like nothing she'd ever known before, and when he'd kissed her, she'd felt the warm explosion inside, intense, like a fire she couldn't put out that blotted out everything except his mouth on hers, and she'd wanted to crawl right inside him and become a part of him.

Lust, she'd told herself over and over again. That's all it was, lust. The yearnings of a young girl who couldn't cope with what her body was telling her. She was almost nineteen now, and it had never happened again. Maybe because she was determined it wouldn't. No man would ever make a fool of her again the way Beau had. No man! Yet . . . she'd never been able to forget what he'd done to her and the wanton desires his hands had kindled that night on the beach. Even now there were times—when she rode horseback, a quick turn against the horse as she straddled it, or sitting upright in a chair if her bloomers pulled too tight—sometimes she didn't even have to move, like now, standing looking out the window thinking of him, and she felt a quickening in her loins, a familiar hint of rapture that swept through her.

Her breathing shortened and she suddenly felt warm all

over, and her whole body began to ache. "Damn him!" she cried to herself as she reached down and spread her hands across her groin, flattening the skirt of her deep blue dress, fighting the natural instincts of her body. "Damn him to hell!" and she turned from the window, scurrying from the room into the hall and hurried down the corridor to the library.

She'd get a book to read—anything to forget—sometimes it hurt so much she wanted to scream!

The library was empty, and she breathed a sigh of relief, trying to push all thoughts of Beau to the back of her mind. The duke had given them permission to read whatever they wanted, so she headed for a shelf of books with fancy leather-bound covers at the far end and began to pull them out one at a time, shoving each of them back after a quick glance at the title. She was so engrossed in her quest that she failed to hear the door open until a voice broke the silence.

"You don't like my late uncle's books?" asked the duke as she pushed another back into its place, to go to the next.

She whirled around and her hand flew to her breast where the low-cut tucked bodice barely covered her, and she drew in a quick breath. "Oh . . . you startled me," she exclaimed breathlessly, then relaxed, her hand falling to her side. She glanced quickly back at the row of books on the shelf. "But I doubt very much if your uncle read these books," she stated, reaching out, pulling one off the shelf, turning it toward him, running her finger across the bold lettering, and Brandon looked amused.

"I daresay you're right," he answered, taking the book from her and skimming through the pages. It was one of the romantic novels of the day that all the ladies were reading. "You don't like to read about romance?" he asked as he handed it back to her and she put it in place on the shelf, tensing up, the hair on her head tightening.

"I detest them," she answered firmly, and he studied her, his brown eyes intent on her face, making her blush as she turned toward him.

"Perhaps it's merely fear of the unknown," he suggested, and her face turned even a more crimson hue.

"Just . . . what is it you're trying to suggest, your Grace?" she asked hesitantly, and he smiled as he glanced first at the books, then back to her face.

"Do call me Brandon," he offered as he continued staring

into her violet eyes. " 'Your Grace' sounds so ancient, don't you think, and I haven't seen my thirtieth birthday yet."

She didn't answer him, but her eyes were still on him.

"Do you ride?" he suddenly asked, and she was somewhat taken aback. "Well . . . you *do* ride?" he asked again after getting no response, and she nodded.

"Yes . . . yes . . . I ride."

"Fine," he answered. "Then may I ask you to join me tomorrow morning for a canter in the park?" and her mouth fell open.

She shut it quickly, feeling like a fool. "But you're in mourning. . . . Your aunt Rachel . . ."

"What is not expedient for Aunt Rachel is not the case for everyone. Men can do almost anything while mourning. Now, what do you say?"

She tried not to look embarrassed. "I'd love to go riding," she ventured, "but you see, I don't know if I should."

"Oh?"

"I'm excellent on a horse," she continued, "but I'm afraid I've never ridden sidesaddle."

"You've never ridden sidesaddle . . . then how?" He looked startled. "You mean . . . you ride straddling a horse?"

"That's right." Her eyes flashed as she saw the look on his face. "What's wrong with it?"

He drew in a quick breath. "My dear girl, it's outrageous."

"Outrageous?"

He leaned forward, frowning. "My heavens," he asked curiously, "What did you wear?"

"Pants! Buckskins!"

"Buck . . . You mean like a man?"

She leaned back, holding her head high. "I can outride some of the best," she answered stubbornly, "and without a saddle."

He grinned, quite amused. "And what else can you do?"

"I can shoot a bow and arrow, fire a pistol, rope a horse, throw a knife, use a bull whip, run like a deer, swim like a fish, and track a snake over solid rock, something my father taught me."

"Aha . . . but can you dance?" asked the duke, tongue in cheek, expecting her to say no, but she stared straight at him, her eyes hostile, and held up her arms.

"Would you care for a demonstration?" she asked haughtily, and he was at a loss as he stared at her animated face, flushed with anger, her eyes sparkling, the soft creamy smoothness of her skin like velvet in the soft lights of the candalabra set about the room; then slowly he reached out, taking her hand, and he began humming.

She moved gracefully about the room in an intricate gavotte; then suddenly he increased his tempo and swung her into his arms, one arm about her waist, and they danced about the library in a sprightly waltz.

Then, quite abruptly he stopped dancing and pulled her closer against him. She could feel his heart pounding against her breasts right through his apricot satin coat and white brocade vest, and the lace at the edge of his cravat touched the hollow at the base of her throat.

"Now, about that sidesaddle," he whispered huskily, and she smirked.

"I'd love to," she answered, and felt his arm tighten about her waist as a slight knock interrupted them.

Brandon released her and turned toward the door. "Come in."

The door opened, and a bewigged butler stepped in, standing tall and straight. "Sorry to interrupt, your Grace," he announced in a deep resonant voice, "but Lord Elton Chaucer is in the main salon and requests your presence and that of Mr. Locke on a matter of the gravest importance."

Brandon stared at him dumbfounded, then glanced at Rebel. "I have a distinct feeling this evening is going to be memorable in more ways than one," he said casually. "Would you care to join me?"

"Why not," she answered, "but what about Father?"

He turned to the butler. "Go find Mr. and Mrs. Locke and tell them Lord Chaucer's here, then tell them to join us in the main salon." He turned back to Rebel and held out his arm as the butler bowed and walked away. "Shall we?" he asked, and she smiled.

"This should prove interesting," she said as she took his arm and they left the room.

Quinn, Loedicia, and Rachel were in the garden talking when the butler found them.

"Beg pardon, your Grace," he addressed the duchess, interrupting them, "the duke requests the presence of Mr. and Mrs. Locke in the main salon. Lord Chaucer has come calling asking for you, sir," and he looked at Quinn.

"The devil you say!" exclaimed Quinn, and Loedicia frowned.

"What does it mean, Quinn?"

"It means, my love, that the Chaucer twins evidently have big mouths and Elton is not as stupid as I thought," and they hurried into the house following the butler and went directly to the main salon.

The butler swung the doors open for them, then stepped back to one side, letting them pass, and as they entered, Loedicia caught sight of Rebel across the room standing with the duke and another man. The man had red hair and was elegantly dressed in a blue satin coat, white breeches, silk stockings, and shoes with diamond-studded buckles. Then suddenly, as she watched him, he turned their way, and her face went white. It was as if time stood still and she was back in the wilderness in that dirty bark hut and all the horrible memories of what seemed like another lifetime flooded in on her.

The man who stood now staring across the room at her was the image of Kendall Varrick. Although his hair was a deeper red-gold and he was minus the scar that had distorted Kendall's face, it was like looking at a ghost, and Loedicia's knees felt weak as the man's cold blue eyes looked first at Quinn, then at her, and his eyes studied her from head to toe, resting on her face, which looked even paler against the red velvet dress she wore.

She grabbed Quinn's arm to support herself, and he felt the pressure of her hand and moved closer to her, his hand over hers on his arm.

"Are you all right?" he asked softly as he looked down at her, realizing what was happening, and she nodded, unable to speak for a moment.

"I'm . . . I'm fine," she finally said, and they continued to walk the rest of the way into the room, the duchess at their side, her elaborate dress, yards of gold satin, making a delightful swish as they moved across the floor.

"Ah," said Brandon as he greeted them. "I believe this is the gentleman you've been asking me about, Lord Chaucer." He held his hand out, gesturing. "Mr. and Mrs. Locke, may I present Lord Chaucer, the Earl of Locksley." He looked directly at Quinn. "He's the father of the two young gentlemen we had the opportunity to dine with the other evening," and Quinn nodded as Lord Chaucer smirked.

"Quinn Locksley and I are old acquaintances, Your Grace," Lord Chaucer acknowledged as he stared into Quinn's intense blue eyes and felt the hatred behind their gaze. "It's been a long time, but I'd recognize him anywhere. When Bert and Perry started telling me about the tall blond giant of a man they'd met and said his name was Locke, I was sure only one man could fit the description, and I had to see for myself. Why didn't you tell them who you really were?"

"I didn't think it mattered."

Elton's eyes narrowed shrewdly. "Then you weren't trying to keep your identity a secret for any particular reason?"

"If I had, I wouldn't have used the name Locke, now, would I?"

But Elton wasn't convinced. "You could have thought I wouldn't remember after all these years," he said, looking at Quinn contemptuously, and Quinn felt Loedicia's hand tighten on his arm.

"I know you didn't come just to pay your respects, Elton," he said flatly. "We were anything but friends when we were young, so will it trouble you too much to ask what it is you intend to accomplish by coming here?"

"Just a friendly gesture," he answered nonchalantly. "After all, it seems strange you'd suddenly come to England after all these years."

"I see nothing strange about it. I came to visit an old friend. Unfortunately, he passed away before our arrival."

Lord Chaucer tilted his head back arrogantly. "That's the only reason?"

"I'm supposed to have an ulterior motive?" asked Quinn, and Elton's eyes moved from Quinn's face to Dicia, still standing beside him, holding onto his arm for dear life. There was something wrong here. She was too nervous and pale, and there was a wild look about her, and besides, he wouldn't bring his family all the way to England unless he was planning something. He looked back at Quinn.

"My dear fellow, it takes a great deal of capital to pay the expenses for such a trip merely for pleasure. I thought perhaps . . ." His voice trailed off.

"You thought what?" asked Quinn.

He smiled cynically. "I had the most ridiculous notion that you had come to try to have your grandfather's petition set aside and claim the title from me. I realize it's silly of me to worry after all these years, but one does wonder, you know."

"Indeed."

"Then I have nothing to worry about?"

"You're worried?" asked Quinn, and Elton tried to look self-assured.

"Not really," he answered. "I think you know as well as I that only a fool would attempt the impossible. Especially since there's no way for you to even prove you're a Locksley."

"And what of you?" asked Quinn, his patience running thin. "Are you a Locksley?"

The earl's face hardened and the veins on his neck tightened. "Just what is it you really want here, Quinn?" he asked harshly, losing his pretense at friendliness.

"I think you already asked that question and received a fair reply."

"Rubbish!" His eyes flashed as he breathed deeply, his anger increasing. "I don't know why you think I'm some kind of a fool. There's only one reason you could possibly have for coming here, but you won't get away with it."

"You always did jump to conclusions," remarked Quinn, trying to hold his temper as best he could. If he gave anything away now, it could ruin everything. "I have no intention of, as you so bluntly put it, making a fool of myself, especially since, as you say, I have no proof to base a claim on."

"And if you happen to find proof?"

"Then that's a different story, isn't it?"

Lord Chaucer's jaw set stubbornly. "Speaking of proof, I might as well warn you. Although General Gage claims that my cousin Kendall was killed by a person or persons unknown, I have proof in my possession of what really happened that night in Philadelphia in 1775, and unless you want to hang, Quinn, I suggest you forget any notion of trying to further any claims against me. Do I make myself clear?"

Quinn stared straight at him, the pulse in his neck beating hard, and the duke, who'd been listening to their sparring, frowned hesitantly.

"What are you trying to get at?" the duke asked, and Lord Chaucer, who'd almost forgotten Brandon's presence, turned.

"Let me clarify myself, your Grace," he answered smugly. "You see, my cousin Kendall Varrick, the former Earl of Locksley, who was also Quinn's cousin, on his father's side, was betrothed to the lady who is at this moment tightening her hold on Quinn's arm. Since they were all in Philadelphia at the same time, and since she ended up married to Quinn and Kendall ended up dead . . . need I say more?"

"Are you accusing them of murder?" asked the duke, and Rachel gasped.

"That's preposterous!" she cried. "My late husband knew Quinn Locke for years, and he always spoke highly of him."

"And did he tell you that at one time he was considered an outlaw? That he lived with savages? That he stole money from the king and had a price on his head?" Elton turned to Quinn. "You didn't know I knew that, did you?" he said. "I'd been at Locksley ever since Kendall first went to America, taking care of it for him, and he wrote often, keeping me well-informed. I imagine the king'd be pleased to learn you're in England."

"That was a long time ago," Quinn retorted. "The king's pardoned the men who fought against England in the war."

"But Kendall's murder is another thing."

"And I didn't kill him!"

Lord Chaucer glanced at Dicia, who was still hanging onto Quinn's arm, her eyes round and frightened. "Then why does your wife look like she's about to faint?" he asked, and all eyes centered on Dicia, who wished she could crawl into a hole and hide.

Quinn's eyes softened as she looked up at him helplessly, and he turned back to Lord Chaucer. "Perhaps because you remind her of Kendall," he answered slowly. "She was deathly afraid of him, and the fact that you resemble him so uncannily is a shock. He almost beat her to death once."

"Don't be ridiculous!" He exhaled disgustedly. "He was in love with her, why would he beat her?" His eyes bored into Loedicia's. "You know, your husband could hang for murder, Mrs. Locke," he warned ominously, and saw her hand move slowly to her throat, as if she was pulling at an invisible rope.

He'd noticed the minute she'd walked through the door that she was a fascinating woman with hauntingly beautiful violet eyes, a full sensuous mouth, and a youthful bloom that still clung tenaciously to her in spite of the fact that he knew she had to be well past thirty. She was warm and desirable, and there was a depth in her eyes . . . No wonder Kendall had wanted her, because as he stared at her now he felt a quickening in his own loins that almost caused him to tremble, and he had to turn away quickly, to quiet his body so it wouldn't betray him.

He looked at Quinn. "All right. I'll play your game for the

moment," he acquiesced reluctantly, "but mind you. The day you try to lay claim to the Locksley estates is the day you'll wish you'd never set foot on English soil again," and he turned abruptly as Brandon suddenly interrupted.

"Enough!" Brandon cried, his face flushed as he tried to control his temper. "This has gone entirely too far! This is my house, Lord Chaucer, these are my guests, and as long as they're under my roof, I'll hear no more threats!"

"I'm not threatening, I'm telling," answered Lord Chaucer.

"And I'm telling too," stated the duke. "I'll have no more of it," and he reached over, pulling a tasseled bell cord near the window behind him.

"Then my visit is at an end, your Grace," Elton agreed angrily. "Only I'll caution you. You may regret the day you ever let Quinn Locke set foot in your home."

The doors to the salon suddenly opened and the bewigged butler once more stepped into the room.

"You rang, your Grace?" he asked in his stentorian monotone, and the duke acknowledged.

"If you will show Lord Chaucer to the door, Jarvis," he demanded firmly, "I'd be grateful. And if he should ever come to the door again, you will please advise him that I'm not in," and Lord Chaucer stalked out without saying another word, his face almost as red as his hair.

"You've made an unpleasant enemy," stated Quinn as Brandon watched Elton Chaucer's departure. "I'm sorry. I didn't mean to bring trouble with me."

"No trouble at all," assured the duke. "It was a pleasure. I've been aching to do that for months, only it took your coming to give me the courage."

Loedicia felt her knees weaken as her fingers dug into Quinn's arm, and she tried to speak, but the fear that had gripped her when she'd first set eyes on Lord Chaucer was still in command of her senses. All the while he'd talked to Quinn. The facial expressions, the mannerisms, the arrogant attitude, the lustful eyes—she was watching a dead man come back to life.

"Varrick!" she muttered, her eyes misty, tears beginning to roll down her cheeks. "My God, he's back," and Quinn turned quickly, his eyes questioning, and he stared at the wild look in her violet eyes as she watched the empty doorway, and a sudden fear gripped him.

"Dicia?" he whispered as he bent toward her, removing her hand from his arm and taking her head between both hands, looking into her face, but it was as if she didn't even see him, as if she was in a trance. "Dicia?"

"Did you see him?" she whispered breathlessly. "He looked at me just the way he always used to. . . . Did you see? Oh, God help me . . . God help me," and suddenly it was just too much and she groaned, closing her eyes, and her knees gave way under her.

Quinn caught her and swung her into his arms as Rachel stared dumbfounded and Brandon looked puzzled. "Grab a light and come with me, Rebel," Quinn ordered his daughter as he held Loedicia close, feeling her tremble against him, and he cursed all the way upstairs as she lay sobbing in his arms.

When he reached their room, he walked directly to the bed and set her down, trying to bunch the pillows behind her head, but she clung to him desperately as Rebel began lighting the candles about the room.

"Don't leave me, Quinn," she cried hysterically. "He'll come for me. You saw him. I know he will!"

He held her close against him, stroking her hair, soothing her, trying to bring her back to reality. "Dicia, Dicia!" he whispered softly, rocking her back and forth in his arms, talking to her like he would a baby. "It's all right, it's all right . . . he can't hurt you . . . he'll never hurt you again. He's dead, remember?" and he glanced behind him as Rebel walked up and stood waiting to help. "There's nothing more you can do," he said as he tried once more to pull her out of his arms and laid her against the pillows, and this time she didn't fight him, but fell back meekly, her tearstained face ashen in the light from the candles.

"I won't hang, will I, Quinn?" she pleaded fearfully. "They won't hang me, will they?" and her hands moved to her throat, tearing at it with her fingers, and he closed his eyes, swallowing hard as Rebel knelt beside him, her eyes misty.

"What is it, Father? What's the matter with her?" she asked anxiously as she watched the agony on her mother's face. "Why is she afraid they'll hang her?"

Quinn's jaw set hard. "Because your mother's the one who shot Kendall Varrick," he answered bitterly, his voice strained, and Rebel stared at him dumbfounded.

"Mother?" she gasped, and Quinn reached out, taking Loedicia's hands from her throat, holding them in his as he spoke.

"She did it to save my life," he explained. "It's a long

story, but tonight, seeing Lord Chaucer, brought it all back. That and much more." He reached up, touching Loedicia's face, then took her chin in his hand. "Dicia, it's over, it's all right, my darling," he soothed. "Please. It's all over." And suddenly he saw the warmth begin to filter back into her face and the horrible stare in her eyes was replaced by a sadness that tore at his heart.

"Oh, Quinn," she murmured breathlessly. "I'm sorry. I don't know what came over me. It was like living it all over again. The horror . . . the degradation. It was like seeing him again after all these years."

He nodded. "I know, but he's not Kendall."

She squeezed his hand as she wiped away a tear. "But he's like Kendall. He's vicious and mean. . . ."

Relief showed on Quinn's face. "You're all right now?" he asked, and she nodded, then glanced at Rebel, reaching out to touch her cheek.

"You heard, didn't you?" she asked.

"Yes, Mother."

"I'm sorry, Rebel," she whispered. "I didn't mean to frighten you, dear. But sometimes things happen . . ."

Rebel put her hand up and covered her mother's. "It's all right, Mother," she said as a tear rolled down her cheek. "But I had no idea."

"I know," answered Loedicia. "I never wanted to tell you."

"But now that you do know," added Quinn, "no one else must ever know. You realize that, don't you?"

She nodded. "Yes, Father," and she leaned forward toward her mother, kissing her on the forehead.

"Thank you, Reb," Loedicia said, and Rebel stood up.

"You'll be all right now?"

"I'll be fine."

"But remember," cautioned Quinn, "if the duke or duchess asks you, you don't know what it's all about."

"Yes, Father," she agreed, "and if you need me again, I'll be downstairs," and she leaned over and kissed them both, then left the room.

Loedicia looked at Quinn, her eyes sad. "Quinn, let's forget it," she begged anxiously. "The title isn't worth it. Besides, now with Jules dead, Lord Chaucer's right. You have no way to prove who you really are except the letter your father left you."

He frowned. "I know I needed Jules," he answered, "but I'll find another way. My father had a few friends too.

There're bound to be a few around who remember me. If Elton recognized me, there's sure to be someone else."

"But it's such a risk. What if he keeps his threat?"

"I don't think he will. Besides, he suspects me, not you, so you're in no danger, and anyway, it's been too many years. Who'd listen?"

"And if they do?"

He took her head in his hands and kissed her softly. "Please, my love. I haven't come all this way to be frightened off by a windbag like Elton. Nothing's going to happen. Please, don't ask me to give up now. Not now."

She looked into his eyes, deep with love. They'd lived in danger before so many times. Could this be any worse? She had no right to ask him to quit now, no matter how frightened she was.

"All right," she whispered, "and don't worry, the next time I see Lord Chaucer, it will not be a repeat of tonight. It was just the shock, but I'm over it."

He grinned. "Good."

She smiled back at him. "You're incorrigible, you know that?"

'Mmmhmmm." He leaned forward and buried his face in her neck, his lips caressing her skin softly. "Don't ever scare me like that again," he whispered against her ear, then straightened up and looked at her lovingly. "I love you, Dicia," he groaned. "Oh, God, how I love you," and he kissed the nightmare away.

As she lay in his arms later that evening she prayed hard that Quinn would see his dream come true without any trouble, but at the same time she had a strange foreboding that this time her prayers wouldn't be answered.

11

The morning air was cool as Brandon reined his horse next to a hawthorn bush and glanced back at Rebel, waiting for her to catch up. She had taken to the sidesaddle as if she was born to it, but it hadn't surprised him. She was the most remarkable young woman he'd ever met, with a natural beauty and charm that were captivating.

This morning she was dressed in a deep green velvet riding dress, her fair hair piled atop her head beneath a matching hat with a long green ostrich feather dangling down on her forehead and another trailing down the back of the hat and curled about her neck onto her shoulders, while the chestnut mare she rode pranced magnificently, as if she was pleased to be beneath her.

They'd left the house shortly before sunup, and now, as its first rays topped the trees, filtering into the cool morning mists, a sunbeam fell across her face, making her look almost ethereal, and the duke sighed as he watched her approach.

"Do you realize how lovely you look?" he said thoughtfully as she reined in beside him, and she smiled, blushing.

"Thank you, your Grace."

His eyes caught hers. "That's the second time you've called me 'your Grace' since we left the house," he stated stubbornly, "I told you to call me Brandon."

"But I've never known a duke before, and it's fun to call you 'your Grace.' "

"Coming from you, I hate it," he said, and she studied him boldly, then reached out and patted her horse's head, feeling the sleek, silky coat.

"Why?" she asked provocatively, and he didn't know quite what to answer.

Why did he hate to hear her call him "your Grace"? Was it the way she said it, with a slight intonation of cynicism, or did it make him feel old and worlds apart from her? Why did he worry about what she called him anyway? He'd never worried before about what women called him.

His eyes flicked over her sensuously, and deep down inside he knew why. She was a rarity, and for the first time in his life he knew he was facing not a self-centered, artificial female, but a beautiful sensitive young woman, natural in every way. There was nothing false about her. If you knew Rebel, you knew her. There was no speculation. Nothing pretentious. She was Rebel. Vital and alive.

"Does it really matter?" he asked, and she grinned impishly.

"It might," she whispered as she leaned toward him; then she straightened quickly and flicked the horse's reins, moving forward along the bridle path.

Few riders were out this early, and he moved up beside her so they could ride side by side.

"I saw your father just before we left," he said, changing the subject. "I'm glad to hear your mother's feeling better now. I was worried when they didn't come back down last night."

"I'm afraid Mother was a bit upset," conceded Rebel. "It's not like her, really, but I guess from what Father says, Lord Chaucer looks just like Lord Varrick, and she was deathly afraid of Lord Varrick."

"Did your father tell you why?"

"No," she answered honestly, because he hadn't told her why her mother was so afraid, only that she'd shot Lord Varrick to save his life. "But if you remember," she said, "he did tell Lord Chaucer that Lord Varrick had beaten her once and almost killed her, so I presume that was the reason."

He stared ahead as they rode their horses to the edge of the park and into the early-morning traffic of London. "I wonder why he'd beat her?" he mused, and Rebel frowned.

"I haven't the faintest idea," she answered, and started exclaiming about the traffic that had filled the streets since they'd begun their ride almost an hour earlier, anything to keep from talking about last night.

She'd seen the look on Lord Chaucer's face as he'd stared at her mother, and she also remembered her mother's words as she'd begged her father to keep him from her. It was the first time in her life she'd ever seen her mother afraid to the point of hysterics. Could just a beating have done all this, or was there something else? Something they weren't telling her.

Something so terrible that they couldn't even talk of it. She wondered. . . .

For the next two weeks Rebel went riding every morning with the duke; then on their return to the house he and her father would disappear for most of the day, arriving back close to dinnertime. They were searching for the proof Quinn needed.

Quinn had planned on having Jules vouch as to his identity because they'd grown up together, but now, with Jules dead . . . So far no one they'd contacted had been able to remember Quinn. They remembered that Martin Locksley had had a son, but to identify Quinn as that son was impossible.

"If we could only locate where you were born and find some records, or locate your old nurse," said Brandon one afternoon as they left their horses and strolled into the house. "But the way we're going . . . So far, the only one in England who can swear to your identity is Elton, and he'd deny it."

"How about the servants at Locksley? There ought to be a few of the old ones about."

"We couldn't get near them. Besides, they'd be afraid of retaliation from Lord Chaucer if they spoke up."

They stepped into the foyer and handed their hats to Jarvis, then headed toward the library.

"Maybe there'll be someone at the ball tonight," added the duke. "I think Aunt Rachel asked everyone who's anyone."

"I hope so," answered Quinn. "I'm beginning to think maybe Loedicia's right and I ought to forget the whole damn thing!"

Brandon laughed. He'd become used to Quinn's rough edge. "But you won't," he stated. "You'll never forget it, no matter how long it takes."

"No . . . I guess I won't," he answered, and smiled as he saw Loedicia coming down the hall.

The house had been in a turmoil all week. It was the first entertaining Rachel had done since her husband's death, and the place had been practically turned upside down. Floors and woodwork were polished to a shine, the smell of beeswax filling the air, mingling with the scent of the flowers that overflowed each room, and everything, including the windows and crystal chandeliers, sparkled like new.

And today, since morning, the cooks had been busy preparing the food and maids had been scurrying about nervously getting everyone's clothes ready. The atmosphere was one of confusion, but happy confusion, and by the time the guests started arriving, everything was ready and they all sighed with relief, including Lizette, who, true to her word, was shunning any social life and seemed to be finding enjoyment taking care of Loedicia and Rebel with a fervor, seeing to all their needs with a few choice comments here and there to Quinn and Teak like a mother hen.

Quinn stared at Loedicia as she checked her hair in the mirror before going downstairs. She was wearing the violet dress she'd worn to President Washington's party back in Philadelphia, and he adored her in it, but it brought back so many memories. He wished to God he could forget that part of his past, but little things always seemed to creep up. Here in England, though, things had been better. There were no reminders, at least there hadn't been until tonight, when she'd put on the dress. But she looked so lovely in violet that for once he didn't care, and he pushed all the angry thoughts to the back of his mind and walked over to stand behind her.

She finished tucking a curl in near the nape of her neck, then pinched her cheeks for color and turned to face him. "There, now, how do I look for an old lady?" she said, and he laughed, pulling her into his arms.

"Old lady! Shame on you!" He bent down and kissed her, pulling her close against him, his kiss filled with all the love it could hold. "You'll never be old," he whispered huskily as he finally drew his head back and she toyed with the front of his shirt.

"Do you think the ball tonight will help?" she asked as she ran her fingers across the soft green velvet coat he wore. "Maybe tonight will be as fruitless as your search has been these past two weeks."

He sighed. "I hope not. There ought to be one person left in England besides Chaucer who remembers me."

"And if they do?"

He held her against him, looking down into her face. "If they do, I can have them sign a statement attesting to my real identity, and then the letter Father left me will mean something and I can present my petition to the earl marshal."

"And when Lord Chaucer finds out about it?"

He saw the worry in her face and dropped his hands. "That's a chance I'll have to take." He shrugged as he walked over and took a handkerchief and folded it, putting it in his pocket. "The man's just a blowhard anyway, trying to scare me off. He can't possibly have proof about Kendall's death, or he wouldn't be threatening to have me hung, he'd be threatening you. He's trying to scare us, that's all. Don't you see?"

She frowned. "Yes . . . I guess you're right, but he still scares me."

"Well, he won't be here tonight," he said as he held out his arm. "So shall we join the others? I think I heard guests arriving already, and I told the duchess we weren't going to be late."

She took his arm, resigned to the fact that there was no way she could talk him out of it. He was bound and determined to see it through, no matter what.

Already it was crowded as they approached the doors to the ballroom in the west wing, and music filled the house, making the halls come to life for the first time in a year. The doors to the ballroom were standing open, and Loedicia strained her eyes looking through them, where she spotted Rebel dancing with a rather portly gentleman; then she saw Teak by the table at the back of the room, already stuffing his face with food, and she smiled. Teak looked quite handsome with his midnight velvet suit, and he seemed to be cutting quite a figure, because all the young girls were eyeing him. It wasn't any wonder, for he looked far older than his fourteen years. He looked every bit of seventeen or eighteen, with broad shoulders, slim hips, hair bleached even blonder from the summer sun, and he was so ruggedly tanned.

She watched a young girl blush at him from the end of the table and turned to Quinn. "Your offspring seems to be making a hit with the young ladies," she said, and Quinn frowned as he too spotted Teak.

"Looks like I'll have to have a talk with him," he answered severely. "I think London's going to his head. Last night when I went to get you some warm milk I found him in one of the deserted halls with that little dark-haired chambermaid, and he wasn't being any too discreet."

Loedicia stopped and looked up at him. "Like father, like son?" she asked, and he scowled.

"That's not funny."

"It wasn't meant to be funny. But do you honestly think talking to him will help? He's a great deal like you, you know."

"God help me, don't I know it," he exclaimed. "But I can at least try," and he watched as Teak forgot the food he was eating to wander after a pair of dark brown eyes set beneath honey-blond hair and wrapped up in a confection of white peau de soie and Irish lace.

Loedicia watched too. He was a headstrong young man, big for his age, and brought up with a freedom few young men were privileged to enjoy, and the combination made him willful and undisciplined, and she prayed he'd listen to his father. That is, if Quinn could talk to him in time. However, the way Teak was gazing at the young lady who'd caught his attention this evening frightened her. She'd seen that look in Quinn's eyes dozens of times when he stared at her, and she shook her head.

"Oh, there you two are," exclaimed Rachel, interrupting her thoughts as she and Quinn stepped inside the ballroom, and Loedicia pulled her eyes reluctantly from her son and turned toward their hostess.

Rachel and Brandon were still standing at the doorway greeting people, and Loedicia couldn't get over what a striking couple they made. They looked very little like aunt and nephew, and if she hadn't seen the flirtatious looks Rachel had been giving Quinn lately, she'd swear that Rachel and Brandon were lovers. There was an intimacy about them that intrigued her. Yet . . . maybe it was her imagination; after all, the duke had been rather attentive to Rebel, and . . . She smiled as Brandon greeted them.

He was partial to brocades, and his coat tonight was a multicolored brocade of russets and gold tones with white breeches, white-lace-ruffled cravat, and satin shirt, with white silk stockings and black velvet shoes encrusted with seed pearls. His hair was in the latest casual fashion, and he complemented Rachel, who was wearing a pale persimmon dress with yards of sheer organza tucked and flounced to make her look almost as if she were floating. Tiny seed pearls decorated the skirt of her dress, and the low décolleté revealed almost more than was proper, but she didn't seem to care, and her chestnut hair, piled higher than usual, was entwined with a rope of seed pearls, giving her a look of sophistication Loedicia wished she had.

Loedicia felt out of place in her heavy velvet with its elbow-length sleeves, flounced skirt, and tucked bodice with her hair pulled back simply in a cascade of curls down the back, and her small dangling diamond earrings were nothing spectacular. Most of the other women she saw as she turned quickly and gazed about the room wore light sheer pastel colors for summer with an abundance of petticoats beneath. They were light and airy, the latest fashion, and were enhanced by the family jewels. Oh, well, as long as Quinn was pleased with the way she looked, that's all that counted. But she wondered what it would be like to wear one of the new sheer fashions with all the ruffles and lace. She had no idea that her simple dress and hairdo gave her a natural elegance that outshone every other woman in the room, and she looked at them enviously, wishing.

"My dears, we've been waiting for you," enthused Rachel as Loedicia looked back toward the duke and duchess. "I thought you'd never come down. Almost everyone's here already. You're late," and for the next hour they walked about shaking hands and being introduced.

"My late husband's friends Mr. and Mrs. Locke from America," introduced the duchess as they moved about the ballroom from one person to another, and Quinn smiled, looking for a familiar face or listening for a familiar name.

Loedicia, however, frowned. She was certain, every time they were introduced, that the duchess's eyes, although she tried to conceal it, lingered rather longer on Quinn than was necessary. At first she tried to ignore it, but after a while she began to wonder, especially as she remembered the little flirtatious remarks she'd heard over the past few days.

"My late uncle's friend Quinn Locke and his wife, Loedicia, from the United States," offered the duke less formally when he introduced them as the evening wore on, and Loedicia began to feel even more and more out of place.

There were dukes, barons, marquises, military men, and diplomats, and the women they escorted were well-bred society, the queen's court, the *beau monde,* and Loedicia had nothing in common with them. She had been a titled lady once, but not anymore. She knew nothing of politics, the races, society, wars, or the latest court scandals. And Quinn, who wasn't fond of dancing with anyone but his wife, was reluctantly forced to take his turn about the ballroom floor with numerous ladies. A feat he'd much rather have relinquished to someone else.

A couple of times, however, Loedicia did see him whirling about the floor with the duchess, and he actually looked like he was enjoying himself, but then, so did the duchess. She was gazing up at him flirtatiously, a sickeningly sweet smile on her face, and Loedicia began to fume. It was obvious now. The little bitch was ripe for an affair after her year of mourning, and Loedicia had a strange feeling she'd picked Quinn to have it with.

About halfway through the evening, Loedicia and Quinn were standing to one side talking to the duchess, who was making it a point to practically exclude Loedicia from the conversation, when the duchess glanced toward the door, and her eyebrows raised.

"Oh, good," she exclaimed, apparently relieved, "he's arrived," and they all followed her eyes to the door, where a latecomer was standing, his face turned away from them, looking about, evidently hoping to see a familiar face. "I thought he wouldn't make it, it's getting so late," she said. "I do so want you to meet him," and she put her hand on Quinn's arm. "He's one of your countrymen, you know. I'll bring him right over," and she excused herself, floating across the crowded room to the man who was standing tall and erect, his deep red coat covering a pair of broad shoulders.

Loedicia and Quinn watched as she hurried toward the man, and suddenly Loedicia felt a prickling at the end of her spine and her face paled as the man turned toward them. He stopped looking about and stood motionless, as if turned to stone, and he looked, not at the duchess as she approached him, but past her at Loedicia, and Loedicia's mouth went dry and she swallowed hard as their eyes met. The whole room seemed lost to her as she stared into those dark compelling eyes, and her heart began to pound senselessly.

Her knees trembled as Rachel rushed up to the man and grabbed his hands, kissing him on the cheek, unaware that he was paying no heed to her gesture of affection. His eyes continued to bore into Loedicia's, and Loedicia's face flushed warm as she watched Rachel say something to him that he also paid little attention to, then take his arm and they started across the crowded room toward them.

Loedicia wanted to run. Someplace, anyplace. Anywhere to get away where she wouldn't have to face it, but she couldn't. She could only stand motionless, staring at him transfixed, literally shaking inside.

He walked toward Loedicia as if in a daze, his eyes intent on her, like a moth being drawn to a flame, and Rachel clutched his arm tightly while she talked, seemingly unaware that he wasn't listening, and as they slowly drew near, panic gripped Loedicia and tears began to fill her eyes. She wanted to die!

"Loedicia, Quinn, I'd like you to meet an old friend of

mine," exclaimed the duchess as she stopped abruptly in front of them. "Mr. Rothford Chapman of the United States, may I present some countrymen of yours, Mr. and Mrs. Quinn Locke," and suddenly, as she began to smile, the smile froze on her face, then faded, and she looked startled, realizing Roth and Loedicia were staring at each other as if they were the only two people in the room, and Quinn was staring at Roth as if he could kill him.

Quinn's eyes had a haunted look, yet they were hard and cold, and the air about him seemed to vibrate with emotion. She glanced quickly at Loedicia, whose flushed face and quivering mouth betrayed only too well that something was wrong.

"What is it? What's the matter?" Rachel asked Roth, who hadn't taken his eyes from Loedicia, and Rachel saw a warmth and yearning in Roth's eyes she'd never seen before, and her face reddened as neither man made any attempt to shake hands or answer her. "Will somebody please tell me what it is?" she demanded, flustered, and slowly, reluctantly, Roth's eyes left Loedicia's face and he turned to Quinn.

"It's been a long time, Quinn," he said huskily, holding out his hand, but Quinn only stared at him, and Roth flinched, his voice sounding hollow and empty as he spoke again. "We did part friends, didn't we?" he asked, and Quinn's face grew hesitant as he bit his lip.

"Yes . . . yes . . . I'm sorry, Roth," he finally answered, embarrassed as he took Roth's hand, his voice strained. "I . . . I didn't expect it."

"You two know each other?" asked Rachel incredulously, and it was Roth who finally answered her.

"It was a long time ago, Rachel," he said as he dropped Quinn's hand. "A long time ago," and he looked once more at Loedicia, his heart in his eyes. "You're looking lovely, Loedicia," he said softly, and his voice seemed to tremble as she continued to study him intently, scrutinizing the gray hairs he knew were beginning to replace the black ones, and the extra lines that age had etched into his face, and he felt self-conscious. There were tears in her eyes, and he wanted to take her in his arms and comfort her, but instead he continued calmly, "The years have been good to you."

She swallowed hard, fighting back the tears. He was still so handsome, so vital, and for a moment all the years rolled away and she remembered how he had been—and Heath—and everything was wrong.

"Thank you," she whispered breathlessly. "I . . . I . . ." Her voice choked up. It was too much, she couldn't do it, and she sniffed in hard as tears cascaded down her cheeks. "Excuse me," she mumbled, her hand flying to her mouth, "I need some air," and she turned, pushing her way through the crowd, heading for the French doors that opened onto the garden. She couldn't stay. She couldn't!

As Quinn watched her go, something inside of him died, and he didn't know what to do. He wanted to go after her, but he wasn't sure she wanted him.

"Excuse me," he finally said as he watched her disappear into the garden. "I . . . Excuse me," and he followed after her, making his way across the crowded room, his heart in his throat, while Roth stared after them.

"Will you kindly tell me what's going on?" demanded Rachel angrily as she watched Quinn following Loedicia.

Roth sighed. "I think you'd better ask Quinn," he answered, and his face was hard to read.

"You look like you could use a drink," she offered, and he looked at her for the first time since his arrival.

"A strong one," he agreed, and they headed for the refreshment table.

Loedicia faced a tree, leaning her head against it, the scent of roses all around her, the warm night air almost as suffocating as the ballroom had been, and she didn't hear Quinn behind her until he spoke.

"Dicia, please don't cry."

She tried to sniff in. "I can't help it," she sobbed hesitantly. "Oh, dammit, Quinn, why? After all these years, why? Why couldn't he stay out of our lives? First Heath, now this!"

He reached out and turned her around, looking at her face in the faint light from the ballroom windows. "Is that what you want, Dicia?" he asked softly as he stared down at her. "To keep him out of your life? Because if it is, I'll go now and tell him."

But she shook her head. "No . . . you can't . . . not now, Quinn. Not now. Now that he's here, I have to know . . . Maybe Heath found him, maybe he knows where Heath is. . . ."

His eyes narrowed suspiciously. "Is that the only reason?" and she stared at him, her hand flying to her mouth, and he looked at her bitterly. "I thought as much," he retorted angrily, and he released her, straightening up, his jaw set firmly.

"No!" she cried. "No, Quinn! You don't understand. That's not how it is. I love you."

"And you love him too. You always have. How many times have I heard you say it before? A half dozen, a dozen?"

"Quinn, please listen," she pleaded. "I just want to talk to him, that's all. To find out if he knows where Heath is."

"And what if he's never heard of Heath?"

"Then I'll tell him."

"Why?"

"He has a right to know."

"So he can love you all the more for giving him a son?"

"I can't help it if he loved me."

"The word is 'love,' Dicia—present tense. You saw his face. He's still in love with you!"

She covered her face with her hands and sank to the cool grass. "I wish I could die!" she cried helplessly. "Oh, God! I wish I could die!" and Quinn stared at her, his chest aching with a deep physical pain.

He moved forward and knelt beside her and reached out, touching her hair, remembering how wonderful the past few months had been, and he swallowed hard.

"I'm sorry," he whispered gently between her sobs. "Dicia, I'm sorry," he pleaded. "Forgive me. It was . . . I guess it was the shock of seeing him and knowing." He took the handkerchief from his pocket and handed it to her. "Please. I can't stand to hear you cry like this."

She looked up at him. His eyes were still angry, but there was love in them too, and she took the handkerchief, wiping away her tears. "I'm all right now," she said. "I seem to have turned into a weepy old lady lately." Then she blew her nose hard and straightened the skirt of her dress, but made no move to get up. "Quinn, I don't belong here with these fancy ladies in their frilly clothes and these men of society," she said. "I'm a backwoods wife. I ride bareback, shoot a rifle, can skin a deer, make cornbread, sew buckskins, and speak Iroquois. I don't belong with these people. I left all that years ago when I left Boston. I don't even know what to talk about when I'm with them. And now Roth's here to make matters worse. And how do we explain him, Quinn? How do we explain Roth to Brandon and Rachel? That he's just a man I happened to marry once when I thought my husband was dead?"

"What do you want to tell them about Roth?" he asked,

and she looked down at her hands, at the handkerchief she was twisting viciously.

"Nothing, I guess. I can't tell them about him. I just can't—what would they think of me?"

He studied her face, the pain that crossed it. He loved her so much.

She looked up at him, into his eyes. "I'll be all right now," she whispered as she wiped another tear from her eye. She couldn't hurt Quinn. He was so much a part of her. "It wasn't seeing Roth that made me cry, darling," she said softly. "Believe me. It was just that he reminded me of Heath, and I don't know where Heath is. I didn't mean to cry, but I remembered the day he left . . . Oh, Quinn, believe me. It wasn't seeing Roth!"

"You're sure?" he asked slowly, and she nodded as she sniffed in and looked up at him as he knelt beside her.

"I love you, Quinn. I may have loved him once, but that was so long ago. He . . . he means nothing to me now except that he's Heath's father." She tried to make it sound convincing because she was trying to convince herself too.

He grabbed her hand as she touched his face, and he held it hard, almost viciously. "Are you absolutely sure?" he asked, and she nodded.

"Yes," she said, crying to herself that it was true, it was true. "Yes."

He stood up, pulling her up with him, and his arms went about her. "I love you," he whispered huskily, and kissed her hard on the mouth, trying to erase the gnawing doubt that kept agitating, trying to surface.

"Quinn, I think he should know about Heath," she said as he drew his head back, still holding her. "And I think I should tell him."

"Alone?"

"Alone."

He stared into her face, then reached up, cupping her head between his hands.

"I don't like it."

"I know," she whispered, "but just once think of Roth. Put yourself in his place."

His eyes looked deeply into hers. What if she really was in love with him? What if her reaction hadn't been solely because of Heath? She looked so soft and vulnerable, but he couldn't drive her away. Not again. He had to take the chance.

"All right," he agreed softly. "When?"

"Now . . . tonight," she answered timidly. "The sooner the better. Go in and send him out. I can't go back in with my face all messed up . . . and we can be alone here."

He hesitated, and she looked at him sharply. "Quinn?"

He knew he couldn't fight her anymore, so he kissed her softly, then dropped his hands and turned toward the ballroom.

The strains of a waltz met him, gay and carefree, but he felt like an old man as he stepped into the crowded room. Rachel and Roth were nowhere in sight as he stood surveying the room, so he stopped Brandon and Rebel as they started to dance by.

"Have you seen the duchess?" he asked as Rebel started whirling past, and Brandon pulled her up short, stopping in front of him.

"I saw her and one of her friends heading for the main salon before I ran into Rebel," he said as he held Rebel close. "She said he wanted to get something stronger to drink," and Quinn thanked him quickly, then moved on as Brandon and Rebel once more started circling the floor.

Roth was halfway through his first glass of brandy, and Rachel was irritated at his silence, when Quinn stalked into the salon.

"Why?" Rachel was asking angrily, as she gave Roth a disgusted look. "Why can't you tell me what's going on? I think it's ridiculous. What could be so secret between you?"

Roth took another sip of brandy, then started to reply, but was interrupted as Quinn spoke to him from across the room, ignoring Rachel.

"She wants to see you, Roth," he said coldly as Roth glanced at him, startled; then Quinn walked up, reaching out, helping himself to the same decanter of brandy and pouring himself a drink. "She's still out in the garden."

"And you want me to go alone?"

"I don't, she does," Quinn answered, and he took a big drink of the brandy, then sighed. "Go on, dammit!" he blurted. "Before I change my mind."

Roth stared at him for a minute, then set his glass of brandy down and hurriedly left the room.

Rachel was furious. "Whatever is this all about?" she asked, but Quinn only stared after Roth, then walked over and looked out the front window, his mind miles away.

She studied his back and felt a strange warmth run through

her. Why did he have to affect her like this? He was a big lumbering man, almost crude, but handsome as the devil, and she wondered what kind of a lover he'd be. He leaned his head back and rubbed his neck, and she sighed, unable to stay away from him.

She stepped over, almost shoving herself in front of him. "Quinn, please, tell me what's wrong?" she begged solicitously, staring into his intense blue eyes as he finally turned to her, and a sudden thrill went through her right to her toes as she looked into his eyes. "I don't understand," she whispered passionately, and it was as if he was seeing her for the first time.

Her chestnut hair, hazel eyes that looked almost green. She was a beautiful woman, and she'd been practically throwing herself at him since the day they'd arrived. And right now she was giving him an invitation, and he knew it, so why was it he felt nothing? Her lips parted seductively, but he had no desire to kiss them, and her body felt warm as her breast brushed his arm, yet he had no desire to hold her, and her perfume was intoxicating, but he felt no exhilaration.

"What is it?" she coaxed sensuously as she looked at him, but he drew his eyes from hers and stared out the window again, wondering what was going on in the garden, and Rachel swore. "Dammit," she shouted, "why can't one of you tell me? Why is it so secret?" and Quinn suddenly looked at her again, his eyes blazing.

"May I have this dance, your Grace?" he asked unexpectedly, his jaw set stubbornly, and she was stunned.

"Dance? You want to dance?"

"That's what I asked," he retorted as he turned from her and walked briskly to the liquor cabinet, emptying his glass on the way, then setting it back beside the decanter. "Shall we?" and he held out his arm as if nothing were wrong, and she shrugged.

"Why not," she answered resignedly as she walked over to him, taking his arm, and as they headed for the ballroom, she was even more puzzled than ever.

Loedicia walked farther into the garden and stopped by a rose bush, bending down to smell the delicate fragrance of one of the roses, and she was reminded of Aunt Agatha's bureau drawers back in Boston, with their rose sachets. Boston was so long ago, and so much had happened.

She straightened as she heard footsteps behind her, and her

heart started pounding so loud she felt as if she was suffocating.

His voice was soft and intimate. "Dicia?"

She swallowed hard, turning, and her heart fell to her stomach, where it exploded, making her tremble. In the semi-darkness of the garden, with his red evening coat looking like the British uniform he'd once worn, the years seemed to melt away and she was back in Philadelphia, staring at the man she'd married and fallen in love with.

She closed her eyes a minute, shaking her head slightly, and brought herself back to reality, then opened her eyes again, but avoided looking at him. "Hello, Roth."

His eyes studied her affectionately. The tilt of her nose, her delicate jawline, the sensuous lips he'd longed to kiss so many times. "I had no idea you were here," he apologized softly. "I arrived four days ago on business and received the duchess's invitation yesterday morning. If I'd known . . ."

"You'd have come anyway."

"Yes . . . but I'd have warned you."

"It wouldn't have helped."

"Me either."

She made the mistake of looking up at him, and his eyes caught hers and held, and she couldn't look away as something passed between them that warmed her deep inside.

"Dicia!" he whispered passionately, and she drew in a quick breath, her knees trembling as he stepped toward her, staring boldly into her eyes, his body against hers.

"Roth!" she murmured breathlessly. "Please . . ." Her hands moved to his chest, and she laid her hands on the soft rich velvet of his coat. "Roth, I have to talk to you. . . . It's about Heath . . ."

He stared at her, his eyes puzzled. "Heath?"

"Yes, Heath."

He looked at her curiously. "Who is Heath?"

Her hands fumbled nervously on the lapels of his coat, and her eyes fell before his gaze. "He's . . . he's your son," she murmured so low he could barely hear, and she felt his muscles tense, and for a moment neither of them moved; then he reached up and put his hand under her chin, tilting her head up so she had to look into his dark eyes again.

"Did . . . did you say my son?" he asked incredulously, and her lips slowly parted.

"Yes, your son," she answered, and he stared at her dumbfounded.

"When?"

"Nine months after we left."

His voice was unsteady. "You're sure?"

"Yes. There's no mistake. It probably happened a night or two before Quinn came back. He looks exactly like you."

"Where is he?"

Her eyes filled with tears. "I don't know."

"You—"

"He knows he's your son," she interrupted, trying to hold back the tears. "Quinn made me tell him, and he went to find you, and he disappeared." Suddenly the tears rolled unchecked down her cheeks, and his arms went around her and he held her close, letting her cry.

He felt the familiar warmth of her against him, and his body felt alive for the first time in years. She was the only woman he'd ever wanted, and he'd lost her, yet she'd given him a son. The realization overwhelmed him, and he held her even closer, his hands beginning to caress her, and Loedicia moved in his arms, reluctantly responding to his hands, and her crying slowly subsided, only to be replaced by a longing for him she'd thought she'd left behind when she'd returned to Quinn.

"Dicia," he groaned helplessly against her ear. "Dicia, I love you," and she lifted her head to protest his words, only to meet his lips as they came down on hers, and for a few moments she forgot everything but finding him again.

Then suddenly, as her body began to move against him sensuously, she remembered Quinn and wrenched herself free, pulling herself from his arms, turning away, her lips still burning with desire.

"No!" she cried. "No, Roth! It's over. It was over a long time ago."

"I don't believe it," he said, his lips close to her ear as she kept her back to him. "You can't kiss me like that and say it's over."

She clenched her hands, wringing them nervously in front of her as her whole body ached with longing. She had never dreamed he'd meant so much to her, but he had.

"It has to be, Roth," she whispered. "You don't know what it's been like. When we realized Heath wasn't Quinn's, it was like a nightmare. To look at Heath every day and watch him turning into a miniature of you, and seeing the expression on Quinn's face whenever he looked at him, knowing that he knew another man had fathered him. I love Quinn, Roth, but he's been a hard man to love the past few years, and it's been a living hell watching the hate build up in him until just the sight of Heath was torment to him. He hates you, Roth. You took his older son from him, but he won't let you take his wife."

Roth straightened as he gazed at the back of her head, studying the curls, remembering how he used to twine them about his finger and bury his face in them after he'd made love to her. All these years he'd yearned for her, and now she was here, and he wanted to kiss her again, but he had no right to touch her. It wasn't fair.

"Tell me about Heath," he asked, trying to keep his mind from dwelling on what he longed to do, and she leaned her head back, then turned slightly to face him.

She told him all about Heath, right up to the day he left. "When I saw you tonight, I thought right away of Heath, and I hoped he'd found you."

"The tears were for him?"

She looked down at her hands, flexing them nervously. "Yes."

"There were no tears for me? For what we might have had?"

Tears for him? Oh, God, yes, there were tears for him, and she knew now that she'd only been fooling herself. President Washington was right. It was possible to love two people with the same warmth and desire, and her heart ached. She couldn't answer him.

"What are you doing in London?" she asked abruptly, ignoring his question, changing the subject as she turned away from him again, and he wanted to take her by the shoulders and shake her and make her say it just once. He wanted to hear her say "I love you," but instead he answered calmly.

"I'm taking care of the businesses my father left me when he died ten years ago."

She turned toward him again. "I thought he disowned you when you joined the rebels."

"Fathers are forgiving."

"Then you're living in England?"

"No. I live in Port Royal in the Carolinas. When I left the army, I decided since my father was in the business and I knew all about shipping and shipbuilding that it'd be a good business to get into. So now I own a fleet of ships working out of Charleston, a shipbuilding company in Beaufort, plus what my father left me here in England. The main offices and family home are in Portsmouth, a day and a half's ride from here, but I often have business here in London and stay at my town house."

"You're married?"

"No."

"I wish Heath had found you."

"Doesn't anyone have any idea where he might be?"

"He reached Philadelphia, and no one's seen him since. He just disappeared." She looked up at him gingerly, wanting so much to feel the warmth of his eyes again, and she wasn't disappointed. "I don't even know if he's alive," she whispered, and his eyes tried to comfort her.

Neither of them spoke for a minute as they looked at each other, and then suddenly Roth couldn't take it anymore.

"Don't look at me like that, Dicia," he whispered breathlessly, "not like that. For God's sake, I'm only human, I can take just so much."

She bit her lip and looked away. "Maybe we'd better go in now," she suggested, and he agreed.

"Do you suppose Quinn would be too angry if I had just one dance with you?" he asked as they walked back toward the ballroom, and Loedicia looked at him sideways. "Please," he begged, and she didn't have the heart to say no.

A slow waltz had started only moments before they stepped inside, and she turned to Roth, seeing his face much more clearly in the warm light from the chandeliers overhead, and her heart turned over. He had changed so little. His eyes smiled at her as his arm went about her waist, and he pulled her close, then began moving slowly to the music.

Neither of them said a word, but both were very aware of each other as the music seemed to lift them beyond the room, beyond the confining walls, to a time and place all their own. The pressure of his arm about her waist, the strength of his fingers as they moved, holding her tightly, and the sensuous warmth of his body so close to hers was intoxicating, and his eyes as they looked steadily into hers were like a drug. She could have danced with him all night, and her heart cried as she fought her emotions.

Suddenly she became conscious of the music coming to an end, and Roth stopped, but made no attempt to release her; instead, his arm tightened about her waist.

"Roth?" she questioned softly, and his eyes were bold and intense as he stared at her.

"I can't," he said passionately, his voice hushed so she

barely heard him. "I can't. I turned and walked away from you eighteen years ago, but not this time. He's had you to himself all these years, and I've had nothing but an empty ache inside. . . . I won't do it again. Not now, so soon. . . . I'm going to see you again, Loedicia, for as long as you're in London, no matter what he says."

Then he released her abruptly as Quinn and the duchess joined them, and she had no chance to argue him out of it.

12

It was a little after three in the morning as Loedicia set her hairbrush back on the dresser and walked to the huge double bed, slipping into it, pulling the cool sheets up to her chin. She stared across the room at Quinn as he finished undressing. The passionate anger on his face distorted his features, making him look almost like a stranger. He was ready to explode, and she couldn't blame him.

Roth had stayed the rest of the evening, dancing with her at least a half dozen more times, visiting with everyone as if nothing was wrong, and Loedicia had to make Rebel and Teak swear to keep his part in her past a secret. Quinn wanted no one in London to know, and neither did she. They were afraid the scandal would have an adverse effect on Quinn's claim to the title when the time came, and all evening Loedicia saw the hatred coming to life once more in Quinn's heart.

His eyes never left her when she and Roth danced together, and the rest of the time he stayed beside her like a shadow, afraid she might end up alone somewhere with Roth. Then, to make matters worse, as the guests were collecting their wraps at the door and saying good night, Roth had approached Quinn and asked if he could have a private word with him, and the two had disappeared into the library with the door firmly shut. The whole while they were in there, Loedicia tried to keep her mind on what she was doing, helping bid good-bye to the other guests, but she couldn't mistake the sudden loud outbursts that came from the room, even causing some of the guests to glance toward the library door apprehensively, and she shuddered.

"They'll kill each other," she whispered furtively once to Rebel, but Rebel shook her head and frowned, warning her mother not to say anything she'd be unable to explain to everyone, and when both men finally did return to the foyer, Quinn's eyes blazed fiercely, his anger deepening his voice, making it sound ominous as he took his place beside Loedicia saying good night to the guests.

Roth, however, looked stubbornly triumphant, although his good-bye to Loedicia showed nothing unusual and was no different from his good-bye to Rebel and Rachel, but his eyes just before he went through the door left a promise unsaid, and Loedicia, if she hadn't been so upset by Quinn's anger, would have unconsciously returned the look.

Now, as Quinn blew out the light and slipped into bed beside her, she felt cold and alone. He'd been distant and aloof since they'd come upstairs, hardly saying a word, and it hurt. She hadn't wanted to hurt him. She loved him. Oh, God, what a mess she was making of everything.

Quinn settled on his back and put his hands beneath his head, his body tense, and she knew he wanted to say something, but she was afraid to encourage him. Not afraid physically. He'd never laid a hand on her, although he could rant and rave like a grizzly at times. It was the subtle change she hated to see again. The snide remarks she was afraid of. The change that turned their marriage bed into a battleground as his ardent lovemaking became a vicious game of "see how much better I am" one time, then made her feel like a convenience the next, as his moods prevailed.

She turned to face him in the darkness and cautiously slid over against him, resting her head on his shoulder, a curl tickling his neck, but he didn't move.

"Quinn?" There was no answer. "Quinn, please."

She felt him take a deep breath; then he hesitated, and she thought for a minute he wasn't going to answer.

"Do you know what he told me?" he finally blurted, knowing full well she didn't. "He told me that as long as we're in London he's going to see you whenever he feels like it." He was more than just angry, he was furious. "He said I've had you to myself all these years and he's had nothing, and the least I can do is let him see you and talk to you." He hesitated, and she lay quietly, waiting for him to finish. "The bastard said he didn't think that was asking too much!"

Suddenly his arm moved from behind his head and encircled her, pulling her close against him. "Too much? Dammit! It's asking more than I can give. I told him I'd kill him, and he said he'd been dead for eighteen years already, so what difference did it make." His arm tightened viciously, and she winced. "I won't allow it!" he stated vehemently. "I won't let him take you from me!"

Her stomach tightened into one big knot, and she rested her face against his neck, smelling the familiar masculine smell of him, his skin touching her lips. "Don't be foolish," she whispered tenderly, her lips caressing his neck. "You'll never lose me to anyone. You should know that."

"Should I?" he asked cynically, his fingers hard against her ribs. "You loved him once, and I know there's still something there. Much as I like to tell myself there isn't, I could see the way the two of you looked at each other." His right hand moved up, cupping her head angrily as her hot breath on his neck raised gooseflesh and warmed him deep inside.

"No, Quinn," she said, and now she felt ashamed of her reactions to Roth. Quinn was her husband. She'd made her choice. She had no right to think of Roth in any way, shape, or form, and she felt guilty. She had to show him he was wrong. Her lips nibbled at Quinn's ear, then searched until she found his mouth, and she kissed him deeply, with an intense desire that thrilled him down to his toes. "I love you, Quinn," she moaned against his mouth. "I love you, you're my husband."

He frowned, whispering, pulling his mouth from hers. "What of Roth?"

She straightened, looking down into his face. "I don't know," she said. "I don't know what I feel for Roth, but it's not the way I feel about you. . . . There's a bond between him and me, yes, because of Heath, but other than that . . ."

She tried to reassure him, and for another hour they argued back and forth, and by the time she was through, she even had herself believing that her feelings for Roth in no way matched the feelings she had for Quinn.

"I don't want him near you," argued Quinn.

"But if you make a fuss, everyone'll ask why, then what?"

"Dammit! I can't let another man court my wife!"

"He won't be courting me," she insisted. "He just wants to talk . . . to ask questions about Heath and pass the time of day. Do you suppose if he was trying to take me away from you he'd warn you ahead of time? Put yourself in his place. If the tables were turned, would you be satisfied with a short talk in the garden and a quick dance around the ballroom?"

"He danced with you half a dozen more times."

She sighed disgustedly. "You're as stubborn as a mule, Quinn Locke. Have I yelled because that designing female who calls herself a duchess has been making eyes at you? Have I?" There was silence, and she heard him breathing heavily. "Dancing with you like some calf-eyed schoolgirl and flirting with you as if I wasn't even around. But that's all right, I suppose."

"Don't be silly."

"Who's being silly?"

"You know it doesn't mean a thing."

"That's what you say, but how can I be sure of that?" she retorted. "The way she's been throwing herself at you."

"You're jealous?"

"Why not!" She was staring down at him in the darkness. "I don't know what ever gave you the idea that I didn't care. That you're the only one with a priority on jealousy. I hate the bitch!"

He cursed, and his arms went about her. "All right, you vixen, you win," he acknowledged irritably. "I'll try, but just once let him get out of line, and I'll—"

She put her hand over his mouth to stop him. "You won't lay a hand on him," she finished, and took her hand away, replacing it with her lips, and for tonight the arguing was over as he kissed her back and felt his body respond to her as it always did.

But for the next few days the atmosphere on Grosvenor Square was anything but congenial. On the surface, things seemed just fine, but an undercurrent of tension was simmering just beneath, and it was taking its toll on Loedicia.

Each day that went by she saw a subtle change in Quinn. He and Brandon were making headway in their search for someone who knew Quinn. They had three affidavits from old friends of Quinn's father and were on the trail of Quinn's old nurse. "But it hasn't seemed to improve his disposition any," Lizette complained, reminding Loedicia of her warning when they were in Philadelphia, and as each new day dawned, Loedicia shuddered, watching helplessly as Quinn once more drew further and further from her.

At times he was gay and charming, others moody and irritable, and the fact that they ran into Roth at another party two days after Rachel's party didn't help matters. He danced more with Loedicia than anyone else, and although he tried not to make his preoccupation with her too obvious, Loedicia was worried. It wasn't the easiest thing in the world to hold Quinn in check. His temper was unpredictable, and she even warned Roth.

"And what am I doing wrong?" he asked her as they circled the floor in a slow waltz. "I haven't whisked you off into some secluded spot to make love to you, although the thought is intriguing. And I haven't kissed your hand more than once, and that was when you arrived. If an occasional dance, bringing you a glass of punch once in a while, and talking to you when we happen to meet during the course of the evening is too much, I'm sorry, he's just going to have to put up with it. I think I'm being quite honorable under the circumstances," and he smiled stubbornly, then continued to twirl her about the room while Quinn stood in a corner, trying to hold up his end of a conversation with two gentlemen who were discussing the races, but his mind wasn't on horses.

Loedicia wished she could tell Roth to leave her alone, to go back to wherever he'd been all these years, but she couldn't, and this too bothered her. As much as she fought her feelings for him, they were there, and she knew deep down in her heart that Quinn's anger was justified, and it made her feel worse.

A few days later Loedicia bumped into Roth when she went for an afternoon canter in the park, and the day after that he was in the dress shop where she and Rebel had gone to find her a new dress to wear to another party for the following weekend.

"He's so handsome, isn't he, Mother?" said Rebel, her flair for excitement surfacing its wicked little head. "And he looks so like Heath. I've noticed Father lately, and he's literally in a tizzy. I never thought anything could upset him so," and Loedicia cautioned her to hush so Roth wouldn't hear as he approached.

The next afternoon Lizette waltzed into the main salon with a package for Loedicia, and Quinn hit the ceiling when she opened it to reveal a lace nightgown and a card that read "Wear this in remembrance of me," and Loedicia's face reddened as she read it. Even though there was no signature, she knew who'd sent it.

"The man has the gall of a . . . You'll send it back!" shouted Quinn angrily, as Rachel, who'd been talking with them, leaned forward and peeked into the box at the exquisite lace gown with pale pink roses in delicate embroidery edging the low neckline, but Dicia shook her head.

"I won't!" she stated. "Besides, there's no one to send it back to. There's no name on the card."

"You know damn well who sent it," said Quinn, and Rachel studied Quinn's face.

"Whoever sent it has excellent taste," she said facetiously, touching the lace, one eye on Quinn's face. "I'll wager it's right from Paris, war or no war."

Lizette clucked as she too felt the soft lace between her fingers. *"Oui,"* she confirmed as she glanced quickly at Loedicia's face, then back to the nightgown. "This war is stupid. Men always fight stupid wars."

The war the French and British were waging seemed almost unreal sometimes to Quinn and Loedicia, because it affected them so little, but Loedicia knew Rachel and Lizette were right. The intimate clothing had a definite look of France about it, and she knew only Roth could have sent it, and she was quite sure she knew why.

"I won't wear it, but I won't send it back either," she answered stubbornly, and Quinn frowned.

"Why not?"

"Because it's beautiful, and what harm will it do to keep it?"

"You don't accept gifts like that from a man."

Rachel laughed, trying to sound casual. "Who says it's from a man, Quinn?" she said, tongue in cheek, and glanced quickly at Loedicia. She'd been enjoying the set-to between the two of them. In fact, she'd been very aware of the little disagreements that had been popping up between them for the past few days and she knew that in some way Roth was responsible, only she couldn't understand how. One thing for sure, he was more than mildly interested in Loedicia, and although neither of them said it, she knew the nightgown had come from him. What surprised her most, however, was the fact that Quinn hadn't ordered him to keep hands off. For a man so devoted to his wife, he was being very lenient, although there were times she was sure the words were on the tip of his tongue. The question was, why was he holding back? "Maybe a woman sent the gift," she suggested, hoping one of them would admit it came from Roth, but neither did. Instead they continued to argue, and Quinn finally conceded to let her keep it if she packed it away and never wore it.

"Brandon said you were an unusual man," Rachel said as Loedicia gathered the package and wrappings together and headed upstairs with Lizette in tow. "And I guess he's right at that."

Quinn glanced at her, annoyed. "You know who sent it,

don't you?" he said, watching the expression in her eyes as she watched Dicia leave the room.

"It's obvious Roth's quite smitten with her, but I just can't understand why you take it. Most men would have called him out that first night."

His eyes grew dark. "And risk losing her? She'd leave me if I so much as touched a hair on his head."

"Oh?" This revelation was new to her, and she eyed him curiously.

"You wouldn't understand."

"No, I guess I wouldn't, but there are other women."

He knew full well what she meant, and he straightened confidently, looking directly at her. "Not for me," he said, but she smiled provocatively.

"Too bad," she answered softly, and her eyes gazed back at him boldly. "If you ever change your mind, let me know," and she continued to smile invitingly at him as Quinn stared back, noticing the softness of her body as she leaned toward him. "You know, I don't think she deserves you," she whispered huskily, and his eyes studied her brazenly.

"She may not deserve me," he said, putting a finger beneath her chin, tilting her head up so her eyes looked directly into his, "but she's apparently well satisfied, wouldn't you say?"

She smiled sensuously, her eyes languid. "I'll let you know the next time I see her with Roth," she whispered, and saw the angry gleam in his eye as his finger dropped from her chin.

In spite of the revelation that Dicia was jealous of Rachel, the byplay and flirtation between the two had increased, and Dicia was sure it was Quinn's way of getting back at her and Roth, but it was still provoking and did nothing to ease relations between them.

The following Sunday, with the weather warm and clear, the Duke and Duchess of Umbridge opened their country home a few miles outside the city for a garden party complete with dancing on the lawn and bowling on the green, and everyone at Bourland Hall was invited, and everyone went except Lizette.

Loedicia was resplendent in a new black-and-white-striped poplin dress with a quilted petticoat and a wide-brimmed white straw sun hat perched down on the front of her head, its black-and-white satin ribbons curled about the brim and bunched into a garland resembling roses at the back, and

Quinn looked striking beside her in his black velvet coat, white breeches, black boots, and high silk hat, with a touch of lace at his throat. They rode in the same open carriage with Rachel, who looked frothy and delicious in a sheer dress of pale aqua with numerous petticoats and a wide-brimmed straw hat crushed on top by a cluster of artificial flowers.

Rebel, feeling like a princess in white peau de soie, the tiny violets embroidered on it matching her eyes, sat next to Brandon in the carriage in front of them and held onto her wide-brimmed hat, turning and glancing back.

"I've been trying to decide who looks prettier, Mother or the duchess," she said as she turned back around in the open carriage and addressed Brandon as they rode along.

Brandon, dressed in his usual brocades, this time in varying shades of green, studied her intently, then smiled. He had his own idea who the prettiest one would be at the party, and he'd been tossing the idea back and forth in his heart for days. Rebel was a find. She was so unexpected, and life with her would never be dull, but was he ready for love? Then again, was anyone ever ready for it, or did it simply creep up uninvited? The more he saw her, the more he wanted her, and now, as he stared at her, her violet eyes warm and alive, he knew he was going to have her.

"Like mother like daughter," he said, smiling, and Teak, sitting across from them, rolled his eyes.

He'd been watching Brandon ever since they'd arrived in London, and he'd decided if he ever saw a man completely smitten with a female it was the duke. When they first arrived it was obvious to him by the looks that passed between them that Brandon and Rachel were closer than they should have been, but gradually the intimate looks began to change. In fact, Teak was amused because lately the duchess had been singling out his father for her special attentions instead of Brandon. It was funny really, and he laughed to himself at the inane futility of it. Hell, his father was one of those stupid men who give their heart to one woman and never leave room for another. Quinn Locke and Roth Chapman were two of a kind when it came to women, but it was fun anyway watching the duchess make an ass of herself over him, and he smiled smugly, brushing a speck of lint from his burgundy suit and fluffing the ruffled cravat at his throat, wondering if that pretty brown-eyed lass he'd met at the last party was going to be there today, and he gazed up at the blue, cloud-scattered sky. It certainly was nice looking older than his years, and he sighed as he thought about the afternoon ahead of them and all the lovely, tempting lips waiting for stolen kisses. There were dozens of girls in the world, and all waiting for him to enjoy them. He certainly wasn't going to end up like his father, no sirree.

The lawn party was fantastic and almost everyone who was anyone was there, except Lord Chaucer, that is. Three days before, Quinn and Brandon had found Quinn's old nurse, who'd not only recognized him, but insisted that besides writing a letter for him she'd also appear before the earl marshal if need be and swear to his identity, and on Friday he'd had an audience with the earl marshal, submitting his petition to reclaim the title and lands of the Earl of Locksley as sole living heir. It had turned court circles upside down, and overnight Loedicia and Quinn became the topic of conversation. By this afternoon the whole of London was agog.

Here was a man, an American, dressed like an English gentleman, with the dominant strength of a backwoodsman, claiming to be an earl, and Lord Chaucer, the present earl, detesting the whole affair, had refused to present himself, retiring to his country estate, warning his friends that no one would take his lands and title from him.

In the afternoon, when the party was well under way, Roth arrived on a beautiful black stallion, riding right into the crowd as if he were royalty, and more than one feminine eye turned his way, admiring the cut of his green velvet riding coat and the shine on his boots and the way he handled his horse. But the eyes he caught as he dismounted were the only ones he cared about, and he smiled at Loedicia with his whole heart, causing Quinn to hustle her off to the bowling green.

The day seemed to be going quite well as Quinn kept Loedicia as far away from Roth as possible; then, shortly before dark, while Quinn was busy discussing his petition with their host and a number of other gentlemen, Roth saw Loedicia wandering away from the crowd, and he began to follow her. She moved slowly along the edge of the lawn and through a hedge, ending up at a small summer house partially screened by wisteria that clung tenaciously from its roof like a screen. It was quiet and secluded, away from the hustle and noise.

She was sitting on one of the benches gazing dreamily into space when he popped his head in.

"Hello," he said as he stepped inside, and she frowned, startled.

"I didn't hear you."

He walked toward her. "I know. I didn't want you to."

She glanced away self-consciously and sighed as he stood looking down at her.

"I have a feeling Quinn's stirred up a hornet's nest," he said, trying to keep the subject neutral, and she glanced toward him, but avoided his eyes.

"I know," she confirmed, then turned away to look out an open space in the wisteria, "and I don't like it."

He frowned, remembering their conversation the other evening regarding Lord Chaucer's visit to Bourland Hall. "You think Lord Chaucer'll make good his threat?"

"What's to stop him? He has power and friends."

"But it's been almost nineteen years. He'd be laughed out of Old Bailey."

"Would he?" She stood up restlessly and walked across the room, reaching up, pulling the wisteria aside to look out. "I wish I were as sure of that as you and Quinn."

He watched her shoulders sag. "Right now I'm not sure of anything," he said as he walked up to stand behind her, "except perhaps that you've been avoiding me all day. Why? Why don't you even look at me, Loedicia? What have I done?"

Her hand dropped, and the wisteria fell back into place, blocking out the golden twilight. "Why did you send it?" she asked softly, and he reached out, taking her by the shoulders, turning her to face him.

"Don't you know?"

She couldn't look at him, and concentrated on his lacy cravat, her face troubled, her voice barely audible. "I know why, but . . ."

"The night we were married, you had to wear that faded, threadbare nightgown Polly'd given you, remember, and I made you a promise that someday you'd wear the latest style from Paris, with pink roses around the neck and yards and yards of lace. And when I saw it in the shop the other day, I just couldn't help it."

"Quinn was furious."

His hands dropped from her shoulders. "Quinn was furious, Quinn was angry, Quinn doesn't like it!" He looked disgusted. "What about me? I love you more than life itself, Dicia. I've been honorable. Except dancing with you, I haven't touched you, and this is the first time we've really been alone since that first night in the garden. He has you to himself every night." His voice deepened as he stared at her, aroused by her nearness. His hand moved up and touched her hair, and she drew in a quick breath; then it moved to the nape of her neck, and he ran his finger affectionately to her throat, and she felt it deep in her loins. "He can touch you . . . and caress you all he wants."

She trembled as his hand moved tenderly across her skin, and she couldn't avoid his eyes this time.

"Do you know what it's like just to touch you like this?" he said passionately. "To feel your soft flesh beneath my fingers?" His hand moved down to the valley where her breasts met, and hesitated, clenching into a fist, as if he was fighting himself; then it opened wide again and moved lower, his fingers gently caressing her bosom. "To feel your soft bare breasts beneath my hands again, to let my lips caress them and bring you alive as they used to do . . ."

Her eyes gazed into his as if mesmerized, and she too remembered what it was like. This gentle coaxing, the warm caresses. There'd been no violence in Roth's lovemaking, only his total surrender, and her body throbbed at the memory.

His hand moved back to her throat, his fingers plying her flesh sensuously. "I'm going to leave, Dicia," he finally whispered as his eyes softened. "I'm going back to Portsmouth, then to America," and he saw the question in her eyes. "I have to," he groaned, his mouth now only inches from hers. "Because if I don't, I may not be able to behave myself anymore," and his lips moved closer, inviting her, and she couldn't move away.

Instead, she stared at him, at the warmth and desire in his eyes, and she swayed toward him, her body on fire. She shouldn't be here, but she didn't care. For a few brief moments she was alive again, and there was a promise of heaven in his arms. Her eyes softened, staring into his, and his arms went about her slowly as she welcomed them.

"I love you," he murmured against her mouth, and he kissed her until she felt it clear to her toes.

This time she kissed him back with an urgency driven by a need Quinn had been unable to fulfill lately. She needed love. Lovemaking, to Dicia, was like the air she breathed, necessary for her existence. What Quinn had given her the last few times was the same hollow, bitter lovemaking he'd given her since he'd discovered the truth about Heath, and now she welcomed Roth's caresses like a starving woman.

Finally Roth drew his head back, his eyes devouring her, his heart in his throat. "Now you know why I'm going away," he said huskily. "I thought just to be near you would be enough, but it's not, and I have no right to more."

"Roth!"

He kissed her lovingly. "Maybe if I'm not here it'll be better for both of you," he said. "It was a mistake . . . I shouldn't have stayed."

"What do I do now?" she asked breathlessly, tears in her eyes. "What do I do?" and he kissed her again passionately, not wanting to let her go.

"Oh, God," he moaned against her mouth, and pulled her hard against him as he kissed her, his body burning with desire, and he felt her need too.

Suddenly they were torn apart by Quinn's voice ringing in their ears from the other side of the summer house, and they drew apart abruptly, staring at each other, startled. He was standing tall and straight beneath the arch that was used as a door, his huge frame silhouetted against the twilight.

"Take your hands off my wife," he roared viciously, his eyes blazing, and Dicia's heart leaped into her throat as she pulled away from Roth. Quinn lunged, shortening the space between them.

"No!" she yelled. "No!" But Quinn was already on top of them, reaching for Roth, who stood stubbornly unmoving, waiting for him. She flung herself awkwardly between them. "If you touch him, I'm through!" she cried, her face flushed, lips trembling, and Quinn stopped abruptly, his hand reaching around her, the fingers already on Roth's coat, and he hesitated, staring at her. "I mean it," she gasped. "If you so much as lay one hand on him"—her voice lowered—"you'll never have me again."

Quinn's eyes blazed. The muscles on his neck strained angrily. "I don't have you now!" he shouted bitterly. "I never have. There's always been a part of you missing because of him," and he started to move again.

She reached out and grabbed his arm, holding it, imploring him, trying to keep him from getting at Roth, who was trying to keep her from getting hurt. The two men were well-matched, she knew, but the anger that drove Quinn gave him an edge. This whole thing was her fault. All her fault.

"Please, Quinn," she begged, and her eyes filled with tears. "I'm sorry!"

"Sorry?" He stopped again, staring at her incredulously. "I find him making love to you, and all you can say is 'I'm sorry'?" He flung his arm, wrenching it from her grasp.

"Don't blame her," demanded Roth from behind her. "It was my fault. Blame me!"

Quinn straightened, his face dark, eyes like steel, hands flexing nervously. "I should kill you," he spat venomously, and Dicia shook her head.

She looked at Quinn, wishing she could change things, yet knowing it was futile. "If you killed Roth, you'd kill my love for you with him."

His eyes widened as if in surprise. "Your love for me?"

"Yes, you." She hung her head, crying. "I know you don't think it's true."

He laughed cynically, sneering, his fists still clenching impatiently. "All right. You love me," he conceded. "I'll accept that." His eyes narrowed darkly. "Now you'll prove it." His jaw set angrily as he looked at Roth. "I've let you make a fool of me long enough," he stated through clenched teeth. "Now I'm calling the cards. I want you out of London, and I want it now, and if you ever so much as talk to her again, I will kill you, regardless of her pleading. Do you understand?"

Roth's dark eyes flashed as he straightened solidly. "I don't need her to plead for me," he answered harshly. "I'm not afraid of you, Quinn, I never was."

"Then shall we make it pistols at dawn?" asked Quinn, and Roth accepted, but Dicia shook her head in disbelief.

"No!" she cried, tears running down her cheeks. "No! I won't have it."

This was crazy. Insane! They were both insane. She looked first at Quinn, then Roth, wiping the tears away with the back of her hand. "I won't let you," she stated, stamping her foot on the floor between them, trying to sniff back the tears. "If either one of you hurts the other . . . I hate you . . . I hate you both. You're not thinking of me. You don't love me. If one of you dies—either of you—I couldn't stand it." The tears flooded her eyes, running unchecked down her cheeks into her mouth, almost choking off her words, and she licked them away with her tongue, their salty taste making her wipe her mouth. "Please," she begged, "I love you both!" and both of them stared at her.

"Don't you see," she sobbed, pleading with them, trying to

make some sense out of the mess. "If you fight a duel, people will want to know why." She sniffed back the tears, trying to control her voice. "The whole thing'll come out, we won't be able to hide it anymore, and besides"—she looked first at one, then the other, trying to compose herself—"if one of you is killed, do you honestly think I could go on caring about the other? I'd hate you for the rest of my life."

She straightened up as she saw the frustration in both their faces. "Roth was saying good-bye, Quinn," she blurted helplessly. "He was leaving because he knew it wouldn't work." She threw her hands in the air hopelessly. "But if that's what you want, if neither of you wants me as a person, but only as a possession, then go ahead, kill each other, and to hell with the both of you!" and she turned her back on them, walking away, then stood leaning against one of the pillars that held up the roof, angrily trying to wipe the tears from her eyes, hoping her words would have some effect on them.

Quinn stared after her, gritting his teeth, the sour taste of anger filling his mouth; then he glanced quickly at Roth, whose eyes were filled with pain as he watched Loedicia, and he was at a loss. He could kill Roth so easily without any remorse, yet he held back. Her words pounded over and over again in his brain, and his fists clenched as Roth drew his eyes from Loedicia and stared back at him, waiting.

Quinn straightened even taller, his face like granite, and he stared hard into Roth's eyes. The man wasn't afraid. There was no fear in his eyes, only a determination to do whatever had to be done. He was far from being a coward. He glanced back at Loedicia, then back to Roth. It was up to him, he knew. He was the one who'd thrown the challenge, not Roth. If he killed him, it was over, she'd never come to him again. Yet, if he didn't . . .

"How soon can you leave?" he finally asked savagely, and Roth's eyes narrowed.

"If I go," he answered, his eyes flashing, "I go because of Dicia, not you." He glanced at her quickly, wishing he'd been more discreet and hadn't lost control; then he looked back at Quinn as Loedicia turned to look at them both. "I'm not afraid of you now, and I never have been, Quinn," he answered boldly. "But I realize now that what I've done was a mistake, and I've only made her life miserable. I'll bow out for her sake, not yours, but I'll warn you, you'd better treat her right and give her all the love she needs, or by God the next time I see her I will take her away from you!"

"Get out!" shouted Quinn through clenched teeth, his face livid, and Roth's mouth set firmly. "Get out before I change my mind."

Roth glared at him, not wanting to leave, yet knowing if he stayed there'd be hell to pay, and he didn't want to hurt her anymore. He wanted to say good-bye, to hold her, kiss her, tell her everything would be all right, but he didn't dare for her sake. Instead, he glanced at her quickly, his eyes drinking her in for one last long moment; then he turned without saying another word and walked out of the summer house.

Loedicia watched Roth leave, then straightened up, trying to hold back the tears, relieved, yet dismayed, and Quinn stared at her, breathing heavily, seething with anger.

"Go on. Why don't you follow him?" he asked furiously, pointing toward the archway Roth had just walked through. "Isn't that what you want?" and she turned slowly, her eyes penitent as they looked deeply into his.

She wanted his forgiveness, wanted to see once more the husband she'd grown to love instead of this arrogant, angry stranger she'd been living with the past few days. "Am I never to be forgiven?" she asked hesitantly, wanting forgiveness more than anything in the world, her eyes pleading. "Or will I spend the rest of my life paying for my mistakes?"

He scowled, his eyes cold and indifferent. "I think it's time we left," he said abruptly, conceding nothing, and he walked to the archway, standing like a stern sentinel waiting for her, as he would a wayward child, and they left the summer house, joining the rest of the guests, trying to act like nothing was wrong.

The party was breaking up as they reached the house, and most of the guests were already saying good-bye at the door, so Quinn made sure there was no time lost in their departure. He accepted the good wishes of his host and many new friends, then sat sternly beside Loedicia as the carriage moved off into the darkening shadows.

Rachel sat across from them, beside Teak, staring curiously. Something was wrong. She had noticed it earlier. In fact, she'd noticed a change in Roth too. He'd approached her a short time before on his way to the door, seemingly preoccupied, his dark eyes sullen.

"You're leaving?" she'd asked, and he'd snapped at her irritably, saying something about staying too long already, and left with a brief good-bye to his host, an action so unlike him that the scene imprinted itself vividly on her mind, and now, as she watched Loedicia and Quinn, she was sure she knew the cause. Loedicia was exceptionally quiet, and Quinn's eyes smoldered ominously, even though he tried to act normally.

It was well after dark when the carriage, its street lights lit, swerved through the gates of the mansion on Grosvenor Square. The night was exceptionally warm and balmy for so late in the year, so it wasn't unusual that Teak had ridden home with them, leaving Brandon and Rebel a carriage all to themselves. And it wasn't surprising either that the duke's carriage wasn't even in sight yet, but Quinn paid little attention.

They entered the foyer and Loedicia took off her hat, then stood as if waiting for something.

"Shall we have a nightcap?" asked the duchess as she surrendered her hat to the maid and sighed. "It's been such a long afternoon and I'm afraid the punch the Duchess of Umbridge served was rather flat." But Quinn declined, stating that he and Loedicia were both tired, and Loedicia, without waiting for a suggestion from him, headed wearily toward the stairs.

When they reached the bedroom, Quinn closed the door firmly behind them, then watched as Loedicia walked dejectedly across the room, her hand at her side trailing her hat in it, the ribbons touching the floor, dragging as she moved. She stopped in front of the French doors and stared out toward the balcony into the night, at the light from the moon barely perceptible on the rooftops at the servants' quarters at the back of the house, and the scent of the flowers from the garden below filled the air, and she waited apprehensively, knowing that Quinn's retaliation for her sins had only been postponed until they were alone.

He stared at her, an ache in his chest, his eyes haunted with the scene he'd witnessed in the summer house, and he cursed to himself as he walked across the room to confront her. "I think I deserve an explanation, don't you?" he retorted forcefully, and she winced at the venom in his voice.

"I told you in the summer house," she answered softly, her back still to him, "he was saying good-bye."

"I don't believe you."

She whirled around angrily, resentful of his accusation and his arrogance. "Then believe what you want," she stated flatly. "I don't care to argue the point anymore. I'm sick and tired of the whole mess. For years, since Heath started growing up, I've watched your hatred grow and I've watched you changing from the man I used to know into a man I wish I didn't know. Then suddenly, after Philadelphia, things changed again for a while and I had my husband back, at least most of the time, but even then, the least little reminder and I could see the hatred in your eyes." She paused, her eyes filled with tears. "It's destroying us, Quinn," she whispered breathlessly. "Your hatred is destroying us. I can't help what I feel, but I'll warn you now, keep it up, Quinn, and I won't have anything left to feel."

"And what do you feel?" he asked, his teeth clenching as he reached out his hand, cupping her head, and he stared at her intently. "What do you feel, Dicia, tell me?" he asked again, and moved his hand up, touching her cheek with his other hand, running his finger along her cheekbone as he held her head steady, and he leaned closer, his heart pounding. Even in anger she had the power to arouse him, to fill his body with desires he wanted to deny, but couldn't, and it only angered him more.

"All I want you to do is let me love you, Quinn," she whispered softly. "With no restraints, no recriminations. I fell in love with you a long time ago, and I've never stopped loving you."

"And Roth?"

"I don't know." There were tears in her eyes. "I'm being honest with you. I just don't know. I have feelings for Roth, I can't help it, and you're not helping me either. Every time you take me to bed, you drive another wedge deeper into my heart."

"And what about my heart?" His fingers moved in her hair and tightened, hurting her. "Do you think I enjoy making love to a woman who's constantly comparing me to another man? Do you think I like sharing your heart with him? Well, I won't do it anymore, do you understand?"

Her eyes widened and her face went white as he made one last vicious twist in her hair, then tore his hand from its black silkiness as she stared into his angry blue eyes. "What . . . what do you mean?"

"I mean since you don't enjoy my lovemaking anymore, then the next time you climb into bed, you'll climb in by yourself," he stated bitterly. "I'm through fighting a losing battle," and he turned abruptly, walking out of the room, slamming the door behind him, leaving her staring after him in disbelief.

She stood transfixed, watching the door; then suddenly, jolted into action, she ran across the room, flung the door open, and ran out, down the hall, and to the top of the steps, just in time to see Quinn, hat in hand, leaving by the front door.

Her heart sank. She'd never seen him this angry before. It was the first time his love for her hadn't smothered his anger. He'd never threatened her like this before. She turned quietly, tears running down her cheeks, and walked back to her room.

She loved Quinn. He was her life, the air she breathed, yet more and more her thoughts were of Roth, and when he'd kissed her this afternoon she'd welcomed his arms, responding to him as she had to Quinn before the hatred that was eating at him had begun to kill her response. But, her heart ached for Quinn, for the love they'd shared, and she knew he'd come back as he always had before when they argued, and things would be all right again for a while. He had to come back. He had to.

She slipped into her wrapper and went about the room blowing out all the candles but one that was on the nightstand beside the bed, then took off the wrapper, laying it at the foot of the bed, and climbed into the huge monstrosity, feeling lost in the mound of covers. She bunched the pillows up behind her back, the blanket just covering her breasts, and settled back, prepared to wait for his return.

13

Quinn had been angrier than any other time in his life as he'd slammed the door behind him earlier and left the house. Ordinarily he wasn't much of a drinking man, but tonight he'd hit every ordinary and grog shop in London. Yet, as he returned, lumbering through the gates, and moved reluctantly up the walk, quietly opening the huge door and stepping into the foyer, he wasn't really drunk. Not to the point of insensibility. He had had just enough to keep the anger alive in his mind and body. He was still incensed, and the picture of the two of them together in the summer house, wrapped in their passionate embrace, gnawed at him, eating him up inside.

He swore as he dropped the key, then picked it up, slipping it into his pants pocket as he headed for the stairs. His mind was a bit foggy, but not foggy enough to erase her picture from his mind. She was so soft and desirable. He'd been fighting with himself all evening, condemning her one minute, wanting her the next, and now as he ascended the steps slowly, trying not to stumble and make any noise, he suddenly wanted her more than anything in the world. To feel her beneath him, to feel his hands on her, his lips on her mouth.

He reached the top of the stairs as the clock in the hall struck two, and he stopped, staring down the long hallway that led to the bedroom where he knew she'd be waiting, and suddenly he couldn't do it. He couldn't crawl back to her like a sniveling coward. Damn her! She'd gone too far, he had to make her pay!

He should beat her . . . but he knew he couldn't. His eyes filled with tears of indignation, and he sighed helplessly. She had no right to do this to him. To make him want her so badly. He straightened, then started down the hall toward their bedroom, anger once more driving him, the ale he'd consumed distorting his thoughts, and then he stopped abruptly and his body tensed as he stood in the hall, hardly daring to breathe.

It was there before him. A way out, and he wouldn't have to crawl back to her. Should he? Turning slowly, he stared at the door to Rachel's room, and the hair on his neck bristled as he closed his eyes to steady himself. He remembered her soft, inviting hazel eyes, warm curvaceous body, and sensuous mouth, and he swallowed hard, his forehead breaking out in a cold sweat. She wanted him, he knew. She'd been throwing herself at him since the day they'd arrived. She was there for the taking, and his mouth went dry.

But what if he couldn't? What if his body betrayed him as it had with the half-breed girl Chatte when he'd thought Dicia was dead those long years ago?

Dicia! Again he thought of her, and again his mind, warped from the ale, fought her, infuriating him until he wanted to hurt her, get her out of his system once and for all, and this was the only way. He'd take another woman and prove he didn't need her.

"Damn her to hell anyway," he whispered viciously to himself, and reached down, turning the knob slowly, his hand trembling.

The duchess was asleep, the room in darkness as he entered and walked steathily toward the bed. The heavy red velvet draperies at the window were open just enough to let in the moonlight, and he stopped, staring down at the way she was sprawled on her back, one hand above her head, the other at an odd angle at her side, the sheer nightgown she wore revealing her breasts in the patch of moonlight that filtered in at the window.

He stared at her intently, not thinking of her, but of Dicia, who was probably in their bed waiting for him to come back, as he had in Philadelphia, and his body began to respond at the thought of her.

"I won't!" he whispered to himself angrily. "I won't go to her!" Yet he knew if he didn't get rid of the anger and frustration, if he didn't release the pent-up desires that were overwhelming him, he'd end up making love to her as he always did, and she'd never suffer for what she'd done.

Slowly, methodically he began removing his clothes, his eyes never leaving the silent figure on the bed, and suddenly Rachel stirred, aware that someone was in the room, and she opened her eyes slowly, hesitantly, her heart in her throat.

At first she thought it was Brandon. But as she watched the vague figure beside her bed, there was no mistaking the breadth of his shoulders and the familiar stance. She sighed, surprised, and instead of crying out, she held her breath as she silently watched him, her heart pounding.

He became aware of her eyes on him as he stepped from his pants, and now that he'd committed himself, a cold fear trickled down his spine. What if it didn't work? What if he was unable to take her, as it had been with Chatte? What if he couldn't stay hard? Wouldn't Dicia like that! What a triumph for her to know the power she had over him. He had to go on, if for no other reason that to prove that he could.

He stood for a moment in his underwear, staring at Rachel's figure before him on the bed, and suddenly she spoke. "You intend to rape me?" she asked casually, her voice sultry, but it was more of an invitation than a question, and he felt the blood rush to his head, warming him clear through. The passionate craving the drink had aroused inside him set his blood racing, and he stepped to the bed, dropping onto the covers, leaning over her, looking down into her face.

"Not unless you intend to fight," he answered unsteadily; then he smiled maliciously. "But you won't, will you?" She moved beneath him as if to get away, then sighed sensuously as his mouth came down on hers hard and demanding, and she returned his kiss eagerly.

He lost little time in preliminaries, his anger prodding him on. His hands were rough with their caresses, and there was no love given as he thrust into her over and over again, his kisses bruising her lips as he fought for the escape his body craved. Yet, much to his surprise, she matched him movement for movement, her cravings as savage as his, her body answering him back with an ardent passion that amazed him. Each time he hurt her she moaned in ecstasy, begging for more, her hands grasping, her body pleading, trying to reach the climax that in spite of his urgency seemed to be eluding her, until he thrust hard, forcing a sharp cry from her lips, and he came, exploding inside her, and she wrapped her legs about him, holding tightly.

She felt his huge bearlike body tremble between her legs, and reached up, pulling his mouth down on hers, reveling in the wonder of the moment, in the hardness of his body. She didn't want it to stop, not yet, but as suddenly as it started, she felt him slump against her, and without one word of endearment and only a halfhearted caress, he rolled off, stretched out beside her, and within minutes was fast asleep, the ale on his breath revealing only too well its part in his actions. But she didn't care. She'd had what she'd wanted. He hadn't fulfilled her completely, but what he had given her was wild and wanton, love or no love. She could wait for that.

She reached over, touching his hair, smiling to herself, and sighed, wondering what his precious little wife would do if she knew where he was. Then, still aching because she had been denied her full pleasure, but extremely pleased with what she had accomplished, she snuggled close and closed her eyes, settling against him until she too finally fell asleep.

Loedicia stirred as the first gray light of dawn began to filter slowly into the room. She moved in the big bed, then suddenly, as if someone had slapped her face, she sat bolt upright, her eyes wide, scowling. Instinct seemed to tell her something was wrong. As her eyes fell on the stand where the candle, once long and tall, had burned all night until all that was left was a puddle of cold wax, fear gripped her; then she glanced quickly to the bed beside her, a cold chill tickling her spine. He hadn't come back!

She frowned frantically, slipping from the bed, rubbing her forehead. What time had she fallen asleep? It was almost morning now, and the sun would be coming up soon. She moved to the balcony and stared out into the gradually fading darkness, hiding her naked body behind the heavy green drapes, her heart pounding. What if something had happened? This wasn't like him. He always came back . . . she knew he'd come back, unless something was wrong. What if . . .? He'd had a good sum of money on him. What if he'd been robbed? Or worse yet, Lord Chaucer'd stop at nothing to get him out of the way.

She moved to the chair and hastily pulled on her wrapper, tightening the sash hard about her waist. She could wake the servants. She hesitated, holding the ends of the sash. No! Not that. They wouldn't know what to do, where to go for help.

The duchess! She should know what to do. After all, London was her city. She'd know whom to contact. Something had happened, she knew it. Quinn always came back, no matter how bitter the words had been. He must be hurt somewhere, sprawled in a gutter.

Hurriedly she opened the door and left the room, her bare feet noiseless on the hall carpet. Not even the servants were about at this hour, and it was so dark she could barely see. She stopped at the door to the duchess's room and raised her hand to knock, then thought better of it, afraid the knocking would echo too loudly in the empty hallway, waking the whole household, and her hand dropped, closing about the doorknob.

The room was shrouded in darkness as she slipped quietly in and closed the door, then turned, her eyes taking in the heavy red velvet draperies that hung at the windows and about the bed. She squinted, trying to see better. If the curtains were open all the way it would help, but she shrugged, then softly tiptoed toward the huge ornate bed.

Suddenly she stopped abruptly a few feet from the bed and held her breath as something within its depths stirred and moved and she heard a deep, masculine moan. As she stared, transfixed, she saw an arm slowly raise, followed by a feminine sigh; then, as the figure nearest the edge of the bed turned her way, she found herself frozen to the spot, looking directly into Quinn's drowsy, sleep-filled eyes, and her heart fell to her feet.

She stood for a moment dumbfounded, unable to believe her own eyes, unable to accept what she was seeing; then, unconsciously an agonized groan wrenched itself from her throat. "My God, no!" she cried as tears filled her eyes, and Quinn, his brain still half-drugged from the ale, his body weary from its night of vigorous pleasure, tried to focus his bloodshot eyes, but it was almost impossible.

Then, as if a veil was lifting, he realized something was wrong and began shaking his head as if to clear it, unable yet to grasp what was happening, even forgetting where he was.

Loedicia watched as he stared at her, bewildered, and a sob lumped in her throat, choking her, tears rolling down her cheeks as Rachel sat up beside him, smiling smugly, running her hand up his arm to his shoulder possessively, her eyes never leaving Loedicia's face.

Loedicia's hand flew to her mouth, and she bit the knuckles on the back of her hand between her teeth, trying to fight the humiliation and anger that were tearing her apart; then, unable to look on the sight anymore, she let out a pathetic cry and dropped her hand, running from the room, out into the hall.

It wasn't happening! It couldn't be! She ran breathlessly to her room, flinging open the door, then stepped inside and shut it, leaning back against it, shutting her eyes, trying to blot out the sight. Her body convulsed as she began to sob hysterically, and her knees weakened as she groped her way to the bed, falling facedown, burying her head in the pillow.

It couldn't be happening, but it was! She'd seen him with her own eyes . . . and that bitch! Oh, Quinn, why? Why? Why?

She pushed herself up on the bed, still crying miserably, hugging her pillow to her as a child would cling to a stuffed toy for comfort, her feet curled beneath her, leaning against the bedpost, staring toward the doors that opened onto the balcony, letting the tears fall from her face unchecked.

When had it begun? With Heath? No, not really. It began long before that. It began the first time Quinn made love to her that night he'd returned when they'd thought he'd been dead. She remembered his words now as if it were yesterday. She'd lain beneath him, ecstatic in her love for him, accepting his love again with no restraints as she'd always done before, and it was his lips against her ear that echoed the birth of his obsession.

"You see what it is with us, Dicia," he'd whispered passionately, his voice low, almost bitter. "Tell me, could Roth ever give you this?" and she remembered the sudden sharp pain that swept over her as he'd said it, only she'd ignored the warning, shoving it to the back of her mind. Nothing was going to spoil their reunion. But it had. From that day on he'd fought a battle with Roth in his head. Trying to compete with a ghost from the past because he couldn't stand the thought of another man having made love to her.

Yes, it had begun there, then been nurtured and kept alive as Heath grew toward manhood. It had pulled at the fabric of their marriage and torn it apart, and now . . . She wanted to die!

Her heart ached with a physical pain almost too hard to bear, and she trembled violently, shaking inside. "Not this," she whispered torturously to herself. "Please . . . not this. Let it be a nightmare." But she knew it wasn't. It wasn't! And she cried all the harder. Quinn had slept with the duchess! He'd let the duchess share what she'd known. His hands had caressed Rachel, his lips warmed hers, bringing her rapture she had no right to feel. She had no right to him!

She cried bitterly, cringing at the thought of his betrayal, of his body pressed intimately against Rachel's, letting Rachel know the ecstasy of his fulfillment as she knew it, and she shivered violently in the huge bed.

Suddenly the door flew open and Quinn stepped in. His hair was tousled yet from sleep; he was barefoot and bare-chested, wearing only his pants, with the rest of his clothes hanging on his arm, and he flung them on a chair near the door as he shut it behind him, then stood staring at her.

She glanced up into his cold blue eyes and her heart went dead inside her. She'd seen him like this only once before, the night he'd made her choose between him and Roth, and she hugged the pillow even tighter against her trembling body as she tried to stop crying.

Quinn's knees felt weak, his mouth tasted like sand, and his stomach was doing somersaults against his backbone. The anger that had driven him last night was still nagging at him, his head felt twice its size, and he felt sick inside. He stared back at her, seeing the agony in her eyes, unable to say anything. Unable to put into words what he felt.

What could he say? I'm sorry? How inept! I didn't mean it? But he had. He'd meant it at the time. God damn he had! He'd purposely sought Rachel out. Then what? What could he do to change the look on her face and make love shine in her eyes again instead of the hate he saw now? How could he tell her he still loved her, that he was sick inside over what he'd done? That he wished now he had come crawling back to her because he'd found nothing in the duchess's arms but emptiness. Savage emptiness!

He swallowed hard and straightened. He had to try something, anything. "I'm sorry," he blurted clumsily, his voice husky and strained, and a rush of new tears flooded her eyes as she tried to hold them back.

"Sorry?" her angry voice squeaked unnaturally, breaking on a sob. "My God, Quinn, was my sin so vile?" she gasped. "Did I deserve this?" The pillow dropped from her arms and she leaned toward him across the bed. "Do you really hate me that much?"

"Hate you?"

"Yes, hate me. Why else would you crawl in bed with that woman?"

He looked away. "You wouldn't understand."

"No I wouldn't!"

He glanced back quickly, and his jaw tightened as he stepped to the bed and knelt beside it, looking up into her face. "Dicia, please listen to me, please," he said, and she gulped back the tears.

"Why? Why should I listen to anything you have to say?"

She hesitated, swallowing back the sobs. "You made it clear last night."

He reached out and tried to grab her hand, but she pulled it away. "Dicia, please!"

"Don't touch me! Talk all you want," she cried, "but don't touch me."

He rested his head dejectedly on the bed, facedown on the covers, shutting his eyes, trying to hold back the tears of frustration. He was losing her and he knew it, and his heart was breaking in two.

Then slowly he raised his head again and stared off into space, away from her accusing eyes, and his voice was almost inaudible as he spoke. "A long time ago, when I fell in love with you, Dicia," he began, "I hadn't wanted to. I'd vowed never to give my heart to any woman. Then you were there and everything I fought against overwhelmed me. For the first time in my life I wanted a woman so badly that nothing else mattered. You became my life, the air I breathed, the only thing worth living for. Then suddenly when I thought you were dead, I died too." He hesitated a minute, then went on. "I told you about the half-breed girl, Chatte. I couldn't even perform as a man anymore without you; then I went to Philadelphia, and there you were and life was sweet again . . . almost." He hung his head, still avoiding her eyes. "I thought I could accept what happened between you and Roth. I kept trying to tell myself that you thought I was dead, but it was so hard. Then Heath came along and life was intolerable. Every time I looked at him I died a little inside. I'd loved him, Dicia, but he wasn't mine. He became a reminder of the intimacy you'd shared with Roth. Whenever I took you in my arms, I wondered . . . did he do it like this? Had his lips brought more response than mine? And whenever I thought I hadn't satisfied you, I was so afraid it was because you'd enjoyed his lovemaking more than mine . . . that you'd loved him more than you'd loved me . . . yet, I couldn't let you go . . ." His voice broke and he turned to look into her eyes, but was unable to fathom their depths, and he went on. "When Roth showed up here in London, I saw your reaction to him after all these years, and I wanted to kill him, but I knew if I did I'd lose you. I couldn't lose you. Without you I thought I wasn't even a man anymore. You did things to me no other woman could. To lose you . . ." He gestured helplessly. "I fooled myself into believing there was nothing, then I saw the two of you in the summer house . . . I hated you for that, Dicia." His voice faltered. "At least I kept telling myself I hated you. That's why I stormed out of here and started drinking. I wanted to forget you and the hurt you'd given me."

He stood up and began to pace the floor as she stared at him unmoving; then he stopped walking, facing her again. "You had no right to do that to me," he cried. "You tore the heart right out of me, and all the way back to the house I fought with myself. Part of me wanted to come back to you and take you in my arms and tell you I didn't care. That I loved you and could never stop loving you, but my pride and the drink wouldn't let me."

He dropped to his knees by the bed again. "The other part of me kept telling me I had to get you out of my system, prove to myself that I didn't need you, that it didn't matter, that I was still a man even without you, that I didn't have to come crawling back to you. . . ."

He straightened suddenly, his face taut, almost haggard-looking. "Do you know what I proved, Dicia?" he asked softly, tears brimming his eyes; then he answered himself. "I proved to myself what a damn fool I am! I need you, Dicia, my God I need you," and the tears streamed down his face. "I took Rachel, yes, but there was no love, no warmth, only anger, bitterness, and frustration. It was nothing without you. It was empty and meaningless. I was a drunken fool and now I don't know what to do." His voice choked up. "When I opened my eyes this morning and saw you standing there, then felt her hand on my shoulder . . . Oh, God, forgive me, Dicia, forgive me," he pleaded, and his head dropped to the bed as he sagged against it, crying like a wounded animal.

She stared at his blond head, watching his bare shoulders, the muscles rippling across his back as his body shook with every sob. It was the first time she'd ever seen him cry. This big, brawny creature God had thrust into the wilderness. This magnificent man who'd warmed her heart and her bed, a man with the strength of a bear, yet he was crying like a baby.

She shook her head, tears flooding her eyes again, and she wept with him, shaking her head in frustration, not knowing what to do. "Oh, Quinn," she cried bitterly, wiping the tears from her cheeks with the back of her hand. "I don't know what to do . . . I don't know . . ."

He raised his head slowly as he tried to stop crying, and he looked directly into her eyes. "Dicia, oh, my love, I know I have no right to ask it . . . and I couldn't blame you if you said no, but I beg you, give me another chance. I've never begged for anything before in my life, but I'm begging you now, forgive me. I can't live without you, I know that now more than ever. Please, please . . .?"

He reached out and took her hand, feeling her muscles tense as she started to pull away, but he held it tighter. "Please," he whispered softly, trying not to cry. "Don't pull away from me, Dicia, I couldn't stand it, please."

She looked down at his hand holding hers, then back to his tearstained face. "What do you want of me, Quinn?" she finally asked, her voice bitter, the tears still on her cheeks. "I'm to forget so quickly? You sleep with another woman, no matter the reason, you give her the love only I should have, you let her experience something that should be mine alone, and then you expect a few tears to wash away the sin? I only kissed Roth, Quinn, and it took your adultery to wash away my sin and make you forget. . . . I'm afraid it'll take more than a few tears to make me forget."

He frowned, unable to answer, unable to reason with her because she was right, and he dropped her hand as he stood up, and walked over, pulling a handkerchief from the pocket of his coat, and blew his nose hard, then turned back to her.

"You win . . . you know that, don't you?" he said softly, tucking the handkerchief in his pants pocket, breathing a sigh. "Twice in my life you've reduced me to tears—when I thought you were dead, and now. I love you, Dicia, I always will, and I want your forgiveness more than anything in the world, but I won't beg anymore. Right now you're feeling what I've felt all these years, the agony of knowing what you shared with Roth . . ."

"You'd compare that to this? I didn't commit adultery!"

His jaw tightened stubbornly. "The hurt's the same. You think there's a difference?"

She flinched and her eyes darkened as he straightened arrogantly. "All I can do now," he said, "is wait until your heart's ready."

Her eyes flashed. "And if that day never comes?"

"It will," he whispered softly, and his eyes bored into hers.

Something should have stirred inside her as it always did before when he looked at her, but there was nothing, only an empty angry feeling.

"I hope to God you're right," she answered belligerently, "because right now I could kill you!"

He walked over and stood staring down at her, his magnificent body only reminding her all the more of his infidelity, and she couldn't stand it anymore. She had to lash out, do something to ease the pain.

She threw her head back, and her teeth ground together viciously as she clenched her fists, closing her eyes. "Get out!" she whispered hoarsely, her heart breaking into little pieces; then she opened her eyes again and stared at him furiously, her voice rising in volume. "Get out, I can't stand to look at you," she sobbed. "Get out of my sight, leave me alone. I'll never forgive you, never! Do you hear? Nothing will ever repay what you've done to me." And she leaped toward him, almost falling off the bed, stumbling against him, her fists pounding his bare chest, trying to hurt him any way she could, and she sobbed against him bitterly, pleading, "Get out of my sight!"

But instead, he grabbed her wrists and pulled her against him, wrapping his arms about her, holding her close.

"Let me go," she cried breathlessly, feeling the strength of him against her, knowing she couldn't fight him. "Let me go, Quinn, I hate you," she sobbed, but he shook his head.

"No!" he said softly. "I won't ever let you go," and suddenly his mouth covered hers and he was kissing her, hard at first as she struggled, then softly as her struggling subsided, his mouth sipping at her hungrily, bringing her to life once more. "I love you," he whispered against her mouth. "I love you," and she knew it was no use.

She'd never forgive him, the hurt and humiliation would always be there, but she couldn't lie to herself either, she'd never leave him. As long as he wanted her, she'd be here. It wouldn't be the same, not for a while, and maybe never, she didn't know, but she'd try, she had to try.

He drew his head back and gazed into her eyes, marveling at how beautiful she was even now. "Please forgive me," he pleaded softly, tenderly. "I swear by all that's holy it'll never happen again," and she nodded.

"I'll try," she murmured, sniffing in, trying not to cry. "I'll try, Quinn, but . . . oh, God . . . I can't promise . . ."

He pulled her closer in his arms. "Thank you," he whispered, and picked her up gently, setting her on the bed, his hands beginning to caress her, but it was too soon.

"No," she cried. "Not now! I can't, Quinn, not now," and he frowned as he saw the look of fear and revulsion in her eyes.

He should have expected it, but it had caught him unawares, and he swallowed hard as he straightened, reaching out instead for her hand. "Then shall we get dressed?" he asked, but she drew back.

"I can't face her, Quinn," she retorted, her face flushed. "I just can't!"

He sat on the bed beside her, looking down at her. "Dicia, before I left her I told her in not very pleasant words that she never slept with Quinn Locke last night, she slept with a drunken fool. Quinn Locke belongs to his wife and always will, and only she'll know the real man, not the sodden imitation who made an ass of himself last night. So hold your head up, my love, and prove to her that I'm right. That my wife is the most beautiful woman in the world and the *only* woman as far as I'm concerned." He reached down and tucked a curl in by the nape of her neck as his eyes watched the valley between her breasts where her heart was pounding; then they moved to her violet eyes, so sad. "I love you. Oh, God, I love you," he whispered, and she swallowed hard. It was going to take a long time. A very long time . . .

The atmosphere in the huge house on Grosvenor Square was strained for the rest of the morning. The duchess, her hair piled high atop her head, her dress immodestly low in front, tried with all her womanly wiles to recapture Quinn's attentions, only to be rebuffed with a cold indifference that left her furious. And Quinn maneuvered between Dicia and Rachel, turning himself off and on like an actor on a stage, trying to convince Dicia that what happened last night was a mistake, being overly solicitous toward her, hoping in his heart she'd forgive him, that he hadn't pushed her too far, yet trying not to make himself appear to be groveling.

But for Dicia each moment was like a living hell. She was exceptionally quiet, her usual warmth and effervescence replaced by a quiet restraint. She spoke only when spoken to, her words as few as possible, and her eyes were often rimmed with tears. It was so hard. Every time she saw the duchess a wave of nausea would sweep over her and she'd try to fight the hate that seeped into her heart. And the more Quinn tried to make her forget, the more she remembered, and she wondered if anything would ever be the same again between them.

The late-morning sun felt good on Rebel's face as she

stood in the garden beside Brandon and reached out, accepting the yellow rose he held out to her.

"Something's wrong, I just know it," she said as she caressed the rose, then smelled its sweet fragrance. "Mother's acting so strangely. Whatever it is, it started at the lawn party yesterday."

"You couldn't be imagining it?"

"You've seen them, can't you tell? Mother looks so unhappy, and father's acting like some kind of a ninny. I know he's always been a bit touched in the head when it came to my mother, but it's ridiculous. He's done everything but breathe for her this morning. As if he couldn't do enough for her. For a stubborn, willful cuss, he's acting . . . well, it's just not normal."

"Maybe they had an argument about something." He hesitated, then looked at her knowingly. "And if my guess is right, it's probably because of Roth Chapman." She glanced at him sharply. "What is he to your mother anyway?" he asked suddenly, and she frowned.

"An old friend of Mother's and Father's, that's all."

"A friend of your mother's, yes, but not your father's."

"It's a long story," retorted Rebel. "One I'm sure wouldn't interest you."

"Anything that concerns you interests me," he said, and she blushed, turning away from him, starting to stroll toward the house.

He watched her intently, the long flaxen hair like spun gold in the sunlight, her lithe figure moving gracefully ahead of him, and he felt a warmth clear to his toes. How many times he'd looked into her violet eyes, almost drowned in them the past few weeks, yet he hadn't even kissed her.

He watched the swing of her hips beneath the folds of her emerald-green dress and began to wonder what it would be like to caress those hips and run his hands up her body, feeling it come alive beneath him, and he swallowed hard. She was a rare contrast of explosive innocence, and he wanted her more than he'd ever wanted any woman before, and he suspected, if given free rein, she'd put Rachel to shame when it came to a bed partner. That is, if you could get her into bed. He had a feeling she'd never let a man lay hands on her outside of marriage. There was a coldness about her at times that puzzled him.

He frowned as he realized he'd been neglecting Rachel lately. It had been weeks since he'd slipped into her room.

Surprisingly, she hadn't complained, but then, her year of mourning was over and she'd had more than a half dozen suitors at her beck and call since the night of the ball. Besides, she'd been too busy making eyes at Rebel's father lately. But maybe he'd visit her tonight. He was getting a bit itchy, and she was better than nothing until he could get what he really wanted. His eyes sifted over Rebel hungrily. God, she'd really be something!

Rebel turned and eyed Brandon curiously, wondering what he was thinking. Ever since that night in the library he'd made it a point to take her riding, escort her to the dining hall at dinnertime, dance with her as often as possible at socials, and catch her alone in the garden whenever he could, but so far, except for the looks he'd given her, he'd said nothing to indicate that he cared, but she was sure he did. The way he squeezed her hand and held her close when they were dancing was anything but platonic. He cared all right, but was it enough?

She'd heard gossip that Brandon Avery, although being eligible, had no place in his life for a wife. It seems more than one young lady had tried to make him come up to scratch, only to discover that his ambitions left no room for love. Oh, he enjoyed the ladies tremendously, but avoided any involvement that would curtail his freedom, and rumor was that if all went well he was to receive a governorship in some foreign territory, a feat not often accomplished by a man so young.

Yes, it would take more than a few smiles and seductive looks to capture the Duke of Bourland, and Rebel realized she'd set herself quite a task. There were other dukes, to be sure, and they'd probably be eager for her hand; some had already let their feelings be known, but most of them were either half again her age or quite unattractive. At least Brandon was good-looking, even if there was a hard core about him that made her wary and almost frightened at times. He had little compassion for anyone, be it servant or peer, and she had the distinct feeling that he'd stop at nothing to achieve his ambitions. But he was a duke, and she'd made her mind up to be a duchess.

"I'm going to the sale at Newcastle to pick out some horses this afternoon," the duke said as he watched her. "Would you care to come?" and she smiled.

"Only if I can help you pick out the horses," she answered, which was no surprise to him, and the rest of the way to the house they talked of horses, and the weather, and everything except what was really on their minds, and as they entered the main salon they were confronted by the butler, Jarvis, who looked very unnerved.

"What is it?" asked Brandon as he took Rebel's arm and escorted her toward Jarvis.

"Your Grace," the man blurted, his usual composure seriously shaken, "there are soldiers and men here and they're asking for Mr. Locke, your Grace," and Rebel's heart skipped a beat as the words tumbled out of the man.

"Where are they?" asked Brandon sharply, and Jarvis nodded toward the foyer. The duke looked at Rebel quickly, frowning. "It sounds like Lord Chaucer has decided to make good his threat," he said as she stared at him apprehensively. "I certainly hope your father knows what he's doing," and he turned to the servant, ordering him to bring Quinn to the foyer; then he took Rebel's arm and they followed Jarvis out.

There were four soldiers and two men in plain clothes standing in the foyer, just inside the door, and Brandon didn't like the looks of it as they introduced themselves. The older of the two men had a warrant for Quinn's arrest on a charge of murder.

"This is preposterous," announced the duke as he read the warrant, then handed it back to the man. "Not only has it been eighteen years since Lord Varrick's death, but it took place on foreign soil."

"I believe at the time, your Grace, the United States was under British rule," the man reminded him, and Brandon's eyes narrowed as Quinn stepped into the foyer, followed by Loedicia and Lizette, and he wondered if the thought had occurred to Quinn.

"This sir, is Mr. Locke," announced the duke as Quinn stopped a few feet from the man, and the man handed the warrant to him.

Quinn's jaw tightened hard as he read it, then handed it back. "On whose authority was this written?" he asked sternly, and the man cleared his throat.

"On authority of his Majesty King George."

Quinn hesitated. This was preposterous. He hadn't expected Elton to carry through with his threat. He thought he'd only been bluffing, but now . . . He frowned, wondering what kind of proof he could possibly have shown the king to make him willing to back him on such a stupid play.

He felt Dicia's eyes on him and knew she was thinking: I told you so. Damn Chaucer! How could he have convinced the king? He glanced quickly at the soldiers, and for the first time in his life fear crept down his spine. Chaucer was out to stop him any way he could, even by hanging if need be, and he could almost feel the rope tightening about his throat. He shouldn't have taken the man so lightly, but still, Chaucer couldn't possibly have proof. If he knew what really happened he'd be after Loedicia. Unless he counted on him covering for his wife. Or maybe . . . Anything could happen to a man while in prison, and often did . . . It could easily be blamed on the other prisoners.

"This is ridiculous," stated Quinn. "There must be some mistake," but the men were determined.

"Nevertheless, you'll have to come with us, sir, until it's straightened out," said the taller of the two men. "In the meantime, I'm afraid you're under arrest."

Quinn's eyes flashed angrily as he turned to the duke.

"I'll see what I can do," offered Brandon, "but it may not be easy. Chaucer can really throw his weight around when he wants to."

"And in the meantime I suppose I have to sit in some filthy cell just to please him."

Brandon wished he could help. Quinn wasn't the kind of man to be confined; besides, he needed him out of prison, not in. But his hands were tied for the moment, and Elton had warned him. The charge was legitimate; the only question now was whether it could be proved, and Quinn had assured him earlier that it could not, because he hadn't killed Lord Varrick. For some strange reason, however, Brandon had the distinct impression that he knew who had.

"Shall we go, sir?" asked the tall man as he stared at Quinn, and Quinn flinched as he felt Loedicia touch his arm and he glanced down at her beside him. It was hard to read the expression on her face, but there were tears in her eyes, which were still puffy from her crying the night before.

"Quinn . . . I can tell them the truth," she started softly, only to see his face harden.

"Shut up!" he growled sternly. "I'll get out of it. He can't make it stick. It'll be all right."

"But I can—"

"No! You're not to say a word," he commanded harshly, trying to keep his voice low. "Not a word, do you hear?" and she stared at him hesitantly.

"But I can clear you. It doesn't have to be—"

"Shut up!" His face was white, his lips pursed as his voice

softened. "You'll say nothing, Dicia!" He turned to the man quickly. "May I get my hat and cloak?" he asked, but the man shook his head.

"Can't let you out of my sight, sir, sorry," he said, and Brandon rang for Jarvis, who brought Quinn's black cloak and broad-brimmed hat while Quinn tried to say good-bye to Loedicia and assure her it would be all right, but his good-bye was strained.

Loedicia had still not recovered from last night, and he knew it, but at the moment he didn't care. He slipped his cloak on, grabbed his hat, then turned, pulling her into his arms, holding her close as he looked down into her face.

"You're not to say anything to anyone, do you understand?" he cautioned her, whispering. "He's managed to fabricate some kind of evidence to look good."

"But you can't sit in prison."

"I've endured worse." He tried to smile. "Besides, it won't be for long. I wager Brandon'll have me out by morning." He glanced quickly at the duke. "Won't you, Brandon?" and Brandon understood what Quinn was trying to do.

"I'll get on it as soon as you leave," he said, only he knew Quinn was really worried, by the look in his eyes.

He kissed Loedicia and Rebel and said good-bye to Teak, who'd slipped quietly into the room while they talked, followed by the duchess. And when all the good-byes were said, with an extra reassurance to Loedicia that things would be all right, he was escorted from the house into a large covered carriage, and Loedicia stepped outside after him, watching stoically from the top of the steps as the carriage lumbered down the front drive and out the wide gate.

She was still angry, hurt, and upset and it felt like her insides were having a battle of their own to keep her breakfast down. She loved him. Watching him go, as he marched tall and erect with the men in black in the lead, a soldier on each side and two soldiers behind, he towered over them all, proud and handsome, and she knew she still loved him, but the hurt he'd given her was a deep wound, and she was afraid it was going to leave a wicked scar. She could feel it twisting inside, the physical ache that made her almost hate him, yet her heart went with him as he left the house.

Rebel stepped up behind her and watched too as the carriage disappeared through the gate. She glanced quickly at her mother, watching the straight stance, wondering what her mother was feeling. There'd been a hesitancy in the reaction to her husband's kiss that had not slipped by Rebel.

The duke stood beside Rebel and addressed Loedicia. "May I speak to you in private, Loedicia?" he asked, and Loedicia turned around slowly, and Rebel winced as she saw the tears on her mother's cheeks and the pained look in her eyes.

Loedicia wiped the tears away hurriedly as she acknowledged the duke, and they left the others, entering the library at the end of the hall.

Brandon closed the door behind him, then walked over to Loedicia, who stood by the desk, her hands clasped together firmly as she waited for him.

"Back there you said you could clear Quinn," the duke began without any preliminaries, and he scowled. "Just what did you mean?"

She bit her lip as she stared at him, then turned her back. "I can't tell you."

"Do you realize how serious this is?" he asked as he watched her closely. "Elton's not playing games. He's playing for keeps and he has the king on his side. That means it doesn't matter whether Quinn's guilty or not, they can maneuver it any way they want."

"But they'll have to take it before the magistrate."

"With paid witnesses and a judge who'll be instructed ahead of time on what to say as per the king's orders."

She whirled around. "They can't do that," she blurted.

"They can and they will. How do you think the king rids himself of his enemies?"

Her eyes suddenly came to life. "Can you get an audience with the king?"

His eyebrows raised.

"Well, can you?" she demanded, and he scowled.

"Maybe . . . I guess."

"Good. Do it."

"What good will that do?"

"If the king knows the truth . . ."

"What is the truth?"

She looked at him speculatively, remembering Quinn's vehement order to keep her mouth shut. But if what Brandon said was true, she had to tell the truth, she couldn't let them hang him. "I want to know what proof they have against Quinn first," she answered, and Brandon exhaled.

She was as stubborn as Quinn. "I'll see what I can do," he said. "But I wish I knew what was going on."

"Please . . ." Loedicia held out her hand and touched his arm. "Please, trust me."

"I haven't much choice, have I?"

"Quinn didn't kill his cousin," she stated emphatically.

"So he's told me before." He turned to walk away. "I'll send a messenger and see if the king will see us," he said, then left the room.

Loedicia turned and walked to the window, looking outside across the front lawn to the gates, where carriages hurried along on the crowded streets, and wished with all her heart she'd never set foot in London.

14

The palace of St. James's was more than Loedicia dreamed. Such wealth and beauty, yet it was like a fortress, and walking its halls was a privilege for the very few, and she thanked God that at the moment she was one of those few. She'd dressed in her best today. The already cool air was working its way toward winter, and her violet dress and black velvet cape seemed quite appropriate for the visit, but as she walked beside the duke, resplendent in a deep blue brocade coat, a deep blue velvet cape hanging from his shoulders, with velvet shoes and a diamond stickpin in his cravat, she felt inadequate and her heart was fluttering so nervously it weakened her knees. What if the messenger had made a mistake? What if the king had changed his mind? Yet, they'd been escorted this far.

The duke had requested a private audience and was rather pleased, yet surprised, when they were escorted to the king's private chambers, where only the king and his secretary waited.

Loedicia stared curiously as the king greeted them. She hadn't known what to expect, but was surprised to see a man quite small in stature compared to her husband, with an arrogant face, paunchy body, and rather wild eyes that looked her over minutely from head to toe as he lounged on the plush royal chair, his long ermine-trimmed robe sprawling majestically about him.

"Well, and who is it we have here, Brandon?" he asked as he greeted the duke, and Brandon watched his eyes shine as they studied Loedicia. The king always did have an eye for women, and Brandon had to admit Loedicia Locke was still a very beautiful woman.

"May I present Loedicia Locke, your Majesty," he introduced cautiously, and the king's eyes narrowed slightly as he looked at her.

"Locke? The name's familiar," he acknowledged purposefully. "I believe I authorized the arrest of a man named Locke just this morning on the recommendation of Lord Chaucer," he said. "Are you a relative?"

Her heart fell to her feet as she bowed in a low curtsy. He looked none too happy. "I'm his wife, your Majesty," she answered truthfully, "and if you'll excuse the impertinence, it was I who asked the duke to arrange this meeting."

"Oh?" He glanced quickly at Brandon.

"Yes," she continued. "If you'd be so kind, your Majesty . . . I can't imagine what makes you think my husband is responsible for Lord Varrick's death."

The king tilted his nose back, looking down at her, then glanced impatiently at Brandon. "You brought this woman here to plead for her husband?" he asked.

"I brought her because she said she wants you to know the truth of the matter."

He looked back at Loedicia. "I already know the truth of the matter," he said sarcastically. "Lord Chaucer has filled me in with the details brought back to him years ago when he sent a man to America to investigate the murder, and at this moment, my dear woman, I have a letter in my possession that was sent to the present earl a short time after Lord Varrick's death, and the letter states that any questions as to the death of one Lord Kendall Varrick can be answered by Quinn Locke, who was present at the time and instrumental in his death."

Loedicia took a deep breath. "May I ask who signed the letter, your Majesty?" she asked, and the king turned to his secretary, snapping his fingers, then holding out his hand, into which the secretary set a piece of yellowed paper.

The king perused it slowly, then looked up at her. "The writing is rather crude, Mrs. Locke," he answered, "but the signature looks to be that of a Mr. Ramsey, the same gentleman I believe who gave Lord Chaucer's agent the original story years ago. He described himself as a friend of Lord Varrick."

Her eyes darkened. "He was no friend, your Majesty," she answered angrily. "He was a backwoodsman who'd betrayed my husband and caused the death of his friends and the burning of Fort Locke. He was there that night, yes, but he was a paid assassin hired by Lord Varrick to kill my husband."

"Those are harsh words, madam."

"But true."

"You have proof?"

"I was there."

The king's eyes widened. "You were there when Lord Varrick was killed?"

Loedicia swallowed hard and wrung her hands nervously, feeling the damp palms pressed together, hot and clammy. There was no turning back now. "Yes," she said softly, and the king grunted as Brandon glanced at her sharply.

"Speak up, woman," retorted the king, gesturing with his hand. "Did I hear you say yes?"

Loedicia nodded. "Yes, your Majesty," she answered loudly, her voice quivering. "I was there," and his eyes widened curiously. "In fact"—she hesitated momentarily, praying for courage—"in fact, I'm the one who killed Lord Varrick, not my husband," and the king sat motionless, his eyes intent on Loedicia's face, and he scowled as Brandon gasped.

"You jest, madam," he blurted arrogantly.

"No, your Majesty, I do not," she answered. "Lord Varrick and his men attacked us in the bedroom when we were sleeping. During the struggle Lord Varrick's pistol fell to the floor, and when he attacked my husband with a knife I grabbed the pistol and shot him."

The king's fingers began to tap irritably on the arm of his plush chair, and his eyes narrowed. "Unbelievable," he said hastily, shaking his head, "quite unbelievable," and he leaned back as he looked at her. "A woman will attempt many things to save the man she loves, Mrs. Locke," he went on, "and your confession was commendable, but not necessary and totally uncalled for. Your husband will stand trial for murder."

Loedicia's eyes blazed. "But he's not guilty, I am!" she cried. "I killed Lord Varrick!"

"And you're willing to hang for it?"

"If self-defense is a hanging offense, then yes," she answered, and he cleared his throat. "But I don't think it is, is it?"

"It isn't," he answered. "But I still can't believe your story, dear lady."

"But you have to!"

He straightened in his chair as Brandon looked sideways at her and reached out to take her arm, but she wrenched it from him.

"Mrs. Locke, I don't have to do anything I don't desire," the king stated haughtily.

Her dark curls bobbed as she jerked her head, looking from the king to Brandon and back again. "Whom would you believe?" she asked quickly, her eyes pleading, and the king settled back smugly.

"You have another witness besides the gentleman who wrote this letter?" he asked as he waved the letter toward her, and Loedicia froze, her eyes staring hard at the letter in his hands.

Another witness? Her heart sank. God, yes, she did have another witness. Roth! He'd been there.

"Well, Mrs. Locke, do you?" the king asked once more, and Loedicia hesitated.

"I . . . yes . . ." she answered slowly, drawing her eyes from the letter to look at his pasty face. "Yes, there is another witness," and King George's mouth slid into a sneer.

"Indeed!" he remarked sarcastically. "And who might it be?"

She straightened her shoulders nervously, as she bit her lip. "There's a gentleman, an American . . . he was here in London only yesterday . . ."

The king reached out and waved his fingers impatiently as she fumbled for the right words. "His name, Mrs. Locke, his name?" he asked, and Loedicia sighed.

"Roth, Mr. Rothford Chapman," she answered softly, and saw a strange look enter the king's eyes as Brandon stared at her, bewildered.

The king straightened and leaned forward, his face intent on hers. "You mean the grandson of the late Earl of Cumberland?" and Loedicia hesitated.

"I . . . I mean Mr. Rothford Chapman from America," she corrected him, but King George nodded his head.

"One and the same, Mrs. Locke," he retorted hurriedly. "His father was the fourth son of the Earl of Cumberland, but tell me, how is it he's your witness?"

Loedicia was flabbergasted. Roth had never mentioned anything about being related to nobility. He'd said his father was a merchant and shipbuilder, but the fourth son of an earl . . . ?

"I . . . we were staying in the same house," she answered

reluctantly, not wanting to say why. "It belonged to friends of his who lived in Philadelphia."

"And he was there when Lord Varrick was killed?"

"Yes, your Majesty," and she related the event as much as she possibly could without revealing her marriage to Roth. Telling how Roth and Burly heard the commotion and ran to help and were there when the actual shot was fired.

"Hmmmm," King George mused when she'd finished, and he settled back again, studying her intently. She was a beautiful woman, and he wondered—could she be telling the truth or was it a dramatic play merely to save her husband's neck? But Roth Chapman? Right now the man had a commission to furnish the Royal Navy with a fleet of new ships; his companies, left to him by his father, supplied the army with over half its equipment; his ships carried food to English troops; and a more trustworthy man would be hard to find. This was her witness? Perhaps there was more to Elton Chaucer's charges against Mr. Locke than he was admitting. After all, the man was petitioning for the earl's title. It could be a way of getting rid of the competition, and the earl was shrewd when it came to business affairs. But he was a friend, a trusted friend. Yet . . . Roth Chapman?

"If Roth were to tell you what happened, would you believe him?" she asked, and he cleared his throat again as he handed the letter back to his secretary.

"If Roth Chapman were to tell me you shot Lord Varrick in self-defense, I would have to believe it in spite of Lord Chaucer," he answered reluctantly. "But I doubt your story is true, and I doubt Mr. Chapman will appear before me."

"And if he does?"

"If he does, my dear lady, I will concede that the letter was written by an enemy of your husband merely to incriminate him, and that Lord Chaucer has been using my friendship for his own personal gain." He stopped and looked at Brandon, then exhaled disgustedly. "Now, if you don't mind, Brandon, I have things to do," he said. "The audience is over," and he leaned back once more, shutting his eyes as Brandon turned to Loedicia, and the secretary waved them toward the door.

They backed out slowly, and the door closed behind them.

"You amaze me," announced the duke as they turned and started down the corridor, and Loedicia took a deep breath.

"So now you know the truth."

"You really shot him?"

"I shot him," she answered stubbornly, "and he's not the only man I've shot. I've fought Indians and British soldiers . . ." She turned to him as they walked. "I know what you're probably thinking. How can a woman who's stood up to a howling Indian and put a bullet right between his eyes get hysterical at the sight of one man, as I did Lord Chaucer that evening."

"It is rather contradictory."

"And a long story. One that I'd rather not discuss," she answered. "Let it suffice to say that Lord Chaucer may as well be a reincarnation of Lord Varrick as far as I'm concerned, and Lord Varrick was the devil himself." She waved her hand as if dismissing the subject. "Now, can we see Quinn?"

He stopped, and she drew up short.

"What's the matter?"

"You want to see Quinn?"

"I want to try to talk some sense into him," she stated as they stood talking, while their escort stoically waited for them to continue their journey to the door of the palace. "He's afraid they'll want to hang me if they find out the truth, but you heard the king. Besides, if Roth can speak up in his behalf . . . for some reason I think perhaps he may hold more weight with the king than Lord Chaucer." She frowned. "Do you have any idea why?"

Brandon smiled. "Roth Chapman is not only one of the richest men in England and America, Loedicia, but he's building a small empire for himself that someday will control shipping in almost every port. Even now his ships are the best. To cross him at a time when we're at war with France could be to the king's disadvantage. He was a rich man before his father died; now he's richer. His shipyards have practically put the Royal Navy afloat, but"—he frowned, puzzled—"I thought you knew all this . . . I thought you were old friends."

"When I knew Roth, all he had to live on was a major's pay," she answered calmly. "Now, can we please go see Quinn?"

"You won't like Newgate."

"I doubt I'd like any prison," she answered, and once more they moved toward the door, with their escort leading the way.

Newgate was worse than she could ever have imagined. In the first place, the duke had to bribe the keeper to let them in; then, as they passed through the keeper's house with its small chapel, they entered into a horror that passed beyond man's imagination. The stench was enough to turn the hardiest of stomachs, and Loedicia held a handkerchief to her nose to try to lessen it, and the sight that met them brought tears to her eyes. They stopped first at the turnkey's lodge, where Brandon parted with even more guineas, and the turnkey, a beady-eyed brute with a scar over one eyelid, became their new escort.

They moved slowly through dank corridors where rats scurried unafraid and dirt and slime clung to the damp walls that in places were covered with a form of moldy fungus; then suddenly they stepped into a hall adjacent to a form of courtyard where prisoners milled about in filthy rags, trying to soak up the sun that was becoming scarcer every day as summer waned and autumn reared its unpredictable head.

The building was three stories high, packed with people living in the worst conditions a body could endure. Even now Loedicia stared as they passed the opening to a courtyard and she saw an emaciated man, the skin hanging on his cheekbones like white cloth draped on a frame, his eyes yellowed with fever. He was dying with no one to comfort him or ease his pain, only more half-dead faces to stare into. It was pitiful.

They passed two such courtyards, prisoners staring at them wide-eyed and envious, then walked past a flight of worn, rickety stairs and into a large room the turnkey announced was the visitors' room.

Even Brandon had a hard time stomaching the filth and degradation of such a place, and Loedicia wished she could shut not only her eyes but also her ears to the moaning wail that filtered through the walls. It was cold and evil-smelling, not just a prison, but a hellhole.

She glanced at Brandon as they both refused the turnkey's offer to sit on one of the filthy benches. Brandon looked ill-at-ease, and she didn't blame him. Merely walking through the place had made her flesh crawl.

It was some five minutes before the turnkey returned with Quinn, and during that time there was little to say, for the room they were in looked out over another courtyard where two prisoners, separated from them only by bars, filthy language spewing from their mouths, their clothing dirty and bedraggled, were fighting over some trivial thing that under ordinary circumstances neither would have cared about one way or the other. But they were going at each other viciously, like animals, and Loedicia watched, fascinated, unable to take her eyes from them, wondering if they'd kill each other, and suddenly worrying about what might be happening to Quinn.

She gasped audibly a few minutes later as Quinn stepped into the room, and her eyes gave away her feelings. Chains hung from his wrists, and he could do no more than hobble because of the chains at his ankles. His blond hair, usually neat, was ruffled haphazardly, but it was his clothes that drew her attention. Already, in only a few hours, they were torn, almost shredded, and there were scratches on his arms and face.

"What on earth have they done to you?" she exclaimed as she looked at him, and he tried to smile, to reassure her.

"A bit of horseplay," he answered huskily, not wanting to tell her how he had to beat them off him when they threw him in the cell. How the other prisoners, seeing his richly made clothes, tried to get them from him, and they had to put him in these chains so he wouldn't kill them. "The men who share my cell felt I looked a bit too dandy for the likes of the place," he said instead, but she didn't look too pleased with his answer.

She stepped forward and touched a streak of dried blood on his arm that he was trying to conceal from her beneath his tattered cloak. "They play rough," she said calmly, going along with him, but her heart was turning over inside her at the sight of him trussed up like this. In spite of all that had happened, she still loved him so much.

"Hell, I've had worse," he stated boldly. "This is nothing compared to what Little Wolf can dish out."

Loedicia turned to Brandon. "Little Wolf belongs to a not-so-friendly Indian tribe back home," she explained.

"And he's a mean cuss," interrupted Quinn, trying to be nonchalant. "Damn near roasted me alive one time after he'd staked me out all day over an anthill." His eyebrows raised as he looked at Brandon. "I don't think you believe me."

Brandon eyed him dubiously, wrinkling his face in distaste. "Ants?"

"They're a hell of a lot worse than these rats. Running inside your nose and ears, trying to get to your innards. You don't dare open your mouth to yell, and they can bite the flesh right off a man."

"Quinn!" cried Loedicia, her face worried. "Stop it. You're

acting like this is merely a game. They're playing for keeps."

He gazed into her violet eyes, his own eyes darkening. "You think it's fun wearing these?" he said, lifting his hands, holding up the shackles.

"You could get them off."

His eyes narrowed.

"You could tell them the truth," she retorted, and his jaw set hard.

"Never! I can't take that chance." His eyes looked deeply into hers. "I can't risk losing you."

"Oh, I suppose I'm just to stand by and watch you hang."

"They don't have proof. Chaucer's trying to show his power, so I'll back down, that's all."

"That's all?" She looked at Brandon. "Tell him what the king has," she ordered, and Brandon took a deep breath.

"It seems a gentleman named Ramsey sent an incriminating letter to Elton Chaucer," he stated. "He might as well have pointed his finger right at you, Quinn, and Chaucer's been hanging onto the letter all these years."

"Ramsey?" He frowned as he looked at Dicia.

"That's right," she said. "Remember before he was taken away the night Kendall was killed he vowed he'd get even with you? Well, he has. He probably thought that letter'd be used against you years ago, but instead Chaucer's saved it."

"But the king can't believe I'd kill Varrick just because Ramsey says so. The man was a lying bastard."

"And the king's supposed to know that?" She gestured helplessly. "What Ramsey didn't say, Chaucer's evidently filled in, lie after lie, and Lord Chaucer's one of the king's court, a trusted friend."

Quinn stared at her, his eyes hard and angry. "How do you know all this?" he asked suspiciously, and she held her head up stubbornly.

"Because we just came from an audience with the king."

"You . . ." His face paled as his eyes widened. "What have you done?"

"I told him the truth."

"You what?" he cried furiously.

She hesitated. "But he didn't believe me."

He sighed, relieved. "Thank God!"

"Thank God? You'd rather hang?"

"Than let you hang, yes."

"But neither of us has to hang, Quinn. Neither of us!"

He frowned warily. "You said he didn't believe you."

"But he'll believe Roth."

"Roth?" His eyes flashed as his face reddened angrily. "Roth?" he shouted again, clenching his teeth furiously, his nostrils flaring. "What have you said? What have you done? What have you told him about Roth . . . about you and Roth?"

"I told him Roth was there, that's all—that Roth saw me shoot Kendall Varrick, and he knows Roth, he said if Roth comes to London and tells him personally what happened that he'll let you go, that they'll do nothing to me . . ."

She watched him shake his head. "No!" he shouted angrily. "I won't have it. I won't have the whole world knowing."

"The world doesn't have to know," she pleaded. "But he can save your life."

"I'd rather die first!"

She straightened, determined, her shoulders squared. "And if I won't let you?"

"Dicia, don't be a fool. He won't believe Roth . . . it's a lie." He turned to Brandon. "Tell her it isn't true, Brandon. Tell her it'd be useless," but Brandon was at a loss. He'd heard the king with his own ears, and he had to confirm what Loedicia had already told him.

"We can send someone to the coast," she went on. "He'd come . . . I know he would."

Quinn's face was livid, the veins in his neck like taut ropes as he stared at her. "No!" he shouted again. "I won't owe my life to that son of a bitch!" and she flinched.

"You can't stop me," she warned, defying him, her eyes blazing, but he looked at Brandon.

"You can," he demanded, harshly. "I'm leaving it up to you. My wife is not to send anyone after Roth Chapman, do you understand?" but Brandon shook his head, bewildered.

"This is crazy," he said. "The man can clear you."

"And put a noose about her neck."

"Don't be ridiculous. The king's ready to concede . . ."

But Quinn would have none of it. He was adamant in his demand and made Brandon promise to keep Loedicia from sending for Roth. "I'd rather hang for something I didn't do than owe my life to him," he answered, and tears sprang to Loedicia's eyes.

"If you hang, my life goes too," she whispered softly, unable to fight him anymore. "Why are you doing this, Quinn? Why won't you let Roth come?"

He looked at her, his face softening, his eyes filled with

pain. "Because I love you," he confessed softly. "I've been a hell of a husband, I know. I've done everything wrong, and I have no one to blame but myself, but by God I'm not going to make the mistake of letting him near you again. He said the next time he would take you from me. If I have to lose you to him, I don't want to be around to watch. I couldn't stand it. I'd rather die loving you than live and lose you. I'm a coward. I value your love more than my life, because without you there is no life for me."

"You think my love's that shallow?" she asked. "You think I don't love you?"

His voice deepened as he stared into her eyes. "I know that after last night I don't dare let you see him. I can't take that chance, do you understand?" he said huskily. "Either way, I lose you, and I choose the honorable way."

Tears rolled down her cheeks as she listened, and Brandon scowled. What the hell was he talking about? Why would he lose her? The whole thing was beyond him.

Loedicia reached out and touched Quinn's hands; they were cold and dirty, his wrists straining against the iron bands that encased them. "You know I'd never go to him if you died on the gallows," she said, and his jaw tightened.

"Wouldn't you?"

"How could I?"

"It'll be easy once I'm gone."

She sobbed, and tears filled her blazing eyes. "I hate you, Quinn Locke," she cried angrily. "You're cruel and heartless and—"

Suddenly he grabbed her wrist and held tightly, his fingers hurting her as he pulled against his shackles. "I love you," he whispered, halting the words that were tumbling from her mouth. "I love you, goddammit!" and she stared at him, crying helplessly as he bent forward, his lips hard on hers, and there was no use fighting him. He wouldn't listen. He was so sure that what he'd done last night had killed the love she had for him. How could she explain what it had done to her? The love was there, would always be there, even though sometimes she wished to God it wasn't, but nothing would ever change the way she felt toward him, no matter how angry he made her. What she did she'd have to do on her own, whether he liked it or not, because she wasn't about to sit idly back and watch him hang.

He drew his head back and looked into her flushed face.

"Now, do you still hate me?" he asked softly, and she nodded hesitantly.

"I hate you . . . for making me love you," she answered, and Brandon, who was silently following the byplay between them, shook his head in disbelief as he saw a look pass between them. A look of fire and intimacy that no one could penetrate.

Quinn reached up and took her face in both his hands, holding her head still so she had to look at him, but he addressed the duke.

"I want a promise, Brandon," he said firmly, his eyes looking deep into hers. "In no way will you let her get in touch with Roth Chapman, is that understood?" and the duke drew in a quick breath as Quinn looked at him sharply, still holding her head still. "I want a promise."

"All right . . . all right." He nodded. "It's a promise, but I think you're crazy. I think you're both crazy."

"Then go right on thinking it," answered Quinn. "Just make sure Roth Chapman stays out of London. I'll get out of this predicament myself," and the duke acquiesced. But by the time they left the prison, Loedicia had already decided what she was going to do and how she was going to do it.

It was pitch dark as she slipped from the house on Grosvenor Square and moved through the shadows, headed for the front gates, pulling the cloak tighter about her. She was wearing boy's clothes beneath the cape. Clothes Lizette had managed to acquire for her from one of the stableboys, with a promise she'd return them mended and clean. Beyond the walls and the front gate a soldier friend of Lizette's was waiting for her with a horse.

"And that was not easy, *ma petite*," Lizette had said as she'd stood in the bedroom earlier while Loedicia was getting dressed and handed her the map her friend had also given her. "I almost had to sell my soul." She rolled her eyes. "These men have but one thing in mind," and Loedicia'd winced, agreeing with her as she tried not to think of Quinn with the duchess. It was over and done, and she had to forget it.

She ducked beneath a hawthorn bush, slipped to the side of the stone wall that stretched between the road and the lawn, then moved to a small door beyond the gatekeeper's house. She lifted the latch as quietly as possible and prayed it wouldn't squeak as she pulled it toward her.

The door opened easily, with hardly a sound, and she sighed as she tiptoed through, then pulled it shut behind her, and her heart was pounding as she started slowly down the deserted street toward the corner, keeping in the shadows.

"My friend will be standing at the corner of the stone wall," Lizette had told her, "and he'll escort you to the edge of the city, but from there you are on your own." Her eyes had pleaded with her. "I wish you wouldn't do this, *ma petite,*" she'd begged. "There must be another way," but Loedicia had assured her that Brandon was keeping his promise to Quinn and would never let her out of the house alone.

"I must do this, Lizette," she'd said. "Lord Chaucer is determined to hang Quinn, and he's such a stubborn fool." She gazed at her friend helplessly. "Why did I have to fall in love with him, Lizette? Why can't I hate him? Why can't I just forget he ever existed and let him hang?"

Lizette's eyes warmed. "Because he's a part of you, *ma petite* . . . because the fire is strong inside you and will never die, because he's your love."

"Yes, he's my love," she whispered now to herself as she reached the corner and spotted Lizette's friend.

He was a soldier she'd met at the park one afternoon, and he'd been dropping in to see her off and on since they'd been at Bourland Hall, and although Loedicia had met him a few times, he didn't recognize her in the boy's clothing and mistook her for one of the stableboys.

"Lizette says you're runnin' a special errand for the duke," he said as he handed her the horse's reins. "I sure wonder sometimes what gets into these dandies, sendin' stableboys out in the middle of the night on secret errands."

She swallowed hard and hesitated a minute, then jumped into the saddle and checked to make sure she still had the map Lizette had given her. She had a long ride ahead of her.

"Let's go," she said, disguising her voice as best she could, keeping the hood of her cape pulled down over the hat she wore so he couldn't see her face, and he climbed into the saddle, leading the way.

The streets were practically deserted, dark and quiet, as they made their way toward the southern end of the city, weaving in and out of alleys, their horses' hooves echoing loudly in the quiet night. The only ones about were the homeless, wandering here and there, trying to find a place to rest their heads, eking out a meager existence from the unwary wayfarers who happened to cross their paths, and Dicia was glad she had Lizette's friend with her.

They crossed the bridge over the Thames and moved slowly onward, soon leaving the houses and cobbled streets behind.

"Well, this is as far as I go," he finally said as they reached a bend in the road and pulled up rein. He sat back in the saddle and stared at her dark figure beside him. "You sure ain't very talkative, lad, I'll say that," he said wearily, as he realized the boy'd hardly said a word since they'd started. Then he turned in the saddle and studied the sky. "Must be close to five o'clock in the mornin' by now, and I'm due back at my post at sunup, so's I'd best be on my way back." He sighed. "You know the rest of the way? You got the map?"

She nodded, and he wheeled his horse about. "Then good luck to you lad," he called, "and Godspeed," and he spurred his horse, heading back toward the city as she watched.

Well, this was it. She couldn't turn back. She didn't even know the way back, or ahead for that matter; she'd have to use the map for that. For the first time since she'd left the house she pushed the hood of her cape back and felt the cool night air on her face. Her hair was pulled back to look like a young boy with a queue, and she pushed the small tricorn hat down farther on her head so it wouldn't fly off; then she pulled at the horse's reins, digging him in the ribs, and he moved abruptly, breaking into a gallop as she lifted her head, feeling the wind in her face as she raced down the road. It was wild and exhilarating and she felt like a girl again. Like riding the wind, with not a care in the world. She fled down the highway for a long stretch, her face into the wind, her heart pounding; then suddenly she straightened in the saddle and pulled on the reins, slowing her horse. At this rate he'd never make it to Portsmouth.

She slowed the horse to a steady, even pace and eased back in the saddle. There was so much to think of. So much to remember, yet most of it she wanted to forget.

By the time the late-September sun came up, taking the chill from the air, she was miles from the city. Lizette had strict instructions to tell everyone she was sick in bed and didn't want to see anyone because it could be something catching, and she hoped the ruse would work. She'd die if the duke came charging after her.

She had a little under a hundred miles to go, and each small town she came to she checked the map, noting her progress and rubbing her rear, hoping she wouldn't get blisters. She hadn't ridden astride since their cross-country journey to Philadelphia, and she knew how easy it was to get sore after so many months away from it. Well, if she did, she'd handle that too.

Around noon she stopped at a small market in one of the towns and bought a loaf of bread, some cheese, and a small bag of apples, filling her stomach, washing it down with water from the town well. Then, putting the excess in a bag fastened onto the back of the saddle, and after a short rest, she took off again down the road, an inconspicuous figure in her boy's clothes, the black cape now rolled up and tied on the back of the saddle, since the sun had warmed the air.

The English countryside was like life to her, and it felt good to be out of the city. She was used to the clean fresh air and the forests at Fort Locke, and it did her heart good, if anything could do her heart good, just to be here. Then she thought of Quinn holed up in Newgate, and it took the joy from the day, and the light from her eyes.

How many times she'd questioned her love for him. Wondering what magic he possessed that held her so. There was a fire in him, a magnetism that drew her against her will. There always had been, even when she'd first met him, and although they argued and fought sometimes like bobcats, there was a strength and wonder at his touch that always amazed her. She'd been unable to fight it right from the start, so instead, she'd languished in it, giving her very soul to him, until the love was so strong between them that sometimes it frightened her. But why did God have to send the bitter with the sweet? Why did he mix the taste of gall with the taste of honey? Why couldn't it be velvet and roses all the way?

She stopped occasionally to give the horse a break and let him graze a bit, then continued on, checking the map each time to make sure she hadn't made a wrong turn in the road, checking landmarks Lizette's friend had written down, and when dark caught up, she still had a long way to go. The road she was on was isolated, in the middle of a wood. She'd hoped to find a better place to spend the night, but this would have to do.

She reined the horse off the road, through the trees, until she was out of sight of the highway, then slid from the saddle, tethering her mount on a bush close by. The air had cooled considerably and she was wearing the cape again, pulled tight around her. She had never slept alone like this before, even during her years with Quinn. He was always there, or someone was there, but she wouldn't be afraid, she couldn't be.

It was so dark she could hardly see her hand in front of her face as she made out a small patch of grass near a fallen tree and walked over, dropping onto the ground, curling up, pulling the cloak about her, resting quietly, hoping to get some sleep. A few hours would help, and she'd start out again before dawn. But the ground was hard, the night cold, and the darkness frightening, making sheer exhaustion the only thing that finally made her give way to slumber, and she nodded off, the low nickering of her horse gently falling on her ears.

The next day, shortly after the noon hour, she rode into the borough of Portsmouth with a tired horse and a gray sky overhead.

She reined up in the middle of the main street of the village and looked about. The map had brought her here, but would take her no farther. She'd have to ask someone the directions to Roth's house. There were few people about as she looked around, but one old man sitting in front of a shop sharpening knives at a grinding wheel caught her eye.

She gently nudged her horse and moved up to him, reining in a short distance away, then tried to lower her voice to make it sound masculine as she spoke.

"Excuse me, sir," she addressed him, "I'm looking for a gentleman named Rothford Chapman. Can you help me?"

The man stopped his grinding and glanced up, staring at her curiously. Probably wondering if she was really a boy; then he smiled as he cleared his throat.

"Straight down the road, turn left at the sign of the rooster, and follow your nose," he answered. "It's the big stone house on the hill overlooking the Spithead—they calls it Windward Hall. But you'd best make it fast, lad. I hear tell he's leaving sometime today for America."

She stared at the man, her heart pounding. He couldn't! He couldn't! Oh, God, he couldn't, and her heels dug into the horse's ribs and she called a quick thank-you over her shoulder as she galloped away furiously, cloak flying as it caught the wind.

Some ten minutes later, her heart was in her throat as she slowed down, approaching a huge boulder some ten to fifteen feet high with the name "Windward" chiseled into it. It sat at the side of the road, a patch of well-cut grass beneath it and a drive curving from each side, coming together behind the boulder, where the main drive led back toward a huge stone house poised atop the cliffs, the landscaped grounds around it like something from an artist's dream.

She bit her lips and pulled the horse's reins, turning him, patting his sweat-streaked neck as she moved up the drive, hoping she wasn't too late.

No one was about as she tied the horse to the hitch rack and walked up the slate steps to the large oak door and raised the knocker, looking about at the majestic beauty of the place, and it was some minutes before the door was opened by a tall gray-haired servant, his breathing labored as he stared at her.

"Something we can do for you, lad?" he asked, and she straightened her shoulders, determined.

"I'm looking for Mr. Chapman," she said breathlessly, not bothering to disguise her voice anymore, but before the man had a chance to answer, Roth spoke from behind him.

"Loedicia! What on earth . . ." and the servant stepped aside as she rushed past him, then stopped abruptly, staring.

He was wearing breeches of midnight blue with a full-sleeved shirt of silk open at the throat showing a mass of dark curly hair, and his polished boots shone with a high luster. He looked ruggedly handsome, and her heart did a turn as she looked into his eyes.

"I had to come," she whispered self-consciously, seeing the frown crease his forehead. "They've arrested Quinn."

He dismissed the servant quickly and took her by the arm, ushering her into a room midway down the hall. "You look done in," he said as he sat her in a chair, then walked over, pouring her a small brandy from a decanter in the liquor cabinet. "Now, tell me what happened."

"Lord Chaucer's persuaded the king that Quinn killed Kendall Varrick, and he's in Newgate Prison."

He stopped for a minute, then continued pouring the drink and brought it to her. "You rode all the way from London by yourself?" he asked, and she nodded as she took the glass from him and took a sip.

She swallowed it, then felt its warmth as it began to spread through her. "Roth, you have to come back to London with me," she said as she sat on the edge of the chair, leaning toward him. "If you come they'll set him free. You have to come."

He knelt on one knee in front of her, reaching out, taking

her free hand. "Whoa, slow down, Dicia. Let me get my breath," he said softly. "Now, tell me what this is all about."

She told him of Quinn's arrest and her audience with the king. "Why didn't you tell me you were the grandson of the Earl of Cumberland?" she asked suddenly as she handed the empty brandy glass back, and he stood up, twisting the glass in his hands as he looked at it.

"I didn't think it mattered," he answered, and she shook her head.

"It doesn't, to me. . . . I was just surprised, that's all."

"My father was the youngest son," he explained as he took the glass back and set it down, then walked back to her. "Under the circumstances, he used his brains instead of waiting for a title that had little chance of ever being his, and he had a good head for business. I think he'd almost forgotten he was the son of an earl. I know I'd never paid much attention to it."

She looked up at him, her eyes pleading. "You will come?" she asked, but he didn't answer. "Roth?"

"Did he send you?"

She hung her head. "No."

"I thought as much."

She lifted her head to look at him. "He'd be furious if he knew I was here, but I can't let him hang, Roth."

"He hasn't been tried yet."

"But the evidence . . . he doesn't have a chance."

"You're sure?"

"I'm sure."

Roth turned away and walked to the window, pulling back the long heavy moss-green draperies, and looked out, his hand on the draperies clenched so tightly the knuckles were white. What on earth did she think he was, anyway? Like an old shoe she could toss aside, then pick up and wear again whenever she felt like it . . . He was a man, a man in love, and God, how he loved her. She was asking him to save the life of the man who stood between them, the man she preferred to him, or did she?

He whirled around. "What is there in it for me?" he asked abruptly, and she stared at him, her face pale. "Well?"

"I . . . I don't . . ."

He walked over and stood looking down at her. "What is it you expect of me, Dicia?" he asked, his voice strained. "You ask me to save the life of the man who's taken you from me, and you expect me to ask nothing in return?"

Her lips parted as she stared at him, and tears filled her eyes. "I have nothing to give."

His eyes hardened. "You could give yourself." But she shook her head, her voice faltering.

"I . . . I could never leave him, you know that."

"But you could leave me."

"Roth, please." She reached up and wiped away a tear. "That isn't fair."

He knelt down and took hold of her chin, looking deep into her eyes. "What is fair, Dicia?" he asked softly, his voice low and intimate. "I love you so much I choke up inside at the sight of you, but I can't touch. Do you know what that's doing to me? Do you think it was easy for me to walk away that day in Philadelphia, and then again in London? Do you think I can go on popping in and out of your life like this without it cutting the heart out of me? I can't do it, Dicia."

She reached out and put her hand on his cheek, and her fingers tingled at the touch. "Oh, Roth, I don't know what to do. I can't let them hang Quinn. I love him. I can't help it, I never could. It's like the air I breathe, I can't explain it."

"And me?"

She sighed. "Oh, God . . ."

"Do you feel anything, Dicia?"

Her throat tightened as she gazed into his eyes, those dark, compelling eyes. Did she feel anything? God, yes! What was it that coursed through her every time she saw him, was it love? The same passionate vibrations filled her when he was near, the same vibrations she always felt when Quinn held her. When Roth caressed her, it was the same as with Quinn. And his mouth, his lips, right now she wanted to kiss them, lose herself in them, yet, what of Quinn? She was so mixed up. She didn't want to hurt either one, yet she had to hurt this man, this gentle, loving man, because Quinn was there first in her heart.

"Do I have to answer?" she begged softly, her fingers moving to his mouth, caressing his lips lovingly, and he closed his eyes for a moment, kissing the tips of her fingers, and his hand dropped abruptly from her chin as he opened his eyes and stood up.

He turned from her and walked back to stare out the window. He knew it was useless. Everything she did was for Quinn, but then, that's the way it should be, shouldn't it? He was her husband, he'd found her first. "How soon is the trial?" he asked abruptly, as if nothing had happened, and she held both her arms in front of her, hugging herself tightly to try to keep her voice steady.

"It's the day after tomorrow."

His head leaned back as if he was thinking; then he turned slowly. "That doesn't give us much time, does it?"

She shook her head, trying not to cry.

"Do you think you can make the journey back on horseback again after a bit of a rest?" and she nodded as he went on. "Good. We'll put some decent food into you, get you a fresh horse . . . I'll cancel my plans." He walked over and pulled the bell cord, then stepped over to her, staring down at the woebegone face, the violet eyes warm with thanks. "But this is the last time, Dicia," he said forcefully, his face determined. "I can't take it anymore. When this is over, I'm leaving and I don't ever want to see you again. I can't." He shook his head. "I just can't!"

She couldn't answer. There was a pain in her heart, a physical ache, and she wished she'd never been born.

Roth turned abruptly as one of the servants entered, and her agony was momentarily forgotten as he started giving orders, canceling his departure for America, ordering food for lunch before they left and horses to be ready out front in an hour's time.

While lunch was being prepared, she was taken to one of the bedrooms, where she washed up but declined to change her clothes.

"I ride better and faster in these," she explained to him over a late lunch of hot chowder, baked chicken, and sweet cakes. "Besides, I think it wiser that people seeing us traveling together go on thinking I'm a boy. It isn't exactly the fashion for a man and woman to travel about alone unescorted, is it?" and he smiled as her face flushed.

"Are you thinking of my reputation or yours?" he asked, and she smiled back, not realizing how irresistible she looked.

"Yours," she answered impishly. "Mine was ruined years ago," and the tension between them eased as he laughed.

They were friends again, and after lunch, before they left, he took her outside to the back of the house that overlooked the waters of the Spithead.

"Exhilarating, isn't it?" he said as they stood at the top of the cliffs, gazing out over the far horizon at the deep blue waters that were churning violently as dark clouds rolled across the sky, and Loedicia thought of Heath. He'd always loved the lake, even when it was violent, and Roth loved the water too. She could tell by the way he watched it. Father and son were so much alike. She tried to shove the thought away.

"It looks like rain," she mentioned, gesturing toward the sky, and he nodded.

"Maybe we can outrun it. It's a long way off. We should be able to reach an inn somewhere by nightfall." He looked down at her and pulled his cloak a bit tighter against the wind. "Well, are you ready?"

"Ready," she confirmed, and they headed for the front of the house and their horses.

15

Storm clouds continued to rumble about them all afternoon as they rode, yet not a drop of rain had fallen, and they'd been traveling for a good five or six hours. It was almost dark now, and they were in a long stretch of road in the middle of the downs, with not a building in sight, when suddenly Roth glanced up as the sky grew even darker and the wind whipped up stronger.

"I think it's finally coming," he yelled to her as the wind tried to catch his words to keep her from hearing, and she nodded vigorously as the first few drops of cold rain hit her face.

Within minutes they were soaked to the skin as the rain pounded them, and they tried to move their horses faster, hoping to see a house or an old barn, but there were none in sight.

"We should have stayed at that last inn back there where we ate," he said as he reined in close to her, trying to keep the rain and wind from his face. "I shouldn't have let you talk me out of it. It's almost dark now, and God knows where we can find another."

"But there was so much daylight left, and we don't have that much time."

"If we both catch fevers, we'll never see London," he answered, and she looked downcast, making him feel guilty for blaming her.

The rain was pelting them hard as they rode along, almost drowning them in its violence, and their horses were moving at a snail's pace now against the onslaught of water and mud.

They moved along like this for what seemed like hours, and still the rain wouldn't let up. It swept across the dark fields, driving everything in its path as they huddled together, continuing to move forward as best they could, trying to stay on the road that was now a sea of mud.

They were completely drenched, and it was almost three hours later when Roth let out a low cry.

"There! Through the trees," he said as he stopped his horse and pointed, and Loedicia sighed.

A faint light shone up ahead through the rain and darkness, and they guided their weary animals on, pulling into a posting house, all its windows dark save one.

He helped her down, feeling her tremble from the cold and wet as he held her against him; then he fastened their horses and helped her to the door. He flung it open and was greeted by a startled innkeeper, standing in front of a blazing fire, poking it, stirring the red-hot coals generously.

"God save us, you scared me near to death," the man exclaimed gruffly as he eyed the bedraggled pair, and Roth pushed back his hood, taking off his riding hat, wiping the dampness from his hair with his free hand.

"We need two rooms and a place to dry out," he ordered as he watched the water drip from his hat, but the innkeeper shook his head.

"Sorry, sir," he apologized, "but about two hours ago a stage broke down not a mile from here, and every room but one's taken. That's the best I can do for you." He looked at Loedicia, the hood of her wet cape partially covering her face, but the boy's clothes visible beneath it. "You and the lad can share the room, though. It's got a good feather ticking and you can hang the wet clothes on chairs in front of the fireplace," and Roth frowned as he turned and glanced at her, his eyes catching a slight glimpse of a scowl on her shadowed face.

But there was nothing else he could do. If he didn't get her dried out . . . It must be close to eleven by now, and he looked about. There was no place to sleep here. The place was small, only a few tables and chairs. So he accepted reluctantly. The innkeeper led the way up the stairs for them, and Roth let her go ahead of him, but she kept the hood up over her head and partially covering her face, not saying a word.

He ushered them into a small room with two straight-back chairs, a bed in one end, and a low, glowing fireplace in the other, promising to bring some food up if he could find some.

"The kitchen girl's gone to bed already," he complained as he started out the door. "But I'll see what I can find," and he left, closing the door quietly.

Roth stared at Loedicia's back as she stood in front of him, and suddenly he saw her shiver. He reached out and turned her around, shoving the hood from her head, and he sighed.

"My God!" he exclaimed. "You're nearly frozen. Your lips are blue," and he reached out, trying to undo the tie on her cloak.

She reached her fingers up to help him, but they were numb, and he brushed them away as he finished untying the cloak and threw it aside onto the chair; then he reached down and started to unfasten the top button of the jacket she wore.

"No," she whispered softly, her voice shaking. "No, Roth, you can't," and he stopped, staring into her eyes in protest.

"If I don't, you'll be sick by morning," he said, and once more brushed aside her hands as he continued to unbutton the jacket.

He slipped it from her shoulders while she protested; then he pulled the camisole she wore beneath it off over her head as she stared at him wide-eyed. He felt a quickening deep inside as he caught sight of her bare breasts, the nipples hard and firm, and he had to fight the impulse to lean down and bury his face in them. Instead, he picked her up and carried her to the chair, where he set her down, pulling off her wet boots, and threw them in front of the fireplace one at a time.

"Now, off with the pants," he said, and she shook her head.

"Roth!"

But he ignored her cry. He reached out and stood her up, feeling her body trembling beneath his fingers, seeing the gooseflesh rise on her skin as he loosened the trousers and pulled them down, her wet underwear peeling off with them.

When she was completely stripped, he stared at her for a brief second; then, not trusting himself, he turned quickly toward the bed and grabbed the blanket from the top, bringing it over, and he wrapped her inside it like a butterfly in a cocoon.

"There," he said as he held the blanket beneath her chin. "Now, go stand by the fire while I do the same thing, and I'll find something for us to sit on."

She started to speak, then changed her mind and walked to the fire, standing facing it, feeling its heat begin to warm her, while all the time she was aware of Roth's noisy movements behind her, knowing he was stripping the wet clothes from his body.

She took a quick, furtive glance once and trembled, a strange feeling in her loins as the firelight fell on his long, lean body, strong and muscular, the dark hair on his chest reminding her of another night, another time, and she looked away. It wasn't right. She shouldn't feel like this. She shouldn't be here. She should turn and run, but there was no place to go.

"I'll spread our clothes out on the chairs," he offered from behind her, and she turned slightly to see that he'd wrapped the sheet about himself, leaving his shoulders bare, and he was draping the clothes on the chairs; then he pulled the chairs close on each side of the fire. "Move back by the door a minute," he ordered as he headed for the bed, and she stepped back, then watched curiously as he lifted the ticking and slid it across the the floor, placing it as close to the fire as possible, but not close enough where they'd be scorched. "Now. Come sit down," he said, and she stared at him.

"Do I have to pick you up and carry you again?" he asked, but she shook her head violently as she moved gingerly across the room. As she sat down in the middle of the mattress, there was a knock on the door, and Roth hurried over.

He came back with a loaf of bread, a plate of cold mutton, and a bottle of wine with one glass hanging over the neck of the bottle. "This is all he could find at this hour," he said as he sat down at the edge of the mattress, close to the fire, and set the plate and bread on the floor beside them. "You can use the glass, I'll drink out of the bottle," and for the first time since he'd undressed her, he looked into her face.

It was flushed and warm in the firelight, and her eyes were steady on him, studying him intently, and he felt all warm inside. He broke off a piece of bread, slapped a slice of cold mutton on it, and handed it to her, trying to ignore what her nearness was doing to him.

She took it from him and tried to eat, but only nibbled at the food, her stomach doing flip-flops. He poured her some wine, their fingers touching as he handed her the glass, and she felt a tremor run through her clear to her toes. The effect he was making on her was unnerving, and she flushed again self-consciously. He turned around quickly, and she raised the glass to her lips, washing down the food that was sticking in her throat.

The wine warmed her inside, and she watched from the middle of the mattress where she sat as he began eating some of the mutton and bread, following it with the wine, warming his hands with the heat from the fireplace as he ate.

When he was finished he turned, avoiding her eyes, and offered her more, but she declined, handing him back the glass, and he set it aside with the leftovers on the plate. He sat quietly for a minute, staring off into space, feeling the warmth from the fire on his bare shoulders, the wine moving through his body, relaxing him, yet making him even more aware of her.

He turned back slowly and looked at her, catching her watching him, and suddenly he couldn't resist anymore. He reached out, his hand moving up behind her as she held her breath, and he loosened the ribbon that held her hair in the queue, pulling it free, letting her hair fall on her shoulders, damp and curly.

"There," he whispered huskily, his eyes devouring her. "That's the way you should look," and they stared at each other silently, the only movement in the room the beating of their hearts and the small dancing tongues of flame in the fireplace, and something passed between them. Something that couldn't be put into words.

"I shouldn't have come with you," he finally whispered, breaking the silence, his voice strained, but she protested tremulously.

"You had to."

"I should have insisted we stay at the other inn where we ate earlier."

"I know."

He reached out and touched her shoulder where the blanket had slipped down, and he ran his fingers across her soft skin. It was like velvet to his touch, and he felt her tremble.

"Are you cold?"

"No."

"Oh." He took his hand away, but continued to look at her, his eyes warm with desire. "You'd better get some sleep."

"I don't feel like sleeping."

"What do you feel like?"

She was staring back at him, her face flushed. "I don't know." And she didn't. Part of her wanted to melt into his arms and beg him to make love to her, and part of her kept shouting "No!"

"Lie down, Dicia," he suddenly ordered roughly, his voice unsteady, "before I forget you're another man's wife!" and he quickly turned his back on her to stare into the fire.

Tears filled her eyes and a burning desire swept over her as he turned away. She wanted to cry out, but instead she lowered herself onto the ticking and lay quietly, turning onto her back, staring at the ceiling, holding the blanket tightly about her with her fists clenched until the knuckles were white.

The room was quiet except for the soft crackling of the fire and the rain beating against the window. She tried to lie still, but her breathing was unsteady, every nerve in her body alive and yearning. She ached for his touch and her breasts tingled for his caress.

Roth stared into the glowing embers, but he didn't really see them. All he saw were her eyes looking at him longingly, begging for what they both knew wasn't theirs to share anymore. He cursed the day he'd walked out of her life. He should have fought Quinn for her. A quick death would have been better than the slow torture he was going through now. He reached over restlessly and took the poker, stirring up the fire a bit, then set it back and tried to relax, but it was useless. The room seemed to vibrate with their awareness of each other.

He glanced back quickly, hoping she was asleep, but her eyes were on him again, and he groaned helplessly as he felt himself hardening all the more. "You're not even trying to sleep," he complained, and she looked back up at the ceiling, holding back tears.

"I can't."

"Maybe if you quit watching me."

"I'm not."

"Dicia! For heaven's sake, you are. How much do you think I can take?"

She looked at him again, her body trembling, her eyes soft and misty. "How much do you want?" she finally cried urgently, forgetting everything but her need for him, and he sighed, his voice hushed.

"All of you," he whispered, and he reached out, touching her, slowly beginning to disengage her hands from the blanket, waiting for her protest, but there was none.

Instead she breathed deeply, her eyes studying his face with anxious anticipation as she lay passive beneath his gaze, letting him take the blanket from her, leaving her naked.

His hand touched her breast, cupping it gently, feeling it soft, yet firm, beneath his fingers as he caressed it. "I can't stop now, you know that, don't you?" he whispered, and her lips parted slowly.

"Yes. I know."

"And you're sure?"

She was breathless. "I'm sure."

He leaned over slowly, his mouth covering hers, and she quivered, feeling it deep inside as he kissed her, his lips lingering on her mouth. Then after a few moments he drew back and looked down into her face, savoring the feel of her as his hands moved down her body.

"I've been wanting you to do that for so long." She sighed, her heart pounding, and his eyes softened.

"Oh, Dicia, my love," he whispered, and his head dropped again, his lips on hers, and this time he kissed her wildly, passionately, and she reveled in the luxury of him, letting him make love to her slowly, deliberately. His hands fondled her, and she gave herself to him willingly as she thrilled to his lovemaking, and as he entered her gently, thrusting forward, she felt a spreading warmth and ecstasy that captured every nerve in her body, making her flesh want to cry out.

He kissed her over and over again, whispering to her tenderly, coaxingly as he caressed her, as if the years between had never been, moving and thrusting inside her until they climaxed simultaneously, bringing them both an ecstasy of sweet rapture that left them trembling and breathless.

Roth's mouth moved against her as he quivered from the violence of his release, and his lips sipped at hers hungrily as she clung to him. "I love you," he whispered against her mouth, and her whole body throbbed.

"No!" Her lips moved against his. "Don't, Roth. Don't love me," she begged. "I'm not worth it." She turned her head, avoiding his mouth, and he drew his head back as she whispered, "I've used you tonight . . ."

He stared at her flushed face, still warm from his kisses, and he frowned. "What do you mean, you've used me?" He reached up, pulling her head, trying to force her to look at him. "What are you talking about?"

She could feel his body hot against hers, and she trembled. "I've betrayed you and I've betrayed Quinn . . . and I'm not worthy of either of you," she cried softly, but he stopped her as he slid from her and lay on his stomach, looking down into her eyes.

"Hush. You betrayed no one."

"But I did."

He stroked the hair from her forehead affectionately, his eyes warm with love.

"When I leave here tomorrow I'm going back to Quinn," she whispered softly, and saw the pain in his eyes.

"I know," he answered, his voice breaking. "I've known it from the start."

"Yet . . . you can still say you love me?"

"Maybe I'm hoping after all this is over he won't want you anymore."

She scowled. "You'd tell him . . . about this?"

He shook his head. "Never. But I have a feeling you will." He'd been holding her hand, and he raised it to his lips now, kissing her palm, and she felt a throbbing deep in her loins. "What happened between you two after I left?" he asked as his hand tightened on hers. "Something happened. What was it?"

She bit her lip and there were tears in her eyes.

"Well?"

"He slept with the duchess that night," she murmured, and she saw his eyes darken.

"Is that why you let me make love to you?"

"No . . ." She sighed. "It made it easier, but that's not why. I wanted you . . ." She pulled her hand free and reached up, touching his cheek, moving her fingers to his lips. "I needed you like a thirsty man needs water."

"And any man would have sufficed?"

"No . . . not any man. I didn't even want Quinn, Roth. I wanted you. I wanted to feel again what we had before."

"And now?"

"I still want you, yet I know that in the morning I'll go back to Quinn and it'll be like it was before and I'll want him too. Sometimes I feel like two different people." She looked away from his piercing eyes and stared at the wall where the glowing embers from the fireplace were casting shadows. "You see, Roth. I'm no better than a common whore."

"You're in love with me."

She looked at him sharply. "No!"

"Yes." He bent down and kissed her sensuously, and she moaned pleasurably beneath him. "Say it, Dicia," he coaxed, his lips on her mouth. "Just once let yourself go, let me hear the words. Let tonight be ours, Dicia. Give me this one night to remember always," and she moaned again, her body on fire.

"I . . ."

"Say it!"

"I . . . I love you," she sighed slowly, breathlessly, and he wanted to explode.

"Say it again," he demanded passionately, and this time she threw her heart into it, her words sure and steady, eyes warm with desire.

"I love you . . . I love you. Oh, yes, I do love you!" she cried, and he kissed her again, then lay back, pulling her to him, into his arms.

"Was that so hard, my love?" he asked, and she trembled, moving closer. "Tonight is ours. Tonight we're together again."

"And tomorrow?"

"For us there is no tomorrow," he answered softly, and she understood as she moved against him. He was right. For them there would never be a tomorrow, and he kissed her again passionately, making love to her, and neither of them mentioned Quinn anymore as the storm raged outside and the embers in the fireplace burned low.

With the morning came clear skies and a wet, muddy countryside. Roth opened his eyes and shivered as he put one arm outside the blanket, then put it back under quickly. The fire was almost out and the air chilled. As the night shadows began to disappear, they were slowly replaced by a few brief rays of struggling sunshine.

He felt Loedicia's body against him warm and soft, and he didn't want to move, ever, but he knew it was useless to dream. He'd had his night, and he looked down into her sleeping face, remembering the ecstasy they'd found together. She was cuddled in his arms, her head resting on his chest, the blanket almost covering her head, her face tilted toward him, and he lifted the blanket, bending down, kissing her lightly.

Dicia felt something brush her lips, and sighed, slowly opening her eyes; then suddenly she let out a cry and buried her face in Roth's shoulder, her whole body shaking. It was over, and this was tomorrow!

"Dicia!" His arms held her close. "What is it?"

She felt his warm skin against her, and a physical pain made her shudder. "It's over, isn't it?" she asked, and suddenly he understood.

"We have to face reality," he answered. "But it'll never be over, not really. We've had a son together, you and I. There'll always be a bond between us, and as long as there are memories, it'll never be over for us. I'll love you until the day I die."

She swallowed hard and held her head up, looking down into his dark eyes. "Forgive me, Roth," she whispered softly. "I didn't want to love both of you."

"I know."

"Do you?"

"Yes."

"And I'm forgiven?"

"Yes."

She sighed. "Thank you." She bent down and kissed him, her lips lingering on his for an exceptionally long time.

"We have to go," he said breathlessly as she drew her head back, "or I'm liable to change my mind," and she sighed.

They dressed in silence, their clothes still damp in places, and Dicia's heart felt like it was breaking inside. She was hurting him, and she knew it, but there was nothing else she could do.

She should feel guilty for what she'd done, but for some reason she didn't. Roth had been her husband once, and to let him make love to her had been a natural thing, even after all these years. But now there was Quinn, and the interlude was over.

She fastened the cloak about her shoulders and started to pull up the hood when Roth stopped her.

"One more kiss to last me a lifetime?" he asked passionately, and she stood still with her hands on the back of her hood ready to lift it.

She looked up at him and there were tears in her eyes. His arms went about her and he pulled her close. "For eternity," he said softly and kissed her long and hard, her arms moving up about his neck, his mouth moving against hers fiercely as she kissed him back, neither wanting to let the kiss end.

Finally he drew back and looked into her face. "Now, if we're going to save that stubborn cuss of a husband of yours from hanging, we'd better be on our way," and he pulled up her hood, tweaked her nose, and held the door open for her. It was his way of relaxing the tension between them, and she looked deep into his eyes for just a moment, then turned on her heel and headed out the door. The ride the rest of the way to London would be the longest ride of her life.

Rebel was looking out the window. She'd been looking out the window since late afternoon when she'd first discovered

Lizette's deception. Sick! Her mother sick? Her mother had always been one of the healthiest women around, but then Lizette had said she'd caught something when she'd been to the prison, and it seemed logical at the time. She should have known better.

If she hadn't wanted to borrow one of her mother's perfumes and slipped into her room, she'd still think she was lying in bed sick and feverish. Damn Lizette anyway. She could at least have told her, but as it was she'd alarmed the whole household without thinking, and now she regretted it, because the duke had been furious and for the first time she had a glimpse of his temper.

She turned and glanced behind her where he was stretched out lackadaisically in a chair, his head resting on his hands as he studied her; then he moved slowly and stood up, stretching.

"She should be back by now," he said as he walked toward her, and she eyed him with apprehension.

"Maybe it takes longer to reach Portsmouth than we figured."

"If she reached Portsmouth."

"My mother can ride like the devil himself," she answered. She looked back out the window. "She made it, I'm sure of it."

"And if she didn't, what do I tell your father? When I told him she was sick in bed, he suspected something. Evidently he knows how your mother's mind works. He wanted me to make sure, but that French tiger your mother calls a friend wouldn't let me near the room and I couldn't find out a thing. When I saw your father this morning, he was anything but congenial. I don't dare tell him she's gone. I gave him my solemn promise."

"If you had known my mother better, you wouldn't have," she answered. "She's unpredictable and quite independent."

" 'Stubborn' is the word."

"She's in love with him. Did you expect her to sit back and do nothing to save him?"

"Most women wouldn't know what to do."

"Most women aren't my mother."

"So I've noticed." He eyed her curiously. "Did you know she shot Lord Varrick?"

"Yes."

"I thought so. That's why the hysterics when she met Elton Chaucer, isn't it?"

"Yes."

"But where does Roth Chapman come into it?"

She didn't like being questioned, and as far as Roth was concerned, that was her mother's business. "Roth Chapman was a friend, that's all."

"Oh, come now, I heard your mother tell the king her story, yes, but it was obvious she was leaving something out."

"Oh?"

His eyes steadied on hers. "She was too nervous in her acknowledgment of him, and your father has reasons for hating him that I think go beyond a slight flirtation with his wife, doesn't he?"

She wasn't about to oblige. "You'll have to ask my father."

"I have. He only stares at me with those cold eyes of his and tells me it's his affair."

"Then I guess it is," she answered, and his face hardened.

Somehow he had to find out why Quinn was so afraid of Roth. It could prove useful someday. Besides, he didn't like people having secrets from him. It irritated him. He frowned. He'd have sworn when he met Quinn that the man wasn't afraid of anything or anyone, and he tried to remember the conversation between Quinn and Loedicia that day at the prison. From what he could remember, it wasn't really Roth Quinn was afraid of, but the influence Roth had on Loedicia. He was afraid of losing his wife to the man. But why? Was he that unsure of her love? The thought was ridiculous. He'd have sworn they were very much in love; at least they'd acted like it until Roth appeared on the scene; then suddenly the atmosphere between them had changed and he'd noticed a tension building up. A tension Rachel had been using to her advantage.

Ah, yes, Rachel. She'd been flirting outrageously with Quinn. A fact that should have bothered him, but didn't. He glanced at Rebel as he thought of Rachel. The two couldn't be compared. Sleeping with Rachel was like sleeping with any common whore. She knew all the tricks, but there was nothing personal about it. And sometimes her savage surrender left him uneasy.

She had welcomed him to her bed last night after his long weeks of abstinence, without a question asked, but for some reason, this time, he found no pleasure in their coupling, and he had a feeling she'd have to find herself another bed partner.

He stared at Rebel hungrily. Now, there was a piece of

woman. There was something wild and untamed about her, yet to look at her was to think of a fragile doll. She intrigued him.

Rebel could feel the duke's eyes on her, and she almost smiled to herself. More and more each day she could see the subtle change in him. His eyes seemed to follow her constantly, and he seemed restless, yet there were times—like when he'd gotten angry this afternoon—he could be frightening. She straightened her shoulders. She wouldn't think of it. She turned back to the window suddenly as a noise in the growing darkness caught her attention. As she strained her eyes she saw two figures on horseback turning in at the gates out front, and she held her breath anxiously.

"It's Mother. I know it is," she cried softly as she watched the dark figures make their way down the drive. "And he's with her," and she turned to leave, when the duke caught her wrist.

"You think your father will stand for it?" he asked as he held her for a brief moment.

"I don't think he'll even know about it until it's over," she answered. "If I know Mother, she'll ask for an audience with the king for first thing tomorrow morning and they'll release my father before it even goes before the magistrate."

He stared into her violet eyes. "And there'll be the devil to pay."

She wrenched free of him. "At least he won't hang," and she hurried from the room with the duke close behind.

Loedicia hesitated as she stood in front of the door, wanting to open it, yet prolonging the moment.

Roth straightened beside her, his body tense. "What is it?" he asked, looking down at her, and she turned to look up into his face.

"I have to forget now, don't I?" she said, and his heart went out to her.

"But will you . . . will you ever forget me, Dicia?" he asked, his voice hushed, and her eyes misted, his face clouding before them as the door burst open, and she was unable to give him an answer as Rebel engulfed her, hugging her ecstatically, almost crying.

"Don't ever scare me like that again, Mother," she admonished as she held her tight, then stepped back and stared at Loedicia's tired face. "I was so worried. To do a foolish thing like that . . ."

"It's not foolish," explained Dicia as she glanced up at Roth, her face flushed. "He came."

"And you'll clear Quinn?" asked the duke from behind Rebel as he addressed Roth, and Roth nodded.

"I'll clear him."

The duke looked at Dicia. "Your husband's going to explode."

"It won't be the first time, nor, I doubt, the last," she said, trying to act confident as she and Roth stepped inside, shedding their cloaks with some assistance from the crowd that was beginning to gather as Teak and the duchess joined them, along with the servant Jarvis, who announced that dinner was served.

Loedicia and Roth ate as they were except for a bit of washing up, and the conversation was heated as Brandon expressed his dislike of her underhanded tactics. But after a good deal of assuaging on Loedicia's part, some fiery comments from Rebel, and an assurance from Roth, they agreed that it was better to have Quinn alive and fuming than hanging from the end of a rope.

"And as soon as we're through eating," offered Roth, "I'll leave for my town house and have one of my servants take a message to the king. Loedicia wants an audience for as soon as possible in the morning," and Rebel glanced at the duke with a knowing smile and Brandon wondered if perhaps she knew her mother so well because she was so much like her, and he smiled back, acknowledging her earlier prediction.

16

Quinn stirred in his cell and kicked his foot out, sending the brown furry rodent scurrying from the blow; then he shifted his weight onto the other hip and relaxed again against the cold, damp wall. His feet felt like ice inside his boots, and he rubbed his hands, shoving them in what was left of his pockets, trying to keep warm as he pulled the cloak tighter about him. It helped some, but the cold seemed to go right to the bone. He winced as he thought of Dicia being sick; then he scowled, wondering if she really was. He glanced across the small cell toward the door, where one of the men lay, his face gaunt and pale with fever, lips cracked and blistered. There was sickness and fever all about him, and he closed his eyes. It could be possible. She could have picked up something the other day, but he had a gnawing suspicion she hadn't, and he wished to hell he knew what she was up to.

But then, if she really was sick . . .

He took a deep breath and stirred again restlessly, hoping Brandon would come early this morning with news that she was better, because he had some news for him in return, and he smiled to himself as his eyes settled on a surly character in the far corner of the room.

The man was stocky, his face scarred, with eyes like hot coals that could stir even the bravest man's complacency. He'd been thrown in last night ranting and raving like a madman, and it was a word here and there Quinn caught that had registered.

His questioning of the man during the night had been subtle, skillfully done, and now, for the first time in weeks, he had something to hang onto. The man was a smuggler working for Elton Chaucer. He'd been in a fight in a grog shop and killed a man, an incident indirectly connected with his smuggling activities, and he'd talked freely, cursing the fact that he'd been caught. Not only was Elton smuggling food, clothing, and jewels in from France, but men. Spies! Enemies of England.

At last he had something, if he could just stay alive long enough to use it. The man had dropped names and places during his ranting, and Quinn tucked them neatly away in his memory for future use.

The trial was to start this afternoon, but if Brandon came this morning he could set things in motion and maybe by afternoon things wouldn't look quite so bleak. With this new knowledge, not only could he discredit Elton with the king, but prove him a liar and a traitor, perhaps vindicating himself from the murder charge and securing the earldom for himself.

He smiled as he watched the surly man leaning against the wall. How ironic. If Elton Chaucer hadn't had him arrested, he'd never have learned the truth. At least not as easily. He'd covered his operations well. Now, where the devil was Brandon?

He shifted again and stood up, trying to stretch, feeling the grit and dirt that were being ground into his skin. No wonder so many never left these walls. The stench alone was enough to sicken a body if the guards and other inmates didn't kill you first, and the food, if you could call it that, was appalling, watery and full of maggots.

He glanced about at his cellmates. They were a ghastly lot. Most of them were uneducated, many of them born and bred in poverty and squalor as bad as they were in now. Trying to struggle out any way they could, which often meant stealing and murder. The rest were men of wealth who'd fallen on bad times or gambled away the fortunes left to them by their benefactors and could no longer keep the creditors from the door. It was the only place in London where the poor felt as rich as the richest man there, and who, for a few guineas, could feel even richer.

Reaching out to one side, he felt for the edge of the raggedy cloak and began trying to pull it about himself to help cover his tattered clothes and try to get a bit warmer. If he didn't have to wear these goddamn shackles. His fingers slipped and he grabbed it again as a man came shuffling down the damp corridor and stopped at the door to his cell. Glancing up, Quinn watched as the turnkey opened the door; then he straightened in surprise as the man called his name.

"Well, come on, come on," the turnkey ordered impatiently

as Quinn hesitated. "I 'aven't got all day, fella. Get yer arse out 'ere afore I 'auls yer out!" and Quinn, staring at him bewilderedly, shuffled awkwardly to the door and out into the corridor as the man shut the door behind him and gave him a shove.

They moved down the hall to the gatekeeper's office, and Quinn had no idea what was going on. It couldn't be visitors, because they were going in the opposite direction.

At the gatekeeper's house two men waited. They were dressed in black, older men, and they studied him from head to toe, their faces sober as the turnkey had him hold out his hands and he began to unlock the shackles on his wrists.

"What the devil's going on?" exclaimed Quinn, quite at a loss. "It surely can't be time for the trial yet. Besides, they never take the shackles off a prisoner," but the turnkey only shrugged as he bent down, unlocking the irons that encased his ankles.

"These 'ere gents brought a summons from 'is Majesty," explained the gatekeeper. "Seems 'e wants to talk wi' yer," and he nodded to the gents in black. "Mind 'e, men," he warned, "this 'ere gent's strong as a bull and 'e may not go easy," but Quinn straightened, rubbing his bruised wrists, a cynical smile twisting his lips.

"On the contrary, sir," he said, addressing the gatekeeper politely, and his spirits rose as he thought of the surly dark-haired man back in his cell. "If they're taking me for an audience with the king, he's just the man I've been wanting to see all morning. But may I warn you," he cautioned. "Take good care of that raving gentleman they threw into the cell with us last night, will you? I have a suspicion the king will want to see him too, and I'd hate for him not to be here when he's summoned."

The gatekeeper eyed him dubiously, then frowned. " 'E'll be 'ere," he answered gruffly. "Now, off wi' the likes of yer," and Quinn nodded to the two men in black.

One led the way, with the other in the rear as they entered the street and escorted Quinn to a covered carriage that waited outside the door. The ride to the palace of St. James's was brief, and as they alighted and he was escorted through the corridors, Quinn frowned, wondering what the hell this whole thing was all about. He was glad for the opportunity, but something just wasn't right.

Much to his surprise, they escorted him first to a small

chamber, where he was ordered to bathe and clean up and one of his own suits was waiting for him to change into.

Slowly, as he bathed, then pulled on the clothes, straightening them, making sure he looked all right, a gnawing suspicion grated at the back of his mind, and he felt the heat of anger begin to seep into every nerve of his body, and some of his enthusiasm began to wane. If his suspicions were right . . .

He finished dressing hurriedly now, then opened the door to be confronted once more by the two men in black. They escorted him down a maze of corridors to where two tall, white-wigged servants stood guarding massive doors that swung open at their touch; then Quinn stood staring at the assemblage before him.

The king sat on his throne engulfed by massive ermine-trimmed robes, his jeweled crown sitting rather precariously atop his head, and on either side of him were his two secretaries and a few advisers.

Standing before the king, her shoulders straightening defiantly, looking more lovely than ever in a dress of gold velvet, was Dicia. Quinn's eyes caught hers instantly as he stepped into the room, and he stared at her, then suddenly he knew. In that silent moment he knew what she'd done; he'd been right, and his eyes moved reluctantly to Roth standing at her side. His fists clenched involuntarily as the veins stood out in his neck, and his jaws tightened angrily as he tried to hold his composure and realized the king was addressing him.

"Mr. Locke," the king was saying as Quinn moved stoically across the floor, "do you have any idea why I've summoned you?" and Quinn turned abruptly from Leodicia to face the man on the throne before him.

He bowed deeply, his lips firm. "I believe I have an idea, your Majesty, yes," he answered huskily as he straightened, and the king sighed.

"Good," he said. "Then may I say that due to the charges levied against you by the Earl of Locksley and with the evidence he brought forth, I was quite willing to have you tried for murder and hung, but after hearing the testimony of your wife and your friend Mr. Chapman, I am inclined to feel that Lord Chaucer was overstepping his bounds and using his friendship with me to secure his hold on the earldom, of which I believe you've set claim, am I right there?"

Quinn's face was hard as he nodded. "Yes, your Majesty."

The king smiled cynically. "I think it was honorable of you to wish to spare your wife any grief, Mr. Locke," he said.

"But there was really no need. Since she killed Lord Varrick in self-defense, there would have been no question of her hanging. Your chivalry was quite meaningless."

Quinn flinched, but held his temper. "Under the circumstances, your Majesty, and with Lord Chaucer willing to go to any extent to eliminate me, I felt it quite necessary. Besides, I was not merely being chivalrous. Even if I had told the truth, no one would have believed me."

King George leaned back, the crown on his head tilting forward as it hit the back of the throne, and he straightened it.

"You're right, Mr. Locke," he said, then looked toward Roth. "However, now that Mr. Chapman has vindicated you . . . I wished to apologize for the inconvenience to you in person. That's why I insisted they bring you here rather than wait to have the magistrate release you, and since I have spoken to the earl marshal and learned that you indeed are the son of Martin Locksley, who would have become the earl had he lived, I wish you luck in claiming the title."

Now, thought Quinn, strike while the door's open. "Perhaps, your Majesty, I can further my ends there also," he said as he addressed the king cautiously. There was a gentleman, or shall I say, a ruffian, thrown into our cell last evening who can shed a great deal of light on Lord Chaucer's activities of late. Perhaps you've been wondering recently how French imports manage to be reaching the sales markets in England and how it is that military secrets and some of your own closely guarded secrets have been reaching France."

The king straightened, frowning. "What are you implying, sir?" he asked urgently, and Quinn went on.

"A man is at this very moment sitting in the cell back in Newgate, your Majesty," he said. "He's told me that Lord Chaucer is not only the brains behind a smuggling ring plying the English Channel, and might I say at a great profit, but he has been instrumental in infiltrating French spies into the country and into your very court. A practice the French pay well for and a situation I believe Mr. Pitt has had suspicions of, but been unable to prove. If I hadn't been thrown into Newgate, the information would probably have died on the gallows with the man, since he's in for murder and I doubt if anyone else would have listened and paid heed to his rantings."

"You believed him?" asked the king hurriedly, and Quinn nodded.

"There's no reason for him to lie. He had no idea he was talking to anyone who could use the information to advantage. The man was merely complaining of his predicament and the reasons thereof. He may even deny it if brought before you, but I doubt it. He seemed the sort that would relish taking others with him if given a chance. However, I have an excellent memory, your Majesty, and I believe I can remember enough to direct your soldiers to a number of places and people who also can point the finger at Lord Chaucer, in case the man's reluctant to speak up."

The king's hands clenched on the arms of his throne savagely. "And to think that I thought Lord Chaucer a trusted friend. No wonder he's been so solicitous." His eyes shone angrily as he stared at Quinn. "If all you claim is right, perhaps I can help the earl marshal in his decision," he said dramatically. "Now, I had you brought here—against your wife's wishes, might I add . . ." He glanced at Loedicia. "She wanted to meet you at the prison alone." He glanced back to Quinn. "Regardless"—he waved his hand to dismiss the thought—"I had you brought here because I wanted to meet the man who could bring Roth Chapman galloping back across the downs to save him from the noose. He's a unique man and a busy one, with little time for friendships. I know the man well. You should be eternally grateful."

Quinn straightened hesitantly, then glanced toward Roth, trying to conceal his anger, wondering how much the king knew of their true relationship.

Roth stood tall and firm, eyes unyielding.

The duke, who'd accompanied Loedicia and Roth, watched the eyes of the two men as they met, and he sensed the animosity between them.

"Then I presume I must thank you," stated Quinn, his voice low and vibrant, and Roth nodded coolly.

"It's the least I could do," he answered awkwardly, then turned to the king. "Now, if your Majesty will excuse me. My ship was in the harbor ready to sail to America. If I might beg your leave, if I ride right away, we might still sail before the week's out."

But the King had other plans. "Nonsense," he said rather provocatively. "I'm having a dinner party this evening and I wish you all to attend," and at his words Brandon's eyes shone wickedly, because he knew there was no way they could refuse. Especially Quinn. Not if he wanted to claim the title, and the duke glanced quickly at Loedicia, who looked uncomfortable. The evening promised to be interesting.

They left Roth at the steps of the palace with little said as he climbed into his carriage, and all the way back to Grosvenor Square in the duke's carriage the conversation was stilted. Loedicia was waiting for the explosion, knowing it was building up, watching the tensions growing, but he held off until they were dressing for the king's party.

She was alone in their room, wearing her blue dressing gown, the deep burgundy dress she was to wear tossed across the foot of the bed. Her dark hair was piled atop and to the back of her head, with the curls hanging at the nape of her neck, making her look much younger than her almost forty years, but she felt ancient as she worked her fingers deftly, fastening the diamond teardrop earrings to her ears.

Earlier, when they'd returned, the duchess had gushed over Quinn disgustingly, and there was no mistaking the invitation she held out to him with every gesture. Rachel was a strong-willed woman, and her mere presence was unnerving at this point, with Dicia's emotions already at a dangerous upheaval.

Loedicia fastened the last earring, then stared at her reflection. Whom was she trying to fool? It wasn't Rachel's presence that bothered her, it was the fact that Rachel reminded her of her own indiscretion with Roth. But Roth was different. Roth had been her husband once. They shared a son. It was no light flirtation. She shook her head. No . . . there was no comparison. She had slept with only two men in her life, Quinn and Roth. The duchess had probably slept with dozens. No . . . she wasn't like the duchess. She could never be.

Suddenly she was jolted from her daydream as Quinn opened the door noisily and stepped into the room, shutting it behind him with a deliberate firmness.

"Now we talk!" he said angrily as she whirled around, and she winced at the look on his face.

He'd been downstairs with Brandon and had only now come up to dress, and it was the first they'd been alone since his return. He stared across the room at her, and her hand moved slowly to her throat, the pulse in her neck beating wildly.

He lurched forward abruptly and stood looking down at her, his brilliant blue eyes hard and cold. "Why?" he asked viciously. "Why did you do it?"

She raised her head defiantly, her face flushed. "Because I didn't want you to hang!"

"You didn't . . ." He laughed cynically. "You mean you wanted to see him again."

"I didn't!"

"Didn't you?"

"No!"

"Then why didn't you listen? Why didn't you trust me? I told you when we first came to England I wouldn't hang."

"You told me?" She stood up and walked to the bed, then turned to face him. "You told me they wouldn't arrest you too, do you remember?"

"That's beside the point."

"Oh, is it really?" Her eyes mocked him. "The last words I remember you saying were that you'd rather hang than let them hear the truth. You'd rather die than take the chance on Roth coming back to London, but now you say you didn't intend to hang."

"I would have gotten out of it."

"How?"

He stared at her furiously. "Brandon had suspicions about Chaucer. He'd have come up with something."

"I was to take that chance?"

"You had to go after him, didn't you? You had to make me beholden to him?"

"Don't be ridiculous."

"What do you call it? And leaving the way you did!"

"Well, what else was I to do? You gave Brandon strict orders."

His eyes studied her slowly from head to toe. He'd never seen her lovelier or more radiant, but there was something else about her. She seemed edgy, unsure of herself. Then he remembered the duchess, and his stomach tightened into knots.

"You still haven't forgiven me, have you?" he asked, and she stared at him, unable to answer. He looked disgusted. "Well, maybe I haven't forgiven myself," he added harshly, but she still stared at him speechless. He walked to her slowly, hesitantly. "What's the matter?"

She frowned. "N-nothing."

His eyes held hers, and he saw something he'd never seen in them before, a look that was alien to her. She looked guilty, but why? Of what? "Well, have you forgiven me?" he asked again, and her mouth felt dry.

"Yes."

His voice lowered. "Why?"

"What . . . what do you mean, why?"

"Why is it you can suddenly forgive me?"

"I don't know." She wrung her hands nervously. "I don't know. . . . Maybe I don't really forgive you. Maybe I'm only saying it?"

He looked at her, his eyes suddenly curiously alive. "Then let's find out," he whispered, and he reached out, his arm circling her waist, and as he pulled her into his arms, she felt a sharp pain run through her and her knees weakened.

He could feel her heart beating against him and he felt his body responding to her. His eyes bored into hers, looking deeply, and she took a quick breath; then he brushed his lips across hers ever so lightly. She trembled as his lips touched hers, and he held her tighter, but there was something . . .

Suddenly he stared at her, transfixed, his eyes widening. "That's it!" he cried passionately, his face pale. "I should have known," and she gasped as he thrust her away from him violently and she fell across the bed. "That's what's been bothering me all along, ever since I saw the two of you standing there together." His voice was bitter, like a sword cutting into her. "You and Roth. That's it, isn't it? I knew . . . I knew something was wrong. You rode cross country together. You and Roth!"

Loedicia lay on the bed trembling, tears in her eyes.

"That is it, isn't it?" he demanded as he took a step toward her. "He cuckolded me while I was in prison. . . . You let him make love to you, didn't you?" He reached out and grabbed her, pulling her up by the shoulders as she still lay on the bed, shaking her until she thought her head would come off. "Is that why you said you could forgive me? Is it?" he yelled, and she nodded.

"Yes!" she yelled back. "Yes . . . yes . . . yes," and he stopped abruptly, his eyes hard and cold, staring into her flushed face, and his heart lurched inside him at her confession. "Yes," she sobbed again softly as he held her still, his hands on her shoulders, staring into her face. "I let him make love to me," and she saw the pain on his face as his hands eased and he let her fall back on the bed.

"This time I'll kill him," he swore as he started toward the door, and she gasped as she reached out, trying to stop him, falling half off the bed.

"No!" she screamed. "No, Quinn, you can't, please!" she yelled, tears streaming down her face. "No, Quinn!"

Then, as he reached the door to fling it open, she yelled defiantly, "I didn't kill the duchess, did I?" and her voice rang around the room, bouncing off the walls, echoing in his ears like a trumpet, filling his head, and he stopped abruptly, his hand on the doorknob.

She saw him hesitate and her heart stood still. "I could have killed her," she yelled desperately, tears wetting her cheeks. "I wanted to. Oh, how I wanted to. I wanted to push in her smiling face and tear her limb from limb, but I didn't." She slipped the rest of the way off the bed, pulling at the sash of her wrapper nervously as she stumbled toward him, pleading with him. "Quinn, don't do this, please," she sobbed. "I couldn't help it. . . . I didn't mean for it to happen, neither did he. . . . We got caught in the rain on the way back and had to take refuge in an inn. Neither of us meant for it to happen, but I was alone and hurt because of what you'd done, and . . . somehow it was as if the years had never been. . . . I'm sorry, Quinn. I'm sorry," and she stood behind him now, staring at his back, still turned to her.

Quinn's eyes closed as his fingers eased on the doorknob, and his head fell back, his voice strained. "So now we're even, is that it?" he asked, and she sighed as she gestured helplessly.

"I don't know, maybe that is it."

He held his breath, then turned on her violently. "Damn you, Dicia!" he cried passionately. "Damn you! I can't live with you and I can't live without you," and he took a step toward her, then pulled her into his arms roughly, his eyes devouring her. "Why do I have to love a hellcat like you? Why couldn't I have kept my heart free?"

Her eyes were misty, her lips quivering. "Is that what you want?" she asked, her mouth only inches from his. "To be free?"

He sighed. "God, no! That's not what I want," he answered. "I want you, but I want all of you, not just the part you want to give me."

"Then let's start over again," she whispered. "Let's forget the past, Quinn. Let's pretend there's no one in the world except the two of us."

"That won't work, and you know it."

"We can try."

"And fall on our faces again."

"Then let's just love each other," she pleaded through her tears, "because I do love you. I can't help loving you, any more than I can help anything else I do. You're in my blood, a part of me."

"And Roth?"

"Don't ask me about him," she pleaded tearfully. "He's an interlude, a part of me that has no right to exist. Please, Quinn," she pleaded, her eyes warm as he held her close. "Let's forget about the duchess and Roth and everything but each other. Let's start over again."

"We can't go back, Dicia," he whispered sadly. "We can never go back."

"But we can go ahead." She reached out and touched the gray at his temples, then ran her fingers through his hair. "Forgive me, Quinn. I forgive you . . . please, now forgive me. . . ."

His lips found hers and he kissed her hungrily. How could he do anything else? She was his life, his love, and he had won out. She'd gone to Roth, but she'd come back to him.

He picked her up in his arms and carried her to the bed, gently laying her down, and the war between them became a truce and the wound began to heal as he made love to her passionately, and she accepted him once more with an intimate longing, loving him as always, and that night when they left for the palace of St. James's there was a new bond growing again. It was a bit strained at times, especially when Rachel made herself felt during the course of the evening and Roth made his appearance, but it was there. The love that had seared itself into their hearts those long-ago years in the wilderness was growing again in spite of everything.

At the end of the evening as they stood by the carriages with the rest of the guests saying good-bye, Roth turned to Loedicia, who was standing beside Quinn. His eyes looked strained, his face sad, and a lump was in his throat as he realized what he was leaving behind. He knew she'd told Quinn. He could tell by the look on Quinn's face, and he'd purposely avoided contact with them all evening as much as possible, rather awkwardly at times, but wisely. However, at the moment, there was no way to avoid saying good-bye.

He swallowed hard as he stared into Dicia's violet eyes, and there was a warmth there for him that was unmistakable. He hated this moment, but knew it had to come. "Good-bye, Dicia," he whispered softly; then his eyes moved slowly to Quinn's face. It was intense and demanding. "I'm not sorry about anything, Quinn," he said huskily, his voice filled with emotion, and Quinn's lips tightened as Roth went on. "The only thing I'm sorry about is that it couldn't last. But I guess she always was yours deep in her heart."

Loedicia sensed that Quinn was ready to lunge at him, and she reached up, taking his arm, holding him back.

"Don't worry," continued Roth. "It's over, for what it's worth. I'll say good-bye now and step out of your lives for good. She's yours, Quinn, unconditional surrender. Just make sure you take good care of her, though, and give her all the love she deserves, or, by God, I'll come back and beat the hell out of you!" and he turned abruptly, without looking back at either of them, and entered the closed carriage that was waiting.

Loedicia watched the door close and the carriage start up, knowing that with it went a part of her. A part of her that she couldn't quite understand, nor could she explain, but he was gone, and she squeezed Quinn's arm harder as his hand covered hers. He was gone for good this time and she knew it, and there was a sadness in her heart, yet she glanced up at her husband, strong and firm, and her heart turned over inside her. This was as it should be, this was right, he was her love, and she blushed, remembering the ardor in his lovemaking earlier when they'd made up.

It would heal. The wound would heal and things would be right again. They had to be, and she smiled as Quinn looked down at her. "I love you," she whispered softly, and he took a deep breath, straightening his shoulders proudly.

"I know," he said, "I love you too," and they watched silently together as Roth's carriage disappeared from sight.

17

In the whole of London there was never such an uproar as was caused when the king's men started investigating the charges Quinn had brought against Elton Chaucer, and during the next few weeks arrests were made in some of the most unlikely places. But the man they wanted most, Elton Chaucer, slipped through their fingers and suddenly dropped from sight, taking his wife and sons with him.

"Fled to France, no doubt," suggested Brandon the day Quinn received word that his claim for the title had been honored; and only a few days after Quinn stood before the earl marshal in his crown and ermine-trimmed robe and accepted the earldom, he, Loedicia, Teak, and Rebel moved from the house on Grosvenor Square to the mansion at Locksley near the English coast.

The estate was beautiful, with its own lake, elegant gardens, and riding stables, and a twenty-room house overrun with servants galore. The house had a fifteen-foot-wide staircase in the foyer, ancestral portraits gracing the landing that separated the east and west wings, and each room wore its ornate furniture with a pride built in over the years. It was Quinn's ancestral home. He'd been raised here, and because of that, Loedicia accepted it, although she would have been much happier with less.

The first thing Quinn did was to lengthen their last name back to Locksley; then he swung into the work at hand, interviewing the tenants, changing the rules, and within a month's time the lovely mansion with its gracious towers saw, surrounding it, a village of happy tenants with a zest for living equaled only by the man they looked up to. The new Earl of Locksley, and the beautiful wife he adored.

Quinn found enjoyment riding about Locksley with Teak in tow, teaching him everything he had to know, and Teak, eager for the title he'd always hoped would be his someday, listened intently, drinking in everything, learning as much as he could.

As the months passed, only Rebel seemed discontented. Winter was on them and the social season was over in London, but still she hadn't managed to get a proposal from the duke, and she had heard that he was leaving shortly after Christmas for Grenada, in the West Indies, where he was to take over the post as the new governor. And now she was stuck out here miles from London with nothing to do but watch her mother and Lizette trying to keep themselves busy.

Unless, that is, she wanted to follow Teak about, trying to keep him out of trouble. Somebody should. Twice now she'd caught him with one of the chambermaids. If he wasn't so blasted good-looking! And he knew how to treat the ladies, too. He had a suave charm that seemed to fascinate them. The trouble was that he knew it.

It was early in the evening two days before Christmas, and Rebel was restless as she stood in the back salon and watched lazy snowflakes falling outside. They reminded her of the snowflakes back home. Home! It seemed so far away. She'd been talking to her mother only that morning about home and wasn't surprised to discover that she too was getting restless. Her mother also missed the log house with its huge fireplaces and Sepia singing in the kitchen, and suddenly, as Rebel stared into the night, it was as if she could see a pair of dark green eyes staring back at her, and she trembled as she cursed to herself.

Would she never forget him? She wondered. Where were they tonight, Heath and Beau? Would she ever see them again? And once more that strange yearning filled her loins as she thought of Beau. She'd tried to forget him, but it wasn't that easy. He haunted her dreams, even after all this time.

She reached up and touched the windowpane, tracing her finger in the dampness that clung to it as the heat from the fireplace in the room made it sweat. It was cold, almost ice already, and she knew the temperature outside was dropping fast.

Suddenly she heard a commotion behind her and turned toward the hall. Her curiosity aroused, she left the room and headed for the foyer, then stopped abruptly as she saw Brandon handing his snow-covered cloak and gloves to the butler.

"Hello there!" he called as he spotted her at the end of the hall, and she smiled.

"Where on earth did you come from in this weather?" she asked as he approached her, warming his hands with his breath, and he straightened, squaring his shoulders.

"I want to talk to you," he said anxiously, taking her arm, ushering her back toward the salon, and when they were inside, he shut the door behind them, then stood looking at her.

She was wearing a heavy dress of deep rose-brown velvet with lace about the high neck and long sleeves, and it made her look fragile and demure. Deceiving, he thought as he looked her over warmly. She was going to be just like her mother, and he knew it—unpredictable and stubborn, with a mind of her own—but he didn't care. He'd tame her. She was what he wanted, had been since the day he'd first laid eyes on her.

"Did your father tell you I'm leaving?" he asked abruptly, and she cocked her head sideways as she looked at him.

"I think he did say something of the sort, yes."

"I'm sailing right after the first of the year."

She smiled coquettishly. "Is that why you came? To say good-bye?"

He frowned seriously as he watched her reaction. "I came to ask you to go with me," he said huskily, and saw her eyes suddenly freeze as she stared at him, and she had the strangest expression on her face. "Oh, come now, is that the way you're supposed to act when a man proposes to you?" he asked, and she swallowed hard.

She'd wanted it. She'd even worked hard to achieve it, but now, suddenly, as she stared at his handsome face, listening to his words, something inside made her stomach tighten. Yet . . . What was the matter with her? He was asking her to marry him. She studied him, taking in his tawny hair, cool brown eyes, and placid face. There was nothing to repel her, yet . . . there was nothing about him to attract her, either. She felt no exhilaration when he was around. No warmth or desire.

True, he was a dominant person. Rather bossy, to be truthful, but she could put up with that if she had to. It was something else that made her wary. He possessed a ruthlessness when it came to the feelings of others. The few times he'd kissed her, she sensed that he took rather than gave in the exchange. His pleasure came first, above all else, to the expense of his partner, and left him with little tenderness.

Her lips parted as she stared at him, unable to answer, and suddenly she found herself in his arms and he was holding her close.

"You must have known," he said as he held her. "It shouldn't be that much of a surprise."

She sighed, trying to brush aside the doubts. "I . . . I had no idea you felt so strongly," she whispered as his lips sought hers and he kissed her long and hard.

"I intend to ask your father," he said as he drew his head back, "but I wanted your answer first. Do you mind?" and she shook her head.

"No . . . I . . . that's all right."

"Then you'll say yes?"

"I . . . I'm not sure. I . . ." She pushed herself back in his arms. "Do you really have to go to those islands?" she asked.

"You don't want to be wife of the governor?"

She reached out, toying with one of the gold buttons on his suit coat. "It's so far from everything."

"But we'll be together."

It's what she wanted, wasn't it? What was she hedging about? Just because she didn't get all weak and giddy inside when he kissed her or looked at her. Suddenly a pair of dark eyes loomed before her, and she trembled. Not again. Never again, she cried to herself, and she glanced up at Brandon. She had decided to become a duchess, and that's what she'd be, and a cold hardness swept over her as she looked deliberately into his eyes.

"I'd be glad to go with you," she answered firmly, and he kissed her again as she pretended to respond to him, but inside she felt as if a cloud of ice had suddenly encased her.

A few minutes later she stood in the library gazing at the walls of books surrounding her, listening as her father and mother discussed the aspects of Brandon's request for her hand.

"But she's not even nineteen yet," argued Loedicia.

"And to go so far from home and family," added Quinn.

"She'll have money and position," offered Brandon, and the argument went back and forth while she listened stubbornly, her mother protesting, the duke demanding, and her father floundering as mentor.

"I can't just say yes," countered Loedicia heatedly, as the duke pressed her. "You must understand, Brandon. Rebel is the only daughter I have. I have to make sure it's what she wants."

Rebel's eyes hardened as her mother looked at her. "It *is* what I want, Mother," she stated, but Loedicia shook her head.

"I want to be sure," she said, and Rebel balked.

"I'll marry him with or without your permission," she said angrily.

"You'll do no such thing," yelled Quinn.

"I'm told there are chapels at Bath where a family's consent isn't even necessary," Rebel suggested, "and they'll marry you in one day. So you see, we don't really need your blessing."

Loedicia was at a loss. She'd heard of the chapels too, and Bath wasn't all that far away. She'd been standing next to Quinn's desk and now she reached over and touched Rebel's arm. "Reb, please, I don't think the duke had that in mind," and she looked at Brandon. "I think he'd much rather wait for our blessing, since his position as governor of Grenada could be jeopardized if you eloped."

Rebel turned to Brandon for support, but instead he agreed.

"She's right, my dear," he said, and he turned to look back at her father. "But I was hoping you'd say yes. I really don't know what your objections are."

Quinn glanced quickly at Loedicia, then to Rebel. "You really want this, Reb?" he asked, and she nodded stubbornly.

"Yes."

He glanced at his wife. "Loedicia?"

She sighed, defeated. What was the use? Rebel would get her own way eventually anyway. "All right," she finally conceded, but there were still no definite plans settled when Brandon slipped into his cloak and headed across the snow-swept fields toward Grantham Hall. However, he left behind an affirmative to spend Christmas Day at Locksley, at which time they'd make the wedding plans.

As the huge house quieted for the night, Rebel slipped off her dress and tossed it on the chair, then finished undressing and put on the pale blue flannel nightgown the chambermaid had set out for her. The room was so cold. Even the roaring fire in the fireplace wasn't much help. If her bedroom wasn't so gigantic, it might be warmer. She glanced up at the huge bed with its blue velvet draperies and satin bedspreads, then thought of her old bedroom with the small bed, patchwork quilt, and log walls, and wished she were in it snug and warm.

Her feet felt frozen as she pulled back the covers and climbed onto the bed, slipping beneath the cold sheets, putting her feet on the hot bricks the maid had wrapped in a blanket and tucked in at the foot of the bed.

She lay for a long time, curled up in a ball, trying to get warm, but it was no use. Finally she threw back the covers and made a dash across the floor to the fireplace, holding her hands out to its red glow and her feet up, trying to get them warm as the blizzard outside continued to gain in momentum.

Suddenly she straightened as she heard a knock on her door. "Who is it?"

"It's Mother," answered Loedicia, and she called for her to come in.

"They can say all they want about these big English mansions," stated Rebel as her mother entered, closing the door behind her, "but they certainly aren't very snug and warm."

"I'll agree to that," replied Loedicia as she too reached out toward the glowing fire to warm her hands. She was wearing slippers, her blue wrapper, and had her hair down, and Rebel stared at her for a minute as the firelight reflected off her and she marveled at how young and pretty her mother looked. But there was a worried look in her eyes that was unmistakable.

She glanced at her daughter and caught her staring. "Rebel," she began, coming right to the point, "why did you consent to marry Brandon?" and Rebel's eyes narrowed warily.

"What do you mean, why? He's been courting me for months. Doesn't it seem the likely thing to do?"

"That's not what I meant, and you know it." Loedicia folded her arms, scrutinizing her daughter's face. "Back in Philadelphia you told me you were going to marry for money. That you didn't care about love. That you were going to be a duchess!"

"So?"

"So is that what you've done?"

"And if it is?"

Dicia shook her head. "Oh, Reb . . . do you think that's fair to Brandon? Do you think he wants a passive wife, void of emotions?"

"So I can pretend."

"Pretend? You think it's that easy?" Her fingers tightened on her arms as she spoke. "You're different from most young girls your age, Reb," she cautioned. "You've grown up with a freedom few girls ever know. Most girls your age have only a vague idea of what happens in the marriage bed, but because of the life we lead, you know what's expected of you. It's something you can't pretend."

"I can and I will!"

"Reb, do you have any feelings at all for the duke?" and Rebel's face hardened. "Because if you don't," Loedicia went on, "you'll cringe at his touch, believe me. I saw your eyes in the library when he took your hand. There was no warmth in them. You looked like you wanted to run."

"That's not true."

"Isn't it? Does being a duchess mean so much to you . . . can you honestly tell me you can let him make love to you without hating every moment? Marriage is so private, Reb, he's not just putting a ring on your finger, he's taking your body too. Can you accept that?"

"If I have to."

"You don't know. You have no idea," Loedicia replied, and Rebel glanced at her sharply.

"And you do? Oh, Mother, it's an act, that's all, like kissing. You've had two men in your life, Mother, Roth and Father, and you loved both of them. How could you possibly know what it's like with someone you don't love?" and Dicia flinched, her face reddening.

"I've had three men, Rebel," she answered huskily, and there was a sob in her voice as Rebel stared at her mother, puzzled. "Lord Varrick raped me, Reb," she confessed deliberately. "So I do know what it's like. He had to beat me almost unconscious to do it, but I still knew what was happening, he made sure of that. I could feel everything, and, God help me, it was something I'll never forget."

Rebel held her breath as she watched her mother's face. So that was why he beat her. That's why she was so frightened.

"You have no idea," Dicia went on. "It's horrible."

"But rape is different, Mother."

"Is it? Is it so much different, Reb? When there's no love given, it's still a violation. Without love there's no joy in it, only degradation."

"Others have done it."

"And been happy?" She reached out and touched Rebel's hands. They were cold, like ice, even with the heat from the fire. "It takes a special kind of woman to be able to let just any man take her, Reb. A cold woman, devoid of love, her emotions dead. She's like an animal without feelings. Are you that kind of a woman, Reb? Money won't compensate for the loving touch of a man's hands. You can't cuddle up to money and feel its warmth and let it caress you."

"But love isn't everything, Mother. Love can hurt."

"Oh, I know that only too well, dear," she replied, squeezing her hands. "Love can hurt terribly, but it can also keep you alive. It can be as vital as the air you breathe."

Rebel pulled her hands free. "Mother, I've already promised Brandon I'd marry him," and she turned back to the fire.

"You can say you've changed your mind."

"Never."

"But you're not in love with him."

She shrugged. "I can learn to love him."

"I don't think he'll be an easy man to love, Reb. He's rather demanding and selfish, and I don't think you'll be happy."

Rebel stared into the fireplace, watching the flames as they licked at the huge log, and it was as if she could see Beau's face in them. The dark green eyes, that cynical smile that always set her blood racing. She turned back abruptly, and there were tears in her eyes as she looked at her mother. "Then I guess that's my problem," she replied. "Because I intend to marry him, Mother, and become the Duchess of Bourland," and Loedicia gave up.

What was the use? She was as stubborn as her father. She watched as Rebel turned back toward the fire again, warming her hands. Something had happened to make her bitter. It wasn't natural for a young girl to be so bitter about love or to act as if it was so unimportant. Not a girl with Rebel's temperament anyway. The mousy creatures London society was turning out, yes, but not Reb. Somewhere along the way she'd been hurt, but how? By whom?

Loedicia turned, cautioning her to get some sleep, then bid her good night and left. All the way back to the master bedroom she walked slowly, her mind going over everything that had been said and done today. There had to be a solution somewhere. She couldn't just let her jump into marriage so recklessly.

When she opened the door to the bedroom, Quinn was already beneath the covers, only his head sticking out. She walked to the window and stared out, watching the snow swirl about and dash against it, listening to the crackling of the fireplace that accompanied the wind as it flew haphazardly against the house.

Quinn stuck his head up, watching her for a minute, then sighed. "Aren't you coming to bed?"

"In a minute," she said as she continued to watch the snow; then, after a few minutes she turned toward the bed and walked over, slipping off her wrapper, tossing it across the foot of the bed, crawling in as Quinn swung back the covers for her.

"Get in here. It's freezing," he said as he reached out, pulling her down against him, and she snuggled close in his arms, feeling his soft skin against hers, the warm strength of him beside her, and the masculine smell of him that always aroused her. He buried his face in her neck, nibbling at her ear affectionately as he ran his hand from thigh to breast, making her blood flow like liquid fire.

This is what Rebel should feel, Dicia thought to herself. This is what lovemaking should be for her.

"Quinn?" she whispered as he kissed her neck, sending shivers down her spine, and he murmured something against her ear in response that sounded like an answer, but she wasn't sure with her feelings so intense. "Quinn, I want to go home," she whispered softly, and suddenly felt his lips cease their searching, and he waited, wondering if he'd heard right. "I want to go home," she said again, and this time he wasn't mistaken.

"I thought you were beginning to like it here," he said as he held his head up, looking down into her face as she lay back on the pillow, and she sighed.

"I'm tolerating it, that's all. We've been here since August, and everything's settled and running smoothly now. You have a good trustworthy agent in Mr. Briggs to handle things for you, and I was hoping we could go home."

"But . . . why all of a sudden?"

"It isn't all of a sudden. I've been thinking of it for days." She touched his shoulder, running her hand down his arm, feeling the hard strength of him beneath her fingers. "I miss the house and the lake, and believe it or not, I miss everything about Fort Locke, even the Indians."

He grinned. "You miss Telak?"

"And his wives."

"Don't let those staid ladies at St. James's hear you say 'wives,' Countess—they'd be mortified."

"I don't like being a countess."

"But I like being an earl."

"Better than being plain Colonel Quinn Locke?"

His eyes warmed as he looked at her. "Not really. At first I did. It was fun watching things change. Watching the tenants turn from ragged, half-starved slaves into happy, contented people, but now . . ."

"Now all you do all day is ride around looking at things." She sighed. "Wouldn't you love to follow a trap line again and camp out under the stars, or swim in the lake?"

"In winter?"

"We could be home by summer." Her finger traced one of the muscles in his arms as she talked coaxingly. "If we left now, we'd be home in time for late spring. Can't you just hear the redwings and see the forest coming to life? I'd love to pick violets again and watch the sunsets on the lake."

"You really want to go, don't you?"

"You did promise, you know."

"I know."

"Besides," she said, "I thought what we could do is"—she took a deep breath—"we could go to Grenada first with Rebel and Brandon and see things went right, then sail back up to Philadelphia."

He looked at her curiously. "Grenada?" he questioned almost beneath his breath.

"Quinn, she doesn't love him," she explained. "We can tell them that the engagement can be announced now, but the wedding is to take place when we reach Grenada, and maybe by then she'll have changed her mind and she can go on home with us."

"You have it all thought out, haven't you?" He leaned on one elbow. "What if Brandon doesn't like the idea?"

"If we refuse to let them marry unless it's our way, his only other alternative would be to elope, and we both heard him on that score."

"And Rebel?"

"She'll balk at first, but I think she'll go along with it. I don't think she's really all that anxious."

"She seemed anxious enough earlier."

Dicia frowned. "Someone's hurt her, Quinn," she stated. "I don't know how or when, but she's bitter, and it isn't just because of the trouble we've had. Someone's hurt her terribly, and she's going to ruin her life because of it."

"You think stalling the marriage will work?"

"It'll take us at least three months or more to reach Grenada, and maybe by then she'll realize the mistake she's made."

"And if she doesn't?"

"Then at least I'll know I tried. That we didn't give in without a fight."

"Then we sail for home?"

"Please, Quinn?"

He stared into her violet eyes, then reached out and touched a curl that lay against her temple, brushing it back. "All right," he answered, sighing. "We'll go home like I promised," and he bent down, kissing her softly.

"By way of Grenada?" she asked against his mouth, and he laughed lightly.

"By way of Grenada," he confirmed, and he kissed her again, until she forgot everything but her love for him.

By Christmas Day the storm had ceased, leaving the countryside almost buried under a blanket of white. The house was festooned with boughs of holly, colorful garlands hanging about the walls, and silver bells suspended from every chandelier, with the smell of plum pudding, chestnut stuffing, roast pig, and glazed duck filtering out from the kitchen.

They had started Christmas morning with a small service in the private chapel, a breakfast of sweet rolls, honey, rice pudding with cream, ham slices, and an egg soufflé, then retired to the main drawing room overlooking the gardens at the back of the house, its bushes topped with snow like cream whipped to a peak and dropped on in gobs with no concern for strength of branches, as they almost touched the ground in places.

"Maybe Brandon won't be able to make it with the snow so deep," said Teak as he and his mother played whist while Quinn read and Rebel paced the floor.

She was wearing a new red velvet dress with black lace ribbons and bows and had her hair piled atop her head like her mother's, hoping she'd look a little more sedate and less nervous. At first when her mother and father had told her of their plans she'd been furious; then slowly she realized that it would give her a reprieve. After all, what did it matter how soon she became a duchess, just so she became one? The only thing that bothered her now was Brandon. Would he be willing to wait? Maybe he'd call the whole thing off, but he didn't.

All her pacing was for nothing. He was irritated and put out at first, but in the long run, when Loedicia explained how thrilled his subjects on the island would be at his marriage and the subsequent celebrations, he bowed to their authority and the wedding date was set for a week after their arrival in Grenada.

There was still one dissenting member of the family, however. Teak had put up a battle, claiming they were ruining his life, taking everything from him he'd always dreamed about. Like going to Oxford.

"Then go, by hell!" yelled Quinn as he threw up his hands at his son's stubbornness. "Stay in England and go to Oxford if that's what you really want," and Loedicia gasped.

"Now, how on earth can he do that?"

"He can stay here," answered Quinn firmly. "I've taught him everything he has to know, and Mr. Briggs is not only a good agent, but I think he's responsible enough to handle the boy."

"But we can't leave him behind."

"I don't want to go, Mother," he protested. "I'm sick of the woods and living like a—"

"Watch it," cautioned Quinn. "There's nothing wrong with the way we lived," and Teak's face reddened.

"Well . . ." he apologized, "I didn't mean anything. I just mean I like having my boots shined, and my bath drawn, and having my clothes tailor-made."

"Your clothes *were* tailor-made," quipped Rebel sarcastically. "Mother and I made everything that went onto your back."

"That's what I mean," he retorted. "I'm sick of buckskins. . . . Besides, I want to study law and military strategy. Someday I may even buy a commission in the army."

"British or American?" asked Reb, and Quinn frowned at her.

"That's enough, Reb."

"Well, he makes me sick. He's so conceited."

Loedicia stared at Teak. He was so much like Quinn, always wanting to try something new, always a new adventure or challenge. She wasn't as close to him as she had been to Heath, but still the thought of leaving him here hurt. She knew, however, by the stubborn look on his face that she could no more change his mind than she could change Heath's mind two and a half years ago. He was determined not to go.

"All right," she finally conceded softly, her voice faltering. "You'll be fifteen in a couple of weeks and eligible for Oxford, and I'm sure there's no reason why your father can't sign you up. We'll leave Mr. Briggs in charge. Only, I'll warn you, young man," she said, almost feeling ridiculous as she stood looking up at her son, who towered over her, "if you don't behave yourself, your father'll come after you and drag you home by the scruff of your neck!"

Teak reached out and grabbed her, picking her off the floor, laughing as he twirled her about as if she were a feather, and Loedicia laughed too. What did you do with such a rascal? She glanced quickly at Quinn as Teak twirled her, and he was grinning from ear to ear.

Her men, she thought as he set her back down, giving her a big kiss, and she straightened her dress as she scolded him playfully. What would she do without them?

It took a week to make arrangements because of the heavy snow, but by New Year's Eve they were in London at Locksley Hall, Quinn's town house, all their bags packed, awaiting the arrival of the ship that was to take the new governor of Grenada to his post, and they rang the old year out and the new in at an engagement party thrown for the young couple by Rachel.

"It's the least I can do for them," she said as she told Quinn and Loedicia about it the afternoon before. "After all, Brandon did say I was welcome to stay at Grantham Hall or Bourland Hall for as long as I like. He invited me to Grenada, but I declined, since he'll be getting married and won't need me anymore."

"How generous," remarked Loedicia cuttingly, but the duchess seemed undisturbed as she smiled sweetly at Quinn and went on with her arrangements.

The party was a success in spite of Loedicia's coldness toward Rachel, and two days later, with their baggage tucked aboard the HMS *Wayfarer*, they stood at the rail and watched as the city of London was left in the distance and they headed down the Thames toward the sea.

Loedicia was frozen. They spent most of their days bundled up in their bunks with the covers pulled as far up as they could go. Heat on the ship was scarce, and the wintry wind made sailing anything but agreeable. The days dragged on, and Loedicia wondered how in God's name the crew could keep going, but as the ship made its way through the channel into the open sea and headed south, slowly, with each new day, the weather turned warmer.

"My God, I do believe I can climb out from under these covers," she exclaimed one morning as she watched Quinn open his eyes, and he laughed.

"You're the one who wanted to come," he reminded, and she shivered.

"I know. I'm just glad things are getting warmer. I feel like I'm sewed into my clothes," and she lifted her hand outside the covers, feeling the air, which was a good deal warmer than it had been the day before.

Within a few days the weather was warm enough to walk about without getting frostbitten, and they were able to sit at their table to eat breakfast. The *Wayfarer* was a military ship and the captain always invited them to eat dinner at his table, and each evening Loedicia, Rebel, and Lizette nearly froze to death listening to his conversation, which for the most part was quite dull.

"As long as we don't meet up with Thunder," the captain said one evening when the weather was a bit more tolerable and his conversation more interesting.

"Thunder?" questioned Quinn, and Brandon glanced at Quinn, surprised.

"You weren't reading the papers in England very astutely, my friend," he answered. "Captain Thunder is a privateer. He sails for the French in a square-rigger he calls the *Golden Eagle,* and it's armed to the hilt. They say he's uncanny when it comes to smelling out a lone English ship in open waters. There's a price on his head, and there isn't a British captain alive who wouldn't like to see him strung up to the nearest yardarm."

"He's French?" asked Dicia, her curiosity aroused.

"American, from what I hear," answered the captain. "No one knows where he's really from or who he really is, except that he's as wily as a fox and disappears as readily."

Quinn raised his eyebrows. "There's a chance we'll meet him?"

"I hope not, but he picks on lone ships. If we had an escort I'd feel better." The captain glanced at Loedicia, Rebel, and Lizette. "And I don't like having women aboard."

"The women are my responsibility," offered the duke.

"And mine," added Quinn.

"But you're all my responsibility," admitted the captain, "and I certainly hope we can sneak by him. The last two trips, we were three ships and I didn't have to worry. But I don't like the odds this time."

"Would he be this far north, *mon capitaine*?" asked Lizette, and the captain nodded.

"Aye. He's even been spotted in the channel. We could bump into him anywhere from here to Grenada, and half of the French Navy along with him. These are dangerous waters," he affirmed, and two days later a crippled ship from his Majesty's line limped past them after barely escaping French guns a few days before, confirming his statement.

"It's no wonder," said the captain. "We're off the shores of southern France. When we get closer to the Azores, the French won't be so plentiful."

The Azores were beautiful. Held by the Portuguese and as colorful as Portugal itself, they now had balmy weather and warm breezes, and the ladies not only enjoyed their walks on deck, but discarded their cloaks, soaking in the sunshine. The ship stopped at a port in the Azores and took on stores while its passengers watched the activities curiously, then it headed southwest again, and Loedicia gave thanks that they were out of the cold weather at last.

She and Quinn stood one evening near the jib watching the stars before going below to their cabin. The air was warm, the sea sloshing recklessly against the ship, and the wind full as they cut the water.

"It's quite a sight, isn't it?" she said as they moved along at a good pace, and he sighed as he stood behind her, his arms about her, holding her close.

He leaned toward her ear. "Makes you almost feel we're the only two people in the world, doesn't it?" and she leaned closer in his arms.

"Mmhmmm."

He kissed her ear lobe and she sighed. "Have you made any headway with Rebel?" he asked, but she shook her head.

"She's so stubborn and bullheaded."

"Like her father?"

She turned in his arms and looked up into his face, and a warmth went through her clear to her toes. Things had been so right with them lately. It was almost as if England had never happened. She brushed the bad memories away and smiled.

"More like her mother," she replied, and Quinn smiled

back; then his eyes grew soft as the moon peeked out from behind a small cloud and shone on both their faces. "Are you sorry we're going home, Quinn?" she asked, and he shook his head.

"No, not really. I was getting bored in England, and I think you knew it. I'm not much for listening to court gossip, wearing ermine mantles and jeweled crowns, and having people scraping and bowing. I proved my point and gave Teak his due. That's all I really wanted."

"I'm so glad," she said, and reached up, her arms encircling his neck. "I like having my husband back again." She touched his hair, ruffling it in her hands. "I like your hair when it's messed and out of place." Then her finger came down, tracing his jawline. "And you look so handsome in buckskins with your face all tanned."

He reached up, grabbing her hand, and kissed it, letting her fingertips linger on his mouth. "You're a strange one—you know that, don't you?" he said. "Most women would be like Rebel, wanting money and position."

"All I want is love," interrupted Loedicia, "and I've found that with you and I don't ever want to lose it."

"You won't," he whispered passionately, and pulled her closer in his arms. "Not ever! As long as there's a breath in my body, you'll never want for love," and he swung her up, across his arms, carrying her toward their cabin beneath the quarterdeck as some members of the crew on board for night duty snickered, and Brandon, standing beside Rebel a short distance away, stared thoughtfully.

"Your parents amaze me, Rebel," he said as he watched them disappear below deck. "Sometimes I swear they act like newlyweds."

Rebel frowned. "When they're not fighting."

"They don't fight that much. At least I haven't seen one good set-to since we left England."

"I have a feeling they're still making up over something."

"Roth Chapman?"

"Perhaps."

He turned, watching her curiously. Watching the moonlight as it danced in her violet eyes and sifted through her blond hair. Watching the way her full bosom rose and fell with every breath, the way her lips parted provocatively, and his heart beat faster.

He reached out, his arm encircling her waist, and drew her

to him, and his hand moved up her back, pulling her even closer. "Maybe we should make up the way they do," he whispered as he gazed at her, and he felt her body stiffen beneath his hands.

What was wrong with her? Why didn't she respond? He could feel her body warm against his, the scent of her filling his head, and he swallowed hard because there was no change in her eyes. No warmth, only a coldness that frustrated him. Even an innocent fledgling had feelings. Even the shyest girls blushed and grew breathless when made love to, but not Rebel. Her actions said one thing, her eyes another. She always let him kiss her, and once he even grew bolder and caressed her breasts, hoping to bring the warmth to her eyes, hoping she'd let her guard down, but instead she'd acted indignant, putting up a half-hearted attempt at pretending to enjoy it, but wanting to wait until after the wedding. Yet he could see only coldness in her eyes. What did it take to break down her defenses?—because he was sure that beneath the cold veneer was a woman with fire in her veins.

He leaned over and kissed her, his lips sipping at hers hungrily, hoping for a natural response, not the calculated way she always kissed him, never letting herself go, deliberately holding back.

He drew back and looked at her, feeling her body rigid beneath his hands. "Would you like to make up like that, Rebel?" he asked again, deliberately watching her reaction. "Is that what you want me to do? Pick you up and carry you off and make love to you?" and her hands moved to his chest.

"After we're married. . . ."

"To hell with after we're married!" he whispered angrily. "You don't have to be married to want love. To want to feel a man's hands on you."

Her eyes widened.

"Don't look so shocked, my dear," he continued. "You're not some innocent little girl from the *beau monde*, you're Rebel Locksley, you know all too well what the marriage bed's about."

He pulled her closer against him. "What is it, Rebel? Why don't you let yourself go? And you're as touchy as all hell lately. Yesterday you bit my head off for no good reason, the day before that you chewed Lizette out for God knows what trifle, and every time I kiss you I get the impression you're merely tolerating it because it's something you have to do."

His eyes narrowed. "We're to be married, Rebel, remember? That gives me some rights."

She stared at him, her eyes reluctant. "You can take your rights after we're married, and not before," she answered firmly, but he laughed cynically.

"If what I've been receiving is a taste of it, I'd rather make love to an iceberg."

Her heart sank. Mother was right, it wasn't as easy to pretend as she thought. But why? Beau had pretended with her, and he'd been convincing. Why couldn't she pretend with Brandon? It didn't make sense. She had to try harder.

"Do you really want to try the merchandise out, Brandon?" she asked seductively as she tried melting against him. "Do you really want me to forget I'm a lady? Or would you rather wait and have our wedding night what it should be?" and she looked down coyly, avoiding his eyes, staring at the lace on his cravat. "I do want you, Brandon," she lied, "but as my husband."

He put his hand beneath her chin, tilting her head up so she couldn't avoid looking at him.

Think of something, she told herself quickly, think of something you want, think of strawberries swimming in cream, of home, of something, anything but Brandon, and suddenly there were Beau's eyes before her, his mouth coming down on hers, and she melted against Brandon, kissing him back for a brief minute, pretending it was Beau; then the moment was gone and her kiss was cold again, and he pulled his mouth from hers abruptly.

"Don't stop," he whispered passionately against her lips. "For God's sake, Rebel, kiss me like that again," he cried, but she couldn't. Instead, she brushed him aside and wrenched free, turning to stare out at the moon and stars, her body shaking. "Rebel?"

"That's all, Brandon," she groaned faintly. "That's all I can give until after we're married," and he sighed.

"At least I know now that I was right. You have a passion in you I mean to enjoy, my dear," he said huskily. "It'll be like refining gold, watching you bloom, but I must say, for a while you had me rather frightened. I was beginning to think I'd made a mistake and you were one of those cold, unfeeling females who give nothing to a marriage but children—and those conceived in agony." He reached out and touched her hair. "God, how I want you," he said softly. "But I'll be patient. You're worth waiting for, my lovely," and he had no way of knowing the dread that was creeping over her at the implication in his words. Mother was right. It wasn't easy. It wasn't easy at all.

18

It didn't take long for the days to roll into weeks. They fought the elements as summer storms hit them, then drifted aimlessly when the wind died down, refusing to fill the sails. Each day was like the day before, with its endless routine and miles of water, the only change coming from the weather and the size of the waves that broke against the ship.

They were running about four hundred miles north of the British-held island of Barbados just east of the Leeward Islands, confident they'd traveled so far without encountering any French ships. The day was warmer than usual, the sky was brilliant blue, with mounds of huge white clouds scattered about, and the sea matched the sky with its deep brilliance.

Loedicia and Lizette were walking the deck, complaining to each other because neither had been successful in influencing Rebel to change her mind as yet. Quinn and Brandon were talking politics. That is, Brandon was. He was telling Quinn of his plans to invade the French-held island of Tobago, then seize Spanish-held Trinidad for the crown. A plan Quinn found irritating. A plan Quinn hadn't known about before leaving England, and Brandon's ideas on how he was going to do it were astounding. He sounded like a pompous dictator, and Quinn glanced across the way where Rebel sat by herself watching the horizon, and he wondered just what they'd let their daughter in for.

Suddenly a shout hailed down to them from the crow's nest. "Sail ho!" The ship sprang to life, men appearing everywhere, surfacing from below, dropping from the sails, out of every nook and cranny aboard, until the deck swarmed with them.

"She's a square-rigger," acknowledged the captain a few minutes later as he scanned the horizon with his spyglass.

"But I can't see her colors yet," and he handed the glass to the first mate, who took a look for himself.

"She has the lines of one of those new clippers, but she's a frigate . . . has to be," he confirmed. "And she's heavy in the water." He pulled the glass from his eye and handed it back to the captain, who took another look.

The ship seemed deadly quiet now, barely a whisper heard, only the continued splash of the water and incessant creaking as the wind drove her onward, and they all held their breath, watching.

Then quite abruptly the captain lowered the glass and turned, looking directly at Quinn and the duke, who stood behind him now. "Take your womenfolk below now, your Grace," he said gruffly. "It's the *Golden Eagle* and she's heading right for us," and he turned swiftly to the crew. "Sound alarm, all hands! I want full sail!"

"You'll try to outrun her?" asked Quinn, and the captain glanced at him sharply.

"From what I've heard about the *Golden Eagle*, we don't have a chance in a fight."

Quinn frowned as he and Brandon rounded up the women, herding them beneath the quarterdeck to the cabin as the crack of new sails unfurling hit the wind and the clang of chains and rattle of ropes and rigging accompanied them.

"It isn't fair," complained Loedicia as she paced the floor, wondering why men thought all women were weak and sickly and afraid of violence. If it came to a fight, she could fight as well as the rest of them. "No pirate's going to lay his hands on me!" she ranted as she paced. "Or you either, Reb," she assured her daughter, but Lizette laughed.

"Ma petite, s'il vous plaît, you will wear out the floor. These men are not pirates, they are privateers."

She stopped and stared at her friend. "There's a difference?"

"Oh, *oui.*" Lizette threw up her hands. "A pirate works for himself. He will do anything for money. But a privateer, oh, *ma petite,* he works for himself, yes, but in a different way. A pirate, he would burn the ship and kill all those aboard after taking what he wants. A privateer keeps the loot for himself, but turns the prisoners and the ship over to the country he's commissioned by for as much money as he can. The more important the prisoners, the higher the payment. This privateer is commissioned by the French for this sole purpose, and the loot from the ships is an extra incentive, *n'est-ce pas?*"

Loedicia frowned. "It's still not right."

"It all depends on whose side you're on, *ma petite,*" she replied, and Loedicia shook her head, then glanced toward the ceiling, listening to the men scurrying about frantically above them.

Time seemed to stand still as the three women alternately paced the floor, listened, and complained of their confinement, until suddenly Loedicia felt the ship heel about in the water, and a loud boom echoed on the air. She gritted her teeth against the impact she knew must come.

Above deck, Quinn felt helpless as he watched the other ship approach. It was a beautiful ship, sleek in the water, its huge sails unfurled to the winds. The large flag flying at the top of the mast had a golden eagle embroidered on it, and it billowed boldly in the wind. She was magnificent, and the battery of guns staring from her gun ports below deck and lining her decks above, looked deadly. She had caught them in record time and now she started a sweep across the *Wayfarer*'s bow and her forward gun fired another warning shot.

Quinn held his breath as the captain stood staring at the vessel, trying to make a decision. Fight or surrender without a shot being fired. If he surrendered, he'd save the lives of perhaps dozens of his men, but the French would gain another man-of-war. If he fought . . . But he was left with no alternative as the ship turned in the water and came about, beginning its broadside sweep, and this time the whole battery opened up, and Quinn felt like he was back in the war again as wood splintered about them and the captain shouted, "Fire!"

All the *Wayfarer*'s guns answered, but their shots fell short as the *Golden Eagle* made a wide turn, her sails catching the wind, and came back at them with another broadside.

This time the captain was ready and the *Wayfarer* spoke first, but the shot missed as the *Golden Eagle* churned the water just out of range; then she maneuvered in the water gracefully, heading directly toward the *Wayfarer*'s bow, as if to ram it, her sails full.

"He's crazy!" hollered Quinn as he and Brandon watched, but Brandon shook his head, his lips set tight.

"Not crazy, cunning. Like an eagle himself. Watch," he said, and they watched, fascinated, as the big ship suddenly came up into the wind, then hauled about broadside, swooping down on them, her full battery opened up, the guns firing alternately as they crossed the bow.

Wood flew as the top of the mizzenmast broke and the front batteries were blown away, and Quinn flinched, watching the tangle of bleeding men strewn about the deck. They were no match for the privateer. Her captain was shrewd. Her guns were top-grade, with a greater firing range, and she could stay all day just out of reach and slaughter the *Wayfarer*. Quinn wondered how long it would be before the captain was forced to run up the white flag. The ship had already taken a pounding that would have sunk a less sturdy vessel, and yet she still held the water firmly.

Below deck the women were frantic.

"I can't stay here!" shouted Dicia angrily as the guns burst even louder this time. "I'm going up," and Lizette and Rebel stood with her.

The corridor was full of smoke, and the smell of gunpowder was strong as they made their way up to the quarterdeck and slowly eased the door open.

"Oh, my God!" gasped Dicia, and Lizette almost swooned.

"*Sacrebleu!* It is a massacre," she cried as she shoved her head out the door and they stepped out onto what was left of the deck.

Quickly Dicia spotted Quinn. He was helping a wounded man, trying to do the best he could for him while others lifted part of the broken rigging off his legs. The man was barely conscious, and blood streamed from a hole in the side of his head.

Dicia grabbed Lizette and Rebel's hands, keeping them close by, and they picked their way across the splintered wood, stepping over mutilated bodies; then, just as they reached Quinn, and Dicia called his name, a faint volley of cheers floated across the water from the *Golden Eagle* and Quinn looked up into Loedicia's face. As they stared at each other, the ship grew ominously quiet and both of them looked up in time to see a white flag being raised on what was left of the mizzenmast.

Quinn stood up quickly and moved forward, his eyes wary. "You shouldn't be up here," he said angrily. "They'll board us now that the captain's surrendered."

"So what does that matter?" she said. "We can't hide down there forever."

He glanced at Rebel, her face pale, eyes frightened, then at

Lizette, who stood stoically, looking about at the slaughter, shaking her head.

"*Mon capitaine* should not have fought," she said softly. "He knew the battle would be one-sided," and Quinn nodded.

"The captain, I'm afraid, is a military man, Lizette, and unfortunately this is a military vessel, and I could wager if we weren't aboard he'd have fought to the death. At least this way he figures what they do get is a crippled ship, hard to get to a port."

Loedicia glanced at him sharply, then looked away across the deck to where the captain stood with the late-afternoon sun on him waiting for the enemy, who were already on their way over in longboats, and she knew Quinn was right. Having to surrender had gone against the captain's grain. But he'd been given strict orders regarding his passengers, and if it weren't for their welfare, he'd have gladly gone down with his ship.

Quinn put his arm about Loedicia and took Rebel's hand, Lizette following, leading them across the deck, where they were joined by Brandon; then the little group merged next to the captain and his first mate, standing silently now, watching the longboats from the other ship coming closer.

As they watched, the longboats moved out of sight against the side of the ship, and someone called up for a scaling ladder. Everyone backed up as the captain's men flung the rope ladder over the side and amid the smoke and confusion on the *Wayfarer*'s deck the hands from the *Golden Eagle* began to climb aboard. Burly men, egging for a fight, their guns cocked, swords drawn.

They swarmed over the sides, eyes alert, ready for anything. Two men, however, stood out from the rest as they boarded, shouting orders as if in command.

"Captain Thunder and his first mate," stated the captain, and everyone stared at the two men, who at the moment were partially shadowed by billowing smoke. They were tall and swarthy, their clothes the casual garb of the buccaneer, but a bit more flamboyant. Loose-fitting black pants tucked into shiny black boots, full-sleeved shirts open almost to the waist with colorful braid-trimmed frock coats over them, and swords at their sides, with pistols tucked in the belts. On their heads they both wore fancy hats with low, wide brims and gaudy ostrich feathers sweeping clear past their shoulders, giving them a jaunty, devil-may-care appearance, yet a touch of elegance.

Smoke swirled about the two men, and the smell of gunpowder burned their nostrils as they gathered the rest of the crew about them; then they all turned toward the captain, his first mate, and the passengers, and suddenly a dead silence hung in the air.

Loedicia's face went white as she felt Quinn's hand tighten on her shoulder, and Rebel gasped, her heart in her throat.

Standing not twenty feet away, in the persons of Captain Thunder and his first mate, and staring at them dumbfounded, were Beau and Heath.

Loedicia's knees weakened. "Heath!" she cried incredulously, and Heath, his eyes full of wonder at the sight of her, let out a shout of joy as he stepped away from Beau's side, lunging toward the mother he hadn't seen for three years.

Quinn heard the click of the pistol being cocked as Heath rushed toward them, and he jerked his head toward the *Wayfarer*'s first mate, his heart falling to his stomach as he realized what the man was doing. Without thinking of himself, his only thought for Heath, he shoved Dicia aside, yelling as he plunged forward between the two, but it was too late.

Loedicia shrieked, her hand covering her mouth as the pistol discharged, and her eyes widened in horror as Quinn's head flew back, his hands clawing the air, and the first mate watched transfixed. Quinn's fingers groped, then found Heath, and he tried to hang on, but he was slipping forward, already weakening, and Heath tried vainly to catch him.

He bellowed a choked cry, his head convulsing as he gasped for air; then he crashed to the deck, hitting it hard, sprawling on his back, eyes closed. He was hurting like hell, and it was hard to breathe as Heath and Dicia dropped frantically beside him, and a burning sensation seemed to fill his whole body. He opened his eyes slowly and gazed upward, watching as everyone crowded about talking, and he took as deep a breath as he could, trying to swallow, but it hurt too much.

Tears filled Dicia's eyes as she knelt by his side on the torn deck. "Quinn! My God, Quinn!" she groaned in agony, and her hands began touching his face, running her fingers over his forehead, caressing him tenderly, tears flooding down her cheeks.

The first mate, his eyes bewildered, stood behind her, and Lizette's tear-filled eyes flashed at him accusingly. "What did I do?" he asked nervously. "He shouldn't have gotten in the way. The young man was going to kill her," but Lizette cut him off.

"*Non, m'sieur,*" she retorted angrily, her voice breaking, "the young man, he is her son! He was going to embrace her!" and at her words none of them saw the startled look on Brandon's face as he stared at Heath.

Now suddenly he knew. He finally knew the reason why Quinn hated Roth Chapman.

Dicia bent down and kissed Quinn's face as he coughed, trying to get his breath. "Be still," she sobbed, trying not to cry as she saw him try to move, and he looked into her eyes, a smile at the corners of his mouth.

"It won't do any good, Dicia, my love," he whispered huskily, his voice choked. Then his eyes moved to Heath, who was kneeling at his other side. "Heath?" he asked, and Heath swallowed hard, holding back the tears.

"Yes?"

Quinn tried to move his hand, and Heath, seeing him straining, reached out and clasped it. "That's good," said Quinn, and he choked again as he stared into Heath's face. Heath—the boy he loved, who looked like the man he hated. But did he hate Roth? Could he hate him now? His eyes moved to Loedicia's face, and he gazed once more into her beautiful violet eyes, now full of tears. Could he blame Roth for loving her?

"I love you, Dicia," he whispered softly, and she sniffed in.

"You're going to be fine, darling," she sobbed. "We'll get the shot out, and you'll be fine," but he closed his eyes as a warm tingling sensation spread into his limbs and he felt himself weakening.

"No," he gasped, his breath labored. "No, Dicia. There's no way. . . . I'll never see home again." He drew his tear-filled eyes from hers to look at Heath again, and Heath saw the tears. "Heath . . . I want you to promise me something," he whispered breathlessly. "When I'm gone I want you to take her to your father, do you understand?"

"You're not going to die!" Dicia sobbed helplessly, interrupting him. "You can't die, Quinn! You can't! I won't let you!" and her tears fell on the front of his shirt as he turned back to her.

"You'd play God, Dicia?" he asked softly. "No, my love. Maybe this was meant to be so you could be together. God probably wanted you to marry him years ago when you first met him in Boston, but I botched up his plans. Now it'll be as it should."

"I don't want him!" she sobbed, touching his face again, tears choking her. "I want you, Quinn. I love you!"

He looked once more at Heath and felt Heath's hand tighten on his, and there were tears in both their eyes.

"She loves him, Heath," he gasped, his breath more labored. "See that she gets to him."

"I promise," said Heath, his voice breaking as the tears rolled down his cheeks. He didn't want him to die. He'd been the only father he'd known all these years, and in spite of everything, he still loved him, but he knew. He'd seen too many men die.

Quinn half-mumbled as he made him promise again to take her to Roth; then his eyes moved to Rebel, who was on her knees beside Dicia, crying unashamedly. "Listen to your mother, Reb," he advised, his voice faint. "She's right." Then he glanced up at Lizette, who was wiping the tears from her eyes and blowing her nose. "And take good care of them, *ma chère amie*," he whispered. "You always were like a mother hen with all of us." Then his eyes once more rested on his wife as he realized there was no longer any feeling in his legs and a deep, intense feeling flooded through him, making his eyes clouded, as he could barely make out her face.

"Kiss me, love," he murmured softly, his heart in his throat. "Kiss me . . . good-bye," and the last thing he remembered was her mouth warm on his as his lips moved beneath hers; then he closed his eyes slowly while she kissed him, and he was gone.

"No!" she cried hysterically as she drew her mouth from his, knowing instinctively that the life force that had always sustained her had left his lips, and she stared at his face. "Oh, God, no!" and her head fell on his chest. "Quinn, you can't leave me, you can't!" she screamed. Her fists clenched and she pounded at his limp body, praying for life to come back to it, trying to shake him awake. "Quinn, come back, come back, I won't lose you! I can't lose you. Quinn!" Her voice shrieked, echoing through the tattered remnants of the ship, its agony shattering even the hardest of hearts, and most of the men turned away, unable to look.

Heath stood up and watched her as she collapsed, falling helplessly across Quinn's chest, her body shaking with sobs; then he walked about Quinn's body and knelt down, picking her up by the shoulders, and pulled her to him, his arms holding her tightly, and as he held her he gazed down at Quinn's still face, so quiet in death, and vowed to himself that come what may he'd keep the promise he'd made to him.

Beau stood watching Heath as he held his mother; then he glanced down at Quinn. He looked so different in death, this brawny, lumbering man who'd held so many people's lives in his hands over the years. Who'd learned to live with Indian and white man alike. A man who knew the dignity of living free and the responsibility that went with it. What a waste of human life, but was it? If Quinn hadn't stepped into the pistol's path, Heath would be dead now, and Beau looked back at Heath consoling his mother. Yes, Heath was worth it. In the past few years he'd become a man to be proud of, and Beau straightened his shoulders once more, remembering the task ahead of him.

He glanced quickly at Rebel, who had her head buried on Lizette's shoulder crying, then squared his shoulders, turning to the captain of the *Wayfarer*. "This is your first mate?" he asked roughly, motioning toward the man who'd fired the pistol.

The man was staring at him, his eyes frightened, and the captain nodded.

"You surrendered," reminded Beau.

"And I'm sorry for the incident," answered the captain, his voice strained. "However, we do have passengers aboard, as you can see. My first mate was hasty in his action, I agree, but—"

"Your first mate is a dead man," interrupted Beau angrily, and suddenly Brandon stepped forward.

"Are you jesting, sir?" he questioned seriously. "The man had no idea the countess knew the . . . uh . . . gentleman."

Beau's head cocked to one side as he looked Brandon over. "And who are you?" he asked arrogantly.

Brandon's eyes narrowed. "I'm the Duke of Bourland, newly appointed governor of Grenada."

Beau's eyes blazed. "And you think that gives you a right to tell me what to do?"

Brandon blustered. "I presume to do nothing of the sort. I only ask that you consider the circumstances before passing sentence on the man."

Beau pointed to the white flag waving from the splintered mizzenmast. "Do you see that flag?" he asked as his men stood by watching restlessly. "That's a flag of surrender. It means you lay down your arms. A good man is dead because one of the captain's men violated the captain's order of surrender. I say the man's a dead man."

Suddenly Rebel, who'd been listening to the two men as she stood with her head pressed against Lizette's shoulder, turned on Beau as if the years between had never been, and her tear-streaked face flushed wildly. "For God's sake, Beau, let it be!" she cried angrily. "The man had no idea what Heath was doing, and you know it," and her heart began to pound as his green eyes looked steadily into hers, and Brandon looked first to one, then the other, startled.

"You know this man too?" he asked incredulously, and she nodded.

"Yes."

Beau looked at Brandon. "Captain Thunder, at your service, your Grace," he said quickly, then glanced back at Rebel.

Rebel eyed him curiously. So he didn't want anyone to know his real name. She sniffed back the tears as she stared at him, and her face flushed even more crimson.

Brandon took a step toward her and put his arm around her, and Beau saw her tense up. "Then since you know my betrothed, I'm sure you'll forgive her outburst, captain. She's rather impetuous at times."

Rebel's eyes fell before Beau's hard gaze; then she turned abruptly as Loedicia, who'd finally composed herself, joined the conversation.

"Beau?" Loedicia asked, her eyes red and filling quickly again with tears. "Will you let him go for me?" she asked. "Please, Beau? He didn't know. Don't make it worse."

Beau stared at Loedicia, and she had no idea that he was blaming himself more than anyone else for Quinn's death. If he hadn't attacked the ship, Quinn would be alive. Quinn Locke, a man who'd been like a father to him.

Beau nodded, acceding to her wish, then turned abruptly to his men and began shouting orders. When he was finished, he turned to Heath. "Take the women downstairs to get their baggage, Heath, then have them rowed back to the ship," he said. "I don't think they'd enjoy going to Martinique with the prisoners."

"You can't take them with you on your ship," Brandon protested, and Beau shook his head, sighing.

"There you go again, telling me what I can and can't do. You are the prisoner, sir, I am the one giving orders. Besides, they won't be prisoners, they'll be my guests."

"And Brandon?" asked Rebel.

Beau frowned. "Who's Brandon?"

"I am," answered the duke. "My name's Brandon Avery."

Beau's eyes darkened as he stared at Rebel, and he remembered a young girl naked in the moonlight with water dripping from her fair hair. "You're really planning to marry him?" he asked, and she nodded.

"Yes."

"Then I guess he'll have to come along too, won't he?" he replied, and a slight smile moved at the corner of his mouth. "I can't have my guests unhappy."

He turned to Loedicia, who was still staring at Quinn's body in disbelief, and he ordered a blanket thrown over it. "Don't worry," he assured her. "We'll give him a decent burial before we leave the ship."

Loedicia gazed out toward the horizon, seeing nothing but water, the large, lonely miles of water. "He can't go in there, Beau," she cried. "It's so big and lonely, so far away. I won't even have a grave to go to."

"It's better you don't, Mother," replied Rebel as Heath put his arm about her once more. "Father wouldn't want you to mourn. This way he'll always be just . . . somewhere out there."

Tears rolled down Dicia's face, because she knew it had to be. Quinn, who loved the land, who reveled in its fields and trees and cherished even the wildflowers, was going to be robbed of it in death.

He was buried late that afternoon at sea from the deck of the torn ship, along with the rest of the dead, while the captain read a service from his prayer book. Dicia stood tall and erect, with Rebel on one side of her, Heath on the other, and Beau and Lizette behind them. As the captain's voice intoned the words, almost shouting them toward heaven, she wasn't listening; instead she was listening to her heart, remembering how only last night he'd made love to her, and she tried to recapture every moment. How alive he'd been, and now . . .

As the captain finished, she watched transfixed, tears streaming down her cheeks as his body slipped from the deck and plunged swiftly into the waters below, sinking from sight. It was over. Quinn was gone, and part of her had gone with him.

A little over an hour later Loedicia sat by the rail of the *Golden Eagle* staring at the horizon, watching what was left of the *Wayfarer*, its prisoners, and the rest of Beau's crew, as it disappeared from sight; then she glanced at the flag high above her, unfurled to the late-afternoon sun, the eagle on it shining brightly, and she tried to go back over everything that had happened.

Last night Quinn had loved her, now he was dead. It was so swift. From happiness to utter chaos in only a few hours. It didn't seem possible, but it was real. It was real! Tears ran down her face again, and she wiped them away, trying to still the ache in her heart. Oh, God, why did she always have to take the bitter? Where had the roses gone?

For days as the *Golden Eagle* plied the waters of the Atlantic she sat crying, staring off into space, her arms aching from emptiness, her body crying just to feel him once more, but it was no use. She had to accept it. This time Quinn was really dead, and slowly, little by little, with everyone's help, the tears became less and the smiles more frequent, and life began to go on again, but there was one thing about which she was adamantly stubborn.

"I will not do it," she stated one evening as they sat at Beau's table eating. "You can't make me go, Heath. You had no right to promise him."

Heath's eyes hardened. "But I did."

Loedicia exhaled, her eyes flashing. "I will not go back to your father now that Quinn's dead," she retorted. "I won't do that to him."

Rebel sighed. "But, Mother, he loves you."

"That's just the trouble," she said. "Don't you see? I can't make him second best. I gave him up. . . . I left him. I have no right to go back. And I won't!" and she pushed her food aside, standing up, and left the cabin for a breath of fresh air.

She made her way to the deck and stood leaning against the rail, watching the night descend, and she sighed, then turned abruptly as Heath, who'd followed her on deck, walked up behind her.

"Mother?" he asked, and she frowned.

"Yes?"

"Why are you doing this?"

"You mean why won't I let you take me to Roth?"

"Yes."

She reached up and touched his face, and her heart cried out at the way he resembled his father. "Because I love him, Heath."

"But if you love him. . . ?"

She stared at him. He was all of eighteen now and looked much older, but he just didn't understand. "Heath," she began, "when we were in England, your father and I . . ." She wrung her hands. How could she explain to him. "The other day I told you about Quinn being in prison and how I went to get your father to save him. Well, Roth and I were caught in a rainstorm on the way back to London and spent the night together at a small inn. Heath . . ." She looked into her son's eyes. "It was as if the years had never separated us." She blushed as she looked away, back out across the water. "Do you know what I'm trying to say?"

His voice was husky. "You let him make love to you?"

"Yes," she whispered. "But in spite of everything, when morning came I returned to Quinn. Don't you see? I can't go crawling back to him now just because Quinn's dead! I can't ever go back to him," and Heath sighed.

He could argue all night and never make her change her mind. Sometimes she could be so stubborn. He turned and walked away, meeting Rebel as she came up on deck. "What are we going to do with her?" he asked as he watched his sister glance toward their mother. "If she finds out we're headed for Port Royal, she's going to explode."

"She doesn't have to know until we get there," answered Reb. "Not unless someone tells her. I think she's forgotten about telling me where Roth lived in America, and since we haven't asked any questions, she isn't suspicious."

"And what do we do when we get her there?" he asked. "Carry her bodily to him?"

Rebel sighed. "It can't be that bad."

"You know how stubborn she can be." He shook his head. "I think she's got some ridiculous notion that she doesn't deserve him."

"Why?"

He blushed. He had no right to tell her. But then, maybe she ought to know. Maybe she'd know what to do. After all, she was a woman, she'd know more how a woman's mind works, so he told her of their mother's indiscretion.

She stared at her mother as he talked, watching her as she leaned against the rail staring into the growing darkness, and it seemed strange to think that she could succumb to the same passions she'd felt that night on the beach with Beau. But after all, why shouldn't she? She was a woman. Just because she was a mother didn't make her a saint; she was still very human.

"I can't figure out why she feels this way," Heath complained as he finished. "She says she loves him."

Rebel's eyes warmed as she looked at Heath. "You don't understand how a woman's mind works, Heath," she replied. "She's ashamed to go back to him now. When she had a choice, she chose Father over him. To go back to him now would be like saying 'Since he's not here, you'll do.' She doesn't want to take a chance on hurting him, and I think she's afraid, too."

"Of what?"

"I think she's afraid Father's ghost will hang between them, especially because of what you say happened in England."

He exhaled disgustedly. "You women! You sure can get complicated."

"Us? What about you? You probably have a girl in every port. I've heard some of the remarks you and Beau have been making. How can you be so fickle?"

His eyes smiled at his sister curiously. "At least I'm not going to marry someone I can't stand," he retorted. "Why the hell are you doing it, Reb?"

She tensed, and her eyes hardened. "What do you mean?"

"I mean the duke."

Her eyes were hostile. "What's wrong with Brandon?"

"You're not in love with him."

"Who says so?"

"I do."

She threw her head back. "And you're an authority on love, I suppose?"

"I've learned a lot about it in the past few years."

"From whom, Beau?" she asked cynically, and was surprised when Beau answered from behind her.

"Why not? I think I'm qualified."

She whirled around and looked into his green eyes. Beau Dante—Captain Thunder. It was strange to think of them as one and the same. He'd taken the name from his Indian name, and she'd learned that not even his crew knew his real last name. He'd told Loedicia he'd planned to use the money from privateering to buy land in America and become a respectable planter someday. But he didn't want his privateering days to follow him.

His shoulders had broadened over the past three years, his frame had filled out, and he was even more handsome, and although she hated to admit it, he still had the power to make her stomach tighten into knots and her loins ache. She'd tried to avoid him as much as possible, but at the moment she couldn't, and the cynical smile that spread across his sensuous face made her heart start pounding. Why did she feel like this inside? Why did he do this to her? She hated him for it.

Heath laughed. "I learned from a master," he said casually, and she turned back to him, but he only laughed again and walked off, leaving her standing alone with Beau.

She stood silently, watching Heath walk away, but she didn't move. She knew Beau was still standing behind her.

"What's wrong, Reb?" Beau asked softly, his deep voice stirring her. "Is Heath right or isn't he?"

"About what?"

"Am I a master at making love?"

"I don't know," she whispered, her back still to him. "You never stayed long enough for me to find out."

"We can take up where we left off." His voice vibrated through her. "It might be fun."

She turned around slowly, her eyes intense as they looked directly into his. "It might at that," she said bitterly, "if I still had any feelings for you, but I'm not the wide-eyed, naive young girl I was then, Beau, and you were right. I don't want an Indian in my bed. Not anymore."

His eyes mocked her. "You'd rather have a duke?"

She smirked. "I'd rather have Brandon."

He leaned toward her. "Is that why you cringe every time he touches you?" He leaned even closer. "Is that why you freeze up like a ramrod when he takes you in his arms?"

Her heart fell to her stomach. "I don't!"

"I've watched you, Reb," he taunted. "You hate the touch of his hands." He reached out and touched her arm, running his fingers up it to her shoulder, and she went all warm inside. "But you like that, don't you?"

She drew in a quick breath, then swallowed hard as a physical ache filled her breast. "Take your hands off me, Beau Dante," she gasped breathlessly. "I don't want any part of you!"

His arm circled her waist, and he drew her close against him, looking deep into her violet eyes, drinking in their wonder. "Don't you?" he whispered. "Don't bet on it, Reb. All I'd have to do is kiss you to prove my point."

"Don't you dare!" she gasped, her eyes flashing. "I'll kill you!"

"You throw a delightful challenge," he answered flippantly.

"Perhaps I'll take you up on it sometime," and without another word he released her and walked away, leaving her standing alone, her face flushed, nerves rattled, her body trembling.

She watched him walk away, and closed her eyes, trying to hold her temper. If she had something, she'd throw it at him. The arrogant . . . Why did he have to show up again? Why couldn't Captain Thunder have been some big, ugly brute?

Heath had told her how he and Beau had knocked about the world after being shanghaied, from one ship to another, learning all there was to know about sailing, hoping to reach England someday, but instead reaching the shores of Africa and being in the right place at the right time to end up with a ship of their own. Why couldn't he have drowned instead?

"It took a while to make it into what we wanted and put together a crew we could trust," Heath had told her, "but the results were worth it."

Now, as she watched Beau, the shadows of twilight playing across his face as he talked to one of his men, she did so with mixed feelings, and most of them frightened her.

The seas were calm for the most part, warm and balmy, with an occasional storm that proved annoying, but all in all the trip was going well. They reached the Bahamas and it was late one afternoon when Beau approached Brandon.

They'd said little to each other the whole trip, and Beau had merely watched Brandon contemptuously with those maddening intense green eyes of his, which made Brandon feel uneasy. And to top it off, Rebel had refused to tell Brandon Beau's real name. She'd told him about Heath, a story he wasn't sure he believed, but nothing about Beau.

"If he wanted you to know, he'd tell you," she said, and now Brandon watched warily as he approached. He didn't like the man. He was younger by a good five years, but had the bearing of a man born to lead, and the command of a man far more advanced in years.

"Something I can do for you, captain?" asked Brandon as Beau stepped up to him, and Beau turned, looking out across the horizon.

"In a few days we reach San Salvador," he stated. "We weigh anchor long enough to take on stores. I just wanted you to understand your position here," he explained. "Although Mrs. Locke, Lizette, and Rebel are my guests, you unfortunately are my prisoner, and I don't want you getting any ideas about trying to escape and taking Rebel with you."

"Speaking of my future wife," said Brandon irritably, "I want to know just what your interest is in her."

Beau pretended shock. "My interest in Rebel?"

Brandon's brown eyes studied him hard, the gold flecks in them flashing angrily. "Come off it, Thunder," he exclaimed. "I've watched you with her. You seldom take your eyes off her, and I've seen the look in those eyes. It's not a look of indifference."

Beau shrugged. He'd discarded his shirt in the heat of the day, and the muscles rippled arrogantly across his bronzed chest. "Is it a criminal offense to admire a woman?"

"It is if she's my woman!"

"Rebel your woman?" Beau laughed. "Oh come now, your Grace," he said sarcastically. "Rebel isn't any man's woman and never will be. There's no man'll ever tame her. Love her maybe, but not tame her. She's like her mother. A woman like that you don't put a bit on, you neck-rein and hope to God it works."

"You seem to know her quite well." He looked at him sullenly. "Just what were you at Fort Locke, captain?" and Beau straightened.

"My father was chief of the Tuscarora," he answered, and saw Brandon's eyes widen. "That's right, your Grace," he continued casually. "I'm an Indian."

"But you—"

"I don't look like an Indian? Touché. But then you, sir, don't look like a duke, either." He looked him over insolently. "You look more like a little boy trying to play at the game."

Brandon's eyes blazed. "You'll eat those words someday, captain," he said. "But first I want to know what you plan to do with us."

"With us, or you?"

"All right, with me."

He thought for a minute. "I haven't quite made up my mind yet, your Grace. Since you were heading for Grenada and I happen to know that two shiploads of fresh troops arrived in Grenada only a short time back, and since Spain's hold on Trinidad is weakening and the French are in possession of Tobago, I'd say you were readying for an invasion of Tobago and Trinidad to try to accomplish what Sir Walter Raleigh failed to do years ago. But since you're at war with the French . . . really, your Grace, I don't know which country'd pay the most for you, France or Spain."

"You'd turn me over to them? But I thought . . . Rebel . . ."

"You thought I was doing Rebel a favor?" He smiled wickedly; then his eyes darkened. "If I was doing her a favor, I'd have thrown you to the sharks." He sighed, and once more his mouth softened cynically, but his eyes never changed. "Ah, but no, I was doing myself a favor. You see, I knew you were headed for Grenada, only I wasn't sure just which ship you were on, and I might say I was pleased to discover I had the right one."

"You mean you were purposely after me?"

Beau smiled, pleased with himself. "And you never caught on, did you?"

The duke straightened.

"You shouldn't brag so much about your abilities, your Grace," Beau continued. "Word gets around, even from London."

Brandon's eyes narrowed viciously. He didn't like being made to look like a fool. "Why didn't you tell me right from the start?" he asked.

"And spoil the game?" Beau laughed. "Really, it's been fun watching you try to hide behind Rebel's skirts," and Brandon's face reddened.

"You're a madman," he blurted angrily. "You're insane!"

"On the contrary," answered Beau, his broad chest expanding. "I'm a businessman, and right now my business is money, of which at the moment you're worth a great deal. And might I add, dead or alive."

Brandon's fists clenched. The man was an arrogant bastard, and he knew he had him right where he wanted. What a fool he'd been to come along so willingly. He watched as Beau turned and walked away.

He stood for a long time leaning on the rail, staring off over the horizon. If he was turned over to either country, he'd spend the rest of his life languishing in some secluded dungeon, or worse yet, they might kill him. Yet how could he get out of this mess?

Then slowly an idea began tossing itself about as he remembered the captain honoring Loedicia's wish to set the first mate free. Whoever this Beau Thunder or Captain Thunder was, he'd thought a great deal of Loedicia and Quinn. He bit his lip. Why not? It was the only way.

He turned quickly and began his search for Rebel, looking

with disgust as he found her dressed in some cut-off pants and an old shirt of her brother's, with her feet bare, helping the hands with the sails. It had been like this ever since they'd come aboard. She seemed to have forgotten what it was to be a lady, and more times than he cared to remember he'd caught her in her brother's clothes working with the crew.

"Get down here," he shouted as she lay curled about the rigging helping unfurl a sail, and she made a face.

"As soon as we're through," she yelled, but he countered.

"Now! I have to talk to you."

She looked at the burly men beside her, their hard faces suddenly breaking into grins; then she relinquished her spot on the rigging and climbed down, landing expertly at Brandon's feet.

"What's so all-fired important it can't wait till we're finished?" she asked, and he stared at her, shaking his head.

"Good God, Rebel. Do you know what you look like in those?" he admonished, and he reached out, flicking the front of her shirt where she'd lost a button. "You're not even half-dressed. How many times have I told you—"

"I'm not your wife yet, Bran," she exclaimed as she pulled her shirt together, holding it with her hand, then flicked her long flaxen hair back over her shoulder. "And even when I am, that doesn't give you any right to order me around."

"Sure of yourself, aren't you?"

"Maybe I don't give a damn anymore."

He grabbed her wrist and held it, staring into her eyes. "Oh, no, Reb, you're not getting out of it that easily."

"Maybe the captain hasn't told you, Bran," she answered sarcastically, "but we're not headed for Grenada anymore."

He sneered. "It doesn't have to be Grenada, Reb. Not anymore," he said, and her eyes narrowed as she looked into his, seeing the desire in them as he went on. "We can be married here on board ship. I can't wait any longer, and it's senseless to try, Reb. I'm in love with you, and it's driving me crazy not being able to touch you." He sighed. "The captain can marry us, Rebel. Now, tomorrow. You and your mother can talk him into it."

She was speechless as she looked at him, then slowly pulled her wrist from his hand, listening closely to every word, a stunned look on her face as if he'd slapped her.

"I'd forgotten about it," he continued as he watched her closely. "We don't have to wait for anything."

Rebel swallowed hard. She'd never dreamed he'd think of something like this, and suddenly she was scared. Grenada had seemed so far away, but tomorrow? She saw his jaw tighten.

"Rebel?"

Her voice was barely audible. "Yes?"

"Well?"

She shook her head. "I don't know. It's . . . it's . . ."

"Don't you dare say it's so sudden."

"Oh, I'm not . . . I'm not," she answered quickly. "It's just . . ." She turned from him, still clutching the blouse in front, and started toward the quarterdeck, with Brandon following at her heels. She flung the door open and descended the steps, making her way along the corridor to her cabin, then turned, leaning against the door. "Brandon," she began, brushing a wisp of hair from her forehead, "when we were headed for Grenada, we were headed for a future. . . . Here we have nothing."

"I'm still a duke," he stated. "If we don't go on to Grenada when he sets us free, we can go back to England."

"You think Beau will let you?"

"That's what I'm trying to ensure," he replied; then he reached past her and opened the door to her cabin, and she had no choice but to step inside. It was empty. Lizette, who shared it with her, had gone up on deck earlier. He explained to her about his conversation with Beau, coloring his story in his own favor and making it look like Beau had used her too, making sure she got the impression that Beau thought her a naive fool. "He's shrewd, this Captain Thunder of yours," he stated as he watched the anger in her eyes. "He knows how to use women to his advantage. He intends to turn me over to the highest bidder, but I have a feeling he has a soft spot for your mother. If you insist on the marriage taking place now, he wouldn't want to hurt her by refusing you, and then, when the time comes, you could get her to talk him into letting us go."

"But getting married here, aboard ship. I wanted a church wedding with a dress and all."

"Does it really matter what you wear for the ceremony or where it takes place?" he asked, and saw her hesitate. "Or has he gotten to you?"

She shook her head. Damn Beau! She might have known. He never did anything without a reason. The looks, the advances. He was only toying with her again, like before. Oh, how she hated him!

Brandon's arms went about her, and he pulled her close. "Rebel, say you'll do it," he whispered. "Don't keep me waiting anymore."

His lips came down on hers, and she closed her eyes, trying to enjoy his kiss, but instead her body was rigid, her mouth unyielding. "Kiss me, dammit!" he said, his mouth against hers, but instead she pushed him away.

"I can't," she murmured. "I can't," and he grabbed her shoulders, holding her so she had to look at him.

"You can't what?" he asked. "Kiss me?"

"Bran, I don't know what's wrong, but I can't do something I can't feel."

"I thought you said you loved me?"

"I do. . . . I did. . . . I . . ."

"Then show it!"

He pulled her into his arms again and began kissing her, and his hand moved inside her blouse, roughly caressing her breasts as he tried to force her to respond, but instead she began to fight him, pushing against him, until he flung her to the floor, where she lay in a heap at his feet.

She hung her head forward, covering her face with her hands, tears of frustration pushing out between her fingers.

He stared down at her for a few minutes, trying to compose himself. He shouldn't have pushed her, not yet. She was such a maddening creature, but he couldn't scare her off, not now. Too much depended on it. He knelt beside her, his breathing short and heavy. He'd been passionately aroused by her protest, but he had to control himself.

"Rebel," he whispered softly, apologizing, "I'm sorry. I didn't mean to scare you. I think I understand. There are some women who can't let a man touch them outside of marriage, and you're one. When you know you're my wife, it'll be different and I'll be gentle with you. You'll see. It'll work out."

He reached down and put his hand under her head and tilted her tearstained face up to his. "You will marry me tomorrow, won't you?" he begged. "It's the only way."

She looked up at him and thought of Beau. He didn't care about her. If he had, he would have stayed at Fort Locke three years ago. What a fool she was, letting him affect her. Well, he wasn't going to spoil this. He wasn't going to use her anymore. She'd still be a duchess. She could do it . . . she could!

"Yes, I'll marry you," she whispered, her voice shaking. "The sooner the better," and he smiled, but there was something malicious about the way he smiled, and suddenly she was afraid.

19

Rebel lay in her bunk listening to the creaking of the ship as it made its way through the water. The night seemed endlessly long, and she'd been tossing and turning for hours. Tomorrow she was to marry Brandon. She remembered the look on Beau's face at dinner that evening when Brandon had broken the news, and the hour she spent arguing with her mother and Lizette, and the next hour she spent in heated battle with Heath. They just didn't understand. But did she?

She closed her eyes and all she could see was Beau's face staring at her. Why couldn't she sleep? Why did he haunt her like this?

Quietly, so as not to wake Lizette, she climbed from the bunk and grabbed a wrap, slipping it on, then made her way to the door. The passageway outside was deathly quiet, not even a lantern lit. She reached the stairs, ascending them quickly, and opened the door, then breathed deeply, smelling the fresh ocean breeze as she stepped on deck.

The night was still and full of stars, with only a slip of crescent moon that barely peeked from behind the sails. She made her way to the rail and stood looking off into space, trying to think some meaning into what she was doing. How could she keep pretending that Beau didn't matter? If he didn't matter, then why did she feel the way she did whenever she looked at him? It could just be lust; yet, if that was it, she'd have felt the same thing for Brandon, but when he'd put his hands on her she'd hated the feel of them, and she reached up now, touching the end of her breast where his fingers had touched her, and she shivered involuntarily.

"Are you cold?" asked a deep voice from behind her, and she spun around, looking directly into Beau's eyes.

His hair was ruffled, his chest bare, and she stared at him

fascinated, watching the soft dark hairs on his chest that moved slightly as the muscles beneath his bronzed skin rippled with each breath.

"You scared me." She sighed and he took a step closer.

"I couldn't sleep either."

"Oh?"

He reached out and touched her hair, twisting one of the curls about his finger. "I keep remembering a sea nymph, her body wet and sleek, her lips inviting."

"No!"

"She was full of fire, and her kisses sang a song all their own that lifted me clear to heaven and back again."

She shook her head. "No! Stop, please, Beau," she pleaded, but he reached out, pulled her into his arms, and began kissing her until she went limp all over; then he picked her up, cradling her in his arms. "No, Beau!" she tried to protest, but the strength of his arms about her and thc warmth invading her body took all the strength from her.

He carried her below to his cabin and opened the door, shutting it deftly behind him, then laid her gently down on his bed, bending over her, and he stretched out beside her, burying his face in her neck, sending shivers down her spine.

"This is where you belong," he whispered softly. "I need you, Reb," and this time when his mouth came down on hers, her lips were waiting, opening to his, and she felt his tongue exploring the sweet corners of her mouth, teasing her senses until she wanted to crawl inside him, and he slowly removed her wrap, his fingers caressing her gently.

His hands fondled her, bringing familiar sensations she remembered from before, setting her body on fire. With each caress she moaned ecstatically, her senses warm, alive, and wanting. His mouth sipped at her body, coaxing her nipples, firming them, teasing her lips as he kissed her over and over again until she forgot everything but her need for him.

This was what she'd wanted to feel ever since that night on the beach, and as he made love to hcr, moving over her, and the first sharp pain of entry was over, she lost herself in his embrace, giving herself to him shamelessly as she arched up to meet him, her senses reeling, wanting to be a part of him.

He thrust into her over and over again, passionately, yet gently; then suddenly she felt a peak of pleasure so strong it made her cry out, and seconds later he made one last lunge, then his body shook violently and he groaned, relaxing against her.

She lay beneath him, marveling in the rapture the violent release had brought to her and the total surrender it had brought to him. He was no longer the all-powerful Beau, the cynical stone-faced captain feared and hated by every British sailor who sailed the Atlantic. He was the man who'd brought her to life, and she touched his shoulders, feeling the smooth velvet of his skin, and as his lips caressed her neck softly, she sighed.

"I knew it would be like this," she murmured. "I knew. . . ."

"Are you happy?"

"Ecstatically."

"You're quite a woman, you know that."

She took his head between her hands and her lips found his, kissing him long and hard, feeling his body still against hers.

"What do I do now?" she whispered softly, and he sighed as he kissed her back.

"What do you mean?"

"How do I tell Brandon?"

His breath was warm against her mouth. "Tell him what?"

A slow fear rankled at the end of her spine, and her mouth stopped against his. "That you and I are going to get married," she said hesitantly, and she felt his muscles tense. She swallowed hard as he lay above her, motionless, looking into her face.

"Who said we were getting married?" he asked, and she felt a cold weakness sweep over her.

"But you . . ."

"Did I mention marriage, even once?"

She closed her eyes, her heart pounding. "Oh, God, no," she cried, and he slipped off her in the darkness, and she shivered as the night air touched her body, naked and sweating where he'd lain.

"I'm in no position to marry anyone, Reb, not now," he explained, cutting the heart out of her. "All I have to my name is this ship. I couldn't ask you or any other woman to share my life. Besides"—he reached over and grabbed his pants, pulling them on—"I'm an Indian, you're the daughter of an English earl. No, Reb. Our lives are worlds apart. I could never marry you."

"But love . . ."

"Love doesn't enter into it."

"Then why?" she asked, tears streaming down her face, and he sat down on the edge of the bed and touched her cheek, running his fingers lovingly to her mouth, barely visible in the darkness.

"Because I didn't want your first lovemaking to be at the hands of that selfish incompetent who'd have ended up raping you. I wanted you to know what lovemaking can be." He hesitated a minute, then bent down and kissed her mouth, savoring its sweetness, knowing he had no right to it, yet loving every minute. "Besides, I wanted to be the first. I may not be able to marry you, Reb, but you'll always be mine now, and your duke can never take that away from me."

"I hate you," she whispered against his mouth, and he sighed.

"I don't think so." He straightened and stood up, looking down at her. "You'll curse me and yell at me and marry Brandon to spite me, but you'll never hate me, Rebel," he said. "As long as there's a breath in your body, you'll never hate me."

She stared at him, speechless, her face flushed, tears on her cheeks; then she pulled her nightgown down and clutched the wrap about her as she slipped from his bed and pushed him aside, stumbling to the door.

"Reb," he said softly as she pulled the door open, "someday you'll thank me," but she tried to block his words from her mind as she left him standing alone in the darkness and made her way back to her cabin.

She climbed quietly into the narrow bunk and lay on her stomach, her face buried in the pillow, trying to stifle the sobs, and she wanted to die. It seemed like the tears would never stop; then suddenly they were replaced by a bitter anger. She turned onto her back and lay quietly gazing into the darkness.

She could still feel the thrill of his hands on her and remember groaning ecstatically beneath him, welcoming him to take her; then she bit her lip, almost drawing blood. She'd show him! She'd marry Brandon and they'd get away and go back to England or Grenada and she'd forget Beau Dante ever existed. Suddenly she shivered violently. How could she ever forget him now? How!

The next afternoon, with the crew assembled as witnesses, a solemn-faced Rebel married the Duke of Bourland, with the captain of the *Golden Eagle* officiating, his dark green eyes uncommonly cold and unfeeling, his voice harsh as he intoned the words.

Heath watched Brandon walk away after the ceremony with Rebel's arm tucked in his, and he turned to Beau. "Why did you let her do it, Beau?" he asked quietly as he saw the pain in his friend's eyes. "Why didn't you tell her how you feel?"

"And how do I feel?" he asked cynically, his eyes hard.

"Come on now, Beau," retorted Heath. "You never have forgotten her. I don't know what happened between the two of you three years ago at Fort Locke, but whatever it was, I was hoping it was forgotten."

"You think I should have married Rebel instead of him?" he asked.

"Why not?"

"You're as crazy as she is."

"What are you talking about?"

Beau stopped stock-still and looked directly at Heath. "I'm an Indian, Heath, you seem to forget that," and Heath cursed.

"I wish to hell you would," he said. "For the past three years I've watched you crawl in that shell of yours and pull it in after you. You won't let anybody get close, and I was hoping Reb—"

"Let's forget about Rebel," he interrupted bitterly. "She's a married woman now." He turned to his crew and began shouting orders, and Heath shook his head. Some people sure could mess up their lives, and he turned toward his mother, watching her and Lizette as they talked. Well, maybe he could keep her from making a mess out of her life anyway, and he wondered what was going to happen when they reached Port Royal. He was anxious to meet the father he'd never known, but cringed at the thought of unleashing his mother's temper. Oh, well. He shrugged. They'd have to take that chance.

That night, as the wind died a little and the sea becalmed, Loedicia moved in with Lizette and gave her cabin to Bran and Reb, because it was the only other cabin with a larger bunk, besides the captain's, and he wasn't about to move out.

Dinner that evening was atrocious. The food stuck in Rebel's throat, and she choked three times, then spilled her glass of wine as Heath called a toast to the captain who performed the ceremony, and she caught a glimpse of Beau's eyes and suddenly she wanted to die.

There was something in them. Pain, hunger, hurt, all wrapped up in one, and in that instant she knew he really loved her. He'd never said it, but it showed in his eyes for one split second, then was gone, and she swallowed hard. Why? Oh, God, if he loved her, why?

It was late when Brandon finally walked her down to the cabin and shut the door behind them. She stood silently, every nerve in her body tense. This was it. She couldn't fight any longer. This was her wedding night, and she was supposed to enjoy it.

He walked up behind her and put his hands on her shoulders, feeling her body stiffen beneath his fingers. "There's nothing to be afraid of, Reb," he whispered softly. "I'll be gentle. I promise."

She gulped back tears. She didn't want him to touch her. Not after Beau, not now, not ever, but there was nothing she could do about it. He was her husband now.

She straightened her shoulders. "I'm not afraid," she whispered to him and to herself.

He reached up and unfastened the back of the pale blue dress she wore, letting it slip off her shoulders, then began unfastening her underthings, taking them off as she stood with her back to him.

"Go lie down," he whispered breathlessly against her ear as she stepped out of her bloomers, and she closed her eyes, praying for courage, then opened them and walked to the bed.

She lay down, waiting in the darkness for him, willing her body to do his bidding. She could pretend. She would pretend, she told herself, and then suddenly he was beside her, his clothes off, his hands pawing her clumsily, hungrily. There was no gentleness as there had been with Beau. No coaxing, no sensuous buildup, no wonder and delight, only an animal instinct that seemed to drive him, taking no heed to her needs, only his own, and when he climaxed, it left an empty feeling inside her, not the wondrous rapture she'd felt with Beau.

She'd pretended as best she could, especially as he entered, making him think it hurt, remembering how it had been with Beau, the movements, the sighs, and she tried to emulate them, but it wasn't the same. It would never be the same. So in the end she just lay beneath him, hating the very act, feeling dirty and degraded, and used, but Brandon, not seeing her face in the darkness, sighed, pleased with himself.

He'd been so wrapped up in his own pleasure he hadn't been aware that she responded more like a frightened animal than a woman in the throes of love, and he merely chalked up her weak efforts at response to inexperience. She was still a bit edgy and tense, but that would go in time. He'd bring her out little by little, he was sure of it. Somewhere inside Rebel was a fire, and by God, someday he'd find it. For now, though, this was enough; she hadn't fought him, and he sighed contentedly as he lay down beside her, unaware of the tears that fell on her pillow and the ache in her heart.

Two days later they sailed into San Salvador and took on fresh water and food and a load of cargo to sell in the States, then unfurled sail again and headed northwest, sailing into Port Royal Sound on a summer morning in the middle of May, the sun coming up over the horizon turning the landscape into a wonderland of gold. They'd slipped into the sound past Hilton Head and Bay Point at night, and instead of the flag of the *Golden Eagle* flying atop the mast, when morning came she flew a red flag with a white dolphin on it in its place. There were British ships along the coast of the Carolinas, and they all knew the *Golden Eagle*, and now Brandon knew how he slipped away so fast.

The extra guns were cleverly disguised. An intricate scroll design was painted along the sides of the ship, covering the gun ports beneath deck when they were closed, and the deck guns were hidden beneath false longboats and packing boxes. She carried no identifying figurehead, and they even had a way of slipping boards in and out of place to change the name so it read *White Dolphin.*

"Where on earth are we?" asked Loedicia as she saw the land against the morning sun; then she frowned as she saw the look on Heath's face. "Heath! You didn't?" she cried, and he bit his lip.

"I promised him, Mother," he answered, and she shook her head.

"But I can't," she said, her voice breaking. "You had no right. I told you I can't," and she turned, running to the quarterdeck and down to her cabin, from which she refused to budge.

"So what do we do now?" asked Rebel as she and Lizette joined Heath on deck, and he shrugged.

"How the hell should I know?"

"You're not very inventive," said Beau as he joined them. "If you can't take her to him, you bring him to her."

Heath grinned. "See, ladies," he said as he gestured to Rebel and Lizette. "He has all the answers," and Rebel, who'd talked to Beau very little since her marriage to Brandon, gave him a quick glance. His eyes were on her, hard and cold.

"Where's Brandon?" he asked sharply as his eyes bored into hers, and her lips parted hesitantly.

"Over there," she said, and nodded toward the other side of the ship, where Brandon stood contemplating just how far he could push Beau.

"Well, tell him he's won," he answered harshly. "Your skirts make a nice shield, Reb. You want him, he's yours. I can't hurt your mother, and I can't hurt you. Just take him off this ship and out of my sight. I don't want to see the arrogant son of a bitch again." Then he turned to Heath. "Go find your father, Heath. Take Rebel and her husband with you, but I'll warn you, Reb," he said, looking back into her violet eyes, wanting to grab her and pull her to him, but knowing it was impossible, "if he ever tells anyone who Captain Thunder really is, I'll hunt him down and kill him, do you understand?"

There were tears in her eyes. "He doesn't know who you really are, Beau," she explained. "All he knows is that your name's Beau."

He straightened and turned without saying another word to her, and walked away, yelling to Heath as he went, telling him to get ready to leave for shore as soon as they anchored.

Loedicia stayed in the cabin as the ship dropped anchor off Port Royal, and Rebel, Brandon, and Heath got ready to embark in one of the longboats. There was no dock big enough to accommodate them, so they had to row ashore.

Brandon was above deck helping lower their trunks, while Rebel was making a last-minute check of the cabin to make sure they hadn't forgotten anything, when Beau stepped in. She turned around, and he shut the door behind him as he stared at her.

She had on a pale green dress that clung to her figure like a sail tight against the wind, and he swallowed hard as he stared. "I wanted to say good-bye," he said softly, and she couldn't answer.

Her mouth was dry, and suddenly there was an ache in her loins as she stared into his eyes, and in three strides he was to her, his arms about her, kissing her hard; then his mouth softened passionately, lovingly.

"I'm no good for you, Reb," he whispered huskily against her lips. "I had to do it. You deserved better than a backwoods Indian with an uncertain future and a price on his head."

Tears streamed down her face as she felt his warm mouth. "I hate you, Beau," she whispered softly.

"I know," he answered, and kissed her again, and she kissed him back. "Good-bye, Reb," he said, and reluctantly took his arms from about her and left, leaving her standing alone in the cabin, her heart breaking. She'd never see him again. Never! And for a minute she just stood there, her heart in her throat, and let the tears fall.

When she finally joined Brandon and Heath on deck a short time later, there was no sign of tears, and she was trying to smile.

"I sure hope you remember everything he told you," said Heath as the longboat made its way toward shore. "That little town on the bank of the sound doesn't look any too big. You're sure he said he lived in Port Royal?"

"I'm sure," she answered, and as the longboat finally reached one of the small docks, a group of men moved out from the side of some buildings to meet them.

"Give you a hand," offered one, and Heath nodded.

"Thanks," he said, and threw the rope to him.

The man secured the rope and helped them out. Happily, when Heath asked about Roth, the men grinned.

"He's about half a day's ride inland," said one of them. "There's a livery around the corner of that there building. You can hire a driver real cheap."

Heath thanked him, and they started unloading Brandon and Rebel's baggage.

"What's the ship?" one man asked. "Who's she sail for?" and Rebel looked quickly at Brandon.

"She's the *White Dolphin*. Sails for herself," said Heath, smiling. "She's privately owned, carrying a cargo and passengers up from Jamaica."

The men squinted, eyeing the ship curiously, then

shrugged, and Rebel sighed, relieved. Privateers weren't always welcome, and there was always the chance that someone would try to get the thousand pounds the British had on Beau's head. Even neutral waters weren't always safe for a privateer.

They hired a carriage and driver, loaded the baggage on, and headed inland.

"Mr. Chapman's quite a fella," said the wizened driver as they rode along. "He owns a fleet of merchant ships working out of Charleston, shipyards in Beaufort, but he lives down here. Bought the land about two, three years back. Says he likes it better here on the river. Queer duck in a way," he rambled on. "Don't have no slaves. All the fellas on his plantation works for wages, and he ain't too pop'lar with the other landholders." The man glanced at Heath out of the corner of his eye. "You're a relative, ain't you?" he asked. "You looks just like him."

Heath nodded. "Yes, I'm a relation," he answered, but he didn't explain, nor did the man ask.

"Well, here you be," said the driver some weary hours later as he turned in at a gate set between two stone pillars, and Rebel was surprised.

Huge gnarled oaks were scattered along the drive and in the lawn, and the house sat overlooking what looked like fertile bottomland along the river. As they rode up the drive toward the house, she could see long white columns across the veranda and a small balcony beneath the roof that the columns held up. Wings went out on each side, and men hammered away at an addition to one of the wings. It was the start of something big and still looked like it was in the building stage, and toward the back of the house more men were working on what looked like a stable and carriage house.

Men and women were everywhere, scurrying about, working in the yard, children playing, and they stopped, staring as the carriage moved up to the front steps.

"What if he's not here?" said Heath.

"And what if you shut up?" retorted Reb, who'd become rather bossy and irritable since her marriage. "You're just nervous. Pay the driver," she ordered, "and let's get on with it," and before Brandon could help her, she'd climbed from the carriage and was halfway up the steps.

"You come to see somebody?" hollered a little black girl as she bounded up the steps, and Reb smiled.

"Is Mr. Chapman at home?" she asked, and the girl grinned.

"He ain't in da house," she said. "He's out in da fields seein' how things is goin'." Then suddenly she turned and squealed. "Hey, dere he do come now!" she cried, and Rebel turned and stared as Roth rode across another drive that was partially hidden by high hedges and reined his horse close enough so he could get a good look.

He squinted in the sun, not sure he was seeing what he was seeing, then grinned as he dug his horse in the ribs and cantered forward. He was hatless, shirt open at the front, his pants none too clean and boots dusty with dirt from the fields, but he looked just as handsome as he had in England.

"Rebel?" he asked, surprised, and she smiled. "And Brandon?" He was taken completely by surprise; then his eyes moved to Heath, and his face went white. It was like looking at himself, only a good twenty years younger. "Heath?" he asked incredulously, and Heath nodded, a lump in his throat.

"Heath!" he acknowledged as he dismounted, and suddenly Heath found himself engulfed in Roth's arms as he was being hugged vigorously, the strength of the man surprising him. "Well," Roth finally said as he composed himself. "Well!" Then he laughed, easing the tension, and invited them in, brushing the dust from his boots as they went inside.

The house inside was also in the embryo stage, with furniture sparse, no rugs as yet on the floor, and the walls undecorated, but Roth made no apologies, and Rebel could see that when it was finished it was going to be magnificent.

Roth could hardly take his eyes from Heath, and Heath almost wore a hole through him staring. Roth offered them something to drink, and the conversation became stilted.

"Brandon and I are married now," said Rebel as they sat down in the sitting room.

"Congratulations," said Roth. "And your father and mother?" He hesitated at the word "mother" and his voice broke. "How are they?"

Rebel bit her lip. "My father's dead," she answered, and he flinched, his face drained of color.

He was almost afraid to ask. "And your mother?"

"She's fine." Rebel saw the relief in his eyes. "That's why we're here." She told him what had happened. "And father made Heath promise to bring her to you," she concluded, and his eyes softened.

"So where is she?"

Heath sighed, disgusted. "She won't come."

His hand tightened on the glass of brandy he was holding. "Did she say why?"

"She's got some stupid notion that you don't want her."

"That's not it at all, Heath," interrupted Rebel, and she looked at Roth. "She doesn't want to hurt you. She's afraid you'll think she only wants you now because she can't have him. . . ." She gestured helplessly. "It's sort of complicated, but—"

He held up his hand. "I know what she thinks," he said, and he smiled, his eyes warm. "I know her better than you both." He drained the drink in his hand. "Where is she?" he asked, and Heath grinned.

"She's back on the ship," he said, only they had some more explaining to do. "Before we go, may I ask a favor?"

Roth set his glass down, straightening his sleeves. "Go ahead."

"Would it be all right if my sister and her husband stayed here until you come back with Mother? They have to find a place to stay, but in the meantime they can't be carting baggage all about," and Roth smiled.

"I'll have the baggage unloaded," he told Heath. "They can stay here as long as they want. I've got plenty of room, and an empty house, although it isn't quite finished. But if they don't mind the hammering and the lack of furniture, it'll be nice having it full for a change," and Heath sighed as he looked proudly at his father.

Roth didn't even take time to change clothes, only grabbed a hat, and they made the ride back to the ship in record time, just Heath and Roth, leaving Brandon and Rebel back at the house, but it was still dark by the time they arrived. As they rode onto the dock, the few men still hanging around stared sullenly, realizing why the young man they'd helped earlier that morning looked so familiar. The resemblance was too striking. They were obviously looking at father and son, and unfortunately they knew Roth Chapman had never been married, and they eyed him curiously.

Loedicia lay in her bunk pouting. She'd stayed in the cabin all day, refusing to join the others, and when it grew dark she'd slipped into her nightgown and climbed into bed, stubbornly refusing to go on deck until the ship set sail again, and she knew nothing of Rebel, Brandon, and Heath's departure earlier in the day.